The Final Addiction

THE FINAL ADDICTION

Richard Condon

Michael Joseph
LONDON

MICHAEL JOSEPH LTD
Published by the Penguin Group
27 Wrights Lane, London W8 5TZ, England
Viking Penguin Inc., 40 West 23rd Street, New York, New York 10010, USA
Penguin Books Australia Ltd, Ringwood, Victoria, Australia
Penguin Books Canada Ltd, 2801 John Street, Markham, Ontario, Canada
L3R 4B4
Penguin Books (NZ) Ltd, 182–190 Wairau Road, Auckland 10, New Zealand
Penguin Books Ltd, Registered Offices: Harmondsworth, Middlesex, England

First published 1991

Typeset in Monophoto Sabon 11/12½pt
Printed and bound in Great Britain by
Butler & Tanner Ltd, Frome, Somerset

A CIP catalogue record for this book is available from the British Library

ISBN 0 7181 3512 1

Note
In *The Final Addiction* the word 'billion' is
used according to American usage, signifying
'a thousand millions'

For the Hunts, Condons, Weldons,
Jupps, Jacksons, Bennetts

(in order of appearance)

Squinting through the plugged keyhole of the past,
Spying on himself, (as it were),
Lo!
He saw that he had been wearing
Someone else's identity
All the time.

The Keeners' Manual

Chapter 1

Chandler Hazman met his future wife in England when he was on his first overseas tour, at the end of his third year with the Defense Intelligence Agency. He had been recruited into the service directly upon graduation from Eureka College, deepest and richest of mines for American intelligence agents, where he had sung (baritone) in the Glee Club and had been transport manager for the Chess Team. Having been an orphan from four months, six days old, raised by a series of nannies and governesses who were supervised by the law firm which had handled his late parents' estates, little Chandler never developed an ability to relate to other people. He was a remote island of a man who lacked empathy but, on the other hand, also lacked quirks in his emotional character which might have been there had he become over-attached to his mother or fearful of his father.

He would have been judged a handsome man by the standards of the American entertainment/advertising industry. He was lanky; a really good ballroom dancer; had an aura (really an odour) of baked cinnamon when physically excited. It could have been this fragrance which made him attractive to women. His son inherited the aura from him. This attraction was surely not based on the conversations of either father or son. Had either of them been a woman he would have been classified as a dumb blonde, but Chandler Hazman was not dumb, he was only uninteresting except to people who were engrossed in chess and the excitement of chess tournaments.

Throughout his life he retained brisk, creative heterosexual interests. DIA psychiatrists rated him as a Triple A risk, classifying him as 'passive/cooperative', always willing to be persuaded by women into the sex act but never taking the initiative himself. Undoubtedly helped along by his smell, he had run up quite a score this way, being particularly attractive to Tuareg and Tonkinese women. Under ordinary circumstances (if such may be said to exist) it would not have occurred to him to wish to know any woman after he had enjoyed her in a ritualistic way. He had been forged as a natural bachelor by his parents' early deaths in that he had never had a role model for marriage.

On the late afternoon of the day he met Molly Tompkins, they were both attending a pre-Christmas party in a country house near the Dorset-Wiltshire frontier, she as a casual visitor, he as a tag-along with Norbert Gaxton of the US Bureau of Fisheries & Wildlife at the American Embassy in London. The house was half a mile from a tiny village which had one pub, one church, and a post office/grocer's. The house was well set back from a secondary road on a slight rise of ground which overlooked a railway line. It had many outbuildings, most of them containing horses. The hostess, a young woman named Deborah-something, had decided she wanted to live in a smaller house. Norbert Gaxton hoped to buy her installation as a 'safe house' for the US Bureau of Fisheries.

Gaxton left Chandler Hazman on his own while he murmured negotiations with the hostess off in the corner of the main room. There were about a dozen other guests who spoke with one voice about horses.

Chandler Hazman had found a book about steeplechasing among several hundred other books about horses on the shelves of the study and had settled down with the book in a chair on a small outdoor terrace overlooking the garden. He wore a heavy overcoat, a tweed fedora, a muffler, and smoked a very expensive Havana cigar, feeling entirely safe from the gathering neighing inside the house.

He had the permanent expression of a man to whom it had been explained that he must die someday and who was exercising all the patience at his command as he waited for the inevitable to happen. He smoked the long cigar with heavy deliberation, conveying sage potency as cigar smokers are intended to do.

When she materialized like a magician's assistant directly in front of him in the feeble sunlight, he was startled. He took in some cigar smoke the wrong way and began to cough heavily.

'Frightened by the horsey people?' she asked as if she were after important information, as if she were a psychiatrist seeking to lay the right question before him, the answer to which would reveal everything she needed to know about him. She had mid-Atlantic speech. Because she was wearing her hair in pigtails, he was

2

repelled by her, rightly believing that it was something an adult woman should never do, but her manner of dress revealed no other signs of cisvestism by which grown women seek to appear as female children.

Hazman struggled to his feet, appreciating the interruption to his study of steeplechasing which, although it held little interest for him, had provided a frame for his handling of the expensive cigar. Women, he thought morosely, did not understand cigars or their need to be smoked in repose. Women, on seeing a contented man smoking a cigar, were impelled to disturb him.

He remembered this first meeting so vividly that he was able to describe it to his son Owney again and again – how she had looked and what she had said, as though he were a movie projector. The time and place never became old in his mind. He always saw it as a pageant of romance, a tableau of stylized sentimentality as if a greeting card were coming to pink-and-white life in his memory. Each time he told the story, his son would ask rapid questions about his mother.

Chandler Hazman would recall that his wife had had blue-black hair and a permanent expression of what appeared to be intense curiosity but which could have been naked ambition. It was her smile, not the woman who surrounded the smile, which had captured Hazman. The smile filled the void from which he had come. She had allowed the smile to exhilarate him for ever, then it was gone. He attended her patiently, waiting for an exact duplication of that smile as he thought he had seen it, the way an astronomer will stare into the firmament for years awaiting the reappearance of a great nova.

'I'm an uninvited guest,' he had explained. 'I don't know anyone in there except Norbert Gaxton.'

'The man with the beefy cheeks.'

'The man with the basso voice.'

'Someone said he was CIA.'

'He's just some functionary at the embassy.'

'Are you CIA?'

He grinned at her.

'You are only an uninvited guest in this house,' she said. 'I am in this country uninvited.'

'Oh?'

'Hungarian.

'A refugee.'

'I am Chandler Hazman.'

'I'm Molly Tompkins. That isn't my Hungarian name because it would be too dangerous to use my Hungarian name. I got my present name from an English music-hall song.'

'I thought Hungarians never lost their accent.'

'I went to school in Canada. My mother was a Canadian.'

It was a pack of lies.

He could still taste her as he told Owney about her. He spoke very slowly, chewing each fragment. Afterwards Owney had ransacked music libraries by mail to London and in New York but he never found the song which his mother had said had given her her name.

Chandler Hazman and Miss Tompkins were married in February 1959 at the Chelsea Register Office in London. Hazman was called back to Washington in June of that year to be planted as a mole inside the office of the Secretary of State. Molly moved into a little house in Meier's Corners, Staten Island, because, as she enchantingly said, no one would think to come to look for her there. Owney was born in March 1960.

In November 1960, Chandler Hazman was seconded to the CIA and stationed in Laos as one of The Outfit's cadre assigned to heroin manufacture, which produced a vast income allowing the Agency to increase their covert funds without having to bother Congress for them. He rose with the fortunes of the war in Vietnam to become an important government narcotics executive. He came home to his wife and son twice a year but it was hard for him to get back inside the family of which he had never been a part. As the war continued, Hazman came home less frequently. He may have inherited the inclination from his own father who, after financial failure, had stepped off the ledge of the fourteenth floor of a Fifth Avenue hotel in New York hand-in-hand with his wife.

Hazman had become an experienced manufacturer of No. 4 heroin, running eight processing plants in the Golden Triangle, with three CIA airlines to speed distribution. He had a dream that, when the war was over, and if he could find the right sort of backing, he would set up protected heroin factories in some forward-looking country and really make his fortune. He fantasized about how, if he could go home with a lot of money, he could re-enter his family as a husband and father, and make things the way they should have been. He felt that endless money might even bring his parents back to him to love him for ever. In the course of his work in Asia he accumulated $673,000 in a Zurich bank account which he had established as a joint account in his wife's name – but his dreams were compromised by the mullahs of Iran, her employers.

His wife had provided her sponsors, the mullahs, with enough hard evidence to have Hazman shot by an executioner sent out from Washington. To prevent that he went to work for the mullahs as a double agent when his son was six years old.

He began to drink after this second enlistment. He was recalled to the States and underwent deep hypnosis in San Francisco under the care of two CIA psychiatrists to whom he disclosed all the details of his employment by Iran, so he was turned again, becoming a triple agent, which is more dangerous work than steeple-jacking.

Chandler Hazman's Iranian masters had given him his wife as his case officer. The arrangement greatly unsettled Hazman because, although he had had no trouble in betraying either the CIA or the mullahs, he could not bring himself to betray his wife to the Americans even though by then he had decided that his marriage had been meaningless.

At last, because he had served God and man at Eureka, because he had fought for his establishment in a world which was crammed full with establishments, he not only told his superiors at Langley about his wife's assignment to run him as an Iranian agent but he told his wife he was going to tell them.

She disappeared on March 2nd, 1969, sixteen days before Owney's ninth birthday, taking with her the $673,000 in heroin profits and the family photo albums. Chandler Hazman collapsed and was hospitalized. In April 1970 he was discharged from the service with a small pension.

He kept the truth about Molly Hazman from her son because he didn't want the boy to think that money had caused the loss of his mother (as money had caused the loss of his).

Owney's father was not the significant monument in Owney's life. Before and after she disappeared his mother was to fill his mind and his life almost entirely.

Chapter 2

In the late spring of 1988, Owney Hazman was working for his father-in-law's company. Heller's Wurst Inc. manufactured and sold frankfurters to people while they watched professionals exercise for them at ball parks and sports arenas. Owney's father-in-law was a native Puerto Rican, whose family, all *Wurstmeister*, had originated in Saxony, Germany. He claimed that his family had invented the novelty frankfurter which was required to be twenty-four inches long with a ring-size of twenty-four. In fact, an executive of The National Sausage Council, the industry's powerful trade association, had informed Owney that spectators had eaten novelty frankfurters while they watched the Battle of Bull Run.

Owney's father-in-law held degrees from Stanford's Graduate School of Business, the Wharton School, and the Alfred P. Sloan School of Management at the Massachusetts Institute of Technology. He was the leader of the free world's frankfurter industry, a tremendous piece of clout given that fifty million frankfurters are eaten every day in the United States, an average of eighty hot dogs per person each year. 'And why not?' as Owney's father-in-law had said again and again. 'They are convenient, available, easy to eat, inexpensive, consistent in quality and size and easily seasoned to suit individual tastes.'

'Lissena me,' Owney's father-in-law proselytized an average of nine times a month before assemblies of women's clubs, sausage experts, and food buyers, 'franks and sauerkraut were sold on milk rolls in the Bowery in New York as early as the late 1850s. Feltman opened his stand on Coney Island in 1871. Nathan Handwerker, who worked for Feltman, the founder of Nathan's Famous in 1916, now has fourteen restaurants featuring the frankfurter and seven franchise operations. And I know what I'm talking

6

about – we got twenty-seven per cent of the national market.'

People around Owney's father-in-law showed respect for frankfurters. He made it clear that he would prefer it if no one referred to frankfurters as 'hot dogs' in his presence, not because he considered the term vulgar, he said, but because the appellation had sprung from illiteracy. 'In 1901,' he had complained to Owney and many hundreds of others, 'when Harry Stevens, the frankfurter vendor at the old Polo Grounds in New York, sought to add colour and pageantry to his wares by yelling out their name as "dachshund sausages", Tad Dorgan, a newspaper man in the press box, didn't know how to spell dachshund so he called them 'hot dogs' and the damned name stuck.' To Mr Heller, when they were wieners they were called wieners, not frankfurters, and *Kalbsbratwürste* were called just that, in the Swiss tradition.

Although the company packed a few additives and preservatives into the product: dipotassium phosphate, sodium silico aluminate, tricalcium phosphate, monosodium glutamate, sodium nitrates, and a pinch or so of BHA oxidant and disodium insonate (factors which Mr Heller referred to only as *'Geschmackverstärker'*), he also explained that they only put in a little to keep the product from turning grey and anyway it was entirely legal. 'Every frankfurter this company produces spends three hours in the smoker and they all have natural casings; no packaging; they are shipped loose, in bulk, the quality way,' Mr Heller told everyone. 'It is a product anyone could be proud of – competitively priced and intended to be served with semi-adulterated mustard on a bun which has a shelf life of 180 days.'

Owney's father-in-law, Francisco 'Paco' Marx Heller, Chairman and CEO of Heller's Wurst Inc., also said, 'Frankfurters, the soul of oral America, are running far ahead of the people, carrying the torch of hand-held fast food into the future. In this nation, which is in a greater hurry to get they don't know where than any other country in the world, the frankfurter has led the way – wrapped in bread, rolls, knish dough, bagel dough, tortillas or fried cornmeal – to almost totally hand-held food eaten around-the-clock in enormously imaginative short cuts to nourishment: six-foot-long Hero sandwiches; sausage *souvlaki*, a Greek sandwich crowded into an Arab pitta loaf with Greek salad; southern Italian sandwiches made of squares of rolled ricotta cheese, *salsiccie*, and sliced boiled spleen covered with grated Parmesan; fat *bratwursts* on exotically seeded rolls; a combination of pork cracklings, steamed plantains and roasted pork knuckles, all devoured while standing. Farfel sandwiches of chickpeas and spice sunk into Holy Land bread with salad topped by paprika. Hot spinach pies. Tacos and *empanadas* of cheese, chicken, and beef and *tostadas* made of refried pinto beans or chilliburgers or bean *burritos*. Counting the daily output of delicatessens – and mobile frankfurter vendors, which we cannot ignore – the City of New York alone consumes 27,852,651 sandwiches a week, almost a billion and a half sandwiches a year, an eating style replicated throughout the country – all of it made possible by the father of all hand-held food: the frankfurter. Americans are too busy or too frightened by their politicians to sit down to eat. They believe in their hearts that money is something you have to make in case you don't die.'

Yet Owney knew, somehow, despite his father-in-law's inspired beliefs, that his own destiny was not to be a frankfurter salesman. He didn't, however, know what he *was* destined to be. He held a degree in Economics from Eureka College, his Dad's alma mater in Illinois. At ten, he had thought of being a fireman. That had gradually given way to perhaps becoming an arbitrageur. But after he was grown up, what he really wanted was to get a job as a national television network anchor man because of the exposure that would bring to him. Sooner or later, being full frame on so many television screens throughout the country would make his mother understand that he was valuable enough, bright enough, successful enough to make her want to come back to him.

He wasn't a snob; he wouldn't have been any more understanding of what had happened to him if he were selling caviar. He appreciated how it had happened that he was selling frankfurters, and in the largest sense he was grateful, but sometimes he wondered why he had accepted his father-in-law's offer when it had materialized. Except that he *did* know why. His entire happiness had emerged from Mr Heller's offer – his wife and his family – or at least eighty per cent of his entire happiness, because the other twenty per cent was an elusive echo of times long past before he had turned nine years old; before his life had changed.

He had been raised to believe that his own father hadn't had an unusual career. Until Owney had been almost a fully grown man he had believed his father was a travelling accountant for the Defense Department. As a profession, accountancy had the dignity and self-expiation which selling frankfurters lacked. Owney believed that passionately for his first few weeks with Heller's Wurst Inc. but, as time went on, when he realized how he was serving, how he had become an integral part of the American culture, he didn't believe that any more. He had become a frank-furter man, heart and soul.

People liked Owney. Whatever it was he had, it sold frank-furters. He didn't think anyone could value their own luck as highly as he valued his, for having been blessed with the wife and children he had. But finding Dolly and his family had meant going into the frankfurter industry where he made more money than he had ever made anywhere else (in a haunted sense, in the sense of the whisper of the promise on which America had been built). Yet a conviction that selling frankfurters was not his destiny persisted.

He and Dolly had had three children so far. The oldest was only three years old and they had been married less than four years ago, when Owney had been twenty-four. Dolly was now twenty-six years old. He was just twenty-eight. That was the only thing that shook him about the marriage. They could end up having eighteen or twenty kids the way things were going. Looked at in an extreme way, having a lot of children was job insurance, he told himself. Every time they had another child he got a $50 rise. Ten children would mean an extra $500 a week; twenty children, $1,000. Grandchildren kept his mother-in-law happy. And when she was happy, his father-in-law wasn't unhappy.

Since he had been nine years old, Owney had had no reason to expect the joy his life had brought to him. It wasn't something to be reasoned because Owney wasn't the sort of fellow who reasoned much. Joy was the miracle that Dolly had performed after what his mother had done to him. He had been all over that old ground with a psychoanalyst in Dixon, Illinois. On the twenty-seventh visit the doctor had explained, 'This is an abnormally strong and prolonged attachment of the son to the mother. There is a clear-cut nostalgia for the mother which exceeds normality with a certain amount of antagonism towards the father. We are going to probe for the parental image of the mother. This must be laid bare if the obsession is to be resolved.'

The transient results of his psychoanalysis had convinced Owney that he shouldn't have used the money on treatment but should have conserved it in case he would need it to hire private detectives to look for his mother. The psychoanalyst had been someone to talk to about his perplexity but the therapy hadn't helped him understand what his mother had done or why she had done it.

He believed without any possibility of dissuasion that the nine years of his life before his mother had deserted him were the

9

happiest of his life, although he couldn't remember them clearly. He could no longer remember what his long-missing mother had looked like, for example. He could remember her dark colouring and how she had laughed and the way she had taken him with her no matter where she went. She had had vivid Canadian speech (she said ruff for roof and hoose for house) and ... but that was as far as he could go. He carried a laminated card in his wallet on which he had had his secretary, Miss McHanic, type words-to-live-by concerning his childhood:

> *We could never have loved the earth so well if we had had*
> *no childhood in it.* (George Eliot)
> *Only child life is real life.* (George Orwell)
> *I love kids.* (George Bush)

To outsiders, it could seem odd that he walked around with those quotes in his wallet and read them over not fewer than twice a day, and perhaps they would have judged Owney to be an obsessed man who thought of little else beyond finding his mother. He realized that he had met very few women (relatively) but still he thought his mother had been the most interesting of all of them. She had been young and pretty and very smart, much smarter than his father, and the best company, perhaps, that he had ever known. Gypsy-dark, quite tall, although he suspected that he remembered her that way from the perspective of a small boy always looking up.

In taking the family's photo album with her when she left she had not only robbed him of herself but of the assurance of the memory of her. He spent the greater part of his days searching his memory to picture exactly what she had looked like so that he could at least have that much, but the memory of her face, the way she had looked and had carried herself, had faded with each year, year after year, no matter how he struggled to keep her image clear and dear in his mind.

Because of the nature of his father's work, Owney and his mother had been alone together most of the time. His father would be somewhere out in the country, or the world, checking the books of defence contractors. In all those years he had never sent them a single postcard. Owney had always thought that he and his mother hadn't missed the man at all because he had his mother and she had him.

Owney had been an easy-going boy; a long, cheerful boy with sandy hair and a beautiful smile. Until he was nine and his mother

10

had gone away, he had liked everyone. After that, in and out of depressions, he was wary and very careful about whom he liked or trusted. He was not easy-going any more, or cheerful, but he still had a beautiful smile when he forgot about where his mother had gone.

In the few weeks each year that his father was able to spend with them at home, Owney would worry that he would stay on and take up even more of his mother's attention. The year after his mother had left them, his father was retired for physical disability and had to spend all of his time at home. By 1978, Owney was eighteen years old and about to start at Eureka so *he* became the member of the family who wasn't home very much.

Owney went back to their two-storey white clapboard house in Meier's Corners on Staten Island every year after his father died, on the anniversary of the day his mother had gone away, to stand outside the house in silent prayer that she would come back to him. After he married Dolly she made the pilgrimage with him and she never said she saw anything strange about it. It had been Dolly's idea to name their first daughter after his mother: Molly Tompkins Hazman, a name whose initials were, to Owney, an acronym for myth.

Dolly was in total agreement with him that they should hire private detectives to find his mother as soon as they had enough basic money put aside in Zero Coupon bonds to ensure college educations for their children.

On the day his mother had disappeared, Owney had come home from school to find the note, just a note, sellotaped to the refrigerator: *Dear Owney*, it said, *You are practically grown up now. I have done all I can for you. Now my turn has come and I am going to find out whether there is any life left on the planet. There is hamburger in the fridge. Love, Mom.*

Owney waited two days for her to come back before he called the special number his father had left in case of an emergency. A man answered. Owney said, 'I am Chandler Hazman's son, Owen. My father told us to call this number if we had to get in touch with him.'

'Will you spell that name, please?'

Owney spelled it.

'What's the problem?'

'My mother isn't here.'

'She isn't *there*?'

'No. Can you tell me where I can reach my father?'

11

'Are you alone?'

'Yes.'

'How long have you been alone?'

Owney shivered. 'Two days.' Logic told him he had been alone only two days but he knew he had been standing beside the kitchen table with her note in his hand for months, even years.

'How old are you?'

'Nine.'

'How much money do you have?'

'About ninety-five cents.'

'OK. All right. We'll get word to your father. Anything goes wrong, you call this number. You understand?'

The voice disconnected. At nine o'clock that night a messenger delivered an envelope which Owney signed for. There were $500 in $20 bills in the envelope. When his father came home three and a half weeks later, Owney still had almost $410 left.

He didn't hear anything from his mother. He went to school. He did the housework and the shopping. Everything was just as neat as his mother had always liked it because at every moment he expected to hear her key in the lock. When he came home from school, in the afternoon, the first thing he shouted (the only thing he ever said in the house for days on end) was, 'Mom? Are you home?'

After he called the special number, he waited for his father to return. When he did come back, and it was pretty quick, Owney thought, considering that he had been working in Asia, he stared at the note from his wife which Owney handed him and began to cry. He *cried*. Like some dumb kid. 'Didn't she even *call* to see how you were?' he asked Owney.

'Well,' Owney said, 'you never call either.'

Owney was graduated from high school nine years after his mother left them, then, out of the blue, his father somehow managed to have him accepted at Eureka College. He lived on campus for four years, coming home at Christmas breaks and all through the summers when, sometimes, his father was there to keep him company. Six years later he was still trying to understand his mother's note. He had decoded it, more or less, but he couldn't understand what it meant or why she had left him. She loved him. He was sure of that and yet she had left him for ever.

Owney had a good mind, which is to say he had a good mind for thinking about where his mother could have gone and why. He didn't use his mind much for anything else. He wasn't exactly dim, but it could be said that he remained mentally fuzzy and this mental fuzziness was to stay with him throughout his life. He was able to dress and feed himself efficiently but he wasn't really a bright young man, or perhaps he had never been mentally organized. He was able to make a living as a novelties salesman entirely because of his smile, his height, his undeniably elegant clothing, and his projection of great, good health. But he never thought of anything in life as a problem to be solved – except the awful loss of his mother.

He couldn't begin to imagine what might have happened to his life or where he might have ended if Dolly hadn't put her arms around him.

But getting Dolly also meant the frankfurter industry. It wasn't that he hated the industry or anything like that. He never said it but he thought, perhaps subconsciously, that being in frankfurters was demeaning for a Eureka man with an MBA and a background in Economics, no matter how much it paid, but he knew that kind of thinking was un-American. Shine at what you do, whatever it is, his mother had said. But his heart ached to find a way to get one of those jobs as a national television news anchor man because he just sensed that would be the most effective way to find his mother.

Anyway, no matter what anyone worked at, he told himself, they were, all of them, only working for money in the illusory sense. In the real sense they were working for the history of mankind. His mother had explained that if everyone put their shoulders to the wheel the world would reach Utopia that much sooner.

Chapter 3

On the third Saturday in May for three successive years, Owney had gone to the racetrack at 5.30 in the morning to see a Mr Olgilvie, who was a two-time widower, a Washington lawyer, and a *very* influential power broker at the highest Party levels, who ran a fair-sized racing stable and also owned a Washington ball club which had missed the World Series by only four games the year before. He was Owney's prime client, not only because of the ball club and his connections with stadium concessionaires (he also owned an NFL franchise) but because he had interceded on Owney's behalf with people at the Belmont and Aqueduct racetracks about the frankfurter situation and he wouldn't take a dime (directly) for his help.

In some measure of return, over and above the indirect commissions which were deposited directly into a numbered account in Aruba, Owney's father-in-law insisted, at the lawyer's suggestion, on being allowed to provide Mr Olgilvie with free frankfurters for his annual party in the grounds of his house in Virginia somewhere near Washington. Mr Olgilvie generated sales of four and a half million ball-park and football-stadium frankfurters and another million-nine at the metropolitan racetracks. Moreover, the company sold an extra 463,000 frankfurters a year due to Mr Olgilvie's political connections.

At 4.30 that Saturday morning in May 1988, Dolly woke Owney by getting into bed with him. That really woke him. After a while she said, 'I hope Daddy appreciates what you do for the company. It isn't fair to make you drive all the way out to that track on Saturday.'

'Saturday is a banner day for franks, Doll.'

'You aren't all that good a driver.'

'Mr Olgilvie is the biggest account I have. How are the kids?'

14

'I haven't looked yet. About the same as last night, I guess. Maybe they gained a few hundred cells.'

'How's your mother?'

'The eyedrops the doctor has her using are too strong.'

'So she'll put a little water in them. Have we got a sitter for tonight?'

'Oh, yes.'

'Then we'll eat downtown.'

They went to fewer and fewer parties because the gatherings were always a mix of the same couples. One of the men, a wag, had made up a form sheet showing what everyone would be doing at each hour of the night from nine o'clock onwards at any given party and it had been so accurate that it had depressed Owney. He didn't like things to be that predictable.

Dolly saw it differently. 'What else can happen at parties with the same people over and over again?' she asked. 'They have to run on form. Everyone is a product of his conditioning. What's wrong with that?'

'It makes me feel like I am wasting my life. *Déjà vu* is nothing compared to *déjà fait*.'

Dolly rolled out of bed and stood over him as she got into a robe. Dolores Guadalupe Hazman-Heller was a tidy package of small bones and tiny tubes, stacked with breathtaking symmetry. She was beautiful in all ways: as vivid as any stand-in for Carmen, with a khaki-and-rose complexion and black, backlit eyes. She had hands as long and as soft as the smoke from a Havana cigar. Her speaking voice sounded as if it belonged in a museum protected by armed guards, insured for millions behind alarm-wired glass enclosures. It was a voice which, at its most dejected, was utterly thrilling and, at its most intensely happy, a glorious religious experience. It was when she sang that the sublime here-after of all the religions of the world seemed to be confirmed. When she sang everyone within earshot was ideally young again, as perfectly young as when, for them, it had been perfect to be young. As rewarding to the beholder as her youthful, compelling beauty was, the sound of her voice was even more healing. It was a voice which dispelled despair in all who heard it, the way sunlight can dispel fear. She was smart about everything she wanted to be smart about and ignored the rest. She loved him.

Owney showered, shaved, and dressed carefully. He still had the rich clothes he'd acquired before he was married. He was a tall, slender man with a perpetual expression of not quite having

15

heard what the world had just said. His eyes were clear and agate-coloured with brush strokes of brown. On a scale of ten his eyes were worth maybe twelve points but it was his smile, when it arrived on his face so totally unexpectedly, which was not to be resisted by other humans. The smile travelled across his face slowly and sweetly, as miraculously distilled as the early morning light of Paris. It wasn't technically achieved as with an incomparable actor. It took an immoderate amount of stimuli to bring it on at all because, with the desertion by his mother always on his mind, Owney was a sombre man.

Owney had lived on Staten Island until he was twenty-one years old, the year his father died, six months before Owney graduated from Eureka College. After his father had retired, Owney had learned that he had not been a travelling accountant for the Defense Department but a counter-intelligence agent for the CIA, the work which had taken him all over the world and which had probably been, Owney thought disapprovingly, recklessly dangerous. The truth had come out because Owney persisted in being puzzled about what sort of an injury could have left his father with two such long surgical scars across his stomach and another across his back. He kept asking his father how things like that could happen in the course of an accountant's work. At first his father had said that he had been attacked by a Filipino electric-toaster supplier whom he had exposed. Finally, he told Owney the truth; that he had been a secret agent.

'Did Mom know that?' Owney asked.

'No. No way. Absolutely not.'

'It could have made life more interesting for her. Maybe, if she knew you were a spy, she never would have gone away.'

'I was not a spy,' his father said wearily. 'Basically, I was a spy-catcher. Although I was given other assignments.'

Owney held his father's hand while he was dying. His mother's nickname for him had been Dad, so Owney called him Dad. Owney leaned down towards the flight of soul which accented the haggardness in his father's face and whispered, 'Why did she do it, Dad?'

His father stared out towards eternity.

'I can promise you this, Dad. I'm going to find her somehow, someday, and I'm going to make her pay.' He knew that was a vainglorious thing to say and a total lie because when he found her he would throw his arms around her and hold her close, doing anything to keep her, but he hoped it would help his father to find final peace.

Chapter 4

When his father's estate was settled, Owney inherited $24,919 in cash, the house on Meier's Corners, the 1970 Dodge, $93,000 in government bonds and a $100,000 government insurance policy on which his father had remembered to keep up the payments. Owney's total (cash) inheritance was $251,268.12, including the sale of the house, the bonds, and the car. This came to him at a time, during the Reagan administration, when interest rates had climbed quite high. Owney had invested every penny of it in money-market funds that earned him as much as $32,000 a year, but he lived on his meagre earnings as a commission salesman of 'luxury' novelties, because he knew he would need all the money he could get if he were ever going to be able to hire the detectives to find his mother. As the money accumulated he kept postponing hiring the detectives because, he told himself, the high interest rates weren't going to last and he had to appreciate his capital while he could.

He moved into an apartment hotel in Manhattan, on Broadway in the high 60s, which, unknown to him (until a shocking incident in the hotel corridor), was a trick factory for hundred-dollar hookers, priced upwards from the going rate of twenty dollars before 1976 when heavy inflation had set in as a result of the Vietnam war and hookers had had to respond to the rising economic curve. As an MBA who had majored in Economics he was keenly aware of those things, just as Ronald Reagan, who had been an Economics major when he had gone to college, couldn't be fooled on the cost of a daily newspaper if he had had cause to buy one, which he did not.

One morning, he left his tiny apartment to take the elevator to the street floor when a man, waiting for the elevator with a young woman, began to punch her about the head then to kick her

18

heavily after she had fallen. Owney rushed to her rescue.

Both the man and the battered woman turned on him. The man tried to choke him and the woman bit his ankles, the woman being far more serious about it than the man. Owney concentrated on dealing with the man because he couldn't bring himself to kick a woman when she was down no matter how badly she was ripping up his socks. Having decked the man twice, Owney was almost certain he could drive off the woman when she leaped to her feet, ran to a nearby apartment door and leaned all her weight upon the doorbell, yelling shrilly for help. Almost instantly, four other women rushed out of the apartment into the corridor and all five of them ganged up on Owney and tried to throw him down the elevator shaft. Their language was terrible. The hotel manager and a house detective arrived and pulled Owney away from his attackers. He was a mess. He couldn't walk because they had struck him repeatedly in the jewels. Three of the women threw shoes at him while he was carried away. The two other women comforted their protector.

Owney settled with the hotel for $6,875 but he had to move out. It was a matter of principle as well as safety. This changed his life and his style of living because nine days later, still limping, while he was eating lunch on a Saturday at the Gitlitz delicatessen on upper Broadway, his small table faced that of a woman who was a vice-president of an advertising agency. When she happened to look at him, Owney was smiling at the waiter because the waiter had mentioned beef-barley soup. The smile destabilized the woman. She transferred her food to his table. After lunch she took him home with her. He lived there, rent-free, for the next five months while he sold novelty enamelled cigarette lighters and mother-of-pearl combs on a door-to-door basis. After that, still making a very slim living, he fell into a pattern of moving into a new woman's apartment at a regularity of about every hundred days. Sometimes the scenes which happened as he was leaving were pretty awful, but he couldn't abide the feeling of permanence which would settle upon him as time went on with the women. He was forced to move from woman to woman from the time he was twenty-two years old until he married Dolly when he was twenty-four.

He wasn't proud of this arrangement but he was fiercely determined not to invade his capital which had grown, due to twenty per cent interest (and the $6,875 settlement) to $343,027, because he knew he was going to need every penny of it for the private

19

detectives. He hadn't moved to start the investigations because he had to get used to the idea. When he had first thought of it, the whole thing made him feel very shy. He couldn't form the first sentence of what he would say to his mother when the detectives told him where she was and he had to confront her. He wouldn't be able to bear it if she stared him down coldly or sent him away. What could he do? He wouldn't be able to make her come back to him even though he'd have to find a way to make her see that she *had* to come back to him. He felt that, within a year or two, he would be ready to put the investigators on the case and to take his chances when the time came for the confrontation.

Dolly insisted that his mother had left the house on some unexpected errand, anticipating that she would be gone only until late in the evening of the day she went away, hence the mention of hamburger in the note, but that wherever she had gone something had happened to her. Dolly said, as gently as possible, that his mother had probably been killed in a car crash or some other crazy kind of accident and that she had not been identifiable when they found her. Owney rejected that analysis because of two meaningful phrases in the note: *You are practically grown up now*, and *I am going to find out whether there is any life left on the planet*. 'But no matter how that is interpreted,' he said to Dolly, 'nine years old is not grown up.'

They talked about it on and off until the first baby came, then Dolly became busy and Owney hadn't wanted to talk about it any more anyway because he just knew what had happened. His mother had deserted him. But she was out there somewhere and some day he was going to find her and make her pay. How he would make her pay he had not determined entirely, but one way he was sure of: he was going to make her tell him, right to his face, looking into his eyes, that she loved him and that a terrible necessity had forced her to leave him.

Chapter 5

Early on, when he lived with the advertising woman, he was
able to save some money out of his rather small earnings from
enamelled-cigarette-lighter sales because, under the new arrangement, he had no outgoings. Winona Nodtze, his first flatmate (and
the random women after Winona), had insisted on giving him
neckties and cufflinks, now and then a suit or two, and he had a
contact with whom he could trade the surplus cufflinks and ties
for shirts, socks, and underwear and the occasional pair of up-
market shoes.

Some of the women were quite good cooks and some were
entertaining in an informal, chatty way. They were all grateful for
his company. Suspended between love and lust, chary of one,
coolly doling out the other, he had developed precise and effective
sexual techniques which, although blindingly efficient, were over-
mannered. In musical terms, he composed classical erogenous-
response scores which he sang during his boa-like movements
before and during copulation, using mews, gutturals, moans, and
ululations to achieve the arias, frequently in duet. Essentially it
was like movie music which had been stolen from old masters.
However, the effect of this music upon the conditioned reflexes of
his partners was to suggest to them that they were exciting him
beyond measure, which drove them into paroxysms in their determination to match his signalled ecstasy, producing buglings which
frequently alarmed the neighbours. He was a mechanistic virtuoso,
all technique, who had found the knack of sustaining erection as
an on-the-job reflex. He became entirely a harmony of action
without emotion.

The reason for breaking up with these good friends – for they
were good friends in every way other than his being able to love
them – was always that the women began to talk to him about

21

marriage. Two of them had also wanted him to share the rent and overheads and he just didn't have the income for that. Selling novelty cigarette lighters was no cinch. He made a block sale to an organization or a company on an actuarial basis of every 21.7 calls, and the franchise company he worked for weren't all that quick about remitting his commissions. Although he had not yet felt that the time had come to touch the capital, he had been searching for his mother since the day he had left the bed of the first young woman, Winona Nodtze (the advertising woman), to move to the next, then the next. For example: there was a *crise de ménage* with a computer programmer he had lived with but Owney didn't have women to bring him trouble. The woman was determined that Owney would accompany her on a ten-day skiing holiday in Vermont. He refused to go. The deadline was two days away and, blindly, he just knew he would have to make some other arrangement.

Having accumulated $183.65 from commissions on the sale of lighters in the previous week, Owney was standing at the far end of one of the central service tables at his bank, making out a paying-in slip to his deposit account, when the bank's alarm bell went off and Owney thought it was a fire drill. He looked up enquiringly just as the hold-up man began to walk rapidly away from a cashier's window. Then the man started to run, with a canvas briefcase under one arm and dangling a pistol from the other. As he reached the far end of the service table he grabbed a young woman bystander by the arm and whirled her around to make a shield for himself. He dragged her towards the bank's main entrance, firing the pistol into the ceiling and shouting that if he didn't get out of the bank he would kill her.

As the two painfully connected people went past him, Owney stuck out his foot between the bandit's legs. The man and the woman fell to the marble floor and slid along it to crash into the bank's single public service, a blood-pressure machine. Owney sprang across the distance between them, kicked the robber heavily in the side of the head and, grabbing the woman by the wrist, pulled her across the floor like a sack of potatoes to the low-walled bank employees' area, crashing the upper right side of her face into a marble pillar as he got her away.

Two bank guards who had been cowed by the thief's weapon rushed in. They seized the bandit and forced him to his feet. One guard snatched away his pistol. The other grabbed the thick canvas briefcase. They frogmarched him to a corner of the bank and held him on the floor like a fleshy rug.

The young woman was stretched out on the carpeted floor, her head in Owney's lap. The right side of her face had begun to swell grotesquely as it built a colossal black eye but Owney, staring down at her, thought she was nonetheless a comely woman.

Police swarmed over the banking floor. Two detectives came to stand around the rowdy burlesque of the Pietà which Owney and the young woman had formed. 'Is she OK?' the thin one asked.

'I'm all right,' the young woman said, opening her good eye and looking up directly into Owney's smile. She shuddered involuntarily. 'What happened?' she asked Owney.

'I stuck my foot out.'

'You saved my life.'

'I just stuck my foot out. I don't think I knew I was doing it.'

In six minutes an ambulance arrived. The right side of the young woman's face was treated. She insisted on going home. She also insisted that Owney go with her. She did not seem to be able to stop staring at him because she had been stunned by his smile. Owney decided that she smelled clean, always a plus with him. He had never known a woman who had bathed as frequently as his mother. The young woman also looked as if she were fighting a compulsion which was ordering her to pull him down on top of her on the floor of the bank. He opened up the smile again and it was as though he had found her Graefenberg spot.

'I am Graciela Winkelreid,' the woman said.

'How do you do?' he said as formally as if they were standing. 'I am Owen Hazman.'

'This is all so unexpected,' she said dazedly. 'I live rather nearby. Please take me home.'

The young woman lived alone in an enormous private house on East 64th Street; quite the most luxurious digs Owney had ever fallen into. He was a young, healthy male who did not want to go skiing in Vermont, so he went home with Graciela Winkelreid.

The following morning, he returned to the apartment of the computer programmer, Dorothy Beardsley, on the West Side, to get his two cardboard suitcases and his belongings. Miss Beardsley, an ectomorph with fiery red high-spots on her cheekbones which could have presaged either a tendency toward tuberculosis or a faulty knowledge of make-up, made a rotten scene about his wanting to leave her, but Owney steeled himself by making himself believe that he was walking out on his mother. It was not something he liked to do to anyone because he knew how it felt to be deserted but he packed the two suitcases silently.

'But *why*, Owney?' the stunningly thin young woman sobbed. 'Is it because of the skiing? You never said anything about not liking skiing. All you had to do was to tell me and we could have gone to Hong Kong or Monaco.'

Miss Beardsley's terror mounted until she was screaming that if he left her she would kill herself.

The suitcases were packed. He turned to face her. 'Women say those things, Dotty, but they don't do them. This is nothing, sweetheart. Think of all the pain in the world. People part. Right now, half the world is leaving the other half.'

He carried the suitcases to the door. Dotty held on to his arm and let both her feet drag as he moved along easily despite her (light) weight. He put down one case and leaned over to give her a stiff karate chop at the pressure point above her bony left elbow, allowing himself to feel that he were striking down his mother. The blow broke her grip. As she fell, making awful noises, he picked up the second case and left the apartment. Owney abhorred cruelty if it were for cruelty's sake, but he had to make a swift clean break, he told himself. It was a matter of survival. At that moment it came to him that perhaps his mother had faced a survival situation, something grim and terrible which had threatened her, so that, in her view, from her own perspective on her predicament, she had felt that she had to make a swift, clean break, a decision which in no way reflected upon the love she felt for him.

Graciela Winkelreid was a mouse-coloured, bombastically pretty woman of twenty-five with enormous blue eyes and intense speech. She was the widow of Terence 'Terry' Winkelreid III, a revolutionary who had blown up himself (and a small building) while experimenting with a time fuse on a bomb which had been intended to destroy his father's bank.

Over the time they were together in Mrs Winkelreid's handsome town house, Owney progressed so far as to be able to admire her, and when their association ended after five months it was because *she* had to leave *him* to study abroad.

One night, while they were computer-charting and imaging the erotic positions they had achieved over the five months they had had together, Mrs Winkelreid broke the news. 'That could have been our last or maybe our next-to-the-last bang, Owney. At least in this series.'

'How come?' Owney asked, bewildered because he had thought she was so in love with him.

'A big opportunity came up for me,' Mrs Winkelreid said. 'My lawyer has found me an opening with the IRA in Belfast. I'm off tomorrow to learn about convenience bombs.'

'Can't your lawyer get you someplace for that in New York?'

'Owney, if I were a painter, a student painter in the Renaissance, and a chance to work under Michelangelo came up – would you say I should take it or turn it down?'

'I see what you mean. Well, good luck.'

'Thanks, sweetie.'

'How long is the course?'

'Only a year. It's a graduate course. Anyway, it was great knowing you, Owney.'

The parting wasn't a wrench to either of them. Mrs Winkelreid was in love with a cause and Owney was bereft without his mother. Over his heated protests she gave Owney $2,500 and left him.

While the relationship lasted Mrs Winkelreid had been the dominant one. She told him when to speak, when to shut up, and instructed him with such regularity that it was altogether as if she were behaving not unlike the way his mother had when she was still there, which gave him the power to admire Graciela. She was the leader and her line of leading was summed up in her stark determination to rid the world of parents, bankers, and the military, in that order. Owney accepted her tenets. If one day they blew up the world together he felt that life would become an eternal Mothers' Day, because he would be blowing up his mother. He even toyed with the idea (temporarily) of not spending his capital on private detectives to find his mother. He would blow her up instead.

As it developed, Mrs Winkelreid had been working along parallel lines. She confided in Owney that her father owned several banks and a great deal else of the country and held an honorary rank as a major-general in the Air Force Reserve. 'So I know bankers,' she said. 'They'd do anything for money. He walked out on me and my mother when I was twelve years old and it nearly killed my mother so, believe me, I know about bankers.'

Owney was tremendously moved. He reached across and put his hand on top of Mrs Winkelreid's. As he stared at her tears came into his eyes. 'My mother walked out on me when I was nine and it killed my father. You know about bankers and I know about women.'

'Owney! Oh, Jesus, Owney, I didn't know.' They stood up simultaneously and took each other into each other's arms, weeping. 'We'll break their fucking backs, Owney,' she sobbed. Then they had tremendous sex together.

The nameless organization which Mrs Winkelreid had formed was also cell-less. It was inter-connected by an elaborate system of coded classified advertisements in *The Wall Street Journal* and the *International Herald Tribune*. There were thirty-two members (sixteen per cent operating in countries overseas), each having a code name (Mrs Winkelreid's name was the Teacher; Owney's name was Periscope), and the advertisements instructed them when and where to meet and what to bring to the meetings. Not only did the entire membership seek the destruction of their parents, but the same parents provided them with the financing to do so in the form of trust funds, stock transfers, and other tax-unburdening cash gifts. The average age of the membership was twenty-three years. All had been over-educated. Four of the thirty-two, including a Portuguese nun, held jobs. Seventeen had attended guerrilla-training camps run by the PLO, the Japanese Red Army, the Tupamaros, Baader-Meinhof, the Hezb'Allah, and the IRA. In the two years of their existence they had planned the ruination of $7,300,000,000 worth of US military equipment, and had projected the assassinations of twenty-nine bank officers, the Secretaries of Defense and Treasury, and thirty-one Senators and Congressmen who sat on Defense or Treasury Committees, though none of these crimes had actually happened yet. There was a danger of a division within the organization because approximately ninety-seven per cent of the membership considered that all politicians and Political Action Committee contributors were the corrupt and murderous link between the bankers and the military and were pressing Mrs Winkelreid for a solution, beginning with the demolition of the Senate Armed Services Committee.

Owney was called Periscope because of his mnemonic ability. The other members were so spaced-out on odd vegetables that Owney must have seemed like a mental giant to them. Only he and Mrs Winkelreid (and she was pretty shaky about it) knew the names and faces of the entire membership. Mrs Winkelreid and her late husband had recruited them.

Not that she considered Owney to be revolutionary material. He was too square. To her he was more of a mascot of the movement, a politically retarded if utterly delightful fellow, an absolutely historic lay, who could not seem to absorb even the most basic principles of terrorism.

'Listen,' Owney had said to her, 'life is a very complicated number. Maybe you can follow it, I can't. But I don't need to follow it. Just tell me what to do and I'll do it because there is entirely too much authority on the scene when a fellow's mother is all the authority he needs.'

Owney had already realized with a terrible clarity that he had reached a time of life when he should have been thinking about (a) its consequences and (b) his probable responsibilities, but he was unable to think with any constancy about anything other than the haunting worry of whether or not he would ever find his mother again. Outwardly, he seemed to be a normal, average young man as free of neuroses as it would be possible for him to be in his time or place, but if a psychic portrait could have been drawn it would have shown a frantic and tormented obsessive who, through the habituation of the years since his mother had vanished, had been consumed by nothing else but the need to find his mother again.

When he and Mrs Winkelreid went their separate ways, she kept in touch with him through classified advertisements in *The Wall Street Journal*, but he had to leave the house on 64th Street. He continued to go to the odd executive committee meeting every three months even if he was never included in its plans. He was there as a verifier, not an activist. But Owney was shelterless, in his second year of moving from woman to woman in order to conserve his capital so that it could grow into an amount which could cover the expenses for the worldwide search.

As crisis points were reached with the succession of women with whom he shared his life, as he was cast out to make his way alone (again), he would look for a replacement by attending ethnic, associational, or church organization functions which were held nightly throughout the city.

Chapter 6

He met Dolly at a dance organized by the Humboldt Society which was named after, not Baron Alexander von Humboldt, the botanist and explorer whose work had influenced Darwin, but Karl von Humboldt, the philologist and writer who had formulated the theory that language expresses the inner life and experience of man, and that languages differ from one another in accordance with the people who use them. It was an intellectual sort of an excuse for a social occasion in the most intensely German sense.

Owney thought Dolly Heller was a German-American girl when he met her at the Humboldt dance. She could have thought he was German, too. He was tall and sandy-haired with the abstracted look which can come with the worry of having to spend one's own money, but which other people frequently confuse with the expression of a deeply involved intellectual.

Dolly was with her two older brothers who were large, silent men with expressionless blue eyes and *Bürstenhaarschnitt* hairstyles. Their speech (when it happened) alternated German and English words in the limited vocabulary of the *Schutzstaffeln Führungshauptamt*. They wore lederhosen but did not dance. They seemed to be there on the orders of some higher command to guard and protect their sister.

Mr Hazman and Miss Heller met for the second time at a dance held by The Friends of Ponce, a Puerto Rican organization. Owney was horrified to meet her again, because he had been so attracted to her at first meeting, knowing instinctively that such a condition, taken to an extreme, could greatly interfere with his lifestyle and threaten his capital. This time the brothers (when they spoke) alternated Spanish and English words in the limited vocabulary of the *Guardia Civil*. They wore sharp-looking suits with pointed shoulders but did not dance. If it had not been for the threatening presence of the brothers (with whom he was now on a nodding basis), Owney could have believed, in a shocked way, that Dolly must be using these dances the way he was, but he could not bring himself to believe that about such a girl.

On the dance floor, well out of the hearing of her brothers, he obtained her telephone number in the last set of the Ponce dance. She had become a woman of importance to Owney and he put all thoughts of his capital out of his head. She was both grave and gay, serious in a committed way, but happy because she was happy with her life. She spoke German and Spanish to her brothers and the most melodious English to Owney. She moved him. He also thought constantly of how he was going to get her into bed, a conclusion which startled him. He had never been required to think like that with the other women because that had been hard duty; this was a vital matter of need.

'What are you doing here?' he asked her as they were dancing.

'I always come to this dance. It's an important occasion for people from Ponce.'

'You come from Ponce?'

'My parents were born there.'

'Then how come you were at that German dance?'

'I'm half German.'

'Then how come you are here?'

'I'm half Puerto Rican.'

'That is really exotic,' he said. They danced every dance. One or other of her brothers began to cut in after the second dance until she managed to get through to them that it wasn't what she wanted.

'You have a beautiful smile,' she told Owney. 'I mean a *really* beautiful smile.'

'You are the loveliest girl I ever heard,' Owney said.

'What do you do during the day?' she asked him.

'I am a sales executive. And you?'

'I just been graduated from Juilliard.'

'Is that a college?'

'Sort of.' Dolly had been all but consumed with the projected plan of devoting herself to a life on the concert stage, playing the cello, and a life off the concert stage, composing music to be played on the cello. 'I've been interested in music.'

'Do you play the piano?'

'Yes.'

'Can you sing the second part in two-part harmony?'

Dolly, who could perform the F. A. O'Connell Variations of switching from harmonic part to harmonic part within a vocal recital of six-part harmony, nodded.

'I think that's a wonderful talent to have,' Owney said.

That evening, on the bus on the way home, he decided he was going to have to dip into his capital. His mother's memory actually became very dim when he was with Dolly. He thought that if he could have Dolly to fill his life, he might never have to think of his mother again.

He bit the bullet, left the woman he was living with, withdrew funds from the bank, and moved permanently into the YMCA. He saw Dolly three nights a week. They went dancing to the music of Czech, Irish, and Finnish organizations which meant expenditures of only two dollars each, plus bus fare. Some evenings they didn't go dancing. They strolled west from Dolly's apartment house to Riverside Park and sat on a bench watching New Jersey and the river with one eye, and the possibility of muggers with the other. Dolly would sing for him. He thought he had never heard anything as thrilling. Her voice had the fascination of a sibyl's: intense with omens, resounding with promises. She knew all the golden oldies, but she sang them in a way that made them sound more beautiful than Owney had ever considered them.

One Wednesday night in the late spring, Owney said, 'You ought to tour with that voice, like the Rolling Stones, or K. D. Lang. You could make eighty or ninety million dollars.'

'My Dad wants me to make records,' she said. 'I thought about it for a while. But not any more. That isn't what I want to do with my life any more.'

'What do you want to do with it?' he asked hoarsely.

'I want a husband and children and a real life.'

'Dolly ... ' He held her hand and stared deeply into her eyes. 'You know about my mom and you must think I'm some kind of a nut.'

'I most certainly do not.'

'I think about her and talk about her too much, I know, so I have to make one thing clear. What I'm going to say has nothing to do with asking you to become some kind of a substitute for my mother – but – from the bottom of my heart, Dolly, will you marry me?'

In answer she turned slowly on the bench, faced him fully, put her arms around him, drew him to her and kissed him slowly, tenderly, and with fulfilling devotion.

*

Seeing Dolly meant calling for her at her parents' huge apartment in the block-square Apthorpe building on West 78th and 79th Streets at Broadway and West End Avenues. The Heller family lived splendidly in a twelve-room apartment on the West End Avenue side. Mr Heller had imported painters and woodworkers from the Italian section of the Bronx and they had transformed the place into replicas of the interior of some of the more baroque rooms of the Nymphenberg Palace.

Mr Heller, a native Puerto Rican, was more German than Otto von Bismarck. As a tribute, his dentures were precise copies of Bismarck's teeth and presented a starkly commanding sight. Dolly's mother was more Puerto Rican than all of East Harlem. Owney could see how handsome she must have been as a young woman but from the time he met her he was taken with her resemblance to the Queen of Spain in Goya's portrait, 'The Family of Carlos IV'. A silent, bulky blond brother stood on either side of Mr and Mrs Heller and, together, they formed a fleshy hedge around Dolly as they moved with her gradually towards the front door, each male member of the family patently apprehensive about having to leave her alone with this stranger.

At the beginning of the second month of courtship, after an intense amount of inner-family wrangling, Owney was invited to dinner at the Hellers'. It hadn't been easy for Dolly to set this up.

'Who is this fellow?' her father wanted to know even before the first date.

'He looks like a rich boy,' her mother said after the first date.

'He ain't a Latino, that's for sure,' Wolfie, Dolly's older brother said before the first date.

'He could be German-descent,' Mrs Heller said. 'The name, Hazman, could have originally had two n's at the end.'

'This is crazy,' Luddie, the younger brother said after the third date. 'Are she all of a sudden going steady with a guy she hardly knows?'

These questions weren't asked directly of Dolly. They were addressed to the entire family and tended to agitate all the male members.

'He has lovely manners,' Dolly said. 'He has a degree in Economics from Eureka College. What more do you need to know?'

'Eureka College?' her father, who had three considerable degrees, snorted.

'A highly-valued President of the United States went to Eureka College.'

'Woodrow Wilson? He went to Princeton,' her father said. 'F.D.R. went to Harvard, so did John F. Kennedy. Nixon went to Duke and Eisenhower went to West Point.'

'I was thinking of Ronald Reagan,' Dolly said sharply.

The first time Owney came to dinner at the Hellers', the two brothers were not there; Mr Heller was wearing the formidable Bismarck dentures; Mrs Heller seemed more than ever a seriously decayed Spanish royal. Dolly and Owney ate pea soup with frankfurter slices and *arroz con salchichas*, sausages made from lean beef and red peppers mixed with *salchicha* slices of veal and pork bangers, raw, salted, and slightly smoked, with nutmeg, white pepper, and rum.

When Dolly and her mother were clearing the table, Mr Heller took Owney into his study, gave him a chair and a Mexican cigar, then asked him, with intent interest, 'So – what do you do?' He had a pronounced Ponce accent with heavy Saxony overtones. Mr Heller had been greatly affected, in a commercial way, by Owney's smile. He saw it, in a vaguely captured manner, as a compelling business opportunity.

'I am an independent sales executive,' Owney said, fixated on Mr Heller's suspended swatches of black eyebags which hung in mourning folds under his pink and blue eyes. Mr Heller was as short and round and as bulky as if, were his clothing suddenly stripped away, he would be found to be formed by rings of giant sausages. He carried his authority in his dentures.

'What do you sell?'

'Luxury novelties.'

'Do you do well? You are well dressed. You appear successful.'

Owney looked him directly in the eye but he did not speak.

'How much do they pay you?'

'Two hundred and fifty a week,' Owney lied.

Elation shot through the canny frankfurter manufacturer. Another of the intuitive hunches which had made him an industry leader was being confirmed. 'I need a specialty salesman,' he said. 'It could lead to sales administration. It could pay you around three hundred a week.'

'I have deep roots in luxury novelties,' Owney answered. 'But thank you, Mr Heller.' The offer had come too fast for Owney's fuzzy mind to be able to understand it, much less evaluate it in all of its meanings, so he had rejected it reflexively.

'That was just a random figure. Four hundred a week.'

Owney beamed his clear eyes at Mr Heller. He allowed a smile of appreciation to demonstrate his fine teeth slowly, in miraculous muscular arrangement, revealing not greed but a kind of thrilling gratitude to the eye of the beholder.

'Well,' he said tentatively.

Mr Heller's small pink and blue eyes drew light into themselves, darkening the heavy swags beneath them as the back-lighting of the sun darkens thunderclouds. He had not become the leading national manufacturer and distributor of frankfurters in the United States and Canada without dedication. When the National Football League had taken demonstration teams to England it had been Francisco Heller's frankfurter vision which had given the sport its American identity. When the bratwurst craze had struck the tennis industry, Heller had been there first with the most bratwursts. He had pioneered cocktail sausages.

Mr Heller breathed deeply, leaned forward, and spoke earnestly. 'Do you know frankfurters?'

'Well, I suppose, I –'

'They aren't just chopped and seasoned meat with 3.5 per cent of specific non-meat additives stuffed into a casing, you know.'

'No?'

'Sausages are human history. Laocoön, who tried to stop the Trojans from hauling the wooden horse inside the walls of Troy, was a prominent sausage merchant of the town who got into an argument with two of his sons about the flavouring in a couple of long links of liverwurst the boys had made and the whole argument ended up with not only the three of them all tangled up in the liverwurst but as a statue, possibly by Athenodorus or maybe Agesander, in the Vatican in Rome. It is an absolute masterpiece of anatomical knowledge.'

He leaned forward yet further with eagerness to impart sausage meanings. 'The earliest North American Indians made pemmican, which is a compressed dried meat and berry cake: your typical sausage. Marco Polo didn't return from China with the discovery of pasta. Pasta had been eaten in Italy long before he was born. What is the word *lasagna* but Latin for the pasta eaten at funerals? Marco Polo came back from China with the frankfurter. It was the invention of the Chinese emperor's *jefe de cocina*. His name was Fan' Fieu Toa. You get it? His name was the origin of the word frankfurter! A great German city was named after him! The wiener, which Johann George Lahner says he invented in Vienna in 1805, is nothing but a bland copy, only skinnier. The frankfurter is an American heritage, more American than Mom's apple pie –

Mom's apple pie! You'll be selling timelessness and five thousand years of human dignity when you sell frankfurters. Who could say that about a Big Mac?'

'I never knew that about China,' Owney said. 'I never thought of the frankfurter that way.'

'*Can* you do it? Do you *want* to do it?' Mr Heller grasped both of Owney's forearms, staring into his eyes as Apollo had stared at the oracle.

'I – I think I can, Mr Heller.'

'You are hired.'

Owney knew, as he shook Mr Heller's hand, that, in a fiduciary sense having nothing to do with what he and Dolly were already determined to do with their lives, he had just committed himself to marrying Dolly, which made him inexpressibly happy because with $400 a week he would be able to support her without depleting his capital. He also knew that, if he accepted the job and, inevitably, he and Dolly got married, it would mean a sacrifice for Dolly, too, and a loss for the world. Although she didn't seem to give a damn about it, she would be giving up a great career as a singer. Her father had spent $1,500, mostly in bribes, to line up a recording date and the result had had such an effect on the record company executives that they had offered Dolly a contract and, when she had refused it, had pleaded with her father to take back the bribes and persuade her to sign with them. But that had happened just two weeks after he and Dolly had met and what with her instantaneous decision to conceive his children, she would have nothing to do with singing commercially.

Owney was bemooned by Dolly. She had graduated summa cum laude from Barnard College with a degree in musical theory when she was twenty then she had gone on to study cello and voice at Juilliard. She could chat comfortably on the faulty philosophical concepts of the Pythagoreans who held that the principles of mathematics were the basis of music, which was a manifestation of mathematical perfection that was independent of the hearing faculty and depended on numbers. 'This was pure philosophical speculation,' she told Owney. 'From the history of thought about music from the Greeks onward, we learn that "science" is a term which has been used inexactly about music in a much wider meaning than it commonly denotes today.'

'Is that so?' Owney answered blankly. He knew that, as a German-Puerto Rican woman, Dolly would make a model wife and mother. The German heritage would make her extremely neat

34

and tidy and the Puerto Rican would keep her from getting too much so, while both nationalities were extremely fertile.

He achieved his answer to Mr Heller. 'I'll take the job,' he said.

The two men rose and sauntered into the living room where Mrs Heller was working a tea cosy in petit-point and Dolly was seated behind a cello.

'Can you play that?' Owney asked.

'Can she play it?' Mr Heller said. 'She can make you laugh or cry or bare your soul when she plays that thing.'

'She is also tremendous on the cellone,' Mrs Heller said.

'That's an instrument which was developed by Selzner of Dresden for the double bass parts in chamber music,' her husband explained. 'Boy! You should hear her go with Schubert's "Trout" Quintet.'

'And the Octet,' Mrs Heller added.

Dolly began to play McDowell's 'Romance' and Owney forgot frankfurters. As she played she filled his mind and heart. He forgot his quest for his mother.

Marriage to Dolly Heller became the main reason for Owney Hazman's life. To win her, frankfurters became the opposing measure of his contentment. They were married and moved into a seven-room apartment in the Apthorpe, one floor below Dolly's parents.

Chapter 7

On Oona and Osgood Noon's honeymoon, an eerily mysterious thing happened. His bride told him that he looked like the young Calvin Coolidge, and Noon was bitten by the Presidential bug, contracting a malaise from which few have ever recovered.

Goodie Noon *was* like Coolidge. He had the same flair for wearing hats, the same eloquent body language, the same endearing expression, the same dulcet voice. He told his dad of his ambitions to seek the White House, emphasizing how he felt that the move could help business, and a separation from the family company was arranged.

Intending to devote the rest of his life to public service, as politics is called at its most profitable level, he climbed the ladder slowly, rung by rung, winning appointments, rather than being elected to the various offices, starting as Deputy Director of the Kansas Bureau of Fisheries, a *sub-rosa* CIA post, advancing to become an aide to the congressman who represented the Highland Park voting district of Dallas, then making his way steadily to become Honorary Chairman of the Committee to Nominate Richard Nixon, a national honour.

After Nixon's election, Noon's contributions to that campaign ($173,983), and his endorsement of the President which said, 'I have absolute confidence as to his integrity', were rewarded by his appointment as Ambassador to Monaco, a newly created post, then in rapid succession he was named Chairman of the National Energy from Toxic Waste Power Commission; Deputy Assistant Chief of Protocol at the State Department (with his own private secretary), and, at last, burst through as a Deputy Assistant Secretary of Commerce in the Ford Administration. He was on the short list of the ninety-one candidates for Vice-President in the first Reagan campaign but he was defeated in that gallant try by vicious, underhanded politics. Nonetheless, he had built up an impressive and enviable political background, which had demonstrated his ability to govern. It was a career résumé which very few men or women in American life would ever be able to match.

After the 1980 elections he shot upwards as his people manoeuvred for and won his appointment to the Chairmanship of the Third American Centenary of 2076. He worked tirelessly at the job until his undeniable talent as a source for funds was recognized by the Republican National Committee, and he was called to the helm of professional politics and put in charge of getting the vote out in American Samoa.

Party leaders tended to try to prevent him from carrying out public speaking chores. As Goodie himself said, 'If I have a tendency, and I confess to it, it is not to go on and on with great eloquent statements of belief.' And, 'America's freedom is the example to which the world expires.'

In a hallowed moment in a speech in Iowa, one of his adopted 'home' states, when he was running (unsuccessfully) for the office of Corn-Popping Commissioner, he orated, 'I was shot down, and I was floating around in a little yellow raft. I thought of my mom and dad. I thought of my faith, the separation of church and state.' As he had said to *The New York Times Magazine*, 'I am not your basic intellectual.'

In all events, Oona Noon had a much firmer grasp of politics (and reality) than her husband. He deferred to her in all matters except those concerning the Flag and the Pledge of Allegiance, where it is possible that no other American or alien expert could ever challenge either his knowledge or his dedication. Since those two subjects, plus a relentless opposition to abortion, were the basis – under the thrilling slogan cried out as if from a modern Henry V by Ronald Reagan on the St Crispin's Day of the Republican Party's soul, *'Get The Money'* – the Noons knew that inevitably Goodie, who had ready access to rather enormous amounts of money, had to be chosen somehow to become a standard bearer for the Party in some area of electoral politics. The die was cast.

There was an innate reluctance to move him any higher at the National Republican Committee, despite the fact that he would have made a great leader, not only because he could not master his native tongue but also because of his wealth, which the Republican Party, as was widely known, tended to abjure.

Goodie Noon was as confused as the voters, never getting any of the issues quite right then fluffing their articulation. E.g.: He was four-square against the American Civil Liberties Union because they were 'too belligerent' about rights of freedom of speech, religion, assembly, political views and the right to be let alone. Furthermore, they opposed the use of assault rifles in schoolyards. He was a Reagan Revolutionary who was determined to preserve for ever the achievement of that venerable leader's record which had 67.8 per cent of national family income going to the wealthiest 40 per cent of Americans.

However, Goodie's own great wealth had its drawbacks. It was a given that the Republican leaders have always been on guard against mixing great wealth and democracy, so Oona Noon put two firms of accountants on the problem and they proved that the Noons owned less than $13,472 in direct capital after the encumbrances of the mortgages on the houses on Bland Island, in the Long Island Sound; Alexandria, Virginia; and the vastly undervalued estate on St Cloud Road in Bel-Air, California, which stood on land that, to Noon's good fortune, still retained an evaluation established immediately after the coming of the Spanish conquistadores in the sixteenth century. The Noon capital was further curtailed, the accountants proved, by his obligation to lifetime leases on a hotel room in Dallas, Texas; a farm outside Des Moines, Iowa; an apartment in Reading, Pennsylvania; and a magnificent estate in Aptos, California, which made him a resident of those great states in the event that one day he would need to seek their electoral votes. 'I am legally and in every other way, emotionally entitled to be what I want to be, and being a Texan, an Iowan, a Pennsylvanian, and a Californian is what I want to be and that's what I am,' Goodie had said forthrightly even though he was born in Massachusetts, grew up in Connecticut, lived in New York, and paid taxes in Maine. Then, abruptly, he changed the subject, bewildering his interviewers. 'On the surface, selling arms to a country that sponsors terrorism, of course, clearly, you'd have to agree it's wrong, but it's the exception that sometimes proves the rule.'

Claiming four states as his home, Goodie had needed to master four separate regional accents. That took time, money, and three of the finest phonetists Hollywood had ever produced. They achieved the effect slowly by teaching him to manipulate his voice to imitate the sound of ripping cardboard as he spoke and that seemed to settle the matter for everyone.

Unknown to her husband, Mrs Noon also maintained a marginal residence in Cochabamba, Bolivia, the world's second-largest producer of cocaine. 'Almost every day there feels like spring,' she had crowed. And so it could have been. Klaus Barbie, who was the Gestapo chief in Lyons, had lived in Cochabamba advising the local dictator (who was deeply into cocaine production) and helping him to plan the highway to the Shrine of the Virgin of Urkupina until he was deported to France.

Mrs Noon had twelve thousand acres of coca leaf under production in the Chapare region west of the city which reduced the cost (to her) of the ultimate product on its journey from maker to wearer by eliminating middlemen. She grew it, processed it, packaged it, then shipped it in her own supertankers to market where the energetic wholesalers and retailers of the Mafia, her partners, took over.

It had hardly been necessary to expose the amount of Noon's 'indirect' capital to the voters which amounted to $2,300,000,092 because that involved his generous share of the limitlessly profitable Noon family business which was in the profession of making large amounts of money wherever it could be found and which had prospered exceedingly under Ronald Reagan. Oona Noon opposed the idea of exposing the amount of this indirect capital to the public because she felt it would only either (a) make them discontented or (b) inflame them. Noon himself bristled when he was referred to as an aristocrat. 'I am a working stiff,' he told his biographer, Abner Stein, 'a tool handler from the oil fields of Texas who gets by with the sweat of his brow.'

Not for nothing was Goodie Noon sometimes nicknamed 'Lucky', an affectionate moniker given out by powerful Administration numerologists, caused by his having more 'windows' in his name than any leader in American history. 'Osgood Otto Noon, seven picture window o's through which the clear and dazzling future can be seen,' the chief White House numerologist/astrologer said. No one, to the family's knowledge, had ever seen the o's as being zeros because Goodie's résumé would have quickly made them a laughing stock.

The charm, beauty, and the considerable personal fortune of his wife emphasized and proved the resonance of the Noons' enormous voter appeal. Seeking the attention of his Party, Noon's campaign contributions had amounted to so much money that it was unavoidable that he be invited to run with the pack of eleven Republican and nine Democratic candidates in 1992, for the office of President of the United States, all of them stuck like infected raisins into a pack of camp followers, pollsters and patch workers,

39

and 1,273 members of the country's committed communications industry which guarded American history. It was the purpose of this entire gypsy army to exhaust any interest the American public might have had in any part of national politics during the two years prior to the Presidential nominating conventions of both parties.

Presidential politics was not a new league for Noon. He had visited the White House twice during the Nixon Administration, so he was in no way overawed by the heights he had reached by gaining the Party's interest in his candidacy. Noon was aware, because his wife had explained it to him several times, that his family company commanded the world's largest interest in American and foreign oil cartels as well as the great aerospace industry, and several of the communications cartels which formed the thinking for the country. He had been hard put to grasp this advantage because for so many years he had been unable to persuade the keepers of the keys to run him for any elective political office even though he had offered generous financing to the State Committee Chairmen of Nevada, West Virginia, and Louisiana to be run for the US Senate from those states or even, in one instance, to be appointed to succeed the one senator who had resigned because of a felony misunderstanding.

For all his yearnings to be called to leadership there had been, despite the profligate availability of campaign funds, something about Noon's grasp of the electorate, of politics itself, of government, even of the actual language spoken by the voters, which had somehow made the professional politicians hesitate to encourage his candidacy for anything except carefully vetted appointive offices, despite the fact that Noon stood for a kinder and gentler Mafia. People in high places told each other that he had a personality problem. Defending his personal style Goodie said, 'What's wrong with being a boring kind of guy? What do they want me to do? Dye my hair green and dance up and down in a miniskirt? Anyway, I kind of think I'm a scintillating kind of fellow.'

The Presidential election of 1992, which was not so far away, would differ markedly from other recent Presidential elections because of the lack of an obvious favourite in either Party and the increased number of early primaries. Therefore the candidates willing to run would face crucial decisions about raising and spending the tens of millions of dollars which were needed to begin and sustain campaigns.

Political strategists said any candidate would need to raise $6 to $8 million for the first year of campaigning alone, to finance the early primary voting efforts and to have any chance of competing for the nomination. Further, as months became years, the fields in both Parties would be whittled down as those candidates unable to raise the $30 to $50 million dollars which would ultimately be needed would have to withdraw from the race.

'Front loading of the primaries demands that fund-raising begin up front,' said Carter B. Modred, Chairman of the Republican National Committee. 'Every candidate will face really serious numbers very quickly.' The Chairman was also quick to point out that a new campaign finance law was on the Congressional agenda as he spoke and that some of the anticipated changes could help lesser-known candidates by allowing them to accept more money from large donors.

The Noons knew of the whole thrilling opportunity in late 1988, some two years before the announcements of candidacies were made. Oona Noon, as though born and bred to politics, began her plotting to win the Presidency for her husband.

Out of the blue, Goodie Noon was a red-hot viable candidate because his analysts had estimated that, in the year of the next election, it would cost Goodie $96 million to be elected as President of the United States and the Party knew that Noon was connected to the largest pools of yearning-to-be-committed money in the entire country, to say nothing of its trading partners inter-nationally: such as the moderates of Iran and the Noriega con-stituency of Panama.

The moment Noon's availability had been made clear to the leaders of the Party, and they saw that Goodie Noon was ready to pull his weight in awesome cheque books, Oona Noon's next exquisitely conceived move was to retain the services of Malachi Olgilvie, the Washington lawyer, one of that handful of sinister men who carried the fearfully compromised reputation of being 'an adviser of Presidents'.

For reasons of tact, inasmuch as Olgilvie was also key adviser to the other Party, Mrs Noon's contact with the lawyer had to be made in deepest secrecy.

Olgilvie was a sportsman: owner of an NFL football franchise; of a baseball team which had almost won the most recent World Series; of casinos in Atlantic City, Las Vegas, the Dominican Republic and the Bahamas; a confidant of the great Mafiosi from whose deep pockets he had been able to finance the wide diversity of his interests. He represented four of the Japanese industrial conglomerates, such as the *nokyo*, Japan's giant association of agricultural cooperatives, three great Japanese over-endowed 'teaching foundations' and one of its great zipper companies. He was Japan's bridge to the US Congress. He was one of the most gallant supporters of The Sport of Kings, American horse-racing. He bred horses, supervized their training, and won with them in the major stake races around the country, so Oona Noon chose to meet him at Belmont Park, in New York, at 5.55 a.m. on a Saturday morning to discuss the early details of the campaign. She did not tell Olgilvie she was coming. He had a reputation for shunning meetings away from his chambers.

Chapter 8

Owney made his way through the muffled light across the walled city of wooden barns and dormitories on his way to the training track. The Pinkertons had just unlocked the gate so he knew it was about 5.30 a.m., but he knew people had their horses out there because he could hear the snorting. He could see dim figures lined up along the outside rail with folded arms or bunching up inside the clocker's stand palming stopwatches.

The ground was alive with thoroughbred horses framed against the high grandstand which was more than a mile across the track far in the background. As Owney came up, Mr Olgilvie was saying, 'Well, he isn't blowing. And he's got his feet under him pretty good.' Mr Olgilvie had a deep furry voice which pushed aside all in its path like a boulder rolling down a hill. He was clocking a horse called Starbinder. He said, without seeming to look at Owney, staring at the running horse, 'Don't bet anything on this one, Owney. He's got heat in his ankle.'

Mr Olgilvie was a model mesomorph with hooded eyes. He was fifty-odd and gave the impression that he could count in nine languages at the same time and come out much better than even with every one of them. His eyebrows could convey orders like a taxi-cab despatcher. He was a big-time Washington lawyer; a man who had plotted his way through dense forests of opportunity; a man to terrify all sensible people, to make them think instantly of the horrors of wars, of great pools of corruption, and of the psalms which were sung to power and greed.

While the lads were covering Starbinder with blankets, Mr Olgilvie and his trainer conferred. The trainer sent the horse back to the barns. Mr Olgilvie took Owney to his car where Allie Melveeny, a riders' agent, was waiting for him.

'What about my boy?'

'We'll put him on Hilary's Doll in the third this afternoon,' Mr Olgilvie said. He and Owney got into the car and drove back towards the barns, angling off the road to avoid a bus which was shuttling hot walkers between stables. He parked the car beside a barn and they got out. 'I'm going to have my Fourth of July picnic at Rockrimmon and I want you fellows to handle the food.'

It would be the third year that Heller's Wurst Inc. had been permitted to handle the food for Mr Olgilvie's picnic; entirely frankfurters and ageless rolls.

'Same as last year, Mr Olgilvie?'

Before the lawyer could answer, a long robin's-egg blue car with a two-seater body by Figoni et Falaschi which had embarrassingly indecent lines drove up slowly and stopped directly in front of them. The directional effect of the car was enveloped in thin, flowing independent pods that were organically and separately expressed from the main form but blended into it. Owney felt himself hyperventilating as he looked at it.

The Figoni vision was driven by a striking woman of, Owney decided, an interesting age. She had a golden tan and wore a V-neck yellow sweater over a scarlet blouse. Her eyes were like Delft dinner plates on a snowfield. Owney decided that the expression she had just slipped into when she spotted Mr Olgilvie was designed to scare the whey out of anyone. She had cheekbones as high and as flat as an Inuit medicine man and short yellow hair which fitted her like an Aztec feather helmet. He made a vivid note to stay out of her way, but she was gorgeous, he gave her that. She wore clothes as if Van Dongen had painted them on her and she had a mouth that looked like a meal in itself.

She stopped the Figoni sculpture directly in front of them but she didn't get out.

Mr Olgilvie said, with enforced courtesy, 'This is Owney Hazman. Owney, allow me to present you to Mrs Osgood Noon.'

'How do you do, Mr Hazman.' She stretched an arm out of the car and they shook hands. She seemed as if she were trying to think of something, anything, to say. She seemed as if she had suddenly run out of words but, holding tightly to the leather-bound steering wheel, she said, 'Are you a racin' man?'

'No, ma'am. Just visiting.'

'Well, you visitin' with the right kinda people.' She was staring hard at him, then she suddenly broke away and spoke to Olgilvie. 'I got to talk to you, Mal.' She tossed a routinely polite smile in

Owney's direction to convey that she had other things on her mind.

Owney thought her voice was like a southern country road. It was rugged and had a lot of ruts in it but it got her there. As he listened to her speak, Owney had a mental association with the proprietary word 'darkies'. She looked and sounded as if she owned thousands of darkies. She also looked as if she owned even more white folks.

Mr Olgilvie smiled (semi-automatically, the expensive lawyer's way), and said, 'Give me five minutes', and turned his back on her. He put his arm across Owney's shoulders and walked him away from the motor car.

As they walked away from her, Mrs Noon looked up into the rear-view mirror and adjusted it so she could see the reflection of her face. Her hand shook as she made the adjustment. She saw that her skin was tanned but that it had no life or real colour in it. Her eyes were as blank as the shock which had taken all expression away. She wondered how she had been able to speak to him after Mal had spoken his name. She knew that if she had had to get out of the car when Mal pulled the curtain away from the past she would not have been able to stand. She had just come face to face with her little boy, her merry, loving, wonderful little boy. He had become a man. She had sent him off to school that morning and, somehow, all these years afterwards, he had found his way back to her. He had come back to her and he had looked at her as anyone would look at a stranger: impersonally, politely, but without interest. Nineteen years. Nineteen years without a day that she hadn't thought about him. Maybe she couldn't ever get him back, but she couldn't let him go either. He wasn't a little boy any more but neither was she the same woman who had done what she was told to do and had left him alone and bewildered, wondering why she had deserted him. She stared out across the horse yard but he had vanished somewhere among the barns.

Mr Olgilvie said to Owney, 'To show my appreciation for what you're going to do for my Fourth of July party, I am going to give you Hilary's Doll in the third race today.'

'Thanks, Mr Olgilvie.'

'It's worth a fifty-dollar bet. No more.'

'Yes, sir.'

'Walk around the barn, then come back here and tell me I have to come to the telephone. Understand?'

'Yes, sir.'

'No matter what Mrs Noon says, you keep telling me what an important call it is. Give me about ten minutes with her.'

'Yes, sir.'

'And, oh, I meant to tell you, I'll get you the frankfurter account for the National Bar Association outing in August. They could eat 7,000 hot dogs. But remember, I take no commissions – directly.' He patted Owney on the shoulder and walked away toward the Figoni.

Owney patrolled around the back of the barn, looking at his watch. He thought about what the odds might be on Hilary's Doll. If the price were 10–1 and he bet a million dollars he could win himself a lot of money. He'd be able to take full page ads all over the world to find his mother. He visualized the television commercial he would run on the networks. It would be a picture of the white clapboard house in Meier's Corners right at honeysuckle time. The voiceover, dreamy and persuasive, would offer a reward of $25,000 to anyone who could give information as to the where-abouts of Margaret 'Molly' Tompkins Hazman, followed by a description of his mother: lustrous black hair, Canadian speech, and a tendency to favour aprons.

He shrugged the vision off. He could probably get fifty bucks together for a sure thing. He would call Meyer the bookie when he got to the office.

He came round the corner of the stable keyed up to deliver the urgent message to Mr Olgilvie but nobody was there except some stable lads and handlers. The Figoni was gone and so was Mr Olgilvie.

Chapter 9

Mrs Noon and Mr Olgilvie talked earnest business as they drove back to New York. To cover up her continuing confusion, she kept a satellite radio going all the way as she half listened to Olgilvie discuss election politics while trying to reach some solution about what she was going to do to reclaim her son. Twice she spoke directly to the captains of two oil tankers; one in the Caribbean and the other off Australia's Great Barrier Reef. Everything they said was intercepted and recorded by the National Security Agency at Fort George Meade, in SIGINT City, Maryland, to be distributed at the order of the Secretary of Defense to effective-eyes-only levels at the White House, the State Department, and the Central Intelligence Agency. She knew she'd be tracked and taped as long as she owned the tankers or until she could get her husband elected President.

'Who was that young man?' she asked Mr Olgilvie. 'A clerk from your office?'

'No. Just a salesman.'

'A *sales*man? At this time of morning?'

'What can I do for you, Oona? Why are we here?' He looked at her more closely. 'Say, are you all right? You look pale.'

'Jes' tuckered, I guess. I been up all hours plannin' on Goodie's future campaign.'

'Campaign?'

'We got the OK from the Party to make the run for President.'

'Well!'

'That was one of the two thangs I had to talk to you about, Mal. And I couldn't risk going to your office or usin' the phone.'

'I should think not. What two things?'

'Well – what is the first thing I should do to get Goodie really started before the primary campaigns?'

47

'Exploratory funds. You've got to pack as much money into pre-campaign exploratory funds as you can raise.'

'Why?'

'Because they are unaccountable funds. No matter how much you can pile into the war chest as exploratory funds, Goodie'll never have to account for a dime of it to the Federal Election Commission. Now's the time to load on the Mafia money, the gun-lobby money, and the tobacco industry money. What's the second thing?'

'I'm thinkin' I'd like to sell off the seventy-nine tankers Nicky left me. If it came out what else those tankers were bringing in besides oil, it could be embarrassing for Goodie's campaign. Cocaine has come to be some kinda political football.'

'You're right, of course. But selling the tankers is sure going to set off a storm with Big Oil.'

'I know. Don't you think I'll ever fo'git what happened when Nicky thought he would sell the tankers to the Saudis.'

'Does Goodie know you've been moving those other cargoes, the – ah – vegetable matter, on those tankers?' Mr Olgilvie asked.

'All he thinks about is the Flag an' how to git elected to some-thin'.'

'What do you want to do?'

'Look at it this way. I took a lotta money out, in oil and in that other stuff, but now Goodie has his shot at the White House after all those years of sluggin' away, servin' his time, playin' musical chairs, and he wants it bad, and I mean bad, so he kin sit higher than his father. So I'm gone sell the fleet.'

'Who to?'

'Well, I gotta go for the best price, don't I, Mal?'

'It begins to sound tricky.'

'Oh, it's tricky.'

'What's your plan?'

'This Monday comin', a new client is gone call on you at you office. He looks Italian but he speaks better English than Prince Charles. He gone make like he a British real estate operator, but jessa same, the govmint spooks gone make him to be a Ayrab an' when they check him out in Riyadh they gone scream because he *is* a Ayrab and that will purely turn their hairs white.'

Oona Noon's speech patterns owed much to the Gullah of eastern South Carolina, from about Georgetown to Charleston and Savannah. It came out of her in choppy, staccato sounds, pitched low but with full resonance. She punished the verbs, slurred the pronouns, and every other statement ended as a question. It was a sensuous blend of sweet and sharp; sounding more feminine perhaps than the good Lord ever meant a woman to be.

'The oilies are gone start up all ovah agin, but this time they'll be runnin' the wrong way. They eyes will be squintin' at the Middle East but we won't be there. They gone think Dr Hassam Atarf will be negotiatin' wif you for the tankers when he'll jes' be talkin' to you 'bout buying some real estate I dangled in front of him that I'm gone let him have cheap. He'll tell you his name is Richard Coomber. He is the red herrin'.'

'If he is the red herring then who is the buyer?'

'The Chinese.'

'The People's Republic of China?' Olgilvie asked with disbelief. He was thinking hard about his main clients, the Mafia, for whom Oona Noon's tankers were importing the most expensive vegetable product ever grown.

'They negotiator will be smuggled inta your house on the Chain Bridge Road at about four o'clock Tuesday mornin'. His name is Mistah Chao Lin Choy. You kin call him Mr Jay. They said he was a geologist an' an engineer but it figures that he holds good rank in their secret police. So you'll see Richard Coomber for an hour or so a day at your office, but the real negotiatin' will happen when you git home at night and sit down with ole Mr Jay.'

'I suppose you know all this is going to make a lot of trouble. The oil companies are going to go bananas because if China gets those tankers there goes the barrel price of oil.'

'But I'm gonna have my two and a half billion from the sale. And I'm not just countin' my dreams. I'm gonna unload before anybody knows what hit them.'

'It's getting complicated, Ravi.'

'Look what they did to Nicky because he played it out in the open.' Nicky Nepenthes had been Mrs Noon's husband before she had married Osgood Noon. 'I owe this one to Nicky's memory. When he found me I was just a wanderer on the face of the earth. The oilies went wild when Nicky made his deal with the Saudis, didn't they? Because he let them know all about it before he set out to do it, they put the Vice-President of the United States on him and the Secretary of State and the Attorney-General on orchestratin' the CIA, the FBI, the Ship Sales Act, AT&T, the world media, and day-and-night surveillance teams on three continents – the power of the world. They had the Minister of Finance of Saudi Arabia embarrass Nicky wif the King. Jay Edguh Hoovuh, hisseff, declared that Nicky was un-American. God, how that maddened Nicky! He carried an Argentine passport and Monacan citizenship so how could he be un-American? They released it to *The Daily News*. Why not to *The New York Times*, the papuh of national record? Their Society Editor never fo'gave me. The oilies filed dozens of law suits against Nicky on three continents, goin' for hundreds of millions in damages, then they had the Peruvian Air Force bomb Nicky's whalin' fleet, but Nicky had insured the ships for nineteen million dollahs, on inside information, befo' it happened. Our tankers jes' rotted at anchor without a charter. It was costin' us 960,000 dollahs a day an' all because Nicky decided to sell his own tankers out in the open.'

'You're a brave lady.'

'The least I kin do, Mal, is git outta the dope business while the oil business is in the doldrums, and help to make my husband President of the United States. The Chinese is the natural buyers, Mal. They found out they got big oil on their land. They don't use cars much and they short on steam heat so they gone have oil to sell. They gotta move it out when it's ready to sell because they need the dollahs more than they need the oil.'

'They could drive the price down to five dollars a barrel,' Olgilvie said reprovingly.

'A-course! That's why we got to let the oilies think you dealin' with a Ayrab who looks like an Italian and talks like an English royal. Then we pull the floor away, Mal. And we go right on to make Goodie our President.'

'I think I like it.'

Mrs Noon took a deep breath, held it, then exhaled slowly. It had come to her how she could go on seeing her son even if he could never know he was her son because her husband had put up with so much just to become President of the United States of America that if it suddenly came out that his wife had a grown son from whom she had been estranged for over nineteen years, it could cost him everything his heart desired.

'We gotta have a dummy middleman to sluice the information through from you to me,' she said slowly, 'or the oilies and the govmint gone stop us before we can make the deal.'

'How do you mean?'

'We got no choice, Mal,' she said. 'Our phones gone be tapped by the Ayrabs, the NSA, the oil companies, the Soviets, the FBI, the CIA, and the Chinese and mosta *their* phones are already tapped by the DDI and the New York banks.'

'One thing is for sure – we cannot be seen together. I'm pretty deeply involved with the other Party and, anyway, there's no sense in letting the spooks know that I'll be negotiating the sale of those tankers.'

'How we gone handle that?'

'Let me think about it.'

'All we need is a go-between. How 'bout that young fella who was with you out at the track this mornin'?'

'Owney?'

'He seemed like a nice, real bright boy.'

'He's nice enough. But we couldn't let him know what we're doing.'

'He could also liaise between you, me an' Goodie on the campaign.'

'I don't know. If the CIA and the FBI shake him hard, he could fall apart,' Mr Olgilvie said.

'We got no choice, Mal. We've got to have a dummy middleman to sluice the information through or we'll be stopped before we can make a deal. And besides, I got a good feelin' 'bout Owney. I know he's a good boy.' She stared at a mote in the middle distance. 'I'm not jes' countin' my dreams, Mal,' she said. 'We doin' the right thing. Now – what do we do about settin' Goodie in the right position to make the best run for the White House?'

'I'll talk to the Governor of Massachusetts about appointing him to the US Senate after I talk to the senior Senator about resigning for reasons of ill health. But it will cost, Ravi.'

'Cost? I'm gone sell my tankers for 'bout two billion five, ain't I? And a good part of that is gonna go towards buildin' Goodie the most gorgeous Presidential Memorial Library any President ever had.'

'Where are you going to site it?'

'Thassa problem. Goodie is officially a resident in four states, an' he jes' hoid about Alaska.'

She drove the car up the ramp of the Queensborough bridge, smiling grimly. She had spent a long time perfecting her plan. She had everything in place in Riyadh to spring the trap which would draw in the Saudis, the Iraqis, the Syrians, the British and Japanese, then the KGB and, at the right moment, pull the American government in the wrong direction, away from any possibility of sniffing out her deal with the Chinese. Then, out of the blue, God had dumped her past on her. Who could figure that her little boy would be left on her doorstep, full grown and fine?

She had to find out all about him. She had to help him. Between her and Mal Olgilvie – and maybe even including Goodie, too – they knew just about everybody who was anybody in the world and no matter what her little boy was doing there had to be fifty or two hundred ways she could help him along in the world.

Chapter 10

===

Owney drove directly from the race track to Heller's Wurst Inc. even though it was a Saturday morning. At 8.12 a.m. he went into the block-long, four-storey frankfurter factory on 12th Avenue. The 52-week-a-year season was into its swing. Employees were forced by law to take Sundays off but they did so begrudgingly because they worked on a profit-participation basis and Sunday was a very big frankfurter consumption day in the ball parks, picnic grounds, and arenas around the country, so a full Saturday work day was normal for them.

Owney entered the details of the Olgilvie order into his work station, then asked his secretary to call Meyer the bookie. He placed a telephone bet of $100 on Hilary's Doll in the third race at Belmont. The morning line was 26–1. As he hung up Miss McHanic reminded him of the 8.30 meeting in his father-in-law's office.

The meeting was just starting when Owney got there. He sat in a corner and listened to the production manager, the executive butcher, and the pork buyer argue. His father-in-law asked him, 'Everything OK with Mr Olgilvie, Owney?'

'The same hundred dozen frankfurters for his picnic, but he is getting us the national jamboree of the American Bar Association in August.'

'Hey – that's about a seven thousand frankfurter event.'

'He asked me what I knew about turkey wieners.' This was a cruel statement which had been planted on Owney by Mr Heller to shake up the executive echelon. Nothing generated competitive feeling with more impact than the most casual mention of turkey wieners.

The pork buyer and the production manager stopped arguing in mid-sentence. 'Turkey wieners?' the pork buyer said with distaste.

'Show me a turkey wiener and I'll show you something you can hardly taste.' This was the traditionalist attitude. Chicken and turkey franks and wieners, introduced in the 1950s, had captured 23.6 per cent of the market.

'What did you tell him?' Mr Heller asked.

'Well – I said they were lower in fat. And that they were seasoned to look and taste like regular franks.'

'You told the man that?' the pork buyer said. 'So maybe they look like the regulars but taste like they don't.'

'Owney is right,' Mr Heller said. 'By blind taste-test.'

'So how come they get only a fair rating on all the taste tests – Consumers' Reports included – when beef franks get an excellent and pork and beef mixtures get an excellent?' the pork buyer said. 'Show me a turkey wiener and I'll show you something you can hardly taste.'

'I agree, Gordon,' Owney's father-in-law said. 'But if Mr Olgilvie wants to try a couple dozen turkey wieners, we gotta supply them.'

The pork buyer threw up his hands. 'OK. All right. Start up and you'll have to buy a chain of turkey farms. Did you ever smell a turkey farm?'

'Well –'

'All right. That's that. Now – do we or don't we make a test run of *Kalbsbratwürste*, Owney's idea entirely, for Heidi-Ho, the Swiss fast food chain which is opening up this market?'

'It is certainly a delicious product,' the marketing chief said.

'Incomparable,' Mr Heller agreed. 'With a beef and veal base, at 1.8 times the bulk of any given frankfurter, it is a very delicious piece of food even if it is dead-white which turns a beautiful golden-brown in the cooking. But I gotta be convinced. A *Kalbsbratwurst* ain't no frankfurter.'

Gordon Manning said, straddling the issue, 'Patriotism is nothing more than the good things we ate in our childhood.'

Everyone sat on the fence, waiting for Mr Heller to make the decision. Owney was sure his father-in-law had decided to make the veal sausages because his mother-in-law had told his wife that he had eaten *Kalbsbratwürste* for breakfast and dinner every day that week which could have been baffling because Mr Heller rarely ate anything but frankfurters. Owney capitalized on his hunch.

'When Heidi-Ho goes national with the *Kalbsbratwürste* this is potentially a 550,000-unit-a-week order, Mr Heller,' he said. 'We should take it.'

Mr Heller moved his glance from face to face around the room. 'All right, then. That's it. All systems go.'

At 4.00 p.m., an hour and a half before he left the office, Owney called Meyer, the bookie. Hilary's Doll had not only won, but it had paid 30–1. For such a thrifty man as Owney Hazman, the realization that he had won $3,000 was almost more than he could bear. Tears flooded his eyes and he resolved to let Dolly have the subscription to *Musical America* magazine which she had wanted so much the year before.

Chapter 11

Jovially, the following Monday morning, Mal Olgilvie received Dr Hassam Atarf in his panelled office with the bullet-proof windows, the sound-transmitting carpet borders, and the Caravaggios on the walls. Olgilvie didn't change his expression when the man came into the room but it was instantly clear that something had gone wrong. Dr Atarf did not look at all Italian. His English pronunciation was closer to Yasser Arafat's than to Prince Charles's and he had not used the cover name, Richard Coomber.

Dr Atarf, although not as handsome as Arafat, was anthropologically the stereotypical Arab who seemed to have been hastily and uncomfortably dressed in Western clothes.

Until his transformation into a businessman, he had been the top car-bomb planner for the Arab Jihad. The real Dr Atarf was being held in Saudi Arabia under intensive interrogation because, at a Michael Jackson video party in Riyadh, he had let drop that he would be leaving the following day for Washington to buy the site for an office/housing/shopping centre in Columbia, South Carolina, from Oona (Nepenthes) Noon. He had mentioned her name rather carelessly because her husband had been so prominent in the international oil shipping business and he thought everyone in the room was in the oil business. Also, he said it that way because that was how he and Mrs Noon had worked out the moves. A Saudi undercover agent whom Dr Atarf had made sure would be on hand had overheard this and had arrested Atarf as he left the party on the charge that he was actually going to Washington to buy the tankers for Iran or for an oil alliance with Nigeria and Indonesia.

After detaining Dr Atarf, the Saudi government, using back channels, had called in Al-Istikhbaratt-As-Souriat (AIAS), the dreaded Syrian Intelligence Agency which operated almost anonymously in the place of the utterly blown Libyan services with fullest KGB resources. Never entirely trusting the Syrians, the KGB had covertly placed the AIAS under the surveillance of KHAD, the grimly appalling Afghan secret police, which was operated and had been trained by the KGB. Nonetheless, and despite the intramural complications it caused, it would not have been possible for the Saudis to take direct action through their own intelligence disciplines because of their warm relationship with Washington.

The Syrians reasoned that, with all those tankers in their possession, they could make a much better deal with Moscow in the long run than if they went running to the Russians right at the start, as if they needed help. It was a somewhat devious high level decision but it ruled out telling the Russians anything about the opportunity until the deal could be consolidated and the Syrians actually had something for sale. 'When we control those tankers,' their leader said, 'the Russians will pay us enough in armaments to destroy every Israeli.'

Everything proceeded according to Mrs Noon's master plan. The Saudi secret police got incomplete information out of Dr Atarf. They learned that he was due to appear in the law offices of Schwartz, Blacker, and Moltonero, Mr Olgilvie's firm in Washington, the following Monday morning. The AIAS had so little time to prepare that they had to send a second-string man to Washington. After a preliminary meeting with Mr Olgilvie in which the false Dr Atarf pressed Olgilvie crudely as to whether Mrs Noon was interested in selling her tankers, the lawyer was ready to report to his client.

Olgilvie couldn't risk a call because the National Security Agency was on the case. He couldn't fly to New York to report in person because his professional calendar was so filled that he had time for only a twenty-minute lunch break at his desk. Until Owney Hazman could be set up as the drop, he would have to turn to the Chinese, as interested parties, and to their resources. They had an enormous intelligence apparatus which could get a safe message to Mrs Noon.

As a two-time widower, Mr Olgilvie lived alone (with four servants) in a 22-room house in McLean, Virginia, just off Chain Bridge Road, overlooking the Potomac. It was an ample, quite comfortable house which had cost $1,438,000 in 1968 and was therefore now valued at $7,912,574, although the Reagan administration had proved over and over again that there had been only the barest minimum of inflation.

Unknown to Olgilvie, despite the financial confidence which the

57

Mafia had shown in him, one of his servants, a houseman named Jilly Pozze, was beholden to the principal crime family of the country because they owned a bank which held notes on a loan his mother had made to buy an apartment house on the Grand Concourse in the Bronx with very short money under very big leverage. In order to prevent the foreclosure which the bank had suddenly threatened, Jilly Pozze had agreed, seventeen months before, to listen to conversations at Mr Olgilvie's house when the lawyer had guests, possibly because Mr Olgilvie never wasted dinners on friends, only entertaining for power and profit.

In the present instance, because Olgilvie had mentioned to his benefactors in the Mafia that Mrs Noon was thinking of selling the fleet of tankers, and because the tankers were a vital supply line of the most popular vegetables the Family had ever distributed, Pozze was told specifically to activate electronic surveillance. If she sold the tankers, Olgilvie would handle the deal. If she sold the tankers, it was a vital business matter to a very, very prominent *fratellanza* family that an entity sensitive to the profits from the valuable vegetables, such as themselves and nobody else, bought the tanker fleet.

Jilly Pozze had prepared the basement room into which the Chinese negotiator, Mr Jay, would move for the duration of the talks that would determine the terms under which the Chinese government would acquire the Noon tankers. In furnishing it comfortably, Pozze had also bugged it well.

At 4.21 on Tuesday morning Mr Jay moved in. No one but the Olgilvie household knew he was there and, of the household, because the meeting room was wired, only Jilly Pozze knew why he was there.

At his first meeting with Mr Jay, Olgilvie shared his own misgivings about the bogus Dr Atarf, asking him if Jay's organization could possibly thwart Dr Atarf. Mr Jay assured him that the problem could be handled.

The basement room was comfortably furnished. It had a splendid Chinese rug of celestial blue and gold, a large work table, two filing cabinets, a sturdy double bed, three chairs, an armoire, a sauna, good lighting and what seemed to be hi-fi equipment which consisted of two Sony 7055As, two Sony cassette recorders, two large Revox tape recorders, and a control panel with many switches. Connected to this amalgam was a bulky metal box.

'This is a late-model Japanese receiver-transmitter. It sends high-speed Morse. It can transmit four thousand characters in a half-second. However, to send your message, I shall use ciphony.'

'Ciphony?'

'Spoken cryptology. In this telephone I have installed tampers with an electrical current which shifts sound frequencies and transposes syllables out of their normal order.'

'Oh, yes. A scrambler.'

'*Scram*bler? You *know* this telephone?' Mr Jay seemed horrified.

'I have one at my office.'

'But – the supplier told us we would have the only operating models in the world.' His jaw muscles bulged. 'Beijing will deal with this,' he added grimly. 'Thank you for bringing it to my attention. I shall communicate through this – scrambler – by using a sixth century Chinese dialect. The NSA will be nine to eleven years in breaking it. By that time Mrs Noon's tankers will long have been our tankers. Please, you must go to bed. I assure you that everything will be achieved.' Mr Jay looked entirely Italian and spoke English as John Huston had spoken it.

'Would it be possible,' Mr Olgilvie asked, 'to install identical equipment – the high speed transmitter, a scrambler and a scholarly Chinese operator – in Mrs Noon's apartment in New York?' Olgilvie had begun to hope that they would have no need for Owney Hazman's services.

'It can be done. But it would take two or three weeks.'

Chapter 12

Mr Jay transmitted the facts about the presence of the bogus Dr Atarf and the threat it constituted to his home-based Intelligence service in Beijing. Eleven hours later, through the New China News Agency (NCNA), instructions from the Chinese Central External Liaison's Department of Investigation (CELD) were received by deeply coded short-wave broadcast which went on the air daily at 9.00 a.m. from Beijing. The CELD orders assigned the Chinese Foreign Intelligence Department (FID), the Chinese equivalent of the American Central Intelligence Agency (CIA), to expedite the matter.

On Thursday night, as the false, jet-lagged Dr Atarf was preparing for bed in the sort of ostentatious suite which was expected of visiting Arabs in a hotel across Lafayette Park from the White House, he answered a knock on the door and admitted the night chambermaid with an armful of linen, who asked, with a shocking Australian accent, if she could turn down the bed. He motioned her into the bedroom.

When she had placed the obligatory imported chocolates on the night table and had positioned Dr Atarf's slippers beside the bed, she went into the living room of the apartment where Dr Atarf was encoding his report for the Syrian Bureau of Fisheries and shot him to death with a sound-suppressed .22 calibre pistol.

When the body was discovered the following morning, because he was a foreign national who had been writing to a foreign diplomat when he was murdered, the Washington police informed an assigned section at the Central Intelligence Agency, the Office of Security, whose responsibilities were to maintain close liaison with police departments within the country to help build security files on almost four million people, including some foreigners, who were or who might be of interest to the CIA. The Office of

Security was the master of the most questionable operations, such as being the Agency's link with the Mafia and procurers of young flesh of both sexes for visiting firemen of every stripe, from heads of state to visiting assassins; the domestic arm of the CIA. It reported directly to the DCI.

At the heart of this black hole in this airless false bottom of democracy was the Security Research Staff (SRS) whose ostensible purpose was to expose Soviet penetration agents but, in practice, was to undertake work which was too secret or too unspeakable for the rest of the organization.

James D. Marxuach, the SRS DC station chief, arrived at the late, false Dr Atarf's hotel within twenty minutes after the call from the DC police. He was a blocky man in his forties who made a profession of patriotism-through-intrigue, embroidering its meaning as the occasion arose. He took the victim's forged passport and the letter to the Syrian Embassy and told the senior Homicide detective on the case, 'We want the body toe-tagged as Michael Joseph Fogarty at the morgue. Hold it there until I release it and hold anyone who claims it. I'll have this stuff back to you in the morning.'

Marxuach took the false Dr Atarf's uncompleted report to CIA analysts at Langley and, because Mr Olgilvie's name was mentioned in the letter to the Syrians, Marxuach asked the DC police to check him out, expecting no useful answers and not getting any. Mr Olgilvie told the police that Dr Atarf had flown in from Riyadh three days before to negotiate the purchase of a shopping mall complex in Columbia, South Carolina.

Marxuach found Malachi Olgilvie in the Outfit's priority files as attorney not only for the widow of Nicky Nepenthes, the late multi-billionaire oil shipper, but as special counsel to the richest and most powerful Mafia family in North America, which told him that he must move very, very carefully so as not to give offence. The files showed that the Nepenthes woman had not only inherited a fleet of oil tankers which were beyond the control of any American oil company, but that she was now the wife of Osgood Noon, a most viable candidate for election to the office of President of the United States. Marxuach knew he would be walking on eggs but he had a job to do.

At 2.21 p.m. Eastern Time, the mole planted within the Saudi secret police by an Israeli organization, Ha Mossad, le Modiyn ve le Tafkidim Mayuhadim (the Special Operations Department of the Central Institution for Intelligence and Special Assignments,

61

Mossad), told his cut-out that the real Dr Atarf was in custody and that the running of the counter-operation had been consigned to the AIAS in Damascus.

At 4.17 p.m. Mossad's back-channel sources in Damascus had established that the bogus Dr Atarf was a mass murderer named Mustafa Bandhar, a subordinate member of the Syrian AIAS, who had been assigned to negotiate the lease/purchase of Mrs Noon's tanker fleet through Malachi Olgilvie. Mossad passed the signal to Langley.

The CIA analysts pointed out to the DCI that a potentially serious decline in Soviet oil production had accelerated to the point of creating a crisis in the Kremlin leadership. The oil production levels which had depended on the Volga-Urals fields had declined, then the production of West Siberian crude which had accounted for sixty per cent of all Soviet oil had fallen far short of normal projections. The Minister for the Petroleum Industry had been dismissed.

More than just meeting the enormous Soviet domestic and industrial needs, oil was the principal source of dollars for the purchase of Western grain and vitally needed sophisticated electronic and industrial equipment as the Soviet leadership undertook the massive shift from a military to a consumer society. The analysis showed that the Syrians were direct clients of the Soviets and that if Syria could buy/lease the Noon tankers to keep them out of the hands of the Russians, Syria would be in a much stronger bargaining position with Russia to secure the arms to blow up Israel.

There were other institutions in opposition to any plan which would have the Noon tankers falling into wrong hands. One of them was Edward S. Price, chairman and CEO of Barker's Hill Enterprises, the 'legitimate' financial arm of the most powerful crime family of Brooklyn which, with other crime families of the country, was a leader in the so-called 'other side' of the American economy, controlling 31.7 per cent of the country's business and industry.

Barker's Hill Enterprises' resources seemed immeasurable by virtue of its reinvestment of virtually limitless capital earnings from organized crime, entirely tax free, from the manufacture, distribution, and sale, by its parent company, of narcotics, pornography, extortion, gambling, prostitution, and labour racketeering. After sixty-odd years of earning an average of

$11.3 billion a year, free of tax, and investing a part of it in the political and law enforcement establishments on the national, state, and local levels, its apparatus had become a foundation stone of both the American economy and society.

Edward Price, the walking holding company for billions of criminally-gained Mafia dollars, a sedate man in his early 60s, played back tapes from the first two meetings between Mr Jay and Mr Olgilvie held in the basement of Mr Olgilvie's Washington house which had been secured for Barker's Hill by Jilly Pozze, Mr Olgilvie's houseman.

'What do you think?' he asked the Prizzi family's *consigliere*, Angelo Partanna. Mr Price had been born a Prizzi.

'I think we should throw an option on the tankers.'

'Those tankers have moved over three billion dollars' worth of vegetables from Colombia, Bolivia and Peru into the American marketplace for us,' Edward S. Price said. 'Not once was a ship searched. Tankers carry oil, or that's what the DEA thinks. If Oona Noon sells the tankers will you tell me where our next three billion will come from?'

'That's what I thought.'

'She's going to have to sell the tankers to some of our people.'

'How much was her end?'

Price waved away the fussiness of the question. 'About three hundred million a year.'

'So it's just a matter of finding out what else she wants outta life, then we give it to her, and our people get the tankers.'

'To sell to the Chinese!' Price shook his head in disappointment. 'A woman with her income, selling to Communists.'

'How much you think she wants?'

'About two billion and a half, give a hundred million, take a hundred million.'

'So we buy an option. Lemme send somebody to talk to her.'

'We won't put up a dime,' Mr Price said. 'We'll use diplomacy. Everybody thinks she is trying to sell the tankers to the Russians. Only we know she wants to sell to the Chinese. Either way, everyone else is going to go crazy.'

'Eduardo – if she's ready to sell to the Chinese, what's the difference? We gotta find out what she wants besides money. We help her get it, and we make a deal.'

'No muscle! This is high level stuff.'

'I have always been against muscle.'

*

63

The directorate of AIAS in Damascus were stunned by the news of the elimination of the false Dr Atarf from the game board. The consensus was that somehow the KGB had found out that the Syrians intended to hold them up for an emperor's ransom and had moved to strike the agent down as an example. After four and a half hours of excited shouting and wailing, a signal was sent to the AIAS team at the embassy in Washington to begin to plan to kidnap Malachi Olgilvie and hold him for ransom or, alternatively, to kidnap Mrs Noon, the ransom for either lift being to secure an agreement to sell the tankers to principals whose identities would be concealed within multiple dummy companies.

The Director, Central Intelligence (DCI), Eddie Grogan, had learned not to see the President alone. No one but the President's wife ever saw him alone because she, by law, couldn't testify against him. Such a thing as leaving the President alone with anyone who spoke English, regardless of their religion, could have violated God's mind. The President was too happy-go-lucky to risk the very strong possibility that someone would try to sell him the Washington Monument, and that he would buy it. If they could break through the high hedge of anecdotes about Jack Holt, Mary Brian, and Warner Oland with which the Commander-in-Chief regaled his visitors they could often get his attention.

The President's Chief of Staff, a charismatic (in the religious sense of that Greek word meaning gift of grace), born-again, down-home-evangelical, television Christian stood guard at the meeting.

After making a show of listening to and chuckling over the river of anecdotes, Grogan was able to hand to the spry old President the agency's economic analysis. The President sat as reposefully as a good child, in blue Dr Denton's and a white woollen robe piped with blue, hair still mussed from his long mid-morning nap, sipping Ovaltine. The report had been distilled into a few sentences of jumbo laser-typing in the hope of holding his attention. It recommended that a noisy show should be made to prove how shocked the American government was to learn of the possibility of the sale of the largest independent tanker fleet in the world to the Soviet Union, that the entire eastern world needed money and that if they had the immediate means to move their own oil out they would dump that oil on the world markets, undercutting oil pricing everywhere and wreaking havoc with Big Oil's profits. Every country in the civilized world took direction from the oil companies so something had to be done. The tankers were the property of an American national, even though they were registered in such countries as Panama, Aruba, Switzerland, and Nepal. The report said the sale of the tankers must be blocked.

'Jeepers!' the President said, reading. 'As I read this, if we don't block this sale, the price of oil will drop, the oil companies will be furious with me, the value of the dollar will soar, which will infuriate big business. But the resulting stronger dollar would worsen the already large US trade deficit – which is bad.'

He looked up from the fact sheet he was reading, startled. 'An already large deficit? When did that happen?'

'Nothing to worry about, Mr President,' Director Grogan said.

Reassured, the President continued his comments. 'This report says that all the countries of the Western hemisphere must join under the one American oil umbrella, by carving out one-fourth of the world market – is that good or bad?'

'The time has come, Mr President,' Grogan said, 'to break up the old gang and protect our own industry.'

'That's all right for you to say, but who's going to tell Margaret?'

'Who?'

'The British Prime Minister. If I am reading this report right, it will ruin the British.'

'Enlightened self-interest, Mr President. The British invented it.'

'God's will,' Dr Toomey, the Chief of Staff said.

'Yes. Sure. But you don't have to sit here and take it when she calls and she certainly will when she finds out about this.'

'We can switch the calls to the voice mimic at Langley. He'll take the heat for you.'

'No. Abolutely not. Mimics never get me right. What's the lowest safe price the eastern bloc can drive the oil to?'

'About fifteen dollars a barrel. That's rock bottom. Even their production costs are too expensive to go any lower than that.'

The President sank his face in his hands and rested there for a long moment. In fact, he fell asleep instantly but Dr Toomey, whose job it was, gently awakened him.

'You could give her a chance to dump and get out,' Dr Toomey said unctuously, after the President had rubbed the cobwebs out of his eyes. 'She's in the oil business in the North Sea. She'll be happy to have an early warning.'

'How nice of you to ring me,' the Prime Minister said silkily.

'Well – something came up,' the Leader of the Free World said.

He told her about the negotiations for the sale of the tankers and of the Saudi, Syrian, and Soviet interests. 'And some of my people here felt that to be fair we should share the information with the NATO alliance and the Japanese.'

Dr Toomey and the DCI listened expressionlessly on extension ear pieces.

'That is no way to run an intelligence operation,' the PM said sharply. 'Nothing has happened that our people can't handle.'

'*Your* people?'

'Our Secret Intelligence Services. I will see that Movement Control puts our best agent on the early Concorde flight tomorrow morning.'

'What for?'

'To liaise with your people.'

'Well – I'd have to clear that.'

Dr Toomey nodded gravely.

'Please don't clear it with anyone. Britain has an enormous stake in this and I must have instant progress reports directly from my own people. OPEC must be brought to its knees and doing that isn't precisely a NATO exercise and most certainly is not a Japanese problem. They're not oil producers, are they? It is *our* problem. *We* face this potential disaster together. If the price of oil dropped to fourteen dollars a barrel there would be a firestorm all the way down. If that happens you're going to have to impose a fifteen-dollar tariff on every barrel of oil imported into the United States and that will need to be passed along to the consumer.'

'A tariff? You mean – a *tax*?'

'Of course I mean a tax.'

'I'm going to have to call you back, Margaret.'

'What about my man? The MI6 man.'

'Well –'

Dr Toomey grimaced and shook his head vigorously, glaring at the President and praying viciously under his breath.

'It's a matter of life and death, isn't it?' the Prime Minister said.

The President shrugged helplessly at his Chief of Staff.

Chapter 13

At twenty minutes to five on the following Friday afternoon, Owney's phone rang. Miss McHanic got it. She put her hand over the mouthpiece and spoke to Owney. 'It's a Mrs Oona Noon,' she said.

'Is she an account?' If Miss McHanic had said the Figoni et Falaschi was calling, he would have remembered.

Miss McHanic shrugged. 'You want me to ask her?'

Owney picked up. 'Hazman speaking,' he said into the phone.

'One moment, Mr Hazman,' an expensive voice said. 'Mrs Noon is calling.' Then that ballsy plantation owner's voice came on the line. 'Mistah Hazman? We met Satdee at the track? With Mal Olgilvie?' Mrs Noon felt light-headed and nauseous at the same time. She had to hold the telephone to her ear with both hands to keep it steady.

'Oh, yes.'

'I want to git a message to him?'

'Well, I'd be glad –'

'He'll be calling you any time now.'

'What's the message, Mrs – uh –'

'Tell him I saw in the papers this mornin' that the Saudi interest in buying my horses is dead.'

'OK.'

'After you talk to him, I want to see you? To thank you an' all? My place at six o'clock?' He had such a beautiful speaking voice! He enunciated as clearly as his father had but there was a richness there, a vitally masculine musical something which just made her want to stand tall. What thrilled her most was that he had distinct traces of the Canadian accent she had used when they had all lived together, which meant that he had to have been deeply influenced by her, the way a boy should be by his mother.

'Your place? Where's that?' Owney said.

'It's in the book.' She hung up before she could start weeping.

Seconds after Owney disconnected, the phone rang again. It was Mr Olgilvie. 'Did she call?' he said.

'You mean – well, yes. I don't get it.'

'Stay with this one, Owney. As a favour to me.'

'She had a message for you.'

'Good. Let me have it please.'

Owney repeated the message.

'When will you be talking to her again?'

'I'm supposed to be at her place at six o'clock but –'

'Good. Please tell her that the Saudi withdrawal has brought considerable interest from the Syrian racing fraternity but that my meetings with prospects are secure.'

'I don't even know where her place is, Mr Olgilvie.'

'Park and 60th. Tell her I'll make a counter-offer next week.'

'But what's the address?'

'It's on the corner!'

'There are four corners. Anyway, why can't you tell her?'

'I have to keep her at arm's length. That's what negotiating is all about, Owney. I'll call you tomorrow morning at eleven o'clock.' He disconnected before Owney could ask for Mrs Noon's address.

Owney stared at the telephone receiver. There was nothing he could do but go along. Mr Olgilvie controlled over one million organized baseball and racetrack frankfurters and a quarter of a million political frankfurters. How could he explain it to Mr Heller if they lost all that business just because he wouldn't take a few telephone messages? He called Dolly. 'I got into something to help out Mr Olgilvie. I'll be a little late tonight.'

'Oh, gosh, Owney.'

'You remember that horse he gave me? Meyer the bookie brought me three thousand dollars this afternoon.'

'Owney! We'll be able to buy another Zero Coupon bond for Bonita's college fund! And Poppa matches every bond we buy for her!'

'Bonita has enough now to get her through graduate school.'

'Anyway, you might as well eat out. Mama brought us a flounder Poppa caught yesterday at Montauk.'

'Thanks for the tip,' Owney said. 'Throw away whatever you don't eat.' (His father-in-law fished for sport then gave the catch away because he never ate anything but frankfurters and the occasional bowl of cold spaghetti.)

He locked his desk, said good night to Miss McHanic, and started uptown.

Chapter 14

Oona Noon reread the newspaper story about the mysterious murder of Dr Hassam Atarf while she waited for Owney to arrive. Obviously the Chinese had done the work on him but the White House was going to be sure the Soviets had done it and the Saudis and the Syrians would be sure the Israelis had done it. She thanked heaven that it was her own Owney who would keep the lines open between her and the Chinese. Thanks, in part, to her own darling son she would soon have the two billion or whatever under her mattress.

She felt herself drifting off into fantasies of how, after Goodie had been safely elected to the Presidency, she could find a way to tell Owney who she was. She would wait until Goodie was off somewhere, threatening the electorate, or busy with the thousand things about the Flag which gripped his mind, and she would bring Owney into the Oval Office, put her hands on his shoulders, look him straight into the eyes and tell him, 'I am your mom.'

She tried to force herself to leave that future behind her because she had to get back to concentrating on business. The stakes were getting higher and higher. She made herself think of Goodie in Air Force One, winging off to yet another wonderful holiday. She thought of the wonderful weekends ahead at Camp David. She allowed herself the luxury of thinking of herself bargaining with all the great dressmakers and astrologers in the land as they pleaded with her to borrow their dresses or to decide her future but her mind kept drifting back to the moment when she could reveal herself to her boy. She would tell him on Mother's Day. She would tell him in the Oval Office on Mother's Day.

It took Owney almost an hour to reach the Noon apartment building on Park and 60th, mainly because of the 14th Street

crosstown bus, then the Madison Avenue bus where a man, suddenly discovering that his fly was partly open and trying to close
it instantly, had got a woman passenger's fur stole caught in the
zip while getting out of the middle door, and then the bus had
started and there was nearly a bad accident as he had sprinted
along beside it for nearly a block and a half.

The traffic had been terrible. There would be seven months until
Christ's Mass but the people were already frantically spending for
Jesus in the stores. He had forgotten to look up Mrs Noon's
address in the telephone book and didn't know which corner of
60th Street and Park she lived on. He had to go into two buildings
to ask for her until it came right in the third.

Although nothing was said about it at the time, Mrs Noon
owned and occupied the entire apartment building. Goodie had
given it to her in the second year of their marriage as a Flag Day
present.

Mr Hazman was expected, the doorman said, then gave instructions to a huge elevator operator who, Owney was sure, was
armed. He had never seen men as large as the two black doormen,
men who must have packed anabolic steroid sandwiches for lunch
every day, until he saw the colossal black houseman in the white
jacket who was waiting for him when the elevator door opened
somewhere near the top of the building. 'Mr Hazman, you are
expected,' the man confirmed.

Every square inch of the Noon apartment was decorator-plotted.
About $700,000 and some change had gone into it. It was so
universally feminine that he decided no Mr Noon lived there, only
the tough-eyed lady who looked like Kristin Lavransdatter and
sounded like Brer Rabbit.

That conjecture was almost wrong. Goodie Noon was in his
third year of learning the 'Tattoo' call on the American bugle
without which, he felt deeply, no lowering of the American Flag
should be allowed to happen. He had been dissatisfied with the
emotional effects the (former) lead cornetist from the New York
Philharmonic had been able to achieve every afternoon at sunset,
so, typical of the man, Goodie was attacking the problem himself.
He had rejected the cornet for the bugle so he could stand with
one hand over his heart as he blew the call. Other than that he
did spend the occasional night in the New York apartment,
between Bland Island where he dreamed The American Dream
and his four other official voting residences.

Owney was led into a study of ellbeemayerian magnificence,

71

fitting for a grandee of the Reagan years. There were more flowers than at the funeral of Napoleon and the entire east wall of the room was covered with a tremendous painting of a gardenia by James Richard Blake. The furniture seemed to be made of exquisitely-turned 24-carat gold and crystal, with deep emerald upholstery. The interior window frames were of solid, highly polished silver. The rest of the décor was off-beat Chinoiserie. From somewhere a tape machine was delivering the exalting sounds of Ray Charles singing 'Georgia', in which the singer had been persuaded to substitute the word 'Carolina' for the title word.

Owney stared at his watch to see if time had stopped.

The houseman filled a crystal goblet with golden champagne from a magnum which stood in a silver cooler, put the goblet on a heavy silver tray and brought it to Owney.

Owney sat alone, sipping the wine, listening to the music, and staring at the fantasy around him. He thought, If my mother hadn't deserted me, I probably wouldn't be here.

Mrs Noon tore into his cocoon by flinging open double doors and almost filling the frame of the doorway. She was wearing a golden *ch'ao-fu* cut in straight lines without a break at the waist. It had long, straight sleeves and blue horseshoe cuffs. Dragons, clouds, mountains, and waves in blue and scarlet were passed across the fabric.

Owney got to his feet slowly, smiling tentatively.

Mrs Noon was stunned by his smile. She had forgotten how handsome her little boy had been and how even more handsome he had matured. She swayed against the lintel of the door, then recovered her poise.

Owney leapt to his feet without spilling a drop of the wine. His incomparable smile was translated by her, as it had been by Owney's father-in-law, into dreams of commercial glory. As a mother, she yearned to take him in her arms, hold him close to her, and tell him that everything had been a mistake, a terrible mistake that she was going to spend the rest of her life trying to put right. But the hopelessness of ever being able to tell him the truth overwhelmed her as she realized that 'the other Party' would savage Goodie's candidacy when they tracked down – as they most certainly would – that she had married Nicky Nepenthes bigamously while Owney's father had still been alive. A freezing laser of dread went through her when it suddenly penetrated her consciousness that she still didn't know whether the man was alive or dead today, which could make her a double bigamist by

72

marrying Goodie. She could see the headlines in the *National Enquirer* on the day before the Republican nominating convention met:

PROSPECTIVE CANDIDATE'S WIFE

A DOUBLE BIGAMIST

As he looked across the room to Mrs Noon's spectacular entrance, Owney was vaguely pleased to see that the haughtiness she had shown at the racetrack had vanished, but, being a professionally passive man (so that he could spend all of his hours thinking and plotting how he could find his mother), that was all he noted. Her sudden faintness and air of near-panic escaped him entirely.

'That is a – uh – beautiful – uh – dress, Mrs Noon.'

'Do you really like it, Mr Hazman?' she said. 'I only jes' recently got innarested in China and a dealer in London was able to get me this little Ming robe from the Victoria and Albert Museum.' If the word burglar had been substituted for dealer the statement would have been even more correct.

She smelled like a wholesale flower market at dawn.

'You sure ought to go into television with that smile,' she said.

Owney blushed deeply. She had reached him where he lived, at the heart of his ambition, his dream of becoming an anchor man on a national network evening news show, his name and face suspended in front of millions of people, including his mother who would then realize her terrible mistake and rush forward to claim him as her own.

'I'm sure it takes much more than that,' he said.

'Good heavens, no. Look at our President.'

The houseman extended a crystal glass filled with champagne to Mrs Noon. 'Thank you, Jeshurun,' she said, accepting the goblet. He left the room.

She sipped the wine, staring at Owney over the top of the glass. 'Jeshurun is an idealistic designation? Of honour and affection for biblical history at the time of Abraham? What did Mal Olgilvie have to say?'

Owney repeated Mr Olgilvie's message.

'Rule one is: don't go horse tradin' with Mal Olgilvie.'

'Horse trading?'

'He's out to buy some racehorses from me.'

'Malachi is an old-fashioned name,' Owney said tentatively.

'It was the name of the last of the minor prophets. It means simply "my messenger".' Her speech slipped further into pure geechee. 'I wouldn't sell him horses if he was Paul Revere and the British were comin' an' I'm not cuttin' no green calabash.'

'I find it hard to keep up with all this, Mrs Noon,' Owney said hesitantly.

'Call me Ravi. All my friends call me Ravi. Fo' *ravissante*. It's sorta a nickname. My last husband but one gave it to me.'

'Ah.'

'I was a widder woman till I married Goodie. The fo'ces of powah purely terrigated Nicky to his grave.'

'I'm sorry to hear that.'

'I cain't figure how you don' know that. Nicky Nepenthes? *Sixty Minutes* covered the funeral and the readin' of the will. Harry Reasoner had tears in his eyes when he did the wrap-up. But why we crackin' our teeth like this? I don' wanna have to talk 'bout Nicky.' Then she went on, intensely, to talk about Nicky as if she wanted Owney to understand how it had happened and what it had meant to her. It was not that she had a need to convey information to Owney. It was a need she had to deviate from any central subject which a visitor might have felt should have been immediately forthcoming; a compulsion to walk all around the business at hand, talking seemingly about anything but the main topic while she sized up her opponent.

'I never could stay on with one man. But there never was anyone like Nicky. I was much more than just stricken when he died on me,' she said rapidly and earnestly, as if she were explaining something very, very important to Owney. 'Until I met him and married him when I was twenty-seven years old, I was just a roamer on the face of the earth. I had him as all my own for seven glorious years. Befo' I met him my idea of heaven had been the notion of one day ownin' a little beach house on Folly Island and lettin' the rest of the world knock itseff out. Then I met him and that was that for botha us. Nicky had his mistresses, a-course, and his little affairs until the day I lost him to the powers of evil, them oil companies. He was a Greek man and that was what was expected of him. My daddy had been like that, and my granddaddy and they wasn't even Greek.' She shrugged lightly. 'Men are men.'

'Nicky was one of the owners of the world, and he got his jollies outta pleasurin' me by buildin' the sweetest twenny-six-room beach cottage ever seen on Folly Island. We spent eight days every year there. When we were on Folly the staff, 'cepting for the three housemen who were our cooks, valets, drivers and bodyguards, stayed on the mainland – or somewhere – then they were all assembled agin to go on to the next house – on the island in the Adriatic or the big house in London, the flower farm on Maui, or the condos in Hong Kong or New York. When Nicky died the size of his gross estate nearly smothered me. The one haffa one per cent he left to old mistresses and servants and other charities came to more than eight million dollahs and the way he had set all of it up there weren't any taxes for me to pay on any of it. God bless Ronald Reagan his wonders to perform. How that man worked day and night so that people could not only hold on to their money, but triple it. You better believe, inheritin' that much powah changed me ovahnight from a Southern gentlewoman into the executive head of an international conglomerate. Nicky had taught me well and I learned fast. But I never agin had the chance to think 'bout much of anythin' else. I managed the fleet of oil tankers, an empire of commodities, gold, constantly manipulated stocks and tax-free bonds, square miles of downtown real estate in the more populous cities of the world, a professional sports team conglomerate which spanned all seasons and with all the gamblin' vigorish that goes with it, a chain of 73 hospitals, 2 national health plans, 6 corporately-owned penitentiaries, 2 fast-food chains, and sundry other responsibilities.'

'Penitentiaries?' Owney said.

She sighed. 'Then I met Goodie Noon. I mean, since the day I met Nicky, then Goodie, I haven't hardly had time to think of where I was comin' from, only where I had to go. I jes' junked the past because I had to learn how to live in new lives.' She sighed again, thinking either of the strangeness of it all or of the strangeness of Goodie Noon. 'So you see what I been doin'. You got some idea of what my life was like all because of the accident of meetin' Nicky Nepenthes.'

Owney stared at her blankly. 'Six penitentiaries?' he asked.

'Maybe you heard of my second husband – my now husband – Goodie Noon?'

'No, ma'am, I don't think I –'

'You will. We gone run him for President.'

'President? Of this country?'

'Oh, it's nice bein' a President, I can tell you. Look at the time the Reagans went down to Barbados for a little five-day visit. Three hundred and eighteen people had to go along with him an' that ain't countin' the crews on the hospital ship and the light

cruiser filled with Marines ready to swarm ashore in case they had
to rescue him from the tourists, and the seven hundred members
of the international press media. Goodie and me are gone have all
that. The Reagans had over a hundred people from the White
House Communications Agency lay cable throughout the island
until there was a phone installed wherever Mrs Reagan might
pause for refreshment and need to call her astrologer. They redid
the Barbados phone system in a very sophisticated way then they
left it there because it was too expensive to haul all that equipment
out and bring it home.'

Mrs Noon wagged her beautiful blonde head with admiration.
'A five-day vacation for two people costin' five million dollahs.
They had three cargo planes haul three armoured limousines for
Ronnie's motorcades – 'cause what's an informal little old vacation
in Barbados without a motorcade? They flew in four more
armoured cars for the Secret Service, and four Marine helicopters –
one for the Reagans, one for the press, and two in case the others
broke down. They even had two fire engines flown in from the
US to stand by at the Barbados airport for when Mr Reagan
landed.'

She exhaled sharply with admiration. 'I'm here to tell you that
bein' an American President the way the Reagans know how to
do it, is better'n bein' a king and queen. Me and Goodie are ready.
Count the Secret Service men wherever the Reagans go. Fifty!
Then there's a gang of people from the Executive Protection
Service who move around through the crowds at the parties and
receptions carryin' metal detectors. The Reagans travel with two
doctors, four nurses, and that fully equipped hospital ship always
standin' by off-shore like I tole you 'bout. They got three photographers and five lab technicians who do the colour work alone
and even the water the Reagans drink – and maybe bathe in – is
hauled down from Washington.

'Sure, the five days on Barbados for two people in love cost the
taxpayers five million dollahs, but think whut Truman, or Kennedy
or Johnson, or Ford or Carter woulda given the people. Jes' the
same old thang – gettin' on an' off Air Force One. Lemme tell you
no other ruler in the world comes even close to the Reagans when
they travel on the taxpayer. Shoot! The Russians let their man
poop along with 110 people surrounding him when he leaves town.
What kind of pomp and circumstance is that? Ron and Nancy
brought along 782 people to make everything work nice in
Barbados. Ron's people figure it is all a marvellous incentive for

the homeless to git up and git goin' so that they kin find themselves a little fun in the Caribbean, too.'

While she talked, Owney was thinking that if a woman with the power of Mrs Noon and a man with the clout of Mr Olgilvie, for whatever mysterious reason, wanted to make him their joint representative, they could get him his shot at television. They probably had the connections to make him a network anchor man who read the national news every night and he could say, 'This is the Nightly Evening News, Owney Hazman reporting', and sooner or later his mother would have to turn on the news show and she would not only see her son right there on tens of millions of television screens, but she would know that he was making a barrel of money and she would get on the phone and call him at the station and the minute he came off the air, some aide would hand him a note saying, 'Your mother called. Urgent' with her telephone number right there on the message pad and he would call her back and they would make a date to meet that night at his house where she would meet Dolly and the children and realize what a mistake she had made.

'Mrs Noon –'

'You married, Owney?'

'Yes, ma'am.'

'Children?'

'Three.'

'Three! An' they all gotta be real little.'

'Well – yes.'

'Then we gotta say you got it made.'

'I don't understand what is going on, Mrs Noon, except I'm pretty sure Mr Olgilvie isn't buying horses from you.'

'Why do you say that?'

'This is not how people buy horses, is it? What's so secret about buying a horse?'

'You right, Owney. It was wrong to tell you that.'

'Just tell me what you want. I'll be more than glad to help you.'

'I cain't say why we doin' what we doin', Owney. But it's a big deal an' we gotta hold it close until we got it made. Anyways, it ain't fair for you to do whut you doin' for us and not git paid.'

Owney protested immediately.

'No, no!' she said. 'We gone make a *lot* of money and you gone git your share. Whatta you do for a livin', Owney?'

'I sell frankfurters.'

'*Frank*foituhs?'

He glared at her. 'I am sales manager of Heller's Wurst Inc.,' he said stiffly.

'How much you makin' sellin' frankfoituhs?'

'About twenty-eight thousand a year.'

'Then we gone pay you ten thousand dollahs fo' two months' work.'

'Ten thousand dollars?'

'It won't innafere with yo' job. If you want, and if it look like it's necessary, Mal Olgilvie will call yo' boss and tell him he needs you now and then as a consultant. You can go see Mal in Washington on weekends, on your time off, and let your family see the cherry blossoms while you talk to Mal.'

'I don't think we could all go to Washington. The baby is too little for that. In fact, they're all too little.'

'You wife ain't too little. Have a second honeymoon. Git a sitter. Your wife gone know all this is the right thang to do. An' I am placin' an oduh for semmeny thousand frankfurters right now for my hospitals, my state prisons, and my tankers. Thass a renewable order. Whatta you say?'

'Your state prisons?'

'Listen – this country got almost a million people in prison right now. It's the new government policy. They keep goin' the way they are an' half the country will be locked up.'

'But how do you –'

'We make prefabricated prison cells which can be connected all up to any size prison a town wants. We git sixteen-five a cell, a good deal for any state. Then when they got a thousand-cell prison all stacked up, somebody gotta operate it efficiently. You cain't leave that to politicians. We operate 'em better'n the govmint. We more efficient.'

'Like hotels?'

'Sorta like that. I mean, we own all those hospitals and they just hotels for pain. Prisons are hotels for shame.'

'There is something much more important to me than ten thousand dollars.'

'Tell me.'

'I – I don't belong in frankfurters. I was meant to be a network anchor man. If you and Mr Olgilvie could help me become one –'

'Lemme think on it,' Mrs Noon said slowly. 'Lemme organize my focus. And if I can hepp you that would be my pleasure. But that got nothin' to do with the ten thousand. That's yo' fee. You gone earn it.'

Owney thought about how much Dolly would enjoy the cherry blossoms. 'OK,' he said. 'I'll take it.'

Owney was trembling because he could see tomorrow. He would be a network anchor man and it would bring his mother back. There wouldn't be a place on North America where she wouldn't see his picture and hear his name every night. She would reveal herself. In his mind's eye he could see the tight shot of himself without Walter Cronkite's moustache but with his awesome, preternatural presence, sinking his piercing but kindly gaze into the camera as he read from the Teleprompter, telling it like it wasn't, directly into his mother's memory and her need. She would be forced to come to him because he would be a certified American celebrity. This was the big chance.

Chapter 15

Freddie Fanshaw had a steak for breakfast on Concorde. He had asked Movement Control to make certain that British Airways had a steak aboard because he really enjoyed a steak for breakfast when he wasn't paying for it, but the steward told him they always carried the spare steak for the really hungover people. Fanshaw boarded the plane, ate the steak, leaned back, closed his eyes, and a few moments later he was on the ground at Dulles airport outside Washington. It was too easy, really.

Fanshaw was thirty-eight years old; in his eleventh year of Intelligence work. He had been a Major, British Army, before that, and at Sandhurst not long before that. He was an orphan. His name was spelled Featherstonehaugh, pronounced Fanshaw, so he had taken Fanshaw as a sort of cover name so that his sisters would never have to know what he did for a living. He had been in the Middle East for the past two years for the SIS; in Hong Kong for two years before that.

When he wasn't on duty, he shaved every other day. He was a fair man with a light beard and he hated shaving. He was middle-sized, lithe, and athletic enough to have played soccer for the Real Madrid team as a cover six years before when he had been assigned to expose a ring of foundation-garment smugglers whose manufacturing operation was in Spanish Morocco. Fanshaw spoke Spanish, Russian, Arabic, and a sort of rough Italian using Sicilian dialects. He took pills to prevent gout attacks and they made his ears itch intermittently but intensely. He dressed at all times like the juvenile in a twenties musical comedy: sleeveless sweaters, baggy grey flannel slacks, polka-dot bow ties, and eight-piece Irish tweed caps. He looked like a casual commuter from Wonersh, Surrey, to a job with a turf accountant in the West End then back to the wife and kiddies, but his wife had left him four and a half years ago because he was home so seldom and there were no kiddies. He had a devoted girlfriend in London – and others in Rome, Toronto, and in Athens. They thought he was a travelling accountant for the War Office.

James D. Marxuach was waiting at Dulles when Fanshaw came through Customs. Marxuach had been with the CIA since 1965, starting in the Special Operations Division. Beginning in '67 he worked in Vietnam in the Provincial Reconnaissance Units programme which had been set up to infiltrate the Communist areas to disrupt, intimidate, interrogate, kidnap, terrorize, and murder. Marxuach was decorated for his proficiency in all these fields to the point of being promoted to the 'Phoenix' operation which was charged with eliminating Communist spies, assassins, and terrorists. Marxuach was credited with over four hundred 'solutions'. When the work in Vietnam was finished he was transferred to the Western Hemisphere Division of the CIA's Clandestine Services section. He had worked for the overthrow of Allende in Chile, had organized terrorists in Germany, and had helped Marcos get established in the Philippines. Later on he had worked in liaison with the British until, in 1980, he was transferred to the Directorate of Intelligence.

Marxuach felt unsympathetically cold and grim about Freddie Fanshaw because he had been ordered to give him the shaft. He had memorized Fanshaw's picture so, when he spotted him, he stood in front of him like a sequoia tree stump, held out both hands and said, 'Hel-lo, Freddie!'

Fanshaw fell all over him with a grinning embrace, although they had never seen each other before except in the covertly taken photographs which they had been required to study. 'James D.!' he chortled. 'Good heavens, it's good to see you.' They moved out to the parking lot, watched by the KGB airport spotter on duty, Fanshaw carrying his own bags. They left the airport in a blue '73 Ford cabriolet.

Marxuach, driving, said, 'They tell me you knew Hassam Atarf.'

'The chap who was shot?'

'Yes.'

'That was the false Atarf. But I knew the real Atarf as well. He had a mahv'less collection of dirty limericks. Spoke English like the actor, Terry-Thomas. The bogus Atarf was a filthy sort of fellow. Awful fingernails. Spoke English like a self-educated dragoman. Stunned by hashish most of the time, I suspect.'

'Did you ever hear of Malachi Olgilvie?'

81

'Only in the file I read last night.'

'He's very connected. Why would he have a car bomber for a client?'

'Well! Why did they switch Atarfs?'

'Who made the switch?'

'Well! The false Atarf was a member of the Syrian AIAS, wasn't he? Obviously, the Saudis nipped the real Atarf and asked the Syrians to carry out the switch.'

'Olgilvie says a man who he thought was Atarf came to him to buy a shopping mall in Columbia, South Carolina. You're a Middle East expert. Does it make sense for an AIAS thug to apply to buy something like that?'

'I've worked in the Middle East for two years but that hardly qualifies me as an expert, James D.'

'You speak Arabic. You knew the real Atarf. And you knew the bogus Atarf, which is a helluva lot more than we knew.'

'What is the point of this, Jim?'

'The Atlantic Alliance needs you to fly to Lebanon this morning.'

'This *morning*?'

'There's an Alitalia flight at 11.50. I have all the details of the assignment in this envelope.' He slipped a fat manila envelope out of the car's glove compartment and dropped it in Fanshaw's lap. Fanshaw stared at it as if it would burst into flames and destroy his manhood.

'Eleven-fifty? From National?'

'You'll have to fly to New York to make the connection.'

'We can hardly make it.'

'We'll make it.'

Fanshaw took a measured breath to control himself. He turned in the seat to face Marxuach. 'We have people in London who are far more qualified than I am to ferret out the background on Atarf, the Saudis, and the Syrians, James D. Best you drop me at a hotel and I'll sort this thing out at the embassy. Clearly, I wasn't sent three thousand miles so I could zigzag back on my tracks another five thousand miles. I must check this out with London.'

'This is a White House-Number 10 operation. You can't get more priority than that. We have an army of agents here, Freddie, but we aren't as strong as we might be in Damascus and you certainly know Damascus.'

Fanshaw knew that most politicians were mad – constant exposure to television lights did it to them – but he was even more sure that orders which had come down from the Prime Minister had to be well thought out because she was very fussy that way. Since the orders had evolved less than twenty hours before as a result of a talk between the PM and the President, he thought it was more likely that the cousins were being devious again. As they rode along toward the National Airport he decided that the British had been at that sort of thing longer than the colonies to the point where he would have to start to be devious himself.

'I'm sure you're right, James D.,' he said. 'I do know people in Damascus who might be able to sort this thing out. What is wanted is clear proof of a Moscow connection – something you can confront Mrs Noon with and make her withdraw. Is that what you fellows have in mind, James D.?'

Marxuach grinned so broadly that it revealed all the dozens of caps on his teeth, as though he'd got a special price from the dentist for agreeing to advertise the man's work.

'That is *exactly* what we have in mind, Freddie,' he said.

'Are the air tickets in this envelope?'

'Air tickets, new visaed passport, new identity garbage, expense money in sterling and Lebanese pounds, and a hotel reservation in Athens.'

'Whom should I contact?'

'Our Bureau of Fisheries man at the consulate.'

'I say – that really is tradecraft.'

'What?'

'How will we rendezvous?'

'Call him. Say your name is George Pappadakis. Say you want some help contacting your cousin in Yakima, Washington.'

'I have a friend in Athens. Beautiful woman. Wonderful company. Good heavens, I hope she isn't your chap's wife.'

'The point is, Fanshaw, you must not contact your own people in Athens, Beirut, Damascus, or Riyadh. It has to be a sealed operation.'

'Oh, definitely, Jim.'

When they pulled up at the National Airport, Fanshaw told Marxuach not to go through the bother of finding parking, there just wasn't any time. They shook hands hurriedly. Fanshaw got his luggage out of the tiny boot and went into the terminal building to the Air Canada counter and caught the next flight for Toronto as Marxuach drove back to Langley. As the plane gained altitude, Freddie stared out of the window thinking that this was going to be a much trickier assignment than had been thought. He sincerely hoped he wouldn't have to kill anyone.

Chapter 16

When Owney got home the children were in bed. That sort of took the keen edge off the $10,000 and the possibility of his becoming a network television anchor man. He went into their rooms and stared down at them for a few minutes, then went back to the living room to read 'Table Scraps', the gossip column in *The Meat Processor*, the industry trade paper, while Dolly made dinner in the kitchen and sang 'Come Rain or Come Shine'. The sounds she made were so thrilling that Owney had to put the newspaper aside. He put his head back on the chair and gave himself entirely to letting her voice enthrall him.

There was no opportunity to talk during dinner because he was hungry and because Dolly was filling him in on what the children had done and said that day, on what her mother had had to say during their two telephone conversations, and on general conditions in Central Park at that time of year. Then she said, 'Did you know that Poppa is starting to eat test runs of *Pinkelwurst*?'

'Oh, God! We're next.'

'Don't you like them?'

'I *like* them, but not three times a day the way your father wants them taste-tested.' He leaned forward and stared at her with even more delight than usual and said, 'You remember Mr Olgilvie?'

'The man who makes you work on Saturdays.'

'Well, he called from Washington and asked me to take a message to his client. Then the client called me and invited me to her apartment at six o'clock tonight – as you know.'

'Her *apartment*?'

'Her name is Oona Noon, she's a –'

'Oona *Noon*? She's Nancy's dearest friend! Jerry Zipkin has walked her!'

'*Walked* her?'

84

'I think it's a euphemism.'

'I guess it's the same woman. It's an unusual name.'

'Is she as glamorous as her pictures look?'

'She has solid gold furniture.'

'I know. It's the only interior Picasso ever agreed to decorate. My God, Owney – what were you doing there?'

'Mr Olgilvie gave me this message on the phone. I gave the message to Mrs Noon. She tried to make out that Mr Olgilvie was buying racehorses from her and I said I didn't think that was how people bought racehorses.'

'What was her apartment like?'

'Later. She admitted it wasn't about racehorses. She said she could see that sending messages through me on the phone wasn't a very good idea. She asked me how I'd like to take my children to see the cherry blossoms in Washington.'

'We couldn't do that, Owney. The children are too young.'

'I told her that. Then she said she'd pay me ten thousand dollars for two months of part-time, sort of weekend, freelance work and that maybe we could get a sitter so I could take my wife to see the cherry blossoms.'

'What?'

'In a suite. And it wouldn't interfere with my regular job. Then she placed an order for seventy thousand frankfurters for her hospitals, tankers, and state prisons.'

'Her *pris*ons?'

'She builds them and runs them for different states.' He shrugged, bewildered. 'That's what she said, Dolly.'

She looked at him thoughtfully.

'What do you think?' Owney asked.

'Well – people like Mrs Noon and Mr Olgilvie couldn't be crooks. I mean, they're too rich. They would have all that behind them. What's the catch?'

'Beats me.'

'We ought to get a house at the beach this summer. We should have done it last summer but you wouldn't let Poppa pay for it. But with the money from Mrs Noon –'

'And the three thousand I won on Hilary's Doll –'

'No, Owney. That really is for a Zero Coupon bond. We could get a nice house for the season and maybe find a girl to mind the kids.'

'I could get there on the weekends I don't have to go to Washington.'

'Long weekends. And if you have to go to Washington then we'll leave the kids with Mama and I'll go with you.'

'Great.'

'I'll call Rita Zendt on Monday and tell her to start looking. How about Point o' Woods on Fire Island?'

'Not too near your father's place.'

'Owney! Daddy only takes Sunday off because everyone else does. When do you start the job for Mrs Noon?'

'I have to call Mr Olgilvie tomorrow morning.'

'When does she pay you?'

'I'll ask her about that tomorrow. This is absolutely sensational food, Doll. What is it?'

'Poppa calls it Ponce Sunday soup. He says if you eat it on Sunday, you don't have to think about food for the rest of the week.'

'*Soup?* What's in it?'

'Three kinds of sausages, barley, beans, beef – all boiled in beer – then an hour before serving you add the pork chops and the large dumplings made with grapes and chopped pears. Poppa says it's a typical Puerto Rican dish.'

'Jesus, it sounds German to me.'

Owney was still in pyjamas when he called Mr Olgilvie at 8.30 on Saturday morning. 'The lady thought it might be a good idea if you and I could have a meeting in Washington,' he said into the phone.

'Right,' Mr Olgilvie said. 'You'd better come down today as a matter of fact.'

'Today?' Owney answered bleakly, staring at Dolly who was sitting on the bed. She caught her lower lip with her upper teeth.

'A lot has been happening and we'll both be tied up all week. I'll have a ticket waiting for you at the Pan Am shuttle desk. Call me from the airport with the flight number. Someone will meet you.'

Owney was aboard the eleven o'clock shuttle. In Washington, Jilly Pozze was at the gate, holding up a sign with Owney's name written on it. James D. Marxuach was waiting three rows behind him. 'Mr Olgilvie will be at your hotel at one o'clock,' Pozze said in a low whisper, brought on by his damaged larynx. 'He's gonna have lunch witchew.'

They walked silently along the concourse while the SRS followed, frustrated in trying to record their conversation with a parabolic microphone. At last, as they were going out the door, the arrow on the sound volume dial, hand-held by Marxuach, jumped. The portable machine began recording. Jilly Pozze said, 'You gonna see the cherry blossoms?'

'I had hoped to show them to my wife but she couldn't get away.'

Marxuach stayed as close behind them as he dared when the Olgilvie limousine left the parking area. He stayed three cars behind in a '79 Chevvy driven by a man wearing a German Army *Feldmütze* cap.

Chapter 17

When Mr Olgilvie arrived at Owney's hotel at one o'clock, he insisted that they have lunch in Owney's suite. He was edgy, nervous, and disturbed. He finished off a dish of eleven jumbo olives, which had come with the pitcher of Martinis he had ordered from room service before leaving his house. While they waited for the food which, for Mr Olgilvie, was two fresh peach sundaes with vanilla ice cream, he said, 'Can you see Ravi tonight?'

'She asked me to be there at six.'

'Tell her that the Dr Atarf who was in the newspapers was not the Dr Atarf I had expected at my office so I asked my boarder to help out then the unexpected happened.' He looked peakish as he said it.

'The unexpected.'

'She will know.'

'If she will know then why do I have to travel a couple of hundred miles on the day I usually spend with my family?'

'Tell her!' Mr Olgilvie snarled. 'Say that the boarder proceeded entirely on his own to have the Atarf problem handled.'

'OK.'

'Tell her he can arrange to have a scrambler-phone operator who will communicate in a sixth-century Chinese dialect installed in her apartment.'

'Mr Olgilvie, this is wild.'

'It's not as inconvenient as it sounds. Ravi's apartment occupies the entire building.'

'That's wilder!'

'Make it a point never even to say the name, Dr Atarf.'

'OK.'

'And never mention Mrs Noon's name to me on the telephone. Talk baseball or frankfurters.'

*

'Well – sure,' Owney said.

Owney got back to La Guardia at five o'clock. He took a taxi directly to Mrs Noon's apartment building. James D. Marxuach followed him in an '80 Oldsmobile Cutlass, driven by a young woman, an SRS agent named Doris Spriggs, who wore a T-shirt with Secretary Donovan's picture printed on it in four colours. She was a pretty, dark-haired woman who did her nails at red-light stops and chewed gum.

'Whatta you do, fahcrissake,' Marxuach whinged, 'go to drama school between jobs?'

'They're never gonna catch me looking the same way twice,' she said calmly. 'So? Who are we after this time?'

'His name is Owney Hazman. It's an improbable name but that's how he registered at the hotel in Washington. Put everything you have on checking him out. I need every who, what, why, where and when you can get.'

Owney was admitted through the barriers of the two armed doormen, the armed elevator operator, and the muscular house-man, to Mrs Noon's presence in the Chinese study. She was wearing a lightweight Javanese ceremonial robe which, in ancient times, had been used for initiations into a sandalmakers' guild. It was stained with the ritualistic colours of beige and blue. She wore a pair of Persian silver peri slippers with curled-up toes, which were marked with the cabalistic signs of the priests of Mazda, in the old, old language of ages and times long gone before which, had anyone living (except two people who were employed by the British Museum) been able to translate them, read: *Please keep these shoes in the company locker when not in use.* To set off all the classicism, Mrs Noon wore the Lavery emeralds, the greatest matched collection of loot a foreign power had ever clawed out of South America.

Owney was aware of a light dusting of freckles across the bridge of her perfect nose which the porcelain make-up was unable to conceal. He wondered if she had bought the nose, it was too perfect to have been a part of her DNA, and since she occupied an entire apartment building in the centre of the exorbitant rent district in New York, he knew she would have been able to afford to have chosen a nose out of thousands of nose shapes. Someday, he thought, if he knew her long enough, God forbid, she was going to wear some kind of a garment that didn't fit her like a flour sack and he would be able to see her figure. He sincerely liked her bone structure and was certain that he would approve whatever it supported.

'What happened?' she asked.

'Mr Olgilvie said to tell you, because he was unable to reach you, that he had had his house guest handle the Atarf situation – whatever that means.'

Mrs Noon nodded.

'This gets crazier, Mrs Noon.'

'Ravi.'

'I read the *Washington Post* on the shuttle. It said the police were still up a tree about the murder of a Dr Atarf a few nights ago.'

'Yes?' Mrs Noon said brightly.

'Well – doesn't that seem to say that Mr Olgilvie's boarder had Dr Atarf killed? I mean, what else can it mean?'

'I don't know right now what else it can mean, Owney, but it surely doesn't mean what you think it means. Mal Olgilvie? Impossible!'

'Mr Olgilvie said to tell you that he can have a scrambler with an operator using a sixth-century Chinese dialect so you can call him wherever he might be. How about that? Is that crazy?'

'Too many people in on it. No scrambler. Tell him you gone be the link, Owney.'

'*Tell* him?'

'Tomorrow's Sunday. Get back down to Washington and tell him.'

'Listen, Mrs Noon – if I have to walk out on my family at the only time I get to see them all week, to ride back and forth to Washington, then this job isn't worth any ten thousand dollars to me.'

'I bin thinkin' 'bout that, Owney. Ten thousand is wrong considerin' the time you gone hafta put in. You gone git fifteen thousand.'

'That makes me suspicious, Ravi.'

'Suspicious?'

'Very suspicious.'

'I'm gone gross 'bout two billion five on this deal.'

Owney nodded just as if the figure had a meaning for him. The words 'a billion dollars' were routine numbers to him because of the intense conditioning he had undergone from the seven years of the Reagan Administration while the old President had slashed expenses and his Secretary of Defense had planned for peace. With a wave of his gnarled hand, the old outlaw had transformed a perfectly usable word, million, into a word with one thousand times more meaning. The Defense Department and the Savings and Loan industry were grateful to him for that. Never in any nation's history had such numbers been slung around within each political working day and never had the price of anything been higher. A billion dollars was what things were said to cost, as routine. Compared to the national deficit by which the elderly President's advisers had arranged to make all the people believe that they were more prosperous, compared to the Star Wars programme which tested a theory of whether a bullet could shoot down another bullet in flight, and which the autochthonal President kept saying might possibly be made to work someday, a billion dollars was light-hearted money and the public had absolutely nothing to say about it because the Federal government had long since gone far beyond the people, was operating so far beyond them that Washington, DC could have been on Alpha Centauri.

'So?' Owney asked.

'Fifteen thousand. Haff now, haff when you done.' She walked to a desk, opened a drawer, took out a cheque book and wrote a cheque. She gave it to Owney.

He stared at the cheque, recognizing the numbers as real money.

'Pick up the ticket at Pan Am tomorrow mornin',' Mrs Noon said.

'My wife might be able to go with me tomorrow.'

'Two tickets, then.'

'That means cab fares to the cherry blossoms and incidentals. Things like that.'

'You think two hunnert will cover it?'

He nodded gravely. She opened a silver cigarette box on the low table in front of her and took out a flat packet of money. She stripped off two one-hundred-dollar bills and handed them to Owney.

'I been thinkin' 'bout how you want to be a anchor man.'

All his doors opened. His pupils dilated. He leaned forward.

'I am gone have five TVs set up fo' you. One for each network so's you can study them. I'm gone give you an apartment in this building to work in. It's gone have a news wire service and a

Fax system. You gotta study anchor-man techniques an' they hairstyles. You got a fine smile, Owney, and that the important thing. But you hairstyle is too doctrinaire.'

'Then what?' he asked, a tad hoarsely.

'Then we got to develop you a speakin' style an' how to shade down your tendency to genu-wine sincerity an' learn you how to projeck a new kind of sober geniality all mixed up with jocular seriousness fo' when you talkin' 'bout wife batterin' an' child abuse. You gotta learn how to grab 'em and hold 'em.'

'How do I learn stuff like that?'

'We git you a coach. He gone drill you. Then, when you ready, we put you on some Joisey station and we git the best anchor agent in the country to watch your work. He'll buy you on your smile alone.'

'What's an anchor agent?'

'An agent. Who books the talent in the anchor industry.'

'What do we need that for?'

'Because, after you shine in Joisey, the agent will set you as a White House correspondent in Washington then move you up to a prime-time spot on a local New York station. That is where he gets you discovered by the advertising agencies. Then he move you up to one of the early mornin' talk shows to build you a national followin' then he move you up into a network prime-time spot as anchor man on the Evenin' News. How does that sound?'

'Jesus, how long does all that take?'

'Oh – figguh 'bout ten years.'

'Ten *years*? I'd be thirty-eight years old before I got started!'

'Up to you intirely, Owney. It's gotta pay 'bout three million a year. But if I was you I'd forget bein' an anchor man an' go into politics. You kin make much more money an' you got a very endearin' personality. But you think on it.'

Owney took the 57th Street crosstown bus to Broadway then the IRT at 59th and rode up to the 79th Street station, almost ga-ga all the way because his most impossible dream of finding his mother was about to come true. His name and his picture would be full-frame on millions of television sets from coast to coast and one of those millions of sets would be the television set his mother watched.

Doris Spriggs, the SRS New York rep, wearing a replica of Colonel North's testifying tunic which had gone on remaindered sale at K-Mart, stayed closely behind him on the bus and in the subway.

Owney didn't dope, drink, or smoke because he knew he had to stay in shape to ride the New York City subway system. He sat warily, his antennae sensitive to all areas around him, looking to the world as if he thought it were still as safe as it had been in 1924. He tried to put Mrs Noon's propositions together. He thought constantly of the $7,500 cheque in his wallet. But he thought even more about one stark fact: if he didn't take a wrong turning he could be on the threshold of becoming an anchor man in ten short years. He fell into a reverie about the wig he would have made which could be shaped into one of those bobbed-teased-fluffy men's styles that were sweeping the US Senate. Nobody would wear anything like that in the street but obviously it was what the networks wanted on camera and certainly the whole look of the Senate depended on mockeries like that. He decided that, since that was what the networks wanted, he would ask Mrs Noon to have a wig made for him right now so he could have a couple of months to get used to wearing it.

He had no idea whether he would be able to continue in the frankfurter industry while he went through the training period because he had no way of knowing how intensive the training would be. He had to have income while he was training. He certainly couldn't be expected to have his family live on his capital, so that was something which would need to be negotiated with Mrs Noon. He wondered whether he should have a lawyer to represent him but he shied away from that because unless the lawyer could negotiate that Mrs Noon pay his legal fees as well, it was out of the question.

There had to be formulae set down in his mind before he could negotiate successfully. If the training was going to take ten weeks then he was going to have to think about arranging for an advance from Mrs Noon which would be ten times his salary of $550 a week or $5,500. His father-in-law was going to have to give him a sabbatical. Dolly could negotiate that through her mother.

Although the network anchor slot would bring in about $3 million a year, a steady $60,000 a week, Mrs Noon had said, suppose it paid only $150 a week in those early anchor jobs, such as at the station in New Jersey?

They could all live on the frankfurters he could bring home in his attaché case, and partly on his broadcasting fees. He knew that Dolly would never OK the plan unless there would be money left over for the Zero Coupon bonds for the children's education.

There was really only one snag. Dolly would be behind him all the way, but how would her father react? Mr Heller was almost certain to think the idea of Owney becoming an anchor man in ten years was crazy. He would make some pretty terrible scenes. Owney shuddered, thinking of his father-in-law's dentures and Dolly's brothers, but he had to go on the air, night after night, from coast to coast, because, if he didn't, he might never find his mother.

Still, no matter what, he faced the problem of breaking in a new sales manager. That was the least he could do. It was a complicated field what with the new *Kalbsbratwurst* contract with Heidi-Ho and the gnawing suspicion that his father-in-law was about to introduce *Pinkelwurst* from left field.

Chapter 18

The Marine VH-3 helicopter, just like the one which took Nancy and Ron to Camp David three times a week, set Mrs Noon down on the family pad at Bland Island. Goodie preferred to use their MH-53J, which he called his Herkybird, an enormous chopper which had been built to carry troops but which Goodie had had fitted out like the interior of the ranchhouse in a movie called *Giant* because even though he had been born a Connecticut man, he lived and breathed Texas. Goodie was such a Texan (in heart, spirit, and leased hotel room) that – in case anyone doubted it in the slightest degree – Goodie had an elderly Chinese round-up cook named Mat Sun standing by to seem to be working at the large cookstove aboard the Herkybird, frying up prairie oysters and flapjacks, turning out hot biscuits and son-of-a-bitch stew or ladling out platefuls of steaming, fiery chilli next to a stack of tasty soda crackers. No one ever doubted that Goodie was a Texan through and through after that experience.

The chopper's interior also had several really good paintings by Grant Wood because, no matter what Wood had painted, it reminded Goodie of his mom and dad.

As she came down the short ladder Oona Noon got into a waiting golf cart and drove directly to a sweetly-designed one-and-a-half-storey brick building. The family called the building either Flag House or Ye Olde Opportunity Shoppe because it had been the source of so many photo opportunities for the inspired craftsman within.

Goodie was at work, as usual, on another typewriter-limned portrait of an American President as part of his series of portraits of Republican statesmen which were intended to become a part of his 'America, the Beautiful' Presidential museum one day, after they had been hung in the White House during his projected terms of office. Each portrait was drawn with repeated typewritten lower-case letters of the alphabet. The effects were startling. The uncanny likeness he had under way was one of Chester Alan Arthur, 21st President of the United States,.

'Hi, hon,' he said.

'What you woikin' on, sweets?' Oona asked.

'I am completing a typewriter portrait of President Arthur. Did you know, Oon, that his career before the Presidency rather paralleled mine?'

'It did?'

'Yes. He held many appointive posts. He was on the staff of the Governor of New York. He was Inspector-General and Quartermaster-General of New York State, both appointments. He was appointed as collector of the Port of New York by U.S. Grant then elected – yes, he was finally elected, as you may be sure I will be one day – to the Vice-Presidency, until, following Garfield's assassination in 1881, he became President.'

Goodie Noon's voice, had Calvin Coolidge ever spoken, which he had not, could have been a nasal match of his hero's speech. It was as though trained people came in every morning before both men arose to pack their sinuses with hot sand through which a dissonant treble wind whistled. It was a voice which would have matched the voice of a grumpily awakened elderly turkey but which, in Goodie Noon's case, often rang with the courage and content of a good child. 'Promote the Flag,' he would say, eyes shining with ambition (for his countrymen), 'and the Flag will promote you.'

'Goodie?'

'Yes, dear?'

'I think I may have been able to retain Malachi Olgilvie to consult – secretly of course – on the campaign.'

'Oona! Oh, that's neat! And I'd like to see us open up that Alaska refuge, and that is important because it was said once, remember, when they built the pipeline, "Don't build the pipeline, you'll get rid of the caribou." But the caribou love it. They rub up against it, and they have babies. There are more caribou in Alaska than you can shake a stick at.'

'And I have a wonderful surprise for you. Mr Olgilvie's suggestion for launching the campaign.'

'Really? I hope I stand for anti-bigotry, anti-Semitism, and antiracism. That, and a zero-option capital gains tax, is what drives me. That is one thing I feel very, very strongly about.' His face, tilting upwards under his right ear, confirmed the findings in Dr John Lynn's scientific paper 'Hand-Face Laterality In Relation to Personality', betraying his hunger to be elected to something, anything.

'The Governor of Massachusetts gone arrange for the retirement of their senior senator,' Oona said. 'He will appoint you in his place. Within a month you will be the Senator from Massachusetts.'

'I'm afraid not, Oon,' Goodie said sternly.

'What?'

'I'm not going to take one more appointed job.'

'But ... ' Oona Noon was flabbergasted. 'Think of what a seat in the Senate will do for your résumé.'

'I already have the longest career résumé in American history. No, dear. I'm going to run from a simple position of strength – gigantic campaign funds. I have a tendency to avoid those on and on and on eloquent pleas. I don't talk much, but I believe; maybe I don't articulate much, but I feel.'

'I'll get on to Mal and try to head him off.'

'What have you been able to get done for the campaign in the funding area?'

'Well, good heavens, Goodie –'

'Under the terms of my dad's will, the estate is ready to match every dollar we can get together for a campaign exploratory committee.'

'Whaaaat?'

'If you raise two million, the estate will have to match it with two million and, as you know, they can also persuade various other oil companies, banks, and insurance and telecommunications industries to chip in. And exploratory committees do not have to file financial disclosure reports with the Federal government.'

'Well, sakes alive, Goodie. Why didn't you tell me that a long time ago?' Oona Noon made a lightning calculation: if she could raise $20 million, and she knew well where she could raise it, then Goodie's dad's estate would have to match it with $20 million and the 'friends' would put up even more matching millions. Goodie's campaign could be over the top before it started; all absolutely legal, and no Federal election snoops would need to know a thing about it. She would also be able to appropriate $12 million from Goodie's own Political Action Committees, those mechanisms which the Congress had legalized so that politicians could bribe each other and be bribed themselves in an above-board manner. While it was purely true that PAC funds could not be used 'directly' in Presidential campaigns, they would be available to finance the candidate's stumping across the country, to see that he ate and slept well as he did the groundwork for his candidacy. And, on top of all that help, Goodie would have the Federal matching funds. She just had to do it. Goodie had to have his chance at being elected to something.

'We've got to do it my way, dear,' Goodie said. 'The country needs me. I have this intense conviction that there are some social changes going on. AIDS, for example, the sale of crack cocaine which is rife in Lafayette Park directly across from the White House, and the Reagans' burgeoning fortune. I don't want my grandchildren to go to X-rated movies. I can influence that from the White House. And everyone realizes that peace through strength works and this is where I make a big difference.'

'I'm goin' right back to New York now and raise them exploratory funds,' Oona said fervently.

'We're in this together, dear, and my plea to the American people is "Values in the schools". I shall run as the Education President because I believe deeply in goals and values – as my work on these typewriter portraits shows – and the people of this country, of course.'

'We'll be fully funded on a non-disclosure basis by this time next week,' Oona pledged.

'Don't ever stop bringing me your ideas, Oon. Let the ideas come to birth, I say, then put them in a family where there will be love.'

Chapter 19

Freddie Fanshaw was fond of Toronto because it was a city that worked in human terms rather than as an eruption which spread itself haphazardly; not just a place to survive in, a place to live. Moving up and across a wide hill from Lake Ontario to the long plateau at the top, it gave the mint-fresh impression of having been built entirely during the night before.

He walked under the enormous skylighted roof of Eaton Centre, around a 6-storey waterfall, under a life-scale mobile of 60 flying geese, across 14.5 acres of enclosed space which contained a church, a city park, 229 shops, and 22 fast-food nosherias to elevators on the west side of the shopping mall. He rode to the fifth floor and went to an office door marked *Uptown Trade Ltd*, opened the door with a brass key and entered.

A young woman with bold boobs and fulvous hair who faced the door as she typed said, 'Hullo, Freddie. What a lovely surprise.'

'Hullo, Gladys. I must call London.' He went into one of the four inner offices, closed the door, sat at a desk, and took up the receiver of the scrambler phone. He got on to Cheltenham and was patched through to London on a protected line. London took the news of his instant disposal to Lebanon by the cousins as being somewhat predictable.

'They weren't awfully keen when Madame made the proposal,' Freddie's case officer said. 'We'll get you another passport and different pocket litter. Go back to Washington and start an independent investigation. Paste on a large moustache or whatever. Just carry on as if the cousins didn't exist. They can't be up to any good.'

'I say, I rushed out of London so fast that I forgot that four books are about to be overdue at the Kensington library. Can you ask someone to break into my flat and handle that?'

'Will do.'

'What about Lebanon?'

'We'll have someone stay in touch with their Fish and Wildlife Service fellow in Athens in your Pappadakis name. Stand by where you are for now. This needs to be passed to the Minister and you may be sure he'll pass it upwards. Have a nice weekend and I'll be back to you Monday at 0700, your time. You may end with the PM as your case officer. Where are you staying?'

'The Four Seasons.'

'What name?'

'Jean-Pierre Blouseau.'

'Was that the name on the American passport?'

'No. I had some old French paper.'

'Who suggested that you must fly at once to the Middle East?'

'A short, quite heavily dimensional type named James D. Marxuach.'

'A bit of a brute, Marxuach. He's one of their steely-eyed chaps in the Security Research Staff so they must be expecting the messiest.'

'Pleasant enough chap, though. Gave me quite a sincere hug at the airport this morning.'

'What's needed is an independent survey. Everything you were looking for when you left London and a little more.'

'A little more?'

'Our masters are certain to want to know what the cousins are up to. Everyone here is alerted to probe their opposite numbers in Washington and in the field as far west as Guam.'

'It is a puzzler.'

'Why did they want you to rush off to Beirut, et cetera? What happened to change the elderly President's views since he talked to Madame? Anything and everything. Find out whatever it is we don't know about the Noon woman and her lawyer. Where does the Mafia fit in? That sort of thing.'

'Alan ...'

'Yes, Freddie?'

'The fact is, Marxuach was rather heavy handed about trying to muddy the waters – working like Hercules to give the impression that the Russians weren't in this at all – as if it were all something the Yanks would be able to straighten out without sweating.'

'That *is* devious.'

'But if the Russkies are involved won't that spell disaster to the cousins' eternal policy of keeping them out of the Middle East?'

'Not really. I mean, if the Russians get the tankers they'll buy them in their wife's name, won't they? The boffins are meeting now to determine what the American perfidy can be about. We are sure of one thing. The cousins want to do us and we can't have that.'

Fanshaw had an exhilarating weekend Mum-and-Dadding it with Gladys Gilpin, the station admin. girl. She had an apartment with an enormously comfortable bed which they tested endlessly until early Monday morning. Freddie was at the scrambler in the floating bug-proof office in the Eaton Centre at 0700 hours Monday morning, rested and glowing, when the call from London came in.

'Freddie?'

'Alan.'

'Everyone here is terribly upset. The PM is flint-hearted about the entire matter. She keeps telling our master that she cannot believe that such a nice chap as the President would do such a thing to her. Pathetic, actually.'

'Oh, well. It *is* hard cheese.'

'She wants you to disem*bowel* them. You are to have an unlimited budget and all the help HM Government can provide and you are to turn up every hard fact concerning what is behind this betrayal, Freddie. Her words.'

'Will do. But I am putting in instanter for surveillance teams, signals units, and researchers. Might as well throw in an armourer.'

'Roger.'

'Both sexes. At least two colours.'

'And – in the hell hath no fury department – if you come across anything which is particularly damaging to the old fellow's administration, be ready to leak it to all the American news media.'

'Alan! If that is my brief, I shan't have a moment in any 24-hour day to do anything else. Particularly damaging items are a way of life in the Reagan Party.'

'Yes. Well, best to give all that a pass then. Now – a courier is on the way with your new pocket litter, et cetera. He will walk into your room at Uptown Trade Ltd in twelve minutes. Use the embassy in Washington sparingly. W.A. Jackson-Bennett of Her Majesty's Fish & Wildlife Service is your contact there.'

'Good chap, W.A.'

'Your base in the DC will be 210A Connecticut Avenue, N.W., Apartment 55. It's a rich American writer's flat. He's in Switzerland most of the time. The embassy will fit the place out with a scrambler and a high-speed transmitter. Rendezvous will be at 11.57 p.m. except Sunday when it will occur at 9.00 p.m. – always your time. Are you equipped for Sundays in Washington, Freddie?'

'I know a positive peach of a girl with British Trade. Lives in Maryland. And I've never been to the Smithsonian Institution.'

'Well, cheer-o.' London disconnected.

Chapter 20

Doris Spriggs followed Owney to his apartment house. She had quiet talks with the building employees and a few neighbours, frightening them into silence and putting lepers' bells on the Hazman family. She was in place wearing an Edwin Meese, jr carnival mask the following morning when Owney walked from the Apthorpe entrance directly to the IRT station kiosk on the corner of 79th and Broadway. They rode downtown on the same subway car to 14th Street, then boarded a crosstown bus together riding west to 12th Avenue. A quite forward, gypsyish-looking fellow with a grotesquely oversized Bulgarian radish grower's moustache attempted to fondle Miss Spriggs' bottom in the packed vehicle. She dropped him to his knees with a karate chop unseen by anyone and, as he fell, broke his jaw with her elbow.

She had changed from the military tunic into a man's exaggerated sports jacket in the oversized Armani fashion wherein everyone seems to be wearing everyone else's clothes, having enormously padded shoulders over an impossibly lumpy tweed skirt and red-and-blue Adidas. Her hair had become bushy and blonde. On the way from the subway to the bus she had become aware of a surveillance team which was competing for Owney, a man and a woman. When Owney entered the frankfurter factory Spriggs rounded the corner then worked her way around the back of the surveillance team who were seated in a Ford saloon. The woman in the team left the car, hailed a cab, and left.

They were obviously Arabs which meant that they could be working for the French Sûreté. Spriggs had been hardship-posted to Libya and she was keen about spotting Arabs no matter how dense the crowd. What were Arabs doing staking out a frankfurter factory? The thought of the content of frankfurters must have rocked them with nausea. Whatever The Company knew about

103

Owney Hazman and his place in the tanker conspiracy, the Arab world, specifically the Syrians and possibly the French government, knew it as well.

She memorized the car's licence number. She called one of The Outfit's regional offices from a telephone booth in a luncheonette and identified herself in code. She gave the licence number, as well as that of the taxi in which the woman had left, and asked that the NYPD pick the Arabs up. She asked for a car to be sent so she could have something to sit on until Hazman came out.

At Langley, James D. Marxuach had asked Central Filing (twenty-two floors beneath the ground floor of the building) for fullest available background on Owen Hazman, Caucasian male, age twenty-eight, et cetera, with the request that it be submitted simultaneously to analysts and to other SRS agents with a need to know. When the biog. sheets came to his desk, the vital information on Hazman would scarcely have filled one page but a second page was needed for the biog. on the subject's parents.

Owen (Owney) Hazman is the only child of Chandler Hazman who was an agent of the DIA and the CIA for 15 years (1955–1970) and Molly Tompkins Hazman aka Mafalda Khomeini, allegedly an Iranian national, said to be 'the eyes in the West' of the mullahs, and who served on the Ayatollah Ruhollah Khomeini's staff in Paris during his exile. (See Photo File H-203-4591.) Molly Tompkins Hazman is rumoured to be the natural daughter of the Ayatollah; said to be a fanatical supporter of the Iranian revolution and a relentless enemy of the United States.

Chandler Hazman was turned by his wife in 1966 and operated as a double agent. He was turned again by the CIA in 1969 following his full (voluntary) confession, to operate as a triple agent against Iranian intelligence whose principal agent, his wife, was a sleeper in the United States and who disappeared in March 1969 (File AT-9-3564-EHC) and is believed to have been returned to Tehran. There is a rumour that she has been executed. C. Hazman received a disability discharge from CIA in 1970. He died of leukaemia January 12th, 1981.

The Hazmans' son, Owen Tompkins Hazman, American citizen born in the Borough of Richmond, City of New York on March 18th, 1960, may now be emerging as an Iranian agent, possibly being run by his mother. He has gained the confidence of Malachi Olgilvie, Washington lawyer, sportsman, and confidant of Presidents, as well as that of Mrs Osgood (Oona) Noon, wife of Osgood O. Noon who will be a candidate for President in the 1992 primaries. Both are considered to be wholly under Hazman's influence as regards the decision to sell the 79 Noon supertankers to the Soviet Union.

Shaking his head with professional dismay, James D. Marxuach fed the report into his desk shredder when he finished memorizing it. He was sure as hell going to step on *that* little bastard.

Chapter 21

Owney burst into the apartment at the Apthorpe to tell his wife the news of his projected schooling to earn $3 million a year as a television network anchor man. He hurried through the apartment looking for her. He found her bending over a bath in a crowded steamy bathroom trying to bathe three small children. He started to talk excitedly but the children all talked at once, overjoyed that he was home.

'You'll never guess what happened –' he started to say.

'Daddy! Daddy! Look at me!'

'Molly, you get out first,' Dolly said to the middle child in the bath. 'Franklin, keep a good hold on Bonita. Good, that's good. Here's your towel, Molly.'

'Dolly, for Christ's sake!'

'Later. Aaaaall right, Bonita.' She took up a towel, put it on her shoulder, and reached down to lift the baby out of the bath.

'Dolly,' Owney said, 'Mrs Noon is going to find an anchor coach for me.'

Dolly dried the baby gently. 'Good. That's nice. We'll talk about it.'

Owney left the bathroom, slamming the door behind him. It was a lucky thing for Dolly, he thought, that he wasn't a wife beater. Still wearing his hat, a black-and-white hound's tooth checked tweed fedora, he fell into a wing chair in the living room which was furnished entirely in Duncan Phyffe reproductions, including a Duncan Phyffe computer stand and a hand-sewn carpet which the dealer had said had been machine woven from original designs by Mrs Duncan Phyffe.

It hit Owney that he and Mrs Noon hadn't settled on which television network he would be working with when the time came.

He wondered what an anchor coach did. How could he be expected to watch five television screens at the same time?

He pulled his copy of the *NBC Handbook of Pronunciation* off the bookshelf beside his chair and began to study it in an effort to keep calm. He tried to remember that network anchor men were forbidden to pronounce the word 'route' correctly but had to say it as 'rout', never to rhyme with 'root' as required by the language.

It took Dolly twenty minutes to settle the kids. While she was getting them ready for bed, the telephone rang. Owney crossed the room to answer it. 'Hello?'

'Dolly?'

He recognized his mother-in-law's voice. 'How could this be Dolly?'

'Who is this?'

'*Who*?'

'Ah – it's Owney. This is Bonita. I'm so proud you got that big order, the lawyer's picnic. Paco is proud too. We are both very proud, Owney.'

'Dolly is putting the children to bed. She can't come to the phone, Momma.'

'I don't need to talk to her. I'll come down with the soup I made.'

'No!'

'Whassamatta?'

'Bring the soup tomorrow, OK? Dolly has to make dinner. I am very hungry.'

'Tomorrow is fine. Tell Dolly I'll call her later.'

'Like nine o'clock?'

'Chew nicely, Owney. God chews with you.'

Owney put his hat in the hall closet then walked to a window on the West End Avenue side and stared out glumly. He could see large apartment buildings, a very small sliver of river and, on the other shore, a fragment of New Jersey. The television station where he would begin his career as a TV newsman was somewhere in New Jersey. Soon he would be seated in front of a camera whose built-in Teleprompter would march living history across its lens and he would begin to read gravely, whimsically, elec-trifyingly (or archly as the case might be), moving his faceless anchor agent to plead with him to consider his next move in the climb towards the top of the national ratings. Every night, somewhere in the fifty states, his mother would stare at the billing on the small screen as the show opened – *reported by Owney*

Hazman – then she would see his head appear and she would cry out in self-pity to think that she had walked away from such a son and his $3-million-a-year (plus expenses) salary.

Dolly called out from the foyer on her way to the kitchen, 'What did you say about Mrs Noon, Owney?'

'Oh, that,' he answered over his shoulder, staring out of the window. 'She's helping me get a job for three million a year.'

Dolly changed course. She whisked herself into the room. 'The anchor spot?' she asked, awed.

'Yeah.'

'Which network?'

He turned to face her. 'Whichever bids the most. It doesn't happen overnight. It's going to take ten years.'

'I should think so.' She sat on the sofa facing the false fireplace and patted the cushion beside her. Owney left the window and sat on the sofa.

'How are those things done?' she asked.

'I can't believe it. She is going to set me up with the same great anchor coach who trained Graham MacNamee and Major Bowes and when the coach says I'm ready she is going to set me as a local anchor on a New Jersey station, then she's going to line up some connection who is going to book me as a network White House correspondent. Then the agent brings me back to New York to anchor one of the big morning shows – then into the big slot.'

'I just can't believe it's going to happen.'

'It had to happen, Doll. That's how I'm going to find my mom.' His eyes went moist.

'I'm so happy for you, Owney.'

'I feel humble. Very, very humble,' he said arrogantly.

'But how are you going to pay the anchor coach? And what about your job? What will Poppa say?'

'There is no reason even to think of leaving the job until the Jersey anchor is set. Your father is just going to have to get used to the idea. Anyway, Mrs Noon is going to pay for the anchor coach.'

'I don't think that's such a good idea.'

'What do you mean?'

'Well! She is a very beautiful, powerful, wealthy woman. You will owe her. I mean – you already owe her.'

'Owe her?'

'You are an extremely desirable man, Owney! Physically and otherwise. Let her pay for those anchor lessons that will place you on the pinnacle in ten years and you will be so beholden to her that you will not be able to turn away her advances.'

'That is absolutely ridiculous. I won't owe her a blessed thing! I'm helping her make two billion dollars. I even offered to do the courier work for nothing in exchange for the anchor coach but she wouldn't hear of it.'

'Well, I don't like it. And I simply will not allow it.'

'You mean, because she's a woman? If it were a man, someone like your father, that would be OK? We've been waiting a long time for this break. What's the alternative?'

'We pay for the anchor coach ourselves.'

'I don't even know what he costs.'

'It doesn't matter.'

'Doll – listen. You know even better than I do that all the money we have in the world is tied up in Zero Coupon bonds so we'll be able to pay the fifty or sixty thousand a year or more that it's going to cost for each kid to go to college. Nothing can get money out of Zero Coupon bonds before fifteen years without paying a tremendous penalty. Be realistic, Doll. Let Mrs Noon, a billionaire, pay for the anchor coach.'

'No, Owney. It's not right. I – I just couldn't live with myself if I let that happen.'

'Then how are we going to do it? I ask you. This is the big chance. If I don't take it now, I'll never get another shot at it.'

'You're going to have your shot, Owney.'

'I will not ask your father for the money and I will not allow you to ask him.'

'Not that way.'

'Are you saying . . . ?' His voice pitched higher into panic. 'Do you mean we should use some of the capital from my father's estate for this? The money that is earmarked for the private investigators to find my mother?'

'No. Certainly not. That money will only be used to find your mother – when the time comes.'

He felt enormous relief. 'Then how?'

'I'm going to call the record company Monday morning and tell them I'll cut two sides for them. They offered me fifteen thousand dollars a side just a few weeks ago.'

'But –'

'It won't interfere with anything. Momma will take care of the kids for the few hours I'll be downtown to sing two songs. With thirty thousand we can work out a deal with the anchor coach

109

and you won't be beholden to Mrs Noon for anything.'

'Doll, it doesn't just end there. You don't just cut two sides and take the thirty thousand. They'll want personal appearances and video and tours and TV shots. The media will be all over you.'

'On my first record? Anyway –' she gave him a foxy smile – 'that's what *they*'ll think. That I will be looking to cut more records after the first two sides. No way. Two sides. Thirty thousand dollars. Then – literally – *finito la musica.*'

'You are some terrific woman,' Owney said.

Chapter 22

The first thing Oona Noon did when she left her husband at his typewriter easel on Bland Island was telephone Owney Hazman to send him to Washington to tell Mal Olgilvie to cancel the plan to have the senior senator from Massachusetts resign in favour of Goodie.

The second thing she did was to make the call to Edward S. Price at his eyrie office on the Avenue of the Americas to suggest that they have a meeting. The income realized from the sale of the cocaine which Mrs Noon's tankers were bringing into prosperous middle-class America from the far countries of South America was distributed by Mr Price's principals and the splendid amounts of tax-free income therefrom were channelled into one or another of the forty-three banks owned by Barker's Hill Enterprises, which Edward S. Price operated for the Prizzi family.

Edward Price claimed to have invented the billions of dollars' worth of junk bonds issued by companies he controlled, then sold to savings and loans, insurance companies and banks – that is, basically to the stockholders of the companies who had bought them – bonds on which the sellers got four per cent, and the lawyers who drew up the indentures got $700 an hour, the public went broke, but no one went to jail. Executives of Barker's Hill companies were also encouraged to give themselves multi-million-dollar wages as they drove their companies into insolvency. Edward S. Price was the inventor of the dream of just writing out cheques with the stockholders' money, made payable to himself, then having his lawyers and bankers certify that it was legal and above board. He had bought huge companies away from their stockholders at far less than real value while using the stockholders' money to hire the lawyers and bankers to help him take away the stockholders' money.

111

When he had explained these procedures, which had become common practice in American business, to his father, the great *capo Mafioso*, Don Corrado Prizzi, the old man had marvelled with admiration. 'You have *really* organized crime, my son,' he said with awe. 'Every year you skim off another two or three billion and the way you got it all figured out, nobody can call a cop.'

'It's just the modern way, Poppa,' Price had said. 'There is no one to bother you. The Congress looks the other way because there is also a big buck in it for them and the Securities and Exchange Commission doesn't make any waves. There are private plaintiff suits, sure, but they all get settled using the stockholders' money – and we come away from every deal richer and cleaner.'

'But you gotta tie up a lotta cash for that.'

'No, Poppa. We borrow from the banks.'

'But that's a lotta interest you gotta pay on loans like that.'

'So sell off some of the companies and fire a few thousand people to pay the interest. The rest is not only clear to us, but we get it all free.'

'Jesus,' his father said, 'and we used to have to use guns.'

So much money had been involved in the business of importing the expensive vegetables in the tanker fleet that Mrs Noon had insisted on doing business at the top. 'It is not that I have anything against hoodlums.' 'Some of my best friends are hoodlums, but I must feel that I am co-opting where the real decisions are made.'

It was a rare thing for anyone, anywhere to be allowed to know Edward S. Price's true function with The Mob but, knowing that Mrs Noon was the wife of an exceptionally wealthy man whose family had made its fortune even before Ronald Reagan had entered the White House, a man who could become a ranking national politician, Price judged that the risk was shared between them. All that and a warm letter of sincere recommendation from the Ayatollah had permitted Mr Price to make an exception in Mrs Noon's case.

'Where shall we meet, dear lady?'

'I certainly can't go to your office.'

'My limousine has purdah-glass windows. Shall we ride round the Park?'

'Please.'

'When will you be ready to leave?'

'I am ready now.'

'I will be in the car at your door in thirty-five minutes.'

*

When Mrs Noon was well settled in the tonneau of the stretched Phantom VII Rolls-Royce which was just a few sweet feet shorter than the locomotive which pulled The Flying Scotsman and which carried saddle-stitched, leather double shotgun scabbards, hand-made at the King Ranch in Texas, on the interior of each front door, Mr Price said, 'My driver and footman are deaf and dumb.'

Price was an angular, exquisitely tailored, aristocratic-looking man whose features had been reset with state-of-the-art cosmetic surgery by Dr Abraham Weiler, Nobelist in plastic medicine, into the cast of the late George Nathaniel Curzon, 1st Marquess of Kedleston and a Viceroy of India.

Price was wearing a casual set of sports dentures which had been modelled on Jimmy Carter's orthodontics. They were deal-making teeth which made him appear amiable, affable, and amorous (in his heart). His speech was entirely languid, conveying, if it were to be compared with the speech of William F. Buckley, jr, that Buckley was from the lower orders and was trying to pass.

As the car turned into Central Park at 60th Street, Mrs Noon, stressed-out as she was from the strain of intending to sell a late husband's fleet of tankers in order to help a present husband become President of the United States, fell into her need for a conversational ice-breaker before getting down to business. She said, 'I don't suppose a man in your position ever really had the chance to eat any really bad food.'

'Oh, I've had my share, I suppose,' Price said languidly. The psychological profile that he had had a team compile on Mrs Noon years before, when they had first contemplated entering into a business relationship, had prepared him for her needs and foibles; her use of ice-breakers.

'I mean *really* bad food. You know, like Disraeli said how he rather liked bad wine because one gets so bored with good wine.'

'I suppose bad eating has its surprises,' Mr Price said.

'The worst single meal I ever tried to eat was the haggis served at the Gloriosa Pizzeria in Palermo. It was the blue plate special. Or have you ever eaten *osso bucco Mailander Art* in Hamburg? Or a French *rutabaga vinaigrette avec pommes à l'huile* in France?'

'I must say,' Mr Price drawled, 'although I am quite familiar with Italian food, I cannot conceive of how anyone could think of ordering haggis in Palermo.'

'Jessa minute here, Mistuh Price. Don't you go attackin' the decent Scottish minority which lives in La MacDougal, the Scottish ghetto of that city. I was faultin' the haggis as they serve it up at the Gloriosa Pizzeria. Lemme say that the haggis offered by Ristorante Il Piccolo Duce in La MacDougal is as good as any in Glasgow. If you can eat haggis.'

'What is this in aid of, Mrs Noon?'

'I am thinkin of sellin' my tanker fleet.'

'Well!'

'I know but, shoot, Goodie wants to run fo' President an' he thinks that somehow my ownin' seventy-nine supertankers will detract from my housewifey image as First Lady.'

'I suppose, in a way, he's right.'

'Jackie an' Nancy didn't convey any housewifey image.'

'No, but they were capable of being trained to seem to be spending their lives adoring their husbands. That is what Mr Noon must have had in mind. After all, if the voting public associates you with running a fleet of seventy-nine supertankers perhaps they might feel that you were preoccupied with the ships rather than with the President.'

'Anyways, I decided to sell.'

'Mr Noon will make a fine President. He's such a patriot. Heavens! What he's done for the Flag and the Pledge of Allegiance alone –'

'Would Barker's Hill like to operate the tankers for the duration of my husband's term in office?'

'*Operate?*'

'The oil the tankers carry does generate a certain amount of money but that is a bagashells compared to the income generated by the vegetable imports. But, a-course, you know that.'

'Our policy is ownership. Outright ownership.'

'I figured that. But I was thinkin', instead of ownership, of grantin' you a hunnert-year lease on the tankers. They would surely be useless after a hunnert years but they would still be my ships so that I would be sole negotiator of the terms for the other import cargoes. Needless to say, with my husband in the White House, the possibility of government interference with those other imports would be remote.'

'Does your husband know about the other imports?'

'Heavens, no. But he listens to me when I suggest things to him.'

'How much did you have in mind for the leases?'

'I was thinkin', if Barker's Hill did all the maintenance, insurance, repairs, and overheads, that I would lease them to

114

you for a hunnert million a year plus a twenny-million dollah contribution to my husband's exploratory campaign fund and a 7.5 per cent increase in my market share of the other imports.'

'A 7.5 per cent increase would raise your share by ninety million dollars a year.'

'More or less.'

'That's a little high for me, I'm afraid. Make it five per cent.'

'Five per cent for the first seven years, then 7.5 per cent.'

'That seems utterly reasonable.'

'We do want Goodie to be elected, don't we, Mr Price?'

'Exactly my thought, dear lady.'

'I'd need the twenny million up front. For the exploratory fund. The rest can follow the leases when they're signed.'

'Right on,' Edward Price said.

Chapter 23

———

Oona Noon wanted Owney to go to Washington to tell Mr Olgilvie that she would meet him at the racetrack at 5.45 the following morning, but Owney flatly refused to make the trip on such a flimsy errand. He agreed to call Olgilvie instead, leaving the message with his secretary and referring to Mrs Noon as 'the lady'. Mr Olgilvie called him right back. 'You'll have to tell the lady we can't go on meeting like this,' he said. 'That goddam car is too easily identifiable and she is married to a man who will soon be in the news.'

'She is?' Owney asked.

'Oh, for Christ's sake, Owney!' Mr Olgilvie hung up heavily.

Olgilvie was in an absorbed discussion with his trainer and a vet when Mrs Noon arrived at the stable yard in the Figoni et Falaschi. He waved to her as she sat in the car and continued his discussion, then, after six or eight minutes, he patted the two men on the shoulders and walked over to join her.

'Even if people didn't remember seeing you here,' he said, 'which is highly unlikely, this is the flashiest, most memory-sticking car ever built.'

'Maybe you right, Mal. Next time I'll rent a Cadillac.'

As he got into the car she started the eighteen-cylinder engine. It sounded like all four motors of a Boeing 747 turning over, then it dropped to the sound of a well-oiled sewing machine, then it sang with silence as it rolled out of the yard.

'What's up?' Mr Olgilvie asked.

'I got to tell you that the sale to the Chinese is off.'

He was startled. 'Off? I don't understand. The negotiations have been going along splendidly.'

'I had to sell yesterday.'

'You sold the *tankers*? Who bought them?'

116

'Barker's Hill Enterprises.'

'*Had* to sell?' Olgilvie knew well who Barker's Hill was. They were one of his clients.

'Ed Price is gone put up twenny million for Goodie's exploratory fund, plus we worked out a good deal.'

'Where does that leave me?'

'I still gotta buy some time till I close with Ed Price, so you gotta keep negotiatin' with Mr Jay, then, after we do close with Price, you gotta keep up a show of lookin' for a customer. I don't want it gettin' out that that Medellín outfit bought my tankers, so you still gone get your three per cent negotiator's fee on the sale, Mal.'

'What about the other imports?'

'You never did come in on that an' you know it.'

'How come?'

'Because you could never have gotten the Chinese to make it a part of their deal, that's why.'

'Don't be too sure.'

'Whutta you think is fair?'

'Well – I don't know – say a half of one per cent override on your end.'

'Thass OK. I can live with that. You headed off the Governor of Massachusetts? About makin' Goodie a senator?'

'No problem. What happened there, anyway?'

'Goodie just dug his heels in. He says his résumé cain't stand one more appointed job. He's gotta git elected to somethin'. That's why he's runnin' for President.'

'The twenty million from Barker's Hill for his campaign exploration fund is really going to get Goodie off the ground,' Olgilvie said. 'The Party will have to take him seriously.'

'You ain't heard nothin' yet. His daddy's estate gone match the twenny million an' they gone get the oil companies, a few foreign govmints, the airlines, the telephone companies, and a handful of dear friends around the world to put up twenny million more – all for that ole unaccountable exploration fund.'

'Well!' Mr Olgilvie said. 'In that case, even I am beginning to take Goodie seriously. What with the normal campaign contributions, the PACs, and the Federal matching funds, Goodie is going to have 150 million to spend on buying himself the Presidency.'

Chapter 24

Early in June, fourteen different departments of ten national intelligence agencies, both covert and economic, were investigating all repercussions from the murder of the false Dr Atarf, and its meaning in relation to the threatening possibility that the Noon tanker fleet would fall into enemy hands. These agencies included the Central Intelligence Agency of the United States (CIA), and its component, the Security Research Staff (SRS); the Defense Intelligence Agency (DIA); the Federal Bureau of Investigation (FBI); the District of Columbia police (DCPD); the Syrian AIAS; the Afghan KHAD who were observing the AIAS for the Soviet Komitet Gosudarstvennoi Bezopasnosti (KGB) and the Pakistani Interservice Intelligence Directorate (IID) who were watching the KHAD for the CIA; Britain's Secret Intelligence Service (SIS) of its Military Intelligence Six (MI6); the Chinese Central External Liaison Department (CELD) operating through their Department of Investigation which was represented in Washington by the Foreign Intelligence Department (FID) and the New China News Agency (NCNA); the Special Operations Department of the Central Institution for Intelligence and Special Assignments of Israel (Mossad), and the Kokka Keisatsu Cho (KKC) of oil-hungry Japan, which was ordered to report directly to the Cabinet Research Chamber, a Brains Trust called the Naikaku Sori Daiijin Kambo Chosa Shitsu (NSDKCS). The KGB, not directly active in the matter, was weighing the information received from its Afghan ally and was frantically monitoring the dramatic increase in telephone and cable traffic between Washington and the Middle East.

The Syrians, most sensitively they thought, had doggedly clung to the notion that it would not be necessary to advise the KGB of developments until the package had been streamlined and made really available. Their most sage spymasters had decided that withholding information until they had everything in hand could mean redoubling the Soviet contribution of future arms and matér-iel by using the leverage of any tanker-fleet-sale information.

Edward S. Price, through his father, Don Corrado Prizzi, had cleared the $20 million campaign contribution to the Noon exploratory committee with the Mafia's New York Commission and the National Council of the twenty-two families and thirty-one affiliates among the black, Hispanic, Oriental, Israeli, and Gay Crime groups involved. In addition to the $20 million, all units were advised to get busy forming Political Action Committees whose accountable funds could be used to elect Osgood Noon on a law and order ticket. All families had their local banks poised and waiting to launder the money which would gush out of the Noon election. It was voted unanimously that Noon would run on an anti-crime, anti-drug, pro-National Rifle Association platform. Clients among police forces around the country were organized to give Goodie their vocal/visual support at any/all campaign print/television appearances.

The Syrian illegals in Washington and at the United Nations, whipped on by Damascus, worked on plans to kidnap Malachi Olgilvie and/or Mrs Noon. By habit, the Mossad watched the Syrians, managing always to stay one step ahead of them.

'The schmucks are going to try to grab Olgilvie and maybe even the Noon woman,' Lev Schlemozle, the Mossad bureau chief in Washington, said to the Premier on a quick trip to Jerusalem. 'They haven't figured out yet that if there is no negotiator there can't be any deal. Do they think they can force the Noon woman to sell her tankers? Either way, it wouldn't work. They force her to sign and she objects as soon as she's free and there is no delivery or the government stops the sale cold. They kill her and what have they got? Nothing. Olgilvie, believe me, figured all that out long ago.'

'But, still, they gotta get inside the Olgilvie house or they'll never know what's happening.'

'Neither will we.'

'So?'

'You want us to get in there?'

'Please, Lev. If the Syrians get the tankers, we'll blow up the tankers, one by one, wherever they are in the world because they stand for violence and violence has got to be stamped out.'

*

The Chinese redoubled their guard of Australians outside and around the Olgilvie house: cruising Australian pseudo-laundry truck drivers, traffic wardens, casual tourists, and itinerant arbitrageurs and merger specialists. The American agencies triangulated the house with radio surveillance beams and were baffled by the sixth-century Chinese dialect. They lost one Security Research person who had been sent to penetrate the house and was never heard of again.

James D. Marxuach personally took charge of the twice daily examination of the Olgilvie rubbish. He was deeply puzzled by the remnants of Egg Foo Yong and Moo Goo Gai Pan which kept coming out. A check of Washington and New York restaurants revealed that Olgilvie was a steak-and-potatoes man who had no record of attending any Chinese restaurant since a long-past flirtation with Anna May Wong when the star had been at her peak. These were the harsh facts because Olgilvie had been under Agency surveillance for twenty-six years.

Marxuach had the Olgilvie domestic staff followed to supermarkets. Not a single Egg Foo Yong or Moo Goo Gai Pan ingredient went into the house yet, day after day, the remnants of Egg Foo Yong and Moo Goo Gai Pan kept coming out in the bins. Marxuach knew that there was something significant in this information but its meaning kept eluding him.

Of all the foreign agents, only Freddie Fanshaw made any progress, such as it was. He thought about the matter long and hard and decided that the Mafia, because of its formalized greed and experience at overtaking, had to be somewhere on the fringes if not at the centre of anything anywhere in the United States which involved more than thirteen dollars and some change. He signalled his people in London to set up a meeting for him with Mafia leaders in New York.

The Minister of State at the Foreign and Commonwealth Office consulted his senior civil servant who produced a small black book from a wall safe in the Minister's office in Whitehall, which contained useful, if arcane, names, addresses, and telephone numbers. Reading from the small book, he informed his Minister that the head of the Mafia in the UK was Lord Glandore, an Irish peer.

Glandore was enjoying the gentling Irish summer with his bodyguards and his cat, Bumpkin Blue, at Winikus Castle, his seat at Leap in County Cork, but he agreed cordially to receive the FO deputy the following afternoon, Glandore's appointments secretary promising scones such as would exceed any in Foreign Office memory.

Glandore, as soon as he understood the financial dimensions of the deal which was the pivot of the FO requirement, said he would be delighted to do anything which would be of assistance to HM Government. He most happily agreed to arrange an immediate meeting between a Foreign Office representative and Edward S. Price in New York.

'The name of our man who will contact your man will be Frederick Fanshaw,' the FO man said.

On his arrival in Washington from Toronto, Freddie Fanshaw was instructed by the Fisheries & Wildlife man at the British Embassy (inside a room which not only floated within the structure but which had been, most recently, swept electronically), to telephone a given number in New York from a public telephone booth in Baltimore and to ask for two orders of Yorkshire pizza to take away.

Fanshaw called the New York number from the phone booth in Maryland, not identifying himself other than asking for the pizzas. The answering voice asked him where he was. Freddie told him. The voice said, 'OK. Check inta the Lord Baltimore hotel. You got it?'

'Entirely,' Freddie said.

'OK. The phone in your room there will ring in one hour and eleven minutes. Now we set the watches.'

The two men synchronized their watches over the telephone. Freddie told the voice that his watch was three minutes slow. The voice insisted that Freddie's watch was three minutes fast.

The voice said, 'I'll toss you. Whadda you take, heads or tails?'

'Tails,' Freddie said.

There was a slight pause. 'You lose,' the voice said. 'We go by my watch. Reset yours.'

Freddie did as he was told. One hour and eleven minutes later, on the dot, the phone in the room at the Lord Baltimore Hotel rang.

'Fanshaw here,' Freddie said into the phone.

It was a different voice; an old man's voice. 'Whatta you want?'

'My dear chap – you are calling me.'

'So?'

'I would like to see Mr Edward S. Price, please. As early as possible at his convenience.'

121

'How come?'

'His British counterpart would have told him how come.'

'Yeah?'

'Well – obviously.'

'Stay in your room. We'll pick you up in eighteen minutes.'

The *fratellanza* people had Freddie in the St Gabbione Laundry in central Brooklyn in ninety-four minutes. He had been driven to a small airport, flown to Floyd Bennett field in Brooklyn, whisked to the laundry to insure against his being followed, slipped into the back of a laundry truck to the Sheepshead Bay heliport, flown by chopper to the East River helipad, then moved in a stretch limousine behind a police escort to the Barker's Hill offices on the Avenue of the Americas for an immediate meeting with Edward S. Price.

Until he reached Price's office the tension had been palpable. During the time when he was being passed from hand to mafioso hand, Freddie could not help but think of the Reuters report he had read which had said that mafiosi suffer worse stress than top business executives, and that, according to Professor Granesco Aragora, a Sicilian pathologist who had spent forty years studying mafiosi cadavers, that the (violently) deceased had thickened arteries, kidney failure, stomach ulcers, and livers that were yellowish, fatty, and chronically short of glucose.

Price, his eight-ounce blue wool suit by Huntsman of London, his shirt, done in a light violet cast by Bejan of Beverly Hills in pure Egyptian cotton which had been spun at 2,831 threads to the inch, wore a Kent & Curwen tie in the lavender and silver stripes which represented the Oxford University Fencing Club for those who had achieved a Blue at fencing (with the stripes descending from the left-hand side, from the heart as it were, in the English fashion). The dentures he was wearing that day had been modelled on the teeth of the late Giuseppe Garibaldi (1807–1882) by Dr Pincus of Beverly Hills. They glistened perfectly. He was affable to a point that would have been starkly frightening had not Freddie had long experience among professional terrorists trained to frighten people for a living.

'What can I do for you, Mr Fanshaw?' Mr Price said from behind the largest Florentine desk ever used by a Medici then exported (illegally) to the United States.

'You know the background?'

Price nodded gravely.

'What is wanted here – what everyone on all sides of the question is trying to do – is to get a man inside Olgilvie's house.'

Mr Price nodded.

'The CIA, or it might have been Mossad, has already lost one man in the attempt.'

Mr Price shrugged helplessly. 'I simply wouldn't know where to begin.'

'Surely you have – uh – ways to reach Olgilvie's household staff.'

'I could suggest to some people that they try.'

'When would you think you might know something?'

Price gave Fanshaw the smile which had made Garibaldi commander of the corps known as 'The Hunters of the Alps' and dictator of Sicily. Emerging from the surgical copy of the face of Lord Curzon, the smile had an awful effect.

'I'll need videotapes and transcripts on every meeting Olgilvie has held in that house,' Fanshaw said.

'Good heavens, man! How do you think anyone could ever get anything like that?'

'We have to know what is happening inside that house.'

'And if my people can find out what is happening, Mr Fanshaw? Is that negotiable?'

'How do you mean?'

'I mean that – sooner or later – you and my people would have to come to some sort of financial arrangement.'

'How much?'

'That depends on the value of the information, doesn't it? We shall have to wait and see, won't we?'

'I am going to have to get back to you on this. It is most certainly out of my hands.'

'How much time do you need?'

'Twenty-four hours at the outside.'

'If I don't hear from you, the people I speak of will sell the option on securing the information to somebody else. Don't worry about it.'

By 3.20 the following morning, 8.20 London time, Fanshaw had an authorization to pay up to $2 million for valid, documented information which would reveal conclusively the nature of the negotiations which were presumed to be going on inside the Olgilvie house off the Chain Bridge Road in Virginia.

Fanshaw telephoned Edward S. Price from the hotel on East

64th Street, at 9.15 that same morning. Mr Price said he would send a car for him immediately.

'You have the authorization?' Mr Price asked when Fanshaw had emerged from the private elevator, entering directly into Mr Price's private office and seating himself across the enormous desk from the great financier.

'Yes,' Freddie said.

'How much are you authorized to offer?'

'That will depend, of course, on the quality of the information.'

'You will understand, I am sure, that my organization is in no way in a position to undertake this.'

'What does that mean, Mr Price? I don't understand. Why are we meeting then?'

'I shall need to find – ah – specialists for the task.'

Fanshaw shrugged.

'If they are successful, a man named Angelo Partanna will contact you at your hotel here in exactly five days' time. He will telephone you at eight ayem and suggest a meeting place. If the evidence he will possibly have been able to secure meets with your requirements, you and he can discuss the value of the information you will have examined.'

Chapter 25

While the national security forces plotted and counter-plotted around them but did nothing because the progress of the negotiations inside the house off the Chain Bridge Road was so immeasurably tenuous (and only Edward S. Price's organization knew for a fact that meetings affecting the future control of seventy-nine supertankers were going on in there), three separate sets of extremely vital decisions were made and executed.

The first was the signing by the two principals of the hundred-year leases on the tankers: by Mrs Osgood Noon and Mr Hugh Pickering, president and CEO of the Ocmara Oil Company, a subsidiary of the Bahama Beaver Bonnet Company, the giant international conglomerate and a secret partner with Barker's Hill Enterprises in various ventures.

Secondly, an aggregate political campaign contribution of $20 million was made available to Mrs Noon, in separate cashier's cheques, by forty-six companies associated with Barker's Hill, and effective operating control of the oil tanker fleet passed into the control of Ocmara Oil. Mrs Noon retained all rights to 'other imports' which the tankers would also be bringing into the United States and other countries as transporter for the organization which owned Barker's Hill Enterprises.

The third extraordinary decision was taken that day by Dolly and Owney Hazman. By doing this they found what historians would have called the climax of their lives because from that point forward, their relationship with each other, for better or worse, would never be the same again; a pity in the best sense perhaps but, in view of the circumstances, cruelly inevitable.

The climax was reached thusly: on the Monday morning following her decision to cut the two phonographic sides, Dolly telephoned the Appleburg Record Company, a subsidiary of the giant Fujikawa Industries. She spoke to John Kullers, its A&R man, and told him she had decided to agree to cut the two sides which the company had been proposing.

'That's tremendous!' Kullers said. 'Jesus! We'll back you up with twenty-two violins. When do you wanna go?'

'I thought towards the end of the week.'

'Hang on, lemme look at my book. OK. Look. We got an open studio on Thursday at one o'clock. You know where? Seventh Avenue and 49th Street?'

'I'll be there.'

'I got your vocal arrangements for three months arreddy. They are terrific. This is music which drips self-pity, masochism, and a sort of vicious nostalgia. Also a twisted kind of sex for the kids. I can feel it in my head. You wanna come down here like on Wednesday about three and we can go through them?'

'Well . . .'

'Baby, you gotta go through the music.'

'Why don't you send them here by messenger and I'll go over them on the piano at my mother's.'

'Listen – anything you say. They'll be at your place in two hours. This is tre*men*dous. I can't believe you are gonna cut for us.'

'Fifteen thousand dollars a side?'

'You got it.'

'As an advance?'

'Advance? Thirty thousand dollars? That is the flat fee.'

'Then I can't do it.'

'An advance against how much?'

'Well – I suppose six cents a side. That seems reasonable.'

'Impossible, Miss Heller. I'll send the contracts with the arrangements.'

'Well, just to be sure – and I apologize that I'm not very experienced at this – make it ten cents a side.'

'Are you outta your mind?'

'What do you think is fair?'

'I think fifteen thousand a side flat is so fair it could break me.'

'I meant in royalties.'

'Nothing, Miss Heller. Who knows you? We are already paying six times the going rate because you kept saying yes, then you kept saying no. This is the music business where they guess about everything. We could lose the farm and you ask what is fair.'

'All right, Mr Kullers. I'll take six cents a side. But with the understanding that that royalty may not prejudice any future dealings we may have. That must be stated in the contract, Mr Kullers.'

'I'll give you haffa cent a side.'

'I can see that I'll have to compromise if we are ever to get this started. Ten cents.'

'All right! All right! Six cents! But they will crucify me in Tokyo for this! I got two new songs and a new singer and I pay royalties for both.'

'If the public likes the records then what's the difference? And if they don't like them you could pay a dollar a side and it wouldn't cost you anything.'

'Two hours, the messenger will be there.'

Dolly ran through the two songs at her mother's apartment that afternoon while the children were napping.

'Very nice. Very sweet, dolling,' Mrs Heller said beaming. 'But where do they get these new songs? What's wrong with the old songs? They couldn't copy them a little?'

'The company has to know *some*thing, Momma.'

'Why?'

'Because that's all they have to do – find the music and hire the musicians.'

She cut the two sides on Thursday afternoon backed up by a percussion combo of piano, guitar, bass, and drums who were backing up four French horns and twenty-two violins. She had never sung with such a solid wall of violins behind her; there only for her. It was exalting. She stood at stage front to the right of the orchestra wearing earphones, a pale blue angora sweater, a yellow blouse and a tweed skirt; fetchingly beautiful with her khaki-and-rose complexion and dazzling teeth; everything about her as gay (in the sense that merriment is gay, not in the sense that gays are gay) as the music itself was not, yet inexpressibly one with the song she was singing, hypnotizing the musicians and the shirt-sleeved men in the recording booth both with what she was and what the meaning of the songs promised all listeners, which was another six-pack and the possibility of suicide.

She thought it all sounded all right when they played it back after five takes on two songs. She understood that modern popular music was designed to sell more beer and whiskey and to encourage the use of marijuana. It was written to celebrate a profound sense

127

of loss of their childhood among people who were too young by at least ten years no matter what their ages were ever to have gained anything. She lost the sense that it wasn't her voice coming through the playback. She recognized the voice but it belonged to a woman she hadn't really met yet, a singer named Dolly Heller. She was Mrs Owen Hazman, a wife and mother who sang around the house. But she was happy in a new way. The only subconscious reservation she had was that she was reluctant to think of playing the records for Owney. She began to understand that her records could be a threat to him when the musicians got to their feet after the last take and applauded her. She liked that and it was disturbing because she had thought that such an ephemeral thing as applause could not have made a difference to her in any way. She rationalized the thrill of it by telling herself that it was recognition by her musical peers. John Kullers said the last takes were 'very nice' but when everyone else had gone home, he and the president of the record company, Dick Gallagher, and the music publisher, Irv Gritsky, took turns laughing and weeping, they were so knocked out by the session.

'We're in at the birth of a great, great, *great* new verce stylist,' Gallagher said. 'With these two tunes, the way she sings them, we'll be producing our own video and wearing rubber thumb guards to count the money coming in.'

Owney worked out the anchor coaching with Mrs Noon the Monday afternoon after he and Dolly had decided how they were going to handle the whole opportunity. The anchor coach's fees were $275 an hour and his assistant got $35 an hour. Owney worked it out on a pocket calculator. For three hours a day, three sessions a week, the coaching would cost $2,790 a week and neither the anchor coach nor Mrs Noon thought it could be done in less than ten weeks. That came to $27,900, plus the rental of the equipment. 'See what I mean, Owney?' Mrs Noon said. 'Twenty-seven ninety a week is a lotta money for a man makin' only five fifty a week. Lemme pay it. It's jes' another tax deduction an' I can use alla them I can git.'

'Thank you – but no thank you.'

'Yo' wife don' want no strange woman payin' yo' bills?'

'Well – that's the fact of it, isn't it?' Owney said grimly. 'We've just got to respect that feeling.'

Mrs Noon tasted the bitterness of mockery. She wanted to help her son because he was hers, and his wife had decided that she was some kind of sex-mad harpy who wanted to do anything to smooth the way. She was helpless to defend herself despite being willing to buy her boy a television network if that were the way to put him firmly in the news anchor position.

She shrugged. 'Whatever you say. But all that money coulda gone to sweeten up the lives of yo' darlin' chillun.'

He did agree to accept a five-room apartment in Mrs Noon's building, with a houseman to serve the occasional sandwich and refreshments, to be used as the coaching studio. The five-screen TV set was installed so that every evening Owney could study the moves and nuances of the national anchor men who told it like it wasn't on the five networks.

Connected to the forty-inch sets was a VCR unit for image and voice recording, for immediate playback of Owney's test exercises if and when the anchor coach decided that they were to be shown. The main camera had a Teleprompter built into it to run the copy across the lens. The camera was operated by Vincent Donahue, assistant to José Turai, the anchor coach, whose own speech was so precise that it was said that he could shave a US Marine's four-day growth of beard with two diphthongs at thirty paces.

Turai stayed just off-camera, facing Owney, during the coaching sessions. He had been a famous star of the legitimate theatre until his feet gave out. He had coached 286 of the 302 great anchor men and women of their times as they pored over their oral scholarship inside the monasteries of their minds, including a hallowed Irish anchor, David Barstow Hanly, after whom a street had been named in Kilmoganny, County Kilkenny. He had made it possible for some very great film stars and eleven CEOs of the great industrial complexes to win extraordinary fees for voiceovers on television commercials plus residuals. He was the elderly President's inflections and gestures coach, shaping the Harold Teen warmth which The Great Communicator projected, through the long days at Camp David where the elderly President had spent one-quarter of the time he had held office, sharing his rest periods with the one-quarter of the remaining time at his ranch in California where a doppelgänger split logs for the television cameras or rode horses, whichever came first. Turai worked a six-day week and a ten-hour day. Owney applied himself tenaciously to learning his craft as an American tocsin.

The irregularly scheduled sessions, over the next few weeks, were always held after Owney's working hours in the frankfurter industry, as though to accommodate him, but were, in reality, scheduled at off-times to make José Turai's presence possible, instead of one of his assistants, as a favour to Mrs Noon. The only thing which could cause rescheduling was the occasional sudden necessity for a trip to Washington by Owney, or to Camp David by Turai. These happened at least once a week and every weekend.

'That word is pronounced "brew-ery", Mr Hazman,' Turai would say, 'not "bew-ery".'

'That's funny,' Owney would reply. 'My father always said "bewery".'

Or: 'May we have a little more of a sense of attack on that line, Mr Hazman? Can you communicate the news rather than merely speak it?'

'I don't know what you mean, Mr Turai.'

'For one thing please say "po-tay-to"; not "bidayduh". Here – allow me – in the style of one of the anchor greats, Barbara Walters.'

He took Owney's place and looked directly into the mirror which was suspended behind the camera. 'Fidel Castro,' he communicated, 'is not only the most physically attractive leader on the world stage today. He is thrilling to interview. I can reveal exclusively tonight that he has just lost thirty-four pounds.'

Turai turned to Owney. 'You took that line, you see, and you gave each word the same value colouration. The *news* here is that Fidel Castro has lost weight and that news item could be of subjective interest to your viewers. Do you see what I mean?'

'I thought I said it exactly the way you said it.'

'Shall we play your reading back?'

'No. I accept your judgement.'

Turai had Owney read paragraphs from the *National Enquirer*, the newspaper of national record, in the manner and timing of Jim Lehrer with pauses for a field correspondent's feed-in. Six beats would be allowed for this, then they would go on to the next item. At the end of a round-up of six items, Turai would have his assistant play back the tape on the television screen, analysing Owney's anchor style as he went along.

'Now, mark this well,' Turai said. 'As you close each broadcast you must stare into the camera lens and say to your audience scattered all across the United States, "I'll see you tomorrow."'

'But that's impossible,' Owney said. 'They see me, I can't see them.'

'That is an iron-clad rule, Owney. We have to work by the rules or we can't work at all.'

In the early days, except for his square hair style, so drab when compared to the exotic Koppel/Rukeyser look, he thought he looked and sounded sensationally professional, but when Turai pointed out the flaws in his work, it was shown that Owney had achieved thirty-four slurs, elisions, or mispronunciations of speech and delivery, and he had continually failed to smile to cheer up his audience with a dazzling grin after reading a disaster/tragedy news item. Owney's confidence began to go and, in subsequent readings, he went to pieces.

'I don't get it, José,' he said. 'Why must I grin after reporting a landslide in Italy which killed 1,236 people?'

'It's a superiority situation,' Turai explained. 'Your smile is giving your audience permission to feel superior because they weren't trapped in that village in Italy.'

By the ninth session of steady pressure Owney was in despair. 'Don't tell me Mr Cronkite went through this torture,' he said.

'Ah – well – Mr Cronkite.'

'I never thought I'd hear myself say this, Mr Turai, but I'm never going to make it to network.'

Turai was kind but firm. 'You are only beginning, Mr Hazman. This work, paying three million dollars a year, takes two or three *months* of hard, gruelling training and sacrifice. You must realize that. You've got to find your technique. There are great anchor men who have trained *weeks* for that. Also, there will be times when you will be offered fantastic sums to do the odd commercial – an entirely different art. How can you expect to hold yourself together without technique?'

Owney was humbled. 'I see what you mean,' he said. 'Let's run it.'

'Try this,' Turai said, handing him a sheet of paper. 'Read it straight into the lens, Mr Hazman. Ready? I say to you, at a press conference in the White House – as a member of the continually baffled Reagan White House press corps – "That wasn't my question, Mr President." I say to you, "You answered a question I didn't ask." Now – please read aloud Mr Reagan's answer.'

Owney cleared his throat. With little head wags and considerable boyish charm he said, 'Well – I'm answering the question because the question you asked is – the answer is so obvious. That obviously, after these years of out-of-control and built up to the level they have, there's no one that pretended that you could – this

131

would then have to go to the States for ratification. There would be a period of time before it was actually put into place. And, in that period of time, you have an opportunity to work out a budget which would not have to penalize people who are dependent now, because, on the Government for help.'

There was an awed pause.

'Ronald Reagan is a master,' Owney said humbly. 'That is virtuosity.'

'Can you imagine being trapped inside that mind?' Turai whimpered, trying not to let his trembling show.

'I carry one of Mr Reagan's quotes in my wallet wherever I go,' Owney said. 'May I read it to you?'

'Good heavens, Mr Hazman ...'

Owney pulled his wallet out of his back pocket and extracted a small laminated piece of newsprint. He faced the camera and began to read. 'You can't have gross national product, here's a thing for the return to the people and so forth on that without it reflecting on those who are paying the taxes.' Owney looked across the room with shining eyes at the dazed José Turai.

After seven weeks of mind-bending work, Owney wanted to play the latest tapes for Mrs Noon. Turai resisted the idea. 'It is a wonderful thing that you feel such confidence, Mr Hazman,' he said carefully, 'but you are a long way from being ready to be seen and heard. In my humble opinion.'

Owney was (nearly) offended. He had run his tapes at home with Dolly again and again, and he *knew* he was ready. He pressed his case. Turai relented.

'I'll have Vincent cut your tape into some Cronkite tapes just to give Mrs Noon a perspective on the progress you've made.'

'Mr Turai! There is no safety in directly comparing me with Mr Cronkite.' Owney now addressed everything in network tones, conveying solemnity and an electrical charge of awe to everything he said.

'We mustn't say safe-ette-tee, Mr Hazman. It's safety.'

'Roger,' Owney said.

'Embedding your tapes within the Cronkite tapes will give just that measure of theatricality to your presentation which will startle Mrs Noon into a suspension of disbelief,' Turai said. 'If you have Mr Cronkite's head telling her like she knows it isn't, then, after the first commercials, your head comes on the screen, she won't have the chance to throw her attitudes into a critical fix – she will respond with a natural reaction.'

132

Owney fixed the anchor coach with his penetrating anchor man's eye and, spelling it out as the men and women of his profession spell out living history daily, measuring man's time against the shortening odds of his doom, he said, 'Thank you, José.'

Mrs Noon looked at the spliced Cronkite/Hazman tape two evenings later. They saw a minute-and-a-half of Mr Cronkite, four minutes of commercials, then Owney's head loomed large in a tight close-up while Owney did his minute-and-a-half. Owney thought it was uncannily like the real thing.

'You need a lotta work, sugah,' Mrs Noon said.

Chapter 26

Freddie Fanshaw was showered, shaved, dressed and ready when Angelo Partanna telephoned him at eight o'clock in the morning five days after he had had his meeting with Edward S. Price.

'Mr Fanshaw?' the suave, hushed voice asked.

'This is Fanshaw.'

'Angelo Partanna.'

'How do you do?'

'We got the stuff you wanted.'

'When may I see it?'

'I'll pick you up at the front door of your hotel at nine o'clock.'

'You have tapes? Transcripts?'

'Everything is on video cassettes. Everything has been transcribed.'

Freddie was at the hotel's entrance seven minutes before the appointed time. A long, black, shiny limousine, the biggest single Rolls-Royce Fanshaw had ever seen, arrived at precisely nine o'clock. It was Edward S. Price's car. It had the same deaf and dumb chauffeur and footman who had so impressed Mrs Noon. Freddie got into the car. He was greeted by an elegantly dressed man who Freddie guessed was in the mid-seventies. He was quite bald and had a nose like a parrot's beak; a smallish man, as dark as a coffee bean, almost lost in the vastness of the tonneau of the enormous car.

'How they hangin'?' the man asked, patting the sofa-length seat beside himself. Freddie sat, the car door closed, the car moved haughtily out into the traffic, heading uptown towards Central Park.

'First, the video,' Mr Partanna said. He pressed a button in an arm rest and a panel rolled away to reveal a nineteen-inch screen in the separation between the driver and the passengers. He pressed another button and the show began.

Freddie sat, fascinated, staring at the pictures of two men, in splashiest colour, one Oriental, the other unmistakably the American lawyer, Malachi Olgilvie, sitting opposite each other at the table in the basement of the Olgilvie house off the Chain Bridge Road. He listened to the complex and multi-layered negotiations to sell/buy seventy-nine supertankers, for what sounded like a figure between $2 billion 300 million and $2.5 billion, entirely unaware that he was being moved around Central Park from 59th to 110th Street and back again, three times, before the cassette came to an end.

He stared at Mr Partanna with a mixture of awe and admiration. 'How did you get this?' he asked.

'Contacts. You wanna look at the transcripts?'

Freddie nodded emphatically.

Mr Partanna opened a suitcase on the seat between them. It was filled with stuffed file folders. 'They're numbered,' Mr Partanna said.

Freddie began to read what he had just heard. When he finished the contents of the first folder, he checked through all the other folders, spot-checking that everything was as he had heard it.

'How much for all this?' he asked.

'Oh, say – two million five.'

'Impossible, Mr Partanna!'

'Whatta you think they're worth?'

'I am authorized to pay five hundred thousand dollars for this information.'

'Forget it.' Mr Partanna took the folder out of Freddie's hand, put it back into the suitcase and closed the case.

'What is your bottom figure?' Freddie asked.

'I couldn't go back to my people with less than two million.'

'Please. I am in a terrible spot here. Make it a million and a half.'

'I'd like to help you but the absolute lowest I can accept is a million eight or else *I'm* in bad trouble.'

'The fact is, Mr Partanna, I have the cheque – certified, of course – in my briefcase. Would you like to see it?'

'Why not?'

'Before I show it to you, I have this to say. I was tootling on the computer last night and several plans occurred to me which might possibly be more attractive to you than a cheque for one million eight hundred thousand dollars.'

'Yeah?'

'Shall I take you through the plans?'

'Why not?'

'Are you up to the rather intricate footwork on this?'

'It's about money, ain't it?'

'Yes.'

'Then I'm up to it.'

'The thing is, after I tell you, I'll have to go back to London to tell my people.'

'First tell me, then I'll say about the cheque.'

'Splendid. This is what I had in mind.'

Chapter 27

Because Owney was the single recurring link between Malachi Olgilvie and Mrs Noon, he and his family were under continuous round-the-clock surveillance, at enormous expense, by the Syrian, Afghan, British, Chinese, Israeli, Pakistani, Soviet, Japanese, and American intelligence agencies and one 'blind' intelligence organization, the Mafia, which had been the sinister presence hanging over all of it from the earliest days of the conspiracy. The *fratellanza's* surveillance was so leak-proof, the information being obtained daily, if not hourly, was so total and self-serving, that if its work were ever to be known, which it would not be, it would suggest to all the other national intelligence agencies that they solve everything by shooting themselves.

Nine copies of Owney's mind-boggling anchor-man training tapes were secured by dark means from José Turai's files by all the national intelligence agencies, and the contents of each one analysed by cryptographers in a desperate effort to try to break down some code. The Afghan operative had a nervous breakdown because he tried too hard.

Because Mrs Noon and Mr Olgilvie had Owney shuttling back and forth between New York and Washington, each intelligence agency had to acquire extended travel facilities to ensure that its teams would be in place to account for his movements. This necessitated block bookings of nine seats for the combined sur-veillance teams on every shuttle flight to and from Washington, an inestimably difficult thing to do because they were shuttle flights and therefore by definition would not accept reservations. But the case officers in Damascus, Kabul, London, Beijing, Jerusalem, Karachi, Moscow, Tokyo, and Washington refused to accept his obstacle. This pressure caused the shifting of four airline personnel rosters. The effect was felt down to the ordering of supplies for the airports' coffee shops for service at odd hours; and the blocking off of ten seats plus the accommodation of nine permanent agents who were stationed at each end of the short journeys in case the assigned surveilling agents could not get aboard, all needing to be wired for recording, together with the installation of nine concealed closed-circuit video cameras to confirm that Owney would be under total surveillance, produced a further strain on the services.

The increased paperwork which was piled upon the case officers in the nine capital cities of the world was an equal hardship. Nine cars and drivers had to be ready and waiting outside Owney's apartment building, Mrs Noon's apartment building, the frankfurter factory, Mr Olgilvie's house, and Owney's hotel in Washington (requiring 45 units of shadow transport) while Owney had to scramble to find a cab or to board a bus. The surveilling agents had to be shifted frequently, to avoid recognition, excepting Miss Spriggs who was deft at disguises. In all, a total of 72 agents surveilling for 9 countries, 18 additional airline and coffee-shop employees, 18 drivers at both ends of the shuttle service, and $229,568 worth of eavesdropping electronic equipment were needed to do the job. The various cost accountants at agencies and embassies estimated that the effort to keep Owney Hazman under surveillance was costing an aggregate of $391,085 a day, but Owney was unaware that he was being observed.

Through it all, the British Cabinet sat in grim and total attention inside Number 10 Downing Street, listening to the tapes and watching the videos of Malachi Olgilvie negotiating the transfer of the seventy-nine supertankers to the People's Republic of China, which could mean that the price of oil would be driven to under five dollars a barrel on the world market, thus wiping out the British economy for it was upon Britain's oil interests in the North Sea fields that her credibility as a economic entity was based.

There was a grieving silence as the last tape played itself out. 'What do you propose to do about this?' the Chancellor asked the PM.

'We must wait upon the outcome of Mr Fanshaw's meetings with Lord Glandore's organization, mustn't we?' the PM said.

'Time is running out.'

'Fanshaw must prevent the sale of the tankers to the Chinese with a little help from me.' Her face hardened frighteningly. 'I shall tell the President that he must issue a directive which forbids the sale of those American tankers to any entity other than total

American ownership even though seventy-eight of the seventy-nine tankers are flagged to countries other than the United States.'

'But can he grasp that?' the Chancellor said earnestly.

'He will have grasped it when I have finished talking to him,' the PM said crisply.

Chapter 28

The false negotiating between Mr Olgilvie and the Chinese government grew denser because the Chinese had no idea that Mrs Noon had already sold the tanker fleet to Edward Price's dummy company, Ocmara Oil. Each night, well into the morning, Olgilvie and Mr Jay slogged through outstanding contracts with ships' officers; comparative international bank rates; insurance schedules and degrees of liability before and after the delivery of the tankers; marine law regarding transfers of ownership on ships which were registered under nine different flags, including two without ports or access to open waters; tax-shelter impediments; anticipated food and fuel inventories at the time of transfer, and a myriad of other things. Although Mr Jay seemed to flower under the intensity of detail, Mr Olgilvie felt the strain because, sooner rather than later, he would have to tell the Chinese that there would be no deal.

He asked Mrs Noon (who referred him to the new owners, who referred him to Edward S. Price, who referred him to Mrs Noon), if he could bring in his partner to lighten the load. Mrs Noon felt that one more high-powered lawyer showing up nightly at Olgilvie's house would tend to double the population of agents on duty outside, as well as putting a strain on the capital's hotel accommodation, so it was ruled that Mr Olgilvie could bring pertinent work to the office in a file to be called 'Harbours, Mines, and Bridges (and other national defence considerations of the Republic of Zaïre)'. Had it not been for the contents of the daily tapes and transcripts, the Mafia plant in the Schwartz, Blacker, and Moltonero law office would never have twigged that all these on-going files relating to the Chinese negotiations were available in downtown Washington.

*

Boris 'Borka' Brodsky, a KGB illegal, a mnemonist assigned as a spotter at the Washington National Airport, had worked in the gambling casinos at Cannes, Biarritz, and Divonne-les-Bains as a 'names and faces' man. For his work as a KGB airport spotter he had memorized the faces (from photographs) of every known intelligence agent in the world's services and although he never forgot a face, he had once fallen in love with a photograph of a code clerk in Ireland's Special Branch (SB) and had so lost his heart to it that he fell into marasmus, a wasting disease, until the KGB (who had certainly advertised themselves as anything but a bunch of romantic softies) had kidnapped her, brainwashed her, and had brought her out for Brodsky to get to know. Within six days he was so tired of her prattle (she had a voice affliction similar to many women on American television which made her sound like a four-year-old child) that he had to apply to have her returned to Dublin, which brought him in for a lot of merciless teasing in the Soviet services.

He was in constant motion, moving suavely, as if knowing where he was going when he knew he wasn't going anywhere, seemingly just another traveller marooned in Washington's National Airport.

He was amused to watch the Mossad man, Moishe Youngstein, watching the Syrian AIAS operative, Moussa Krushen, but as the days went on he realized that they were both following the American SRS agent, James D. Marxuach, who stayed close to Frederick Fanshaw of the British SIS – all of them following the same young man who kept disembarking from the New York shuttle then returning later the same day to reboard the shuttle. When the young man flew to New York, they all flew with him. Most disturbing of all, in an accumulating sense, was the presence of two agents from the Australian Security Intelligence Agency (ASIA), who wore the beard for too easily identified Chinese agents in the queue. After two days of this, Brodsky arranged for discreet photographs to be taken of the entire procession.

When he reported the heavy package of spies to the Fisheries & Wildlife man at the Soviet Embassy, the information was rushed to Moscow. Within nine hours the Chief of the Middle Eastern Directorate of the KGB, Moscow, had summoned the deputy chief of AIAS from Damascus, but instead of arriving alone, the Syrian spymaster brought with him four Syrian generals who entered the meeting wringing their hands, wailing and shuddering indiscriminately.

The delegation was shot in the Lefortova prison, except one. He had been spared to carry the word of justice back to Damascus. The KGB took the AIAS off the case entirely and the Syrian government was told that if AIAS efforts against the Noon fleet of oil tankers showed anywhere, the cities of Aleppo and El Rashid would be bombed forthwith.

The KGB sent a fresh team of thirty-seven illegals to Washington. Leading the new team was a KGB major, Ivan 'Vanitchka' Ramen, but before the new team could take up their new positions, the greatly affronted, wildly vindictive, and (when aroused as they had been aroused) greatly to be dreaded Syrian Al-Istikhbaratt-As-Souriat found they were no longer interested in building information which would lead to a best deal with the Soviets. They sought only to control the Noon tankers in the hope of using them as a bargaining chip to advance causes with the enemies of the USSR. A limitless pride had been grossly offended.

The Israeli unit, Mossad, which had its people inside the KGB's Middle Eastern Directorate, knowing the reasons for the Syrian passion and feeling that the tankers could be more easily controlled in Syrian hands, did not interfere when the AIAS kidnapped Malachi Olgilvie from his own car as he was on his way to his office from Virginia. Mossad agents were nearby when the lift happened, and followed the kidnap team to the hide-out in the Arab quarter of Georgetown.

Simultaneous with Olgilvie's abduction, the AIAS made an unsuccessful attempt to kidnap Mrs Noon in New York in front of her apartment building. All three AIAS agents were shot to death by the doorman of Mrs Noon's building, Elek Fahrami. Mrs Noon was saved from being wounded in the cross-fire (or killed) because it was a chilly day and she was wearing a bullet-proof sable coat. Before the police could arrive, because she was running late, Mrs Noon went on to lunch at La Grenouille where she had an appointment with Harriet Blacker.

She ordered a bottle of Le Montrachet '71 for her guest and herself. 'An' I want the wine from that nine-acre section of the commune, facin' east, you heah?' she said to the sommelier. 'Don't you go bringin' us none of that south-side section stuff.'

She turned to Miss Blacker. 'You gotta warn Mal,' she said. 'An Arab team jes' tried to grab me for good outside my buildin' jes' now so the FBI or the po-leece or both is gone be here to talk about it any minute.'

'Arabs?' Miss Blacker said. 'Does it have any connection with that little gook Mal had shot in that Washington hotel?'

'Thassit. Now, the main thing is if they git me or they git Mal you gotta take over with the Chinese in Mal's place. Git hired guns from one of the security companies. How much longer do you think the hagglin' with the Chinese can be dragged out?'

'About two months.'

'Tell Mal to hole up. No more goin' inta the law offices. An' if anything happens to Mal, that's whut you gotta do, too. Oh-oh! Here they come!'

The maître d'hôtel came to the table to say that two gentlemen of the FBI wished to speak to Madame but, because of the weight of luncheon reservations, it would not be possible to seat them and, alas, there was no room at the bar where they could meet with Madame.

'You tell them to go on out an' sit in my car,' Mrs Noon said. 'Give them cigars, some coffee, and a cold bottle of Krug while they waitin'. An' you make sure they git that genuine Ethiopian coffee from that high Harar plateau, don't you go handin' them any of that other stuff.'

'An ideal solution, madame,' the maître d' murmured.

'Tell them I figure to be finished with lunch inside an hour, then we can all ride around the park an' they can talk they heads off.'

That evening, in Syria, seven hours later by time zones but nearly simultaneous with Mrs Noon's encounter with the FBI at La Grenouille and five minutes after Dolly Hazman had recorded the first take of the first side for Appleburg, and inadvertently simultaneous with Freddie Fanshaw's entrance into the Cabinet room at Number 10 Downing Street, a squadron of the 4112th Wing of Soviet bombers based in Sernyy-Zavod in the Karakumy desert of Turkmeniya, USSR, because of a miscalculation by the lead navigator due to a faulty in-board, computer system, overshot the Syrian target cities of Aleppo and El Rashid, and bombed Beirut, Lebanon, rather heavily, killing 721 people, injuring 2,903, mostly Shiite Muslims, for which the Israeli government was immediately blamed and for which the Israelis not only blamed the Syrian government and the PLO, but sent a combat battalion into Ghecko, a Syrian settlement near the Israeli border, and wiped it out.

Chapter 29

———

Freddie Fanshaw rather expected the silence when he entered the Cabinet room at Number 10, but he did not expect the faces which seemed to be ready to vote for his public hanging.

'Good evening, Mr Fanshaw,' the Prime Minister said. 'Take that chair.'

Freddie marched to the chair and sat himself down.

'What are your recommendations?'

He felt the glare of the Cabinet. He was afraid he was going to faint. He breathed deeply, thinking of the head of his service and what he could expect to happen if he botched this meeting.

'Well, I *have* – ah – conferred with the gentlemen of the American – ah – Mafia – if I may use that term in this room.' He heard his voice rise and fall a full octave. 'But one does have to state that they hold all the keys to this – ah – contretemps, in that they have been – to all intents – eye and ear witnesses to the negotiations between the representative of the owner of the tankers and the government of the People's Republic of China – as you have seen and heard from the tapes and transcripts which you authorized me to buy.' He leaned forward, took up a tumbler and drank down the full glass of water. 'With that in view, alas,' he continued, 'they *are* dealing from a position of strength. Therefore, I recommend – ah – it is recommended that we – ah – you, that is – proceed as follows. One: that you accept that the – ah – Mafia's representative in Beijing, a Mr Al Melvini – a chap they call The Plumber? – be permitted to secure an exclusive sales agency to resell the seventy-nine supertankers to a third party for fifty per cent more than the Chinese would have been able to pay for them – the third party to be approved by the British government – who would then lease them on a flat fee basis to the Chinese government, giving the Chinese a substantial profit over what they would have had to pay had they concluded the negotiations with the tanker representatives in Virginia. All transactions would be commissionable to the – ah – Mafia at a rate of three per cent of the gross – a lease figure amounting to many hundreds of millions of dollars.'

'But why should the Chinese lease tankers which they are already negotiating to buy?' asked the Chancellor of the Exchequer.

'Because the – ah – Mafia has agreed to split the commissions with the People's Republic in exchange for certain concessions having to do with Chinese opium poppy production.'

'Demmed clever,' a voice from the end of the table said.

'The second point, Mr Fanshaw?' the Prime Minister asked.

'Yes. It is respectfully required that Her Majesty's Government arrange for the – ah – purchase, through the – ah – Mafia – at the aforementioned sales commission of three per cent – with the intention that the tankers be leased back to the Chinese after our statisticians have proved to the Chinese that they can once again triple their capital in the project by using the tankers to ship the oil at a price to be fixed by Her Majesty's Government.' Fanshaw ran out of air as he finished the statement.

'I see,' the PM said. 'Of course, the loan to the Chinese to buy the tankers would be handled by a consortium of British bankers and the agreements would be made to guarantee that all funds flowing from the Chinese oil account and the commissions to the – ah – Mafia could remain in British banks to the greater chagrin of Washington.'

'Hear, hear!' was the cry from around the table.

'But certainly,' the PM continued, 'the accredited agents of the Chinese government do not need to be termed as the – ah – Mafia? I am told by most reliable sources that the United States Department of Justice – specifically their Federal Bureau of Investigation under the *intrepid* Mr J. Edgar Hoover – maintained for thirty years or more that there is no such thing as the Mafia.'

'That is true, madam,' the Home Secretary said.

'We must adopt that policy. Neither is there nor shall there be a – ah – Mafia in this country.'

'Hear, hear!'

'Surely, as sales agents, they have a company name?' the PM asked.

'Yes, madam,' Freddie said. 'It is called the Bahama Beaver Bonnet Company, registered in the outermost Seychelles islands.'

'Then, henceforth, we shall be dealing with Bahama Beaver

145

Bonnet who will offer them for lease to the group we will cause to be formed.'

'The lease to go for three billion four,' Freddie said.

'To keep that money and all money accruing in Britain, we should make it *some*how attractive to the Bahama Beaver Bonnet Company by arranging some spectacular sort of tax shelter so that the purchase can be made through a British company with the hope of our people receiving some sort of benefit. Further, as I understand it, it is the intention that we lease the tankers back to the Chinese, thus creating the paper tax loss which would justify the tax shelter. What with British banks cooperating and the Chinese government cooperating on our views of proper crude oil pricing, those people at the White House who forced us into this will fall into despondencies of rue and regret. I should think the pressure on the President will be fiercely unremitting when the news of this transaction comes out.'

'Yes, madam,' Freddie said.

'Thank you, Mr Fanshaw. You have been most helpful. Good evening to you.'

Freddie made his way out of the room without accident.

He returned to New York on Concorde with a written offer from Inter-European Consolidators Ltd, the British government designate, to lease the tankers from the Bahama Beaver Bonnet Company, for sub-lease to the People's Republic of China. He agreed to have Angelo Partanna set up a meeting in New York with a man named Wambly Keifetz who Angelo Partanna had said would represent Bahama Beaver Bonnet in the deal.

Partanna passed the word to The Plumber in Beijing telling him to have the Chinese government instruct its negotiators in Virginia to withdraw any offer which might have been made for the tankers and to open negotiations with the Commercial Attaché at the British Embassy in Beijing.

After expenses Mrs Noon cleared $2 billion 139 million on the transactions. When it was announced that no 'other' nation had been able to buy the tankers from Mrs Noon, and because the lessee, Bahama Beaver Bonnet, an American company, was a known neutral and powerful entity, all teams of surveilling agents were withdrawn, excepting the vengeful Syrians.

Chapter 30

Malachi Olgilvie had been slugged, drugged, then stowed into a large packing case marked THIS SIDE UP and flown with other contents of the Syrian diplomatic pouch to Damascus where he was locked into a suite of rooms which was the interrogation facility of the AIAS, Central Division, in what resembled a quaint native hotel in Scottsboro, Arizona. Heavily dosed with exotic Middle Eastern mind-benders, he was hypnotized and, before any interrogation, it was deeply implanted in his mind that he was deeply in love with a blindingly plain, even cacophonously ugly (but amiable) agent of AIAS named Zuba Tabi. At first he resisted her by telling himself over and over the advice of the old Supreme Court Justice for whom he had clerked when he had been a young man: 'When the chambermaid starts to look good to you, it is time to go home.' It was to no avail.

'You are bewitched by the beauty of Zubayah Tabi, the most desirable woman in the world,' his brainwashers imprinted upon his mind. 'You cannot look at her without needing to adjust your clothing. She is utterly lovely. You met her in Switzerland where you both began what had been intended to be separate holidays. You need, deeply and without surcease, to spend the rest of your life with her.'

Malachi Olgilvie, a 55-year-old lawyer – an *American lawyer*! – was hopelessly, irretrievably, in love.

When, nine days later, the news was flashed through to the AIAS command that the matter of the tankers had been settled satisfactorily, that everyone's friend, the Mafia, would control them, it was too late for Malachi Olgilvie. Inextricably planted within his mind and memory was the fixation that he was helplessly in love with the most beautiful woman who had ever lived, Zuba Tabi, that she loved him as deeply – or would as long as he

147

continued to do as she wished. He pleaded with his captors to let him marry her.

The brainwashing team stayed on, polishing Mr Olgilvie's mind for five more days, even though the Chinese sub-lease on the tanker operation had been confirmed. The team arranged that Mr Olgilvie's memory begin anew at an afternoon on the afterdeck of the lake steamer, the *Anieres*, at its pier in Geneva, recalling how he had been seated at a table in the gentling open air, gazing at the Alps on the port side and at the Jura on the starboard, watching other passengers who were boarding. It was at that precise moment (it was implanted within Mr Olgilvie's mind) that he first set eyes upon the woman he loved.

He remembered disembarking with Zuba Tabi two hours and twenty minutes later at Evian-les-Bains. How he cherished the camera-eye recall of the moment they were married, in his illusion, three days later, by the assistant mayor of the village of Cologny on the outskirts of Geneva.

Before he began instruction in the Muslim faith prior to remarrying Zuba Tabi in a religious ceremony at AIAS headquarters in Damascus, he was allowed to telephone his office in Washington. He talked to his secretary. He made the call three weeks (to the day) after he had disappeared into the District of Columbia traffic.

'Miss Silverschien? This is Malachi Olgilvie. Since I'm in Switzerland, I –'

There was a shriek at the Washington end of the line. Miss Silverschien, who was too emotional to be a legal secretary, had fainted.

'Miss Silverschien?'

A male voice spoke into the phone. 'Miss Silverschien fainted. Who is this?'

'Who *is* this? This is Malachi Olgilvie. What the hell is going on there?'

'Holy shit! It's Olgilvie!' the voice said.

Miss Silverschien snatched the telephone. 'Mr Olgilvie? Are you all right?'

'Of course I'm all right. What's the matter with you people?'

'Did they release you? Did they harm you in any way? Oh, my God. I have to call the FBI.'

'The FBI?'

'Where are you?'

'At the Hôtel des Bergers in Geneva. Where else?'

'Geneva? Geneva, *Switz*erland?'

'The bank merger. The Kastenberg estate.'

'Mr Olgilvie, that was two years ago. The FBI and the police have been searching for you night and day. It's been almost three weeks and –'

'Miss Silverschien – are you all right? Or are you out of your mind?'

'You were kidnapped three weeks ago today. We've been frantic thinking what could have happened to you.'

'Kidnapped?' Mr Olgilvie laughed with enormous pleasure. 'I was married yesterday to a magnificently beautiful Arab woman but that is hardly what you could call kidnapping.'

Miss Silverschien fainted again.

After a stimulating honeymoon, Mr and Mrs Olgilvie returned to Syria (in the groom's mind) and settled in the bride's home town of En Nebk. Mr Olgilvie assumed native Arab dress, in the dashing Yasser Arafat tradition wearing an old-fashioned speakeasy table-cloth for a hat, learned to speak expressively guttural Arabic, qualified to practise civil law, became a leader in the community and, in time, fathered fourteen sons and daughters.

Things returned to what is always judged to be normal, to normality – which all network anchor men, including the aspiring Owney Hazman, called normalcy – except that, in Owney Hazman's case, a lust for success such as he had never felt before had been generated by his concentrated work with José Turai.

Chapter 31

Dolly's single had been a sensational success. Record pressing plants all over the country never stopped working. In release only four days, it was Number 2 and climbing on the charts. So far, it had sold 4,600,000 copies. The press coverage had surely reached every village and hamlet in the country, because people had been calling them on the telephone in the middle of the night until they had to change to an unlisted telephone number.

Kullers and Gallagher had predicted Dolly's share of the sales at somewhere around $300,000 but her accountants certified that the amount due was $2,400,000 as of the period which had ended six weeks before. The record company paid her in full cheerfully with the certified cheque which her people had insisted upon.

Dolly couldn't believe it.

'My God, Owney,' she said, holding a hand to her forehead, staring at the cheque, 'two million four hundred thousand dollars for singing two songs!' Owney wouldn't even think about it.

The unlisted telephone never stopped ringing. They had to put in a phone which only rang when the caller could give a code number. Only Dolly's mother, Mrs Noon, and John Kullers had the code number.

In the flush of instant and unexpected success Dolly agreed to make an entire album of songs for Appleburg. Owney knew in his bones that the day Dolly refused to sign for yet another album, Kullers and Gallagher would see that the code number for the telephone was auctioned off and the incessant ringing would start all over again.

Dolly wanted to buy him one of the new $193,000 Bentleys. He flatly refused it.

'Then what kind of car do you want more than any other car in the world?'

The thought of Mrs Noon's Figoni et Falaschi popped into his head but he said, 'It's not real money, Doll. Two million four hundred thousand for an afternoon's work, no matter how you look at it, is somehow wrong.'

'Owney! They are talking about *touring*! They estimate a ninety-seven million dollar gross and I get eighty-five per cent of the net!'

Perhaps if he had already qualified as a network anchor and had been paid four thousand dollars for a half-hour's work each day, his perspective would have been changed and he would have agreed to dream the American dream with Dolly. But by then he knew that was not to be.

The day after Turai told Mrs Noon that there would be no point in continuing Owney's training, her secretary called Owney at the factory and asked him to be at the Noon apartment at six o'clock that evening. He called Dolly to tell her he would be late for dinner.

'Guess what, Owney,' Dolly said. 'Kullers and Gallagher want me to do an album with Luciano Pavarotti and George Burns singing accompaniment – and doing a solo each, of course. And I get top billing because the other two can't agree who should be first.'

'So they'll toss for it.'

'But then they'd have to agree who would toss first.'

'The same album or another one?'

'Another one.'

'What did you tell them?'

'They told me to read my contract on the album we're going to record tomorrow.'

'So?'

'They have an option to do another album.'

'But this is crazy, Dolly. I mean, when you consider what happened with one single record – I mean that riot in the super-market and the seven hundred fans standing outside our building so we couldn't even take the kids to the park –'

'I know. Kullers and Gallagher want us to move to a less public neighbourhood.'

'That's no answer. Where? What less public neighbourhood?'

'Beverly Hills.'

'*Whaaaaat?*'

'They said either there or Switzerland.'

'What did you tell them?'

'I told them you were on your way to being a network anchor man and that we couldn't move.'

When Owney hung up he was really worried. He just didn't know what he was supposed to do with a rich and famous wife. They were growing apart. He could feel it. She would be zapped away from him just the way his mother had disappeared. Day after day he would stand there as an observer while, little by little, he would lose her. She would disappear into a pink steam of teenage notoriety backed up by twenty-two violins, four investment bankers, and a colossus of Hollywood agents. He would be Mr Dolly Heller which would have been all right, he supposed, if he had been in the music business. Dolly was a sweeter-than-sweet German-Puerto Rican girl who was the mother of his three children. She had no right to make sensationally successful records. She must know that it was the same as leaving him behind while she was changed into something he would never be able to recognize. He would lose her for ever just as certainly as his mother had abandoned him.

Three times a week Owney had been going to Mrs Noon's apartment house on Park Avenue to continue his training with José Turai, but he did not see Mrs Noon. He felt he was making sensational progress with Turai and as soon as the training period was over in two more weeks, he would be able to confront Mrs Noon about setting him up in the anchor job at the New Jersey TV station.

Owney had worked desperately hard to master network anchoring under Turai but, paralysed emotionally by the awful glue of his wife's sudden success, he was freezing on camera worse than ever, in voice and in meanings, as Turai put him through the drills. He sat rigidly, unable to relax. In the ritual 'signing-off' he was forgetting to tell the unseen audience that he would see them tomorrow night. So important in his own proportionate scheme had his ascension to network anchor person become to him because of the three million a year it would pay, even though that kind of money was at least ten years off, he felt that just starting out on the road to anchordom as, say, a White House correspondent, could make him an equal (in his wife's eyes). But the tension/stress that this terrible need produced wouldn't allow him to keep up with the movement of the words on the Teleprompter no matter how slowly they were shown. He mispronounced words which were sacred to the television industry.

'Never mind if it is correct or not, Mr Hazman,' Turai would say. 'The word "r-o-u-t-e" is pronounced as "rout" by all network anchor persons because that is how Mr Paley pronounced it. And you must learn to say "par-tick-oo-ar-lee" for "particularly" or they will all think you are trying to make them look bad.'

At the end of the eleventh week of training, Turai requested a meeting with Mrs Noon. 'It's no use,' he said to her. 'Hazman is not going to make it. Something locks inside him when he faces a camera and he insists on speaking proper English which could only result in confusing his audience.'

'That will be very hard for him to realize, Mr Turai.'

'To continue the training would be a waste of time and money.'

Mrs Noon shook her head sadly. 'It was his most impo'tant ambition.'

'Do you want me to tell him?'

She sighed. 'No. I'll do it. Tomorrow. I owe him that much.'

She was his mother. She had to absorb as many of the shocks which were his lot as was possible but, most of all, she had to substitute something of value for the loss of his dearest dream. She had no idea what the new quest would be but she was going to think of nothing else, all night, because her boy had to regain his pride and the illusion of a certain necessary male precedence over his wife. A woman who had earned six bodyguards, a notoriety beyond even Donald Trump's, and an income of many, many millions of dollars a year could not be blamed for believing she had suddenly become head of her household, over her husband. Whatever it was, whatever she would arrange for Owney to do, it had to be something which Owney's wife would see as slightly more than an equalizing force in their marriage.

It had been many weeks since Owney had made a trip to Washington. No one had ever even told him about the existence of the tankers so he had no idea that the intensity of the intelligence-gathering activity centring on him was over. He had been startled when he read that Mr Olgilvie had been kidnapped, and gratified when he read that he hadn't been kidnapped at all.

Owney knew about people disappearing. His mother had vanished that way and when he read that Mr Olgilvie had married an Arab bride, it suggested to Owney that his mother may have run off with some man. That made him brood for the very short while he had time to brood, because it was the height of the outdoor frankfurter season and Owney spent most of his time on the telephone with customers all over the country.

The only tiny cloud on his horizon was that he would have to tell his father-in-law that he was leaving the frankfurter industry.

Chapter 32

Jeshurun, the Shiite houseman, led Owney into the surveillance-proof Chinoiserie of Oona Noon's living room in New York, saying that Mrs Noon would be there immediately. Owney settled himself in an easy chair made by Benjamin Randolph and Hercules Courtenay in 1771 from Thomas Chippendale's designs in *The Gentleman and Cabinet-Maker's Director*, a supreme expression of curves, ornamentation, and comfort. He inhaled the scent of the flowers and listened to Ray Charles waft through the stereo system, singing his hymn in praise of the Carolinas.

Mrs Noon came through the high doorway from an unknown beyond wearing natural silk overalls in powder pink over a Kelly-green polo shirt. Owney sprang to his feet.

'Siddown, Owney. You wanna drink?'

'No, thank you.'

'I got good news and bad news. How do you want it?'

'Bad news?'

'Bad news first? Thass good. Thass the right order 'cause no mattuh how bad the bad news is, the good news gone cheer you up again.'

'What happened?'

'Turai says you ain't gone make it.'

'Oh no!'

She wanted to weep, standing there, because of the anguish she had brought to him. 'I purely hate to tell you this, Owney, but I have to agree with him.' Her voice trembled. 'In fact, they is nothin' I wouldn't do not to tell you this, but that's how it is.'

'I – I just can't believe it. I mean, I *saw* what we've been doing. My hair was right. I mean, the wigmaker to the US Senate! I read the words wrong just the way the network anchor men do. I never flinched at the different slants of the news Turai handed me to read. I pretended I would be able to see thirty million individual people the following night just like the real anchor men do. I mean, I just don't get it.'

'Look, Owney – please don't feel bad. I put off believin' Turai. I made him give me your best tapes and I took them to a coupla friends of mine who run a coupla networks an' we looked at them together. The fact is, Owney, they agree with Turai.'

Owney dropped his face into his hands. When he lifted it, his eyes were filled with tears. 'I guess I'm never going to be a network anchor man, then,' he said. He saw the seven hundred ecstatically-driven people as they had stood in the pouring rain in front of the Apthorpe in silent reverence, waiting for Dolly to appear. The titles of the only single she had ever made loomed up as large as the sign over HOLLYWOOD: 'My Drippin' Heart' with 'Let Go My Earrings?' on the flip side. God! He would be a midget to the woman he loved. He would be just so much furniture cluttering up her memory.

He had listened in on the extension while a national magazine had interviewed her and had asked her if she preferred Bolivian or Colombian cocaine, because she was the great new rock star and the magazine had fantasized that cocaine was what rock stars did.

He felt just the way he had when he had stared at his mother's note sellotaped to the refrigerator door. Dolly was going to disappear in the new-fashioned way of disappearing. She would seem to be there but only as a voice backed by twenty-two violins and soft percussion oozing out of a juke box or the cover of *Time* magazine. His children would eighteen or twenty before he could break through the bodyguards to hug them again. He would be a frankfurter salesman, not a network anchor man. His own family would be royalty in Oz, but he would be Prince Nowhere.

Mrs Noon took him by the shoulders and shook him gently. 'Ain't you gone ask me whut's the good news?' she said.

'*Good* news? Hah!'

'Yin and Yang, Owney. Thass how it rolls.'

He made a mournful attempt at smiling.

'I been thinkin'. Know whut I mean? It come to me the first time when you smiled 'bout that Chinese robe I had on – the one from the Victoria and Albert? Then I saw you smile on the tape an' it come to me again that you a natural for politics. Thass all the people want – a great smile, a promise, a little fake Jesus talk which the staff will provide, an' sort of a helpless dishonesty. They'll vote you higher 'n' higher.'

'Well, thanks anyway, Ravi. But I'm just too young.'

'You twenny-eight years old. An' it gone take a little time to git you started. Age don't mattuh. My people can falsify all you vital documents – birth certificate, passport, credit cahds, Social Security – all that stuff. Look at whut his daddy done for J. Danforth Quayle. He's only fourteen years old an' he in US Senate.'

'He *is?*'

'The smile is your gimmick, Owney.'

Owney had a flash of what it would be like to be a US senator. He already had the wig. The possibility of his becoming an anchor man to one side (for ever), being a ranking politician in the United States in 1988 was the only kind of national celebrity which could overshadow the importance of being a rock star. Dolly and he would be back on the same level again, except that she would have to look up to him the way Prince had to look up to Ronald Reagan; the way Mayor Koch towered over Michael Jackson in a long-term, dimensional, totally respectable way.

'It – it sounds great, Ravi. But I wouldn't know where to start.'

'Lemme figure it out. I kin buy people for that. First thing we gone do is bring in a man to train your memory power so you kin remember everythin' you read. You'll talk as if you actually knew what you was talkin' 'bout an' you'll be the biggest thang ever to hit the talk shows or the Congress. You'll be sensational in press conferences. You got to look like whut you are, never mind what you are.'

'What do you want me to do?'

'Gimme time to think 'bout it. I'll git back to you aftuh.'

157

Chapter 33

Goodie Noon was polishing his collection of assault rifles and handguns when his wife came into the family's arsenal building in the compound on Bland Island. 'Ran out of pork rinds again, hon,' he said reproachfully after he had greeted his wife with characteristically courtly politeness.

'There's gotta be a shake-up, Goodie,' she said. 'That is purely the result of rotten staff work.'

'I never thought I'd have to go cold turkey on pork rinds. But, while I went through the withdrawal, I was thinking, thank God that this is a country where sportsmen, particularly in the inner cities,' Goodie said, patting the stock of the assault rifle nestled in his arms, 'can have a day in the open air enjoying their guns without a lot of bluenoses trying to keep them from getting off a few rounds.'

'But they are, Goodie. They is lotsa people against guns.'

'Who? Where? Sweetheart, that's impossible. It's in the Constitution. That's what democracy means. The right to shoot guns.'

'Goodie, we gotta talk. Mal Olgilvie got hisseff married to an Ay-rab woman.'

'An Arab, hey?' Goodie said, murky about current events. 'That's really romantic.'

'Gone live in Syria. So we gotta git you a new campaign strategist.'

'We have to get this gun thing straightened out first, dear. I know what I'm talking about. It was right there in print in *The American Rifleman* which is one of the most influential monthlies in this country.'

'Goodie! Will you please listen to me?'

'If it were chemical or biological weapons, that would be different. Remember last summer, when we had my grandchildren with

158

us in Kansas City – six-year-old twins, one of them went as a package of Juicy Fruit, arms sticking out of the pack, the other was Dracula? And Dracula's wig fell off in the middle of my speech and I got to thinking, watching those kids, and I said if I could look back and I had been President for four years, what would I like to have done? Those young kids, there. And I'd love to be able to say that working with our allies, working with the Soviets, I'd found a way to ban chemical and biological weapons from the face of the earth.'

'I think we should make a deal with Wiley Monahan. He's the best an' the roughest. He jabs with a dirty needle every time and plays a great rock tuba. He'll be the rotten partner all through the campaign while you'll be the sweet and reasonable partner who comes off smellin' like roses. Mal Olgilvie was all right, sure, but he was subtle compared to a slime-slinger like Wiley Monahan.'

'God, if only it were still possible to get Ferdinand Marcos to handle the campaign. He not only proved that he knows politics, but how I loved his adherence to democratic principles and democratic processes. God! The way he worked to find ways by which sure profits could be made for President Reagan's blind trust. How thriftily he used resources from his country's tobacco, gambling, banking, petroleum, and construction industries to give seven million dollars through third parties to the Reagan-Bush campaign in 1980. He was a man who understood American politics.'

'Jes' the same, Goodie, Freddie is gone so we face the same old thang. Wiley Monahan, jes' like Mal, is also the principal adviser to the other Party, so, if we decide to put him on, it'll have to be undercover.'

'It's no exaggeration to say the undecideds could go one way or the other,' Goodie answered, staring straight into her eyes. 'And I'll tell you something else. If this country ever loses its interest in sports or fishing, we've got real trouble.'

'Listen, Goodie – stay with me on this – it's time we called the very first meetin' of the Committee for the Election of Osgood Noon. The primaries are only four years away. I see a small meetin' – say myself, Wambly Keifetz, an' General Dewar, the grand ole man of the Party. That committee will be the first Political Action Committee of the 137 PACs that I'm gone have formed by the 119 executives of Wambly's combined 312 companies, plus the 200-odd PACs which General Dewar will see are formed among the bankers, the Mafia, the gun lobbies, an' the oilies. We 'way ahead on the unaccountable funds anyhow, but the voters expect big PACs.'

'Just look out that we don't paint our tails white and run with the antelopes,' Goodie said sagely.

'Then the prime committee would see to the formation of one more committee – say of bankers, the gun lobby, the real estate lobby, and Big Oil – to negotiate a deal with Wiley Monahan. He'll do it if we promise him some off-shore drilling rights. We'll buy him away from the other Party. He knows everybody's price all the way 'long the line and he fears nothin' 'cept being poor again.'

'You really think we need someone like that?' Goodie asked.

'Goodie, you a great candidate, but you need an organization. You the compound candidate. You got the frivolousness of Jack Kennedy – the one thing the voters demand – the cupidity of Johnson, the shallowness of Nixon, the callous indifference of Reagan, and the shoe size of Abraham Lincoln. But you gotta have an organization! Nevuh fo'git that, baby.'

'I meant – well, I don't see how this Wiley Monahan can just walk away from one Party and take on another.'

'People change! They see the light! It might cost us givin' him the right to set up housin' developments in the national parks, because he's a nut on real estate, but we can win his mind and heart. It's jes' gone take a little time.'

'Time for what?' Goodie asked suspiciously.

'Time to convince the people that it was the right transition. Look, Goodie – I'm gone set him up with a stalking horse. A pure, young idealistic candidate. I mean this boy looked me in the eye and said to me, "We never stop blaming the people of Germany for allowing Nazi politicians to carry out the extermination of eight million Jews, but here we are with all the things we can't do anything about either – guns in the streets, drugs, the worst set of politicians ever assembled, dope everywhere you look, blacks being forced to slide backwards, homelessness, and poverty."'

'Politicians? The worst *set*?'

'Like I said – he's a pure, idealistic boy.'

'We certainly don't want anything to do with a commie nut who is against politicians,' Goodie said indignantly.

'Wait! We run him for Congress an' the committee hires Wiley Monahan to run his campaign. While everybody thinks Monahan is workin' on his campaign, he'll really be workin' on your campaign. Then at exactly the right moment, Monahan announces that he gone leave the other Party and, for patriotic reasons, take a stand at your side.'

'What's this crazy idealist's name?'

'Owney Hazman.'

'Well, as I have said – maybe it could work. Remember the promise I made when I turned sixty, three years ago? How I resolved never again to eat broccoli, Brussels sprouts, cauliflower or cabbage? And you know something, Oon? I never did. Let your Owney Hazman think about that for awhile.'

'Truss me, Goodie. You goin' straight to the White House.'

Chapter 34

The summer had flown past. Owney spent long weekends with Dolly and the children. Dolly made her first album which sold 1,891,023 copies within the first four days and, in a very short time, made her the first in her family to earn more than $2 million a week. She had to go to Los Angeles to do a lot of television shows to promote the album while the single was still No. 1 on the singles charts. She called Owney daily, but she called her mother twice and sometimes three times a day to check on the children.

On the morning of her third day, while she was having breakfast with Kullers and Gallagher in a large bungalow at the Beverly Hills Hotel, eleven heads of the great communications conglomerates called to offer her staggeringly complex contracts for movie, television, recording, video, magazine, and newspaper work and to offer astonishing amounts of money for world book rights in her autobiography. A man from one of the great television networks came to the bungalow to talk to her about doing her own one-hour weekly talk-and-song show with guest stars such as François Mitterand, the Dalai Lama, General Noriega, and Joan Rivers. The money was sensational. Her agents, the Morris office, CMA, ICM and the Matson office urged her to take all of them, assuring her that they could get stock options in addition to fees, expenses, a Gulfstream III, and a lifetime of free around-the-clock breakfast, day, and evening wear from any seven dress-makers of her choice.

Dolly thanked everyone but refused everything. She and Kullers and Gallagher had their first argument. Dolly said that since she had made $3,691,000 and some change so far, she shuddered to think what Kullers, Gallagher, and Fujikawa Industries had made. Now that she had cut an entire album for

162

them, she told them, she shouldn't have to work any more.

'Baby, believe me,' Kullers said, 'you are absolutely right.'

'Turn everybody down,' Gallagher said, 'because when the second album takes its death grip on the ears and hearts of the American people you will be able to dictate your own terms for movie and television deals.'

'And don't bad-mouth the tours and the grosses from the tours,' Kullers said.

'And the own-name perfume royalties,' Gallagher said.

'Listen to me and get it right for once,' Dolly told them. 'I am not making another album – or a movie or anything else. I am going back to my husband and my children.'

Before her eyes, Kullers began to weep brokenly. Gallagher tried to jump out of the window even though it was a one-storey bungalow surrounded by grass.

'Stop it!' Dolly yelled.

'We signed, we committed with two great male singers, Pavarotti and Burns. You know what the settlement could run to?' Kullers sobbed. 'Ten, twenty million. We don't have that kind of bread, Dolly. It will break us.'

'You have kids, we have twice as many,' Gallagher said. 'Where are they gonna live when the courts take the houses away?'

'That ain't all with the contract commitments!' Kullers wept. 'We are on the line with Akira Kurosawa to direct the video.'

'Akira Kurosawa?' Dolly's jaw dropped.

'The greatest emotions manager of our time. Can you ever forget *Rashomon, Seven Samurai*, or *Throne of Blood*?'

'Thousands of jobs,' Gallagher said. 'That's what you'll be costing people who are your friends.'

'Kurosawa has agreed to direct the video?' Dolly said dazedly. 'He's over eighty years old.'

'He is teetering on the verge. I hadda hold him off until you said you'd do it,' Kullers said.

Dolly sighed. 'I'd certainly like to work with Akira Kurosawa,' she said.

Although (and because) Dolly did not tell her husband that she had agreed to make a second album, the Hazman family had a wonderful summer on Fire Island. On weekends they had all the days with the kids and all the nights to themselves. Dolly never spoke about the record business and she had hired a local schoolgirl to answer the telephone whenever it rang. She refused to come to the phone unless it was her mother or Owney calling. When they were out of the house – in the village or on the beach – Dolly wore a white paper cone over her nose as a precaution against sunburn so not once all summer, until the time came to take the ferry and go home (when the police had to call out the National Guard to protect the Hazman family and President Reagan sent his own helicopter to fly them out to safety), did the fans recognize her. But the mail was something else.

'The apartment is piled with mail sacks,' Owney told her. 'There must be twenty or thirty thousand letters.'

'Can you get the superintendent to burn them?'

'The post office wants the mail sacks back. And the super is on vacation.'

'I'll call Kullers and Gallagher and make them send somebody to take them all away.'

In the twenty-three days it took temporary help to open and sort the mail at the Appleburg offices, $23,761 in cheques, 231 mezuzahs, a lot of used underwear, 572 mail-order catalogues, 119 scapulars, and 4,117 threats were found among the contents of the envelopes.

The three-part vocal arrangements for the work with Pavarotti and Burns were very tricky because Pavarotti was resting with his family in Italy and Burns was running in the New York Marathon. Kullers sent a rehearsal pianist, an album producer, and a sound cutter to the Fire Island house to work with Dolly. She only let them in three days a week and Owney was never told that they had been there, or that Kullers and Gallagher were negotiating with a television network to tape the album recording session. All Dolly had on her mind was to figure out the right way to ask Owney if he would be her manager. Jesus, she thought, tens of millions of dollars are involved here, who else can I trust besides Owney? She felt almost certain that she could make her father understand why Owney had to leave the frankfurter industry. Having Owney as her manager would be the only way they could ever have any real time together. She loved Owney and she loved only Owney, but she was a woman and that, as the entire culture had explained, meant that she had a right to a life of her own. The whole thing was strictly a pain-in-the-ass situation. What could she do?

Chapter 35

The terrible crisis was faced. Perhaps, if Owney had agreed to be his wife's manager, it would never have happened, because the battle would have been disarmed and deformalized. But when Dolly asked him to take on the job, pleaded with him, he turned her down flatly.

The children were fast sleep. Owney had eaten an entire bowlful of sliced cucumbers which always made him very horny. He looked deeply into Dolly's dark eyes which, as he saw them, were lusting with yearning glints. Her Chinese-red lips looked moister and softer than foam. He leaned forward into them as she leaned forward to him. As they kissed his hands went up to hold her and the uncanny tailoring of her dress allowed itself to accommodate the prevailing spirit by spilling out a boob. Dolly fell back slowly upon the huge sofa with Owney closing over her like a Swiss Army knife. Her anxiety about protecting her money, enforced by the power which needed the protection of inaccessibility, even invisibility, opened her like a rose in the sun. Owney's terrible fear of loss of face gave him an iron determination to be needed without the possibility of losing as much as a freckle. His need for a huge emotional Band-Aid regenerated all of his long-dormant technico/mechanical sexual skills from the days when he had passed himself from one kind stranger to another in order to belong somewhere and to conserve capital. In one prolonged sexual act he etched himself for ever upon Dolly's memory as deeply as would ever be possible for a woman who had the responsibility of actually recording an album and a video with Kurosawa, Pavarotti, and George Burns with an equal share in the royalties but with top billing.

There was a short delay getting her dress, bra, and panties off and while Owney struggled with that, Dolly kept thinking of the wheeze about the hooker who had said to her client, 'If I had known you were in such a hurry, I would have taken off my pantyhose', but all the little delays were worth it because she came, then came again, then came again, like a pibroch of bagpipes.

They had just floated down from the ninth level of bliss when Dolly murmured, lying in his arms, her face pressed into his chest, 'How can you just ignore what could be a potential hundred million dollars?'

He sat up. The magical moment turned into everything detestable, into the horror which he had been trying for weeks to silence or to make disappear for ever. As Dolly's career had soared and she had got more and more scared about protecting their money, she had begun, at first timidly, then more strongly, then flatly, to approach the verge of demanding that he take over the management of her affairs. It had never been as direct as this before; not as starkly, unequivocally direct. Owney disengaged himself from their embrace. He sat, naked, on the edge of the bed.

'That's not what our marriage was supposed to be and you know it,' he answered bitterly.

'Owney, this is America. You're making twenty-eight thousand a year and I'm making over forty million – or will be if the projections turn out. No matter what I do, it's a promotion for the record albums, Kullers and Gallagher say.'

'That's obscene.'

'Would it be obscene if you were the one who was making that kind of money? Would it?'

'Dolly, I just can't do it. It's – it's a reversal of everything we've ever been to each other.' He got up and began to put on his underwear. He got the right leg in the left trouser opening and almost fell over, further scarring his dignity. 'I mean – neither of us can understand what it would be like with you as the star, the bread-winner, the dominator of the marriage – because whoever brings in the money has the power – with me following along behind you, trying to hold your attention while they pour money on you and thirty or forty million people want to touch you – and God knows what else is in their dirty little minds.'

'Owney! We're young! Give us five years at fifty to seventy-five million a year, and we can take the three hundred-odd million dollars and let the other guy knock himself out! Already I've been able to buy five hundred thousand dollars' worth of Zero Coupon bonds for each of the kids. No matter how the price for a college education soars, they'll have at least their Bachelor's degrees protected.'

'Dolly, you've got to see my point of view ...' Owney said as he buttoned his shirt.

'Look – be practical. Who am I going to trust? Kullers and Gallagher? By next year, I'll probably level off at forty-five or fifty million a year. That has to be invested in high-yield tax-free bonds, Owney. I need you to make those judgements! In ten years you'll be handling an investment portfolio of 450 million dollars, bringing in – give or take some change – five million a year extra in tax-free interest. Let some stranger handle that and he'll steal me blind, Owney. Don't you see? I need you. You have a degree in Business Administration from Eureka. I mean, I really need you.'

'I can't do it, Doll. It's not just crap like pride. It's my whole manhood.' He pulled on his socks and got into his trousers, which totally reversed the way he usually did it, overcome with that same terrible feeling he had had years before when the time came to walk out on one of the women who had been so great to him. But this wasn't just another woman. This was Dolly; his Dolly. But she wasn't the same Dolly because something had happened to make her execrably rich and wildly famous.

'Won't you at least say you'll think about it?' Dolly said. She got out of bed, pulled on a robe, and walked around the bed to face him. 'I don't really need to know for ten more days.'

'What happens in ten more days?'

She covered her face with her hands. 'I – I signed a three-picture deal with Paramount.' She bit her lower lip then looked him squarely in the eye. 'And in ten days rehearsals begin on the talk-and-music show that has been set up to run on ABC.'

'Movies? You'll be acting in movies? Slimy actors will be kissing you and grabbing you?'

She nodded. 'The combined agencies got me eleven million a picture to start. Plus a very good percentage of the gross.'

'But how can you make movies and cut records and do television at the same time?'

'It's not simultaneous. They have it all programmed.'

'This is absolutely disgusting.'

'Dis*gus*ting?'

'When are you going to have time to take the kids to the park? Who's going to cook dinner?'

'We'll be a long way from the park, Owney. And that's another reason why you have to agree to be my manager.'

'A long way? From the park? What other reason?'

'Everything in showbiz is in California now, Owney. To cut records, make movies, and do television, we've got to move to California.'

'It will kill your mother!'

'No. Mama's very happy about it. The Morris office was able to get her a deal for free video cassettes.'

'What about your father?'

'Poppa's life is frankfurters.'

'You expect me to drop everything and rush off to California as Mr Dolly Heller? You want me to move into that Lotus Land and eat your money for breakfast?'

'Something like that.' Her eyes filled with tears. 'That's what I'd hoped for. Something like that.' She put her arms around him. 'Owney, do you realize what we can do with fifty million dollars?'

'What?' he said sullenly.

'We can use it to find your mother. No matter where she is in the world, the army of people which fifty million dollars can put on her trail just has to find her. You can have your mother back.'

'You're breaking my heart.'

'Just say you'll give it a try.'

'Dolly – darling Dolly – I can't. It just wouldn't be right.'

She pushed him away. 'Do you think this is the first time in history that, because a woman got luckier and made more than the man, they worked together to keep the money she was making? All over the world, right now, women are contributing money to men and men are contributing love and support to the women.'

All in a rush, Owney remembered Dotty Beardsley, the computer programmer who liked to ski, the advertising executive who had lunched at Gitlitz that day, and Graciela Winkelreid.

'Why are you getting all red in the face?' Dolly demanded.

'Once, a long time ago, I let women buy me things.'

'Things?'

'Like food and clothes and rent. I was trying to conserve what I had so I could use it to find my mother. But that was long ago.'

'But you did it!'

'I didn't care what those women thought of me. I care what you think. I didn't love them. I love you. I'm sorry, Dolly. I can't do it.'

'You're shifting the blame for all this on me, Owney. And I hate it.' She flung a pom-pommed mule at the far wall.

'No. Things will never be that simple again. The fact is you had a choice between me or five hundred million dollars and you chose the money. That's what broke my heart. I never, ever, in my whole life, thought this could happen but it's happening. So I have to say it. Goodbye, Dolly.' He turned slowly, walked out of the room, and shut the door. In a few seconds, just before she realized what had happened and started to weep, she heard the front door slam heavily.

Chapter 36

While Owney sold hundreds of thousands of frankfurters in a dumb, numb daze, living at the 34th Street YMCA, eating at Taco Loco and Pastrami Ink, unable to grasp the stark conception that his life with the only woman he would ever love (except his mother) was over, he was almost wholly unknowing of the dazzling future which Mrs Noon had in mind for him. Wiley Monahan, the campaign strategist who Owney did not know existed, had arranged for the Teamsters' Union, Drexel, Burnham, the National Manufacturers' Association, the Mafia National Commission, Wambly Keifetz, and the Cardinal's office in the New York diocese to pressure the State Chairmen of both political Parties to run Owen Hazman for the congressional seat representing the 101st Manhattan District. The State Chairmen agreed that this would be an effective way to introduce a wholly unknown name and face as a candidate so Owney began his political career with the endorsement of both Parties.

Compassionately, Mrs Noon kept Owney away from all these technical moves and countermoves. He was so new to politics that all of the wheeling and dealing could have set him off on the wrong foot because he had some weird notions about governance. She had noticed that he had been morose and moody lately, so she decided that it would be counter-productive to burden him with new responsibilities. She did tell him, in advance of the bipartisan decision, that an opening had occurred and that, because of a few favours she had deposited in the favour bank, she felt confident that she could secure the nominations for him.

Owney felt he desperately needed to change his identity as a frankfurter salesman if he were going to compete with the kind of cultural fame his wife had achieved – and it was something he must do if he were going to hold her; and, because being an anchor man was a passive manifestation compared to the positive presence of a national legislator, he would be in a still better position to find his mother if he entered the Congress. As a politician, he would be transformed into an effective magnet to draw both Dolly and his mother to himself. The news media had reported little else beyond politics and politicians since Reagan had been elected and had swept into office with Deaver, Gergen, Baker and Darvan and 2,411 other personal press agents. The resulting appearances, photo opportunities, little wars, huge national humiliations and immeasurable corruptions of and by the Reagan government, and the constant, permanent campaigning for the Presidency by hordes of grinning men, had given the American people the impression that there was nothing else to read, look at, or pretend interest in but politicians.

Owney thought of the Capra movies: Mr Smith and Mr Deeds, and whereas he did not compare himself, even *to* himself, with Jimmy Stewart or Gary Cooper (except that they were all tall), he knew that they had commanded enormous respect by bringing democracy to the Congress of the country, if not beyond it and if only temporarily, for the duration of the movie. If he could ever perform the same feat, the media would bugle the news around the world and his mother would be made to realize what she had missed by throwing her boy away like an orange peel.

As a politician he would be on an equal footing with Dolly, a rock musician and movie star. He had the chance of winning Dolly back and of bringing his mother home but, it came to him in a rush of shame, he would be seen as a politician by his children and his peers; he would be cast down into the dust. His children's children would have to carry the shameful onus of knowing the debasement and loss of caste his going willingly into politics would bring. He was only twenty-eight years old even if Mrs Noon's falsified birth documents made him be over thirty, but it could not be measured, in that short time, how far politicians had fallen into the abyss of ignominy.

Owney bit the bullet. If he wanted Dolly and his mother, he would have to sacrifice himself at the altar of sleaze.

'It's an interesting idea, Mrs Noon,' he said distantly. 'Please keep me advised.'

Owney did not attend the power lunch which sealed the launching of his candidacy. It was held high on the eighty-second floor of the Yamamoto National Bank in lower Manhattan. Wambly

Keifetz was Chairman and CEO of the bank. He was a discreet, publicly deferential figure of world politics and finance who was a silent partner with Mrs Noon in many enterprises. He owned vast amounts of loan paper on entire nations, and had helped to re-arm the free world with American weapons systems. In passing, he was also Graciela Winkelreid's father.

At the luncheon it was settled that, because Owney's chosen election district was so heavily Republican, the Republicans should win him, as a signal to the country at large that the tide would be running Goodie Noon's way after he won his nomination. Both Parties would endorse Owney's candidacy, an extraordinary recognition for an unknown candidate, allowing the news media to indicate that Owen Hazman might well be the forerunner of a profoundly meaningful change towards an all-Republican Congress. Under the system, it always took long months of hard, plodding work by the densest sort of media repetition to make evident any differences between the two Parties so the agreement demonstrated by this joint political Party endorsement baffled the public apathy even more.

It was settled at the lunch that Owney would run against Kim Paisley, a middle-aged, Korean-born hunchback woman who would have strong ties with the Socialist Party. Also at the luncheon, Mrs Noon, in a part of her short talk, said, 'If we bring Owen Hazman along, spotless and squeaky-clean with an ever-growing record in the Congress as a fighter for the people; and as the champion of the Constitutional Amendment for a balanced budget, a line veto, and an unlimited term of office for the President; plus the old-fashioned, reduced-taxes promises so that the people kin believe they are paying less when they will be paying more; and a tremendously overloaded defence budget, in two years' time we can move him into the Governor's mansion in Albany, and the good Lord only knows how high after that.'

She took questions.

'What did you have in mind?' Beniamiamo Camardi, the Mafia representative, asked mildly.

'How does no taxes on corporate or individual incomes over two hundred thousand a year strike you?'

'That would allow prosperity to trickle down to the people,' General Dewar said, 'but where would you get the money to run the government?'

'Heavens, Al, we'd tax the welfare beneficiaries, eliminate the Post Office, give the oilies a chance at winning new wells – think of what the coastal rim can bring in if we sell it off. Eliminate Medicare – in fact, gradually eliminate people over sixty-five. Things like that.'

'Those are exciting concepts,' Wambly Keifetz said.

The negotiations with Wiley Monahan were intricate and secret; as secret as Mrs Noon's early meetings with Malachi Olgilvie had been. They met on the foredeck of the Staten Island ferry boat. Monahan pretended an almost hostile indifference to the idea at first, but as Mrs Noon exposed the stages by which it would all be done, so that he could gradually emerge as the campaign consultant for Goodie Noon's Presidential bid, Monahan began to warm up, at least enough to ask what would be in it for him.

Monahan was a cubically square, completely bald man with white-paint sideburns and a strawberry tan, whose teeth had been made by a great artist and whose clothes appeared to have been torn from a scarecrow. He had a reedy voice whose regional accent changed to conform with the speech of whomever he was talking to. As the politician's politician he was a very rich man who called everyone kid, including Presidents of the United States, because he rarely bothered to try to remember anyone's name. 'That old-time card-file-for-a-brain political trick is finished,' he told his assistant, a young blonde woman with a heavy chest and sweet legs like exclamation points whose name (actually) was Jackie Sue. 'Never mind their names. They know their names. Tell them how to get the money and you win their loyalty.'

'We know of your abiding interest in housing, Wiley,' Mrs Noon said. 'Therefore, if you can bring about Goodie's election, how would deed and title to Yellowstone National Park hit you? You could develop that to your heart's content. And really be helping the well-to-do homeless.'

A deal was struck on the return voyage of the second round-trip crossing of the ferry.

The first thing Wiley Monahan wanted to know after his deal was set and he and Mrs Noon had gone over a sketch of his possibilities was, 'Where are Mrs Hazman and their handsome well-bred children? It's an election must.'

'There may be a problem there.'

'How do you mean?'

'Hazman's wife is Dolly Heller, the rock star.'

'Holy shit. I mean – excuse me, Mrs Noon – I mean, no kidding?'

'She is making a movie right now with Nicholson, Redford and George Burns as her leading men.'

'So what's the problem?'

'Mr Hazman doesn't approve of working wives. That may be good for your anti-day-care people, but his wife and children live in California and he lives in New York.'

'But all I need is one photo opportunity with the whole family together.'

'I'm afraid not. He's very bitter.'

'There must be some snapshots. From before she went into showbiz.'

'I'll see what I can do.'

Wiley Monahan was one of the last men in the world, excepting Mikhail Gorbachev, to wear a brimmed fedora hat. He wore it for the same basic reason that other people of the world no longer did, so that audiences would be able to recognize them when television cameras took their pictures whenever they ventured out of doors. Monahan was one of the ninety-three people in the United States who had never been on television. His existence was only dimly known to the news media so he was unknown to the public at large. His extensive knowledge of American demography, cupidity, voter distribution, envy, campaign contributions, and greed had enabled him to elect the past six administrations of the government of the United States. Regardless of Party, all candidates tried to hire Monahan. Whichever side he chose to work with was usually the winner on election day.

Monahan was a rarity. He had no interest in orthodox power. He was a shambling technician in his middle sixties who rarely spoke unless the door were locked and the room had been swept for bugs.

'Living apart while the wife makes a few hundred million could be very understandable to the voters,' he said. 'But no divorce. One thing they will not tolerate is divorce among candidates. They get divorced, themselves, constantly. In fact, anyone who stood in the way of their right to divorce would be lynched by an angry mob, but marriage is sacrosanct with them where their political candidates are concerned.'

'Mr Hazman wanted a divorce, but his wife would not agree to it,' Mrs Noon said.

'Lemme talk to the kid, what's-his-name, Hazman. Lemme size him up. After all, I am going to be his best friend.'

*

174

Owney was briefed on Monahan by Mrs Noon. 'Before PACs came in and evil became a relative thang in politics, Monahan used to be called an evil genius because of the dirty campaigns he ran. But today, dirty campaigns are what people expect an' want so, by sublimating his instincts in what he calls his life-long crusade for good government, Monahan lost his chance to become one of the great organized criminals of all time. He's elected six Presidents. He knows more than anyone about foolin' most of the people alla the time an' how to keep them from thinkin' but always reactin' to what he wants them to git stirred up over.'

'I don't even know how to talk to a man like that,' Owney said.

'Owney – lissenna me – Monahan gone be your best friend. You'll see.'

'Mrs Noon, I can't be expected to give up my job for pie-in-the-sky like this, can I? I mean, even if I were elected, it's only a two-year job, isn't it?'

'Once you in *nothin'* kin git you out. It's called the law of the incumbent. And you'll *be* somebody! What is a frankfurter salesman next to a Congressman?'

'It's a lot saner, for one thing. And a lot more tangible. But no matter what, I have a family to support. I am not going to risk my job for a trunk full of worms like Washington.'

'The committee will pay you a salary while you're running for the job. Say, a flat fifteen thousand dollars?'

'Mrs Noon. I can't run – that is, I can't campaign. For a flat fifteen thousand dollars I'll agree to run, sure, but I can't take time out to make speeches and show up for TV talk shows and shake hands with the workers coming out of the 21 Club. I have to hold my job.'

'I'll make you a deal. A flat fifteen thousand an' you sign a paper that you will campaign with all your might for the three weeks before election day.'

Owney shrugged helplessly. 'I guess that's OK,' he said.

Owney and Monahan got to know each other at a luncheonette on 11th Avenue, near Heller's Wurst Inc. The extraordinary thing that happened was that Owney liked Monahan immediately. The unextraordinary thing was that Monahan genuinely liked Owney. He could sense something flaky there but he was drawn to Owney's smile.

Monahan smoked a long illegal Cuban cigar after lunch. He said, 'Listen, kid, all it takes is a lotta money and some window dressing. You got some very, very big money behind you. But there are certain basics. The American people expect to be screwed if we entertain them in exchange. It's not a matter of keeping a lotta action going, we have to guarantee to keep their hatreds alive, the hatreds they were taught at Mom's knee – the hate-thy-neighbour formula the charismatics on television preach. The job of good government is to keep people at the throats of their neighbours. It keeps them off balance and the beauty part is they don't have to think. They are all afraid of sliding back down to where they think they came from. When you have people who live out an imaginary fantasy like that, then everyone in the country has to see everyone else as his potential enemy. So he builds ramparts against them and calls the ramparts White Supremacy, or Elks, or Conservatives, or Feminists – or whatever – and figures that if he stands well at the centre of any pack like that he can protect his place in the pecking order. All we have to watch is not to interfere with their right to live like all the other people – nine hours of television, the chance to pay one dollar sixty for a loaf of bread but to believe government statistics that there has been only a 4.2 per cent rise in inflation. They want cars that wear out in six or eight months – an entire culture that wears itself out, in fact. They will gladly accept being humiliated by their politicians if the politicians keep them entertained. My God, look at Ronald Reagan! He gave them wars, disasters, scandals, circuses, shamings, corruptions, and the illusion that they were all rich while his people stole them blind. And he did it all with television which is the voters' training course for the grave. It empties their minds and makes it impossible for them to think about anything except what they are told to think about.'

'From what you are telling me, Wiley,' Owney said, 'I am not yet able to grasp how you are going to get me elected to Congress, then somehow make me Governor of New York.'

'Don't worry about it. Just show up on time. We'll do the rest. All you gotta do is concentrate on being tall, smiling into the cameras, and making boyish wags with your head. And you'll only have to do that in the last three weeks of the campaign. So when can I meet your wife?'

'We are estranged.'

'She a very, very big star.'

'I only watch PBS.'

'All I want is a letter of introduction. And don't worry. I'm not gonna rock any boats.'

Chapter 37

Owney plunged into work. Mr Heller wanted to start a national sausage craze. He was even willing to consider spending money to hire publicity people and to have the craze sweep the country as soon as he could decide whether the craze should be about the spicy Hungarian *debrizna* sausage, the *Mexicana*, or the *Paprika-burenwurst* of Austria.

Owney wanted to have thirty-five per cent of the production of the *Wurstwerke* set aside to turn out miles of slimming sausages which were a mere 210 calories, compared to the standard 280, which meant that the 70-calorie saving could make it possible to eat a 70-calorie roll without further risk. Also, the slimming sausage was twice the size of the normal *Wurstel*.

'The whole thing could be packaged with Dolly's record company selling Viennese waltz records,' he said to the combined production/sales meeting, 'a tremendously energetic dance which would also melt the pounds off.'

'It's a nice gimmick,' Mr Heller said.

'It would mock everything we've ever done,' Gordon Manning, the pork buyer, said. 'It would be like saying that every sausage we ever made was made just to put weight on people.'

'Gordon, the *beer* people have gone Lite! *Cake* bakers have gone Lite! The market is demanding it! You want them all to die from cholesterol?'

As at a tennis tournament, all eyes turned to Mr Heller.

Mr Heller made the decision. 'Everybody wants to be skinny,' he said to the meeting of department heads and outside consultants. 'Give them a sausage that will knock off the weight and you'll see a friendly bunch of consumers. But with us, taste is everything. Taste, and sausages the way they are, are what made us what we are today.'

He got to his feet and let his steely glance move from eyeball to eyeball around the table. 'My choice for the new product which will create the craze which will sweep the country is the delicious Magyar masterpiece, the delightfully spiced Hungarian *debrizna* sausage.'

From that day forward, Heller's Wurst Inc. plant and offices were alive with the sound of musing. The staff, executives and wurstmen, were split down the middle, some (personally) supporting the slimming sausage, the others wildly partisan on behalf of the *debrizna*. The slimming sausage concept was cruelly abandoned.

Mr Heller OK'd Owney's proposal that they seek a nomination for the *debrizna* from the Academy of Sausage Arts and Sciences in New Braunfels in the hill country of Texas, which was calculated by international *Wurstmeister* (and Texans) to be approximately at the centre of continental United States, as a part of the ongoing national orgy of self-congratulation which was celebrated by giving dozens of 'best' awards on network television or in the nation's press week after week throughout the year. The Awards would be made the following January. The Academy solicited and encouraged packing houses and individual butchers from all over the world to participate. The great sausage products of the world would be tasted and judged for the sixty-third year on the basis of appearance, texture (not too hard, not too soft, and leaving no trace of fat on the knife), taste and smell and, above all else, quality of the ingredients and workmanship. Andy Warhol had designed the Awards trophy many years before which was known as the 'Weenie'; a gold-plated wurstel, supremely erect, mounted on an ebony pedestal.

The intensive publicity campaign began. The pundits discussed the political meanings of the *debrizna* on the interminable Sunday morning talk shows, heavy-browed men wrote columns about 'the sausage in history'. There was talk of starting a fast-food chain to be called Von Donald's. For the next four months, Miss Dolly Heller, star of stage, screen and video, scarcely showed up in any photo opportunity without a *debrizna* sausage in her hand and the sales curve went to unbelievable heights.

Owney was on the go from morning till night; selling, inspiring the sales staff, talking to every state of the Union on the telephone, pitching himself headlong into work to try to forget that he had lost Dolly. While he worked, the technicians under Wiley Monahan sweated over the campaign with one hundred per cent

178

effectiveness, if the polls were to be believed and there was no reason why the polls shouldn't be believed inasmuch as Owney had the endorsement of both Parties.

Monahan had three long meetings with Dolly – in New York, Nashville, and on the Concorde to London. In the first meeting she made it clear that she would prefer not to discuss her husband. At the second meeting she indicated that she was ready to listen to any sane business proposition, providing that Monahan levelled with her.

'Level? I always level.'

'I still am not sure what these meetings are all about. Sometimes you seem to be a marriage counsellor, then you sound like a broker with an edge. What do you want?'

Dolly was wearing her lion's mane hair-do. Her face was like that of a goddess with a semi-bald head floating in the Sargasso Sea. She wore a champagne-mink kilt, a silver-blue Cossack blouse, and unborn natural calfskin boots halfway up her hips.

'Owney is running for the United States Congress from New York. After that, he'll probably be Governor.'

'Owney? *Owney?* What kind of a joke is that?'

'No man is a hero to his ... et cetera.'

'You – they – somebody – is going to run Owney for *Congress?*'

'That's right, Mrs Hazman.'

'And – if he runs – he needs a wife and family?'

'Entirely correct. It can all be worked out. No one is asking for something for nothing. Take your talk-and-music show. It's only seen in North America. We could arrange to have it beamed to the world in simultaneous translation from the outer space satellites. You'd be seen across the First, Second and Third Worlds. Think of the promotion for your records. And guests for the show. Desmond Tutu? Mikhail Gorbachev? J.D. Salinger? Think of anyone in the world and we can get them for you.'

'I just can't understand why anyone would want to run Owney for anything. He's a lovely man, don't misunderstand me. And he's hard-working, but he's not – not – you know, a heavyweight.'

'My God, is Ronald Reagan a heavyweight? What? Lissena me, Mrs Hazman, your life will go on substantially in the same way. What we're asking won't interfere with your work or your children. You don't have to live with your husband. But there is one thing we have to have: a simple contract – your own lawyers can draw it – that you will make two appearances with Owney in public and hold still for three photo opportunities and, in between, you will live the same moral life you have lived since the separation. That is all we want from you.'

'I just can't get this through my head, Mr Monahan.'

Monahan smiled a kindly smile, or what he thought of subjectively as a kindly smile. It made him seem as if he were wearing a papier-mâché mask; the kind used to frighten children or something from the Macy Thanksgiving Parade. 'When you refused to divorce him you must have had some idea of getting together with him again,' he said.

'I may have thought that once,' Dolly said. 'But I never heard from him again, Mr Monahan. He just turned me off like a faucet. All I could do was wait for a day like today when he would think he needed me and I could slam him into the ground.' She sighed heavily. 'But I never anticipated that he would send a man to work it all out and that the man would make a casual reference to expanding my television show around the world.'

'What else would you like, Mrs Hazman?'

The contract was signed at the third meeting. It provided that a house would be bought for Dolly and the children in Bel-Air which would be situated not less than 17.5 feet higher than the Reagans' on that hill and would have a separate apartment for Owney to which he would always be welcome; that Mrs Hazman would agree to act as hostess at an official reception to be paid for by Mr Hazman and that she would smile not less than sixty per cent of the time in which she participated and one hundred per cent of the time when she and Mr Hazman were on camera. In the event that Mr Hazman were elected to the Governorship of New York, Mrs Hazman would live at the Governor's Mansion for not less than two months a year in increments of one week at a time and would participate in photo opportunities all during her visits. However, if Mr Hazman were to be elected to the United States Senate (or some higher national office), Mrs Hazman would spend an equal amount of time in Washington, DC and neither she nor her agents would accept other conflicting dates.

Mr Hazman was to be allowed to 'romp' with his children as a photo opportunity for four days each year and during one five-day period during school holidays. In return Mrs Hazman was to receive a gift certificate for $500,000 for any internationally famous dressmaker she cared to name, full simultaneous distribution of her talk-and-music television show to the countries of Europe, Africa, Asia, South America and Australia/New Zealand by satellite and full access to anyone living to appear as guest stars on that show.

At the signing, Mrs Hazman said to Monahan, 'You are either insane to be sponsoring Owney or you are the most cynical man in the world.'

'Maybe a little of both,' Monahan said.

'How are you with the Mafia?' Dolly asked.

'Pretty solid. What do you want?'

'Are the Mafia people behind Owney?'

'Oh, I think it's much worse than that.'

The contracts were signed backstage at the Grand Ole Opry in Nashville. To an extent, Dolly and Owney were reunited.

Chapter 38

When James D. Marxuach, head of the Security Research Staff of the CIA, was informed by Doris Spriggs, his Chief of Station New York, that the Sino-British agent, Owen Hazman, had won the endorsement of both political Parties to run for a seat in the US Congress, Marxuach was so consternated that he did the unusual and asked for an immediate meeting with the Director of Central Intelligence, Eddie Grogan.

Within four hours, he was summoned to the Director's office.

'Is this the guy who masterminded the sale of those oil tankers to the British, the Chinese and the Mob?' Grogan asked.

'Same guy, chief,' Marxuach said.

'An Iranian spy is running for Congress and Wiley Monahan is handling his campaign?'

Marxuach gulped and nodded. 'Not only that, chief,' he said, 'but somehow he got the endorsement of both Parties.'

'How can I tell the President a thing like that? An Iranian agent! Even the *word* Iran is barred from the White House. Nancy will go crazy.'

Marxuach shrugged. 'You could temporarily say the man is a KGB agent. The President has been told that he likes Russians now.'

'The NSC or the RNC will handle it. But, in the meantime, I want total surveillance on this rat twenty-four hours a day. Total. Physical and electronic. I want to know everything he says or thinks or does. You take over personally.'

'We'll nail him, chief.'

'Wiley Monahan! Is there no bottom to a politician's greed? And to run slime like that on the *Republican* ticket. I tell you, Marxuach, this could break the President's heart.'

*

Although Wiley Monahan carefully delayed the announcement of Owney's candidacy, his opponent in the race for the Congress, Kim Paisley, the hunchback Korean woman who was running on the Socialist ticket, had been campaigning for three months, speaking wherever she could find a crowd and driving home such radical campaign proposals as saving a half-billion by cancelling NASA's Space Station Program; raising the marginal corporate income tax rate to 35 per cent for a 5-year gain of $3.3 billion; ending postal subsidies for not-for-profit groups to save $2.3 billion; reducing active-duty military strength to 1982 levels for 5-year savings of $5.3 billion, and a lot of blather like that.

After frantic, unrelenting days of organizing the campaign for the Academy Awards, setting the intricacies of introducing the new spicy *debrizna* sausage to the finicky American market, corresponding with chefs, *Wurstmeister*, and meat packers all over the world (and in consequence turning up a fascinating new sausage in Thailand) as well as handling the normal high pressure of frankfurter sales on the North American continent, Owney's evenings were spent with mnemonists who had been hired by the election committee to train his mind to retain any and every factoid which might be imprinted upon it. After the first three months of this, Owney was able to deliver a speech from memory after reading it once. He was able to reel off statistics, quotations, historical data, and legislative citations until he gave the impression of being the best-informed man in the country (but never seeming to be so smart that he didn't say 'bidayduh' for 'potato', or 'rout' for 'route', and 'bew-ery' for 'brewery', all of which increased his popularity among the voters).

Ten days before the announcement of Owney's candidacy, Graciela Winkelreid telephoned him at Heller's Wurst Inc. It had been four years since he had heard her voice and as it had been a lonesome life living at the 34th Street YMCA he was delighted to hear from her.

'When can I see you?' he said into the telephone, remembering vividly the gigantic waterbed in the mansion on 64th Street of what seemed like only yesterday.

'How about late this afternoon?'

'Terrific. Where?'

'We have to be careful not to advertise. I just ducked a crazy woman who is all over town telling people she's going to shred me.'

'Then let's make it Cudihy's Bar on East 46th Street at half past five.'

The telephone conversation was tapped and taped by Marxuach's ELINT people.

It was a fine meeting of old friends. They arrived at the saloon at about the same time and were shown directly to Booth No.3, which James D. Marxuach, between the time of Mrs Winkelreid's call and the meeting, had had time to wire for electronic eavesdropping and in which he'd set his invisible cameras. Mrs Winkelreid was, if anything, even more nuts than she had been in the old days. They both said ecstatically that neither one had changed by one little crease. Mrs Winkelreid certainly hadn't. Every three years she had a very clever Japanese plastic surgeon reconstitute her face and body from nude photographs taken on the evening before her graduation from high school. It had been a wise cosmetic decision for someone who wanted always to look like a young girl in the American way.

They talked, filling each other in on what they had been doing. Owney said he had three children and was a sales manager for a big frankfurter company but he didn't say that he was separated or who his wife had become. Mrs Winkelreid, although slightly spaced-out, did her best to fill Owney in.

'I've been doing lots of active field work with the IRA, Hezb'Allah, the Japanese Red Army, the Islamic Jihad, the Tupamaros, the Red Army Faction, and a few Libyan groups. Learning my trade, the usual stuff: bombings, plane and ship hijackings, airport massacres, and political kidnappings. I think we're ready to overthrow the government here.'

'No kidding?'

'First the Pentagon, then the CIA, then I'll kill my father.'

'The more things change the more they remain the same,' Owney said.

He thought it was a miracle that she looked exactly the same considering what she had been doing, because he knew that no matter how much spiritual peace the Ayatollah urged, that sort of thing can leave its stamp on a person's face.

Owney had changed, he knew, since he and Mrs Winkelreid had lived together in the mansion on East 64th Street. He had worried a lot and had spent endless nights brooding about his mother and his lost marriage; he had ached for his children and, quite naturally, all those things had added dimensional character

184

to his face. Well, that was genes for you, he thought. Lincoln went through it.

'But, business aside, tell me – what else have you been doing?' Owney asked.

'Oh, I dabbled in lesbianism for a while but it couldn't last. Lesbians are too possessive. I am thinking of experimenting with religion but I can't decide which one.'

'Your father is the chairman of my election committee.'

'Oh, Jesus. You were that close to him and you didn't do anything?'

'He's a very pleasant fellow, actually.'

While they chatted James D. Marxuach sat wearing earphones inside a dry cleaner's van parked thirty feet down the street from the entrance to the saloon, clucking with disapproval and dismay, listening to the taped conversation from the remote microphones which a bribed waiter had stuck under the rims of all of the china on which the two old friends were served pretzels, Frito-Lays, and dehydrated pork rinds.

After a few drinks – Perrier for Owney, Coke for Mrs Winkelreid – they went to her house, the same old nostalgia-drenched house on 64th Street, and balled the night away, talking between bangs about the good old days: who had been arrested from the cells of The Organization, who had been blown away by home-made bombs, and how the entire movement all over the world was promising an early demise of parents, bankers, and the military establishment.

Marxuach's people had broken into the house while Mrs Winkelreid was meeting Owney downtown and had made a complete electronic installation which gave Marxuach a firm fix on the conversations after the first hour (which was entirely taken up with sexual activity anyway), working with through-the-wall taps and hover-ball microphones which had been suspended in the air of the hallway just outside Mrs Winkelreid's bedroom.

It was not until late in the evening that Mrs Winkelreid registered that Owney would be running for Congress. She was horrified. 'Are they blackmailing you or something, Owney?' she cried out.

'It's one of those things that happen in life,' Owney said.

'But to be sentenced to be a politician! It's not fair! You'll have to live among those people and – God forbid – be infected by them. Washington is not a city. It is a place on another planet which has nothing to do with life on this planet. Those people are mindless mutants with only one desire in life: to get re-elected.

185

Drunks, crooks, power-mad PAC-takers and chancers, they forgot long ago why they are there. Oh, Owney. I am so sorry. This is terrible. Just terrible.'

Owney's candidacy turned itself into a crazing aphrodisiac for Mrs Winkelreid which she hardly needed. Utterly exalted after many carnal processings which required that Owney summon up technical virtuosities from the distant past, she said, 'Now I can understand why you are making this sacrifice, Owney. It is your way of getting us access to the Pentagon, to blow it to smithereens at last. I could weep with gratitude over what you are doing for us.'

'Delighted to help,' Owney said dreamily.

He smiled at her. To humour her, because he really was fond of her, crazy as he knew her to be, he said, 'I am going to legislate to have the Defense Department and all the Generals eliminated. They have to go.'

Chapter 39

On the Sunday before the Monster Election Rally scheduled to take place on the Great Meadow of Central Park on the weekend following the announcement of Owney's candidacy, the Hazmans, husband and wife, met by appointment at the Seal Pond of the Central Park Zoo.

Dolly wore her lion's mane hair-do and an A-line caftan of red and orange with a collar of amber and rubies. Her long fingernails were painted green to match her eye make-up and the sides of her cheeks had been darkened to lengthen her face and accentuate its bone structure. She wore little fur muklaks with sensible soles and heels. Six bodyguards hovered near her. Owney walked past her twice, seeking her anxiously, without recognizing her. At the third pass-by she stopped him. 'Hello, Owney,' she said shyly. He stared at her until he knew who she was.

'Dolly!'

'Who did you think it was?'

'You look so different in that crazy costume.'

'Crazy costume? Who did you think I was?'

'Would you believe Genghis Khan?'

'Well, you certainly look the same.'

'But – what happened?' he asked with alarm. 'When did you go bald?'

'*Bald*? What are you talking about? I have never showed so much hair. My fans are crazy about it.'

He looked closely. 'There's a lot of hair in the back and on the sides, too, I suppose, but it pulls your forehead up to the top of your head.'

'I look bald? I actually look bald?'

'Well, balding. But it's very attractive, Dolly. I mean that.'

She backed away from him. 'Make it here at three o'clock,' she said, retreating sideways. 'I'll be back here at three o'clock.' She was gone into the crowd, half walking, half running. She ran across Fifth Avenue and disappeared into the Pierre Hotel, the six bodyguards following her.

She rushed into the hotel's beauty salon. She grabbed the first coiffeuse she saw. 'Do you know me?'

The woman gulped. 'Yes, Miss Heller.'

'You have to take me right now,' Dolly said. 'You have to. It's a life and death situation.'

In one and a half hours, her glistening black hair had been washed into straightness and cut into a beguiling Dutch-boy bob with a heavy fringe. She left the hotel, half walking, half running, and returned to the Zoo. It was ten minutes after three. Owney was standing where she had left him.

'Hello, there!' she said gaily.

'Dolly!' He dropped his voice. 'Who are these six guys?'

'Bodyguards. Do you like my hair?'

'What happened? Is that a wig?'

She marked him well in her mind. He was going to pay for that too. 'A wig?' she said, greatly amused. 'Good heavens, no. I just went into the ladies' room at the Pierre and combed it out. I got tired of that lion's mane thing. It was strictly for television.'

They began to walk, as slowly and as rhythmically as two *carabinieri*, around the Seal Pond. The six men fanned out discreetly behind them.

'Well!' Dolly said brightly. 'They tell me you're going into politics.'

'Well, yes.'

'It's a pity you never made anchor man.'

'How are the kids?' he snarled.

'Fine, fine. I've got to tell you though, that Momma is going crazy trying to keep Poppa from finding out that we aren't married any more.'

'We're married.'

'Some marriage.'

'Anyway, why does she bother? It obviously has so little to do with you how can it have anything to do with your father?'

'It has to do with you actually, Owney. Because my father will kill you if he finds out. And he will tell my brothers.'

'What kind of nonsense is that?'

'They are Puerto Ricans. Puerto Ricans never forget.'

'Every one of them is more German than Hermann Goering.'

'Germans are even worse about getting revenge, Owney.'

'Bosh.'

She flared up in anger because he wouldn't take her seriously. 'Listen, Owney. We are here talking only because I agreed to pretend to be friendly because of the global TV show your people offered, which is a terrific record promotion, and the terrific guests, the house in Bel-Air near Ron and Nancy and a couple of favours from the Mafia.'

'I just can't handle this any more.'

'Then stop acting like a fool and come home to your family!'

'Not if I have to share you with ninety million other people.'

She couldn't see anything to pick up and hit him with. So she did the next best thing. 'Owney, I have found a real man. A man who understands me. And loves me.'

'Jesus, let's sit down.'

Owney strode to a bench and fell on it. Dolly, pleased, sat beside him.

'His name is Al Dewar. He's a former Secretary of Housing and Welfare who was in command of all military forces in North America.'

'General Dewar.'

'I suppose so. What difference does it make?'

'He's three times your age, that's the difference.'

'He's – he's wonderful, Owney. He invented Henry Kissinger in his cellar in Scarsdale.'

'He's one of the cement heads on my election committee.'

'I know. He admires you.'

'This is too much, Dolly. This is really too much.' Owney stood up and strode away toward 59th Street.

Dolly smiled. Then she grinned. Then she began to giggle. She signalled to the six bodyguards and they strolled to Fifth Avenue and the two stretch limousines which were parked there illegally.

On the Sunday following the Wednesday announcement that Owen Hazman would run for Congress, Monahan staged a political rally which was a proclamation in tribute to the boundless social, racial, and religious tolerance of the candidate and his universal appeal to voters everywhere. It was a vision of the boiling pot called America at its finest hour.

The greater part of the population of the South Bronx had been bussed to the Great Meadow in Central Park to be entertained by showbiz greats of stage, screen, and television (and by sincere statements from the candidate). What could have been the entire population of Spanish Harlem were rocked, socked, and boffoed by every Latin headliner who had ever learned to sing Spanish phonetically who warmed hearts with *canciones* and *corridas* filled with sobbing *gritos*. Nineteen thousand Irish ethnics from Queens were bribed with thousands of free beer coupons to attend the rally. Hard-eyed country and western soloists were followed by garnet-eyed rock vocal groups who whinnied and shrieked. Then the candidate's wife, the sensation of sensations, Miss Dolly Heller, sang a rock arrangement of a musical interpretation of 'We Shall Overcome', backed by the NY Philharmonic conducted by Yo Yo Ma. Then dozens of little girls from the West Side, wearing buckskin skirts and cowboy hats, came out and played country fiddles, making sounds that no one present, or tenanted in the hundreds of high-rise apartment houses on both sides of the park, would ever be able to loosen from their minds, causing some severe psychiatric damage. The whole bash cost Mrs Noon $1,684,391.14, but on the foreign and domestic TV rights, syndication, and other residuals she made back all but $1,491.35 which was tax deductible.

Then, even though it was a perfect Indian summer day – for there is no free lunch, there is a price for everything – the candidate made his speech. Owney delivered the speech without notes, talking easily, directly into the cameras, ignoring the 332,874 people assembled. The speech was embroidered with folksy allusions which told the enormous crowd and the immeasurable television audience that he was a warm and wonderful man who did not have a greedy or mean bone in his body. That he cared. With all his heart he cried out to share an America pinpointed under a thousand points of light as if to focus the aim of the National Rifle Association.

'Here we are,' he seemed to be saying, 'rocking on democracy's front porch, and talking over our problems like good neighbours and friends.' He gave them one-liners which had worked on the old-time two-a-day vaudeville, more fascinating facts than they had ever heard at one time, and recited with incomprehensible hand gestures ecstatic fantasies of national and international affairs. He did it all as if it were off-the-cuff, an extemporaneous feat which had actually taken months of memory training, and five hours, twelve minutes of rehearsals. A few hundred people out of the three hundred-odd thousand assembled applauded politely. He was followed by Miss Dolly Heller singing a thunderous hit from her own worldwide best-selling rock album, 'Don't Twist My Heart', which brought such screaming and applause from the nearly-hysterical audience that the singing could not be heard. The programme was closed by the barbershop harmonies of a Rainbow quartet, a Black (bass), an Hispanic (alto), an Israeli (melody) and a Navajo (tenor) harmonizing in a C & W arrangement of the national anthem behind Miss Heller who almost ripped her throat out carrying the solo, while Owney faked a guitar accompaniment out front.

Owney closed with: 'To our children who are watching all of this on television in schools throughout this great city, thank you for watching democracy's big day.'

Four hundred-odd city police had to hold back the tide of grateful humanity who tried to climb up on the stage to shake his hand or squeeze his crotch, Miss Heller having been taken off by twenty-two armed guards while Owney made his closing remarks. With all of that and with all the news media coverage which had been minutely planned to follow, he was handicapped by the National Sports Book in Vegas to be a shoo-in for election.

Chapter 40

Five days before election day, James D. Marxuach of the Security Research Staff of the CIA leaked the Winkelreid-Hazman story to the news media.

At 7.17 a.m. on that terrible day, Owney was shaving in his bathroom at the 34th Street YMCA before a big day on the stump, scheduled to go from rally to luncheon to cavalcade. He had finished breakfast of Poland Water, Oatsies, and iced tea and as he applied the shaving soap he wondered how he was ever going to get Dolly back with honour or regain his mother on any terms at all. There was no way that he and Dolly could ever be together unless it was on some equal-status footing. She had flown high and he had stayed right where he was before she left. He didn't see how they could ever be reunited unless he won this election and went on to make history in the Congress. As he yearned for his mother, he began to think that, what with Dolly earning $47 million a year, perhaps, if and when they did get together, he *should* accept a million or so from her and put private detectives to work to find his mother. He was just really warming up to the idea when the phone began to ring.

In order of dialling, the calls were from Wiley Monahan; Oona Noon; his father-in-law, F.M. Heller; and Dolly. He answered all four of those calls in sequence but couldn't get up the spunk to answer the others from all four New York newspapers, two wire services, two news magazines, seven television news desks, three charismatic television clergymen and a lecture bureau.

'Owney? This is Wiley Monahan. What are you trying to do to me?'

'What do you mean?'

'You haven't seen the papers?'

'No.'

'You haven't turned on the television?'

'What happened?'

'Listen to this: front page the *New York Times*.' Monahan read the headline into the telephone. '"CANDIDATE PLOTS GOVERNMENT OVERTHROW WITH TERRORIST".'

'Wh*aaaaaat*?'

'Wait. Listen to the *News*. A screamer on the entire front page.' Monahan read, '"LESBIAN PLOTS PENTAGON DOWNFALL WITH CONGRESS CANDIDATE".'

'I never heard such crazy stuff.'

'You want *Newsday*? You want the *Post*?

'But, how could such a –'

'Is it true or do we sue?'

'Well – yes and no.'

'It can't be yes and no or you are ruined! We are *ruined*. You think Osgood Noon is gonna entice me to handle his campaign with this giant wound festering all over my face? What is this yes and no shit?'

'Yes, I know the woman. Yes, she did dabble a little with lesbians but it didn't work for her. Yes, she does belong to all those revolutionary organizations –'

'Terrorists!'

'Yes, they are terrorists but no to my saying I was going to eliminate the Department of Defense. I was only humouring her. I mean, what was the harm? We were in an – an intimate situation, and she was overcharged, so I just wanted to jolly her along a bit.'

'Look, Owney, the voters couldn't care less if you slept with six wart hogs. But you were endorsed by the Republicans. The White House will take this as a direct affront to the President, a man with extremely dainty morals except perhaps where money and Nicaraguans and his appointees are concerned.'

'Wiley, this is crazy –'

'If the timing had been different and the President had been at the ranch, you would have been swept into Congress by an even bigger vote than I expected. But happening this way, right before the election, just before the President's press conference (which he has a hard enough time figuring out), the rest of the country would be able to criticize New York's morals and, as you well know, no New Yorker can stand that. So you are dead. You could make it in vaudeville if there still was any vaudeville but you are finished in politics. Too bad, because you had a helluva smile.' He hung up.

Owney disconnected in a daze and the phone rang again immediately. It was Mrs Noon. The earpiece was covered with shaving foam.

'Owney? Ravi heah. Owney? You theah?'

Owney breathed into the mouthpiece.

'You OK, Owney?'

'Well, yes. I guess so.'

'Is somebody framin' you, Owney?'

'I – I certainly think so. I just don't understand any of this. Wiley Monahan just called and he went crazy.'

'Well, it's his livin'. Anyways, I called a few friends around here an' Washin'ton an' they come up with the news that the story was leaked by the CIA.'

'The *C-I-A*? Nobody at the CIA even knows I exist.'

'Well, maybe not, but you remember when I was selling all them tankers? And you was goin' back an' forth to Washin'ton?'

'Yes.'

'Well, maybe that was when the CIA got on to you.'

'It – it just doesn't make sense. None of it makes any sense.'

'Come to my house for lunch. We gotta lot to talk about.' She hung up.

Owney hung up, started for the television set to catch the news segment on the *Today* show but the phone rang again immediately.

'Hello,' he said, hopelessly looking around at the walls of the tiny room which seemed to be closing in on him.

'You *verachtungswert* sneak! I just found out you deserted your wife, my daughter! You *papaya*! You have broken the heart of the sweetest little girl in the world. You are fired, you *mandarria*. *Te voy a meter hasta los cojones*! I curse you in Cuban because Cubans can say worse things than any other language can imagine. You will never know when I and my sons will hit you. Whenever you go out on the street you are going to have to look in every direction with every step because my sons are going to be hiding in doorways and behind mailboxes and they are going to jump out on you and beat you to forcemeat, you *tolete*. *Vete al coño de tu madre*.' Mr Heller hung up heavily.

Owney stared at the wall remembering what Dolly had told him, that Germans weren't in it with Puerto Ricans when it came to revenge. He would have to live inside locked cars if he left the house. He hated to live like that.

Then the realization covered him like tar and feathers. He had no job. He was through in politics so his chance of regaining Dolly was gone. He would never find his mother. The sound of the phone ringing directly beside him struck like a spear into the chest. He picked up the receiver.

'Owney, this is Dolly. I have to get out to the airport but I had to tell you that I don't believe one word of anything that is in the papers this morning. Not one word. Aside from being with that woman which is a perfectly natural thing considering that we've been separated, I had to tell you that you are absolutely incapable of doing any of the things they say you did. Got to run now. By-ee!' She hung up.

Owney held the telephone in front of him and stared at it with wonder and joy. Then he sank heavily down on the end of the bed and, because he had no control over it, his eyes brimmed with tears and he began to weep with joy. No matter what, he thought. I have two friends. Dolly and my mom.

Kim Paisley, the first Korean-born hunchback Socialist to be elected to Congress during the Reagan Administration was swept into office by an overwhelming majority. She was to become a dominant figure in the House and would set to work immediately to reduce both the budget deficit and the national debt by raising taxes, greatly embarrassing the other members.

Chapter 41

The Blackfoot Indians had a system of mockery which could make life intolerable and drive any victim out, alone, on a quest either for death or for war honours with which to redeem himself. It had been the most subtle and sophisticated method of mocking ever known until the rituals exercised upon Owney Hazman on that morning which was five days before the election day which was to have solved all his problems. It enveloped Owney in an equal sense of American shame and helpless hopelessness as when Richard Nixon made another triumphant come-back surrounded by the Republic he had betrayed, or when Ronald Reagan had explained his reverential visit to the SS cemetery in Germany by saying that he had been told the SS storm troops buried there had been executed for being kind to inmates, or the shaming moment when he had hustled his disastrous Presidency for $2 million plus 'expenses' as a pay-off from the Japanese, or for a $7 million advance for the rights to publish the apology for his public life, or for the $60,000 plus 'expenses' he got for addressing the hamburger franchise-dealers association of Miami.

By 11.45 a.m., Owney, after sitting on the floor of the bathtub while a cold shower bath poured down on him and the telephone never stopped ringing, managed to drag on his clothes and leave the YMCA through the rear service entrance to avoid the congregation of reporters, photographers and television crews who the management had said were waiting for him in the lobby.

He made a wide swing around the block until he came back to 34th Street, well out of sight of the YMCA. He walked unsteadily to Madison Avenue then boarded an uptown bus to 59th Street. He got to Mrs Noon's building at 60th and Park, walking as if in a trance, at 12.47 p.m. for a one o'clock luncheon.

Each one of the enormous Shiite employees of the building

greeted him with pleasure. Elek, the doorman, was waiting to tell him about the morning he had shot the three Syrian kidnappers, the calibre of gun he had used, and how the men went down. 'I see these men lay hands on my lady,' Elek said, 'and try to drag her into a 1980 Dodge. It were a Magnum revolver I used, sir, an' I shot them through the head. I had never seen such an effect, sir. It was like a great train had laid chains on them and pulled them eleven feet across the pavement. Zap! Zap! Zap! And they were stone cold dead.'

Owney heard the delighted words as through the layers of a hot fudge sundae; as though he were buried under an avalanche of soft fudge and heavy whipped cream, as if he, himself, had become a cold, cold, *cold* piece of ice cream under layer upon layer of the thick congealing sauce of destiny.

Jeshurun was waiting for him when the elevator door opened at Mrs Noon's main floor. 'I must say you are not looking at all well, sir,' he said.

Owney was seated as carefully as a mannequin in Macy's window, a glass of champagne was inserted into his hand as he was arranged to face the doorway through which Mrs Noon would enter. He was unable to think about what had happened to him. There was only a sense of awful loss but it had become shapeless so that it could settle into the crevices of his memory and numb all areas of his body.

Mrs Noon came into the room six minutes later, giving Owney a chance to be soothed by the constant Ray Charles music which sang of the wonders of South Carolina to the tune of something he was sure had been called 'Georgia'. Mrs Noon's expensively stripped hair, which had had all colour removed from it, filament by filament, was arranged in a flawless page boy. Her eyes were large Confederate-grey lazy ovals which seemed to Owney that morning to have been painted on her face by some master of *trompe l'œil*. They were oddly opaque eyes, he noticed for the first time, like the coloured eyes on the statues over graves in Cuban cemeteries. Dully, Owney sensed that the cause of this was that her eyes, like her magnificent teeth, had been capped; the teeth with flawless bonding; the eyes with coloured lenses. The cost of the make-up alone on the surface of that skin, he thought, could have fed a South-East Asian family of six for 22.3 days.

'Hi,' he said listlessly.

'They workin' up a nice tuck-in fo' you in the kitchen. I went in there mahseff. Roast toikey, mashed potatoes, brown gravy –

197

all boys likes gravy – an' a lotta creamy green stuff. You gone love it.'

'I'm not very hungry, Ravi.'

'Shoo! Wait'll you smell it. Drink up yo' champagne an' let's git to dreamin' again.'

'Dreaming?' Owney bolted down the wine and watched Jeshurun refill the glass.

Mrs Noon settled herself with a throw-away air of magnificence upon a settee. She crossed the legs which so many showgirls had attempted to recreate through the miracle of cosmetic surgery.

'The TV anchor thing didn't woik out,' she said sympathetically. 'Now you been screwed outta the Congressional thing. So we gotta figure how to set things straight agin. I mean, you helped make me a bundle of money so it figures that I owe you one.'

'No. Not that I want to sound ungrateful. You've done everything possible that anyone could do but I just didn't have it.'

'How old are you, Owney? I mean – not your real age but your political age that Monahan set up for you.'

'Thirty-something, I suppose. Anyway, he handed me a birth certificate and a passport and a social security card that proved I was of Constitutional age to hold national office.'

'But you really only twenny-eight?'

He nodded apathetically.

'What do you figure you'd like to do?'

'I was fired this morning, Mrs Noon. I can't think. I just can't get a bead on anything.'

'Fired? Fired from you regular job?'

Owney nodded.

'But you so good at it! You musta sold five million frankfoituhs fo' that man.'

'He's my father-in-law. He was upset because my wife and I separated.'

'That jes' breaks mah heart,' Mrs Noon said.

Owney nodded. 'It's a long, sad story, Mrs Noon.'

'You love her, a-course. You love yo' chillun. But her success is more than you kin take.'

'She's making 47 million dollars a year. That's a take-home cheque every week of 903,846 dollars and 15 cents, which is considerably more than I earn – or probably ever will earn. She has to live in California to be near her work. It's no use. We're finished.'

'Owney, lissena me. You may not know how to anchor a news

198

show and you may not be electable to the Congress but one thing you do know is the frankfoituh bidniz.'

'Oh, I know that all right.'

'Then we gone set you up in your own frankfoituh company. How does that grab you? You got any ideas on that?'

'Hazman's Lites!' Owney blurted involuntarily, springing to his feet.

'Whut?'

'We could package and sell an entirely new slimming frankfurter and a *Kalbsbratwurst* packed with Alpine herbs imported from Switzerland made on the same low-calorie formula! They could sweep the country. We could sell twenty, thirty million of them a year.' He stared at her like a man who is looking deep into a vision of the future. 'I wouldn't make them in the *schublig* size that we were talking about in the meeting, I'd make them in the normal hot-dog size and pull the calorie count down another hundred calories to around 110 a sausage! Lites! Slimming frankfurters are a tremendous idea whose time has come, Mrs Noon.'

'Ravi,' she said, smiling happily. 'How much you think it would take to start up?'

'God knows. Two, three million. Finding the factory site would be the important part.'

'I got a factory site in Long Island City. If you could get the machines and the people, you could walk right in.'

'I wonder if I can claim the ball-park and racetrack and football-stadium business – and the bar association picnic and the political rallies Mr Olgilvie lined up for me when I was with Mr Heller?'

'I'm gone send Mal Olgilvie a telegram to Syria right now an' git a clearance from him on that. An' you know you got the weenie order for all my hotels and hospitals and prisons – they been turnin' over a lotta frankfoituhs.'

'We should sell both loose and packaged,' Owney said excitedly. 'The Lites absolutely belong in a package and all the institutional sales should be in bulk. My father-in-law had this idea that quality frankfurters were only sold loose. I mean, how can we get into the supermarkets with the Lites unless they're packaged?'

'A-course. Now, look-a here, we'll do it this way. I'll lend you however much you need to git goin' and after you pay me back plus a fifty per cent profit, you own forty-nine per cent of the company an' I own the other half.'

'I can't take that kind of money from you, Mrs Noon.'

'Ravi. You'll take it because you gotta take it. Plus a contract that gone pay you one hunnert and fifty thousand a year plus expenses. I mean, in a soitain sense I got you inta all this trouble. If I hadn't asked you to be the connection between me an' Mal Olgilvie, you woulda still had both your job an' your wife today. So I owe you. Also, fifty-one per cent is a fair return on my money an' you gotta own something big so you kin go to your wife all even and start up all over again.'

Chapter 42

Early in 1989, Owney left the YMCA and moved into a furnished three-room flat in Sunnyside, Queens, just over the Long Island City frontier from his factory site. He hired his secretary, Emmaline McHanic, away from Heller's Wurst, retained the firm of Schwartz, Blacker and Moltonero as legal counsel for his new company (at Mrs Noon's suggestion) following a cabled correspondence with Malachi Olgilvie in En Nebk, Syria, thus assuring the sporting and political frankfurters, and accepted a revolving fund of $1.5 million which Mrs Noon deposited in the name of Hazman's Own Inc. at the Yamamoto First National bank branch in mid-town Manhattan.

Hazman's Own state-of-the-art equipment itself was far more modern than the equipment used by Heller's Wurst. Within two days he had hired a plant foreman and a manufacturing engineer who secured and installed sausage-making machinery which Mrs Noon insisted be flown without delay from Switzerland. Harriet Blacker personally made lasting arrangements with the Sausage Makers' Union, Local 107, and wurstmen were made available on a fair contract basis to begin two days after the permanent installation of the machinery. Gordon Manning, Mr Heller's own pork buyer, insisted on 'consulting' on the initial meat supply contracts because he felt that Mr Heller had acted with gross unfairness in firing Owney and had told Mr Heller so.

Just weeks after the meeting with Mrs Noon on the day which had marked Owney Hazman's lowest point in life, the first two and three-quarter miles of Hazman's Own Lite frankfurters were turned out, packaged, and shipped. Owney was his own sales manager, aided by three seasoned assistants. Twenty-six hundred and forty supermarkets were the company's first accounts and, within two weeks, this had grown to an account list of 11,783 stores.

The Lites were the national sensation that Mr Heller had expected the Hungarian *debrizna* to be when he spent $263,472.07 on trying to popularize it nationally. When the Academy Awards for sausages were broadcast from New Braunfels, Texas, on January 26th to a worldwide television audience, Owney's two new sausages were nominated and were lightly favoured in the national betting due to the tremendous advance and follow-up news media coverage which included three 1.42 minute shots on the evening national television news.

When the sealed envelopes prepared by Price, Waterhouse were opened on camera, the Lite slimming sausage, made by Hazman's Own, won three of the four performance Weenies awarded: 1. for Best Sausage, a measure of taste, texture, smell, and quality; 2. for Best Performance by a Sausage, an honour measured by its universality of distribution and sales; and 3. for Best Supporting Sausage (the *Kalbsbratwurst* Lite which Owney had quietly introduced).

Owney Hazman, *Wurstmeister*, was also honoured by the acclamatory votes of sausage people throughout the world with the Fan Fieu Toa Award for Greatest Achievement in the Sausage Industry.

Heller's Wurst Inc. received only one performance (as opposed to technical) Weenie, for Best Foreign Sausage, the Hungarian *debrizna* into which Mr Heller had poured so much money and for which his daughter had worked so hard.

The Hazman supermarket accounts doubled, then tripled to serve over 30,000 stores; 117,000 restaurants; 5,634 hotels, airlines, hospitals, delicatessens, street vendors, and prisons. The Department of Defense ordered Hazman's Own Lites for every branch of the Armed Forces. State governors and big city mayors ruled that the Lites had to be included in school lunches. Out of the blue, Dolly Heller, on her wildly popular satellite talk-and-music show, switched from the *debrizna* to Hazman's Own Lites when she urged her guest star, William F. Buckley, jr, to eat a pair on camera with horseradish mustard. Buckley, after three rapid, self-conscious swallows, belched (involuntarily) into Camera No. 3. The nation flinched.

Hazman's Own was shipping 261.7 miles of Lites each week which, at half the rate of gain already established and taking into account the inevitable acclaim from the export market due to the international status of the three Weenies it had won at New Braunfels, would be shipping over 20,000 miles of slimming sausages by the end of the year. However, well before the end of the year, the company would be manufacturing and distributing its revolutionary, improved *kalbsbratwurst*, flecked with imported Swiss herbs, whose popularity would cause an enormous extension of the mileage of sausages from the model Long Island City plant to almost 32,079 miles a year, a distance almost 1.5 times around the earth at the equator.

Mrs Noon's investment of $1,279,632.14 was returned, with her fifty per cent profit, within nineteen weeks. Owney Hazman was as celebrated in *The Wall Street Journal, The Meat Processor,* and *Business Week* as his wife, Dolly Heller, was in *People* and *Billboard.* Owen Hazman was on his way to becoming a multi-millionaire in the neo-Reagan tradition.

When he had become (almost) a half-owner of his company, the first thing he did with his new endowment was to have Schwartz, Blacker, and Moltonero negotiate the purchase of the little house at Meier's Corners on Staten Island where he had known happiness with his mother. When the Hazmans had bought the house in the late fifties, it had cost $13,093.41, but, due to the costs of the Vietnam War, the nation's expenses in the Persian Gulf area, and the steady draining by the Contras and HUD consultants, the 6.4 per cent annual rate of inflation for thirty years, as well as the need to devalue the dollar to cope with the deficit and the trade imbalance, due also to the paralysing size of the national debt which President Reagan had accumulated as he reduced the cost of government by increasing expenditures, and despite the fact that Owney had the shrewdest, hardest negotiators in the country, the Malachi Olgilvie-trained law firm, arranging the purchase, the little house cost $519,284.03.

Owney paid it with a smile. To him, owning that house again was almost the very next thing to finding his mother.

Chapter 43

Dolly sent her husband a warm and loving telegram of congratulations following the Academy Awards broadcast from New Braunfels (which was carried by forty-one countries and translated simultaneously into eighty-nine languages across region after region of the world). She also telephoned him backstage at the Awards auditorium with such sweetness and pride in his triumph that Owney had tears in his eyes. She didn't end the bridge-building there. She followed that up with a letter so personal in its devotion and recall of indelibly intimate moments from their past lives together that Owney was grateful for the huge PERSONAL sticker she had put on the envelope. The towering dam of resentment which he had built up inside himself broke.

He knew who he was now. He stood tall within his international identity as one of the era's great frankfurter industrialists.

He flew to the Los Angeles airport where he hired a chopper to drop him on Dolly's helipad in Bel-Air and gathered her into his loving arms, and (when the servants and bodyguards had been asked to leave the room) blubbered piteously that he had made a terrible mistake and pleaded with her to come back to him.

The Hazmans were reunited. The combined Appleburg-Paramount-NBC press departments flashed the story around the world. The news of such a star of records, screen, radio, television, and product endorsements choosing to rejoin her husband (himself a three-time Weenie winner) exploded like a bombshell. As the flash came over the wires and into the newsrooms, the five networks flew in their anchor men from Bucharest, Medellín, Prague, Beijing, and Washington for a joint informal round table interview with the happy couple and 2,147,893 requests for the 91-page transcript of the interview were mailed out by the networks at four dollars a copy over the next three weeks in response to the greatest public interest yet shown in public affairs. The anticipated ratings caused a postponement of a Presidential press conference from seven to eight p.m. as twenty-seven television cameras crowded into a semi-circle in the enormous sound recording studio which Dolly's recording company and music publisher had built for her on the hill-top Bel-Air estate.

Owney explained that the rift in the marriage had 'all been a misunderstanding'. The transcript (in part) reads as follows:

Q:You are both such fabulously successful people. Isn't there always the possibility that your entirely different careers will pull you apart again?

A (by both Hazmans in one burst): Not a chance. (Laughter. Miss Heller defers to her husband.)

Mr Hazman: Our careers are no longer entirely different. Not only are we both in show business – Dolly in music, movies, concerts and television and I in frankfurters – but as the president and CEO of a Fortune 500 company, I am going to take over the management of my wife's business affairs so we will have a career relationship which will be closer than it has ever been before. (Applause from the assembled television crews.)

Q: But are you still in love? Isn't that what really matters? I mean, isn't this reunion more like a great corporate merger than the re-establishment of a romance?

A (by Miss Heller): If we believed that, we just couldn't go on. I couldn't sing one more song and Owney couldn't make one more frankfurter. We don't only have our love. We have our family and our dog, Captain. That is five human and one canine heart bound together and nothing, and I am saying this from the bottom of my heart, will ever tear us apart again.

To close the show (at the insistence of the President and White House aides who were standing by in Washington to follow the appearance of the Hellers), Miss Heller sang a chorus of 'Bronze Baby Shoes', her latest hit, smiling happily through tears with every thrilling note. Immediately following the show there was a full photo opportunity with the happy couple and their three children. Owney spoke briefly, revealing some of his work with Hazman's Lites and NASA, conveying a come-rain-or-come-shine certainty about the future of the American frankfurter in space (which, after the combined networks show was over, the syndicators took for an enormous cash guarantee), and the entire press corps was lavished with take-home packs of Hazman's Own Lites.

The Hazman family flew to New York in Dolly's Gulfstream IV. They would divide time unequally between the Apthorpe in New York and the house in Bel-Air. They would live in California only as long as Dolly's revised work schedule required. All music recording was to be done in New York. The production of the television show was moved to New York and with only one picture to go on her three-picture contract with Paramount, Dolly said (modestly) that she was determined, if anyone wanted her to make more movies, that they would have to be made in New York.

Owney felt that the arrangements were entirely acceptable even though he had to give up the furnished apartment in Sunnyside and commute all the way from the West Side of Manhattan to Long Island City. He did have the advantage of not having to drive. Dolly's contract with the record company provided a limousine and a driver-bodyguard.

The re-establishment of the marriage brought great happiness to the elder Hellers. Mrs Heller had known all along that the reunion would happen and, even if it happened gradually, she was able to persuade her husband and her sons to see that the little bump in her daughter's life had been just a lovers' quarrel. She had to refuse to cook for or talk to the three men in her family in order to bring them round to welcoming Owney back but through various ways which she called 'concentrating the mind' she cajoled her husband into agreeing to invite the Hazmans to the Heller table for dinner.

'Are you crazy, Bonita?' Mr Heller said. 'First the man walks away from my beautiful daughter, then he walks away with half of my beautiful business. I'm no longer number one because of him. I took him in and he stole my life's blood and you want me to sit down and eat with him?'

'Who's crazy? When you die you are gonna take the business with you? Wolfie is a lawyer. Luddie is an astronaut. So what can you do? You want the business to keep going you gotta let Owney manage it – the only one in the family besides you who knows the first thing about how to run it. And the time has come, Paco. We got a right to go on a cruise, go back to Ponce and show them what success is. The time is now to leave the business and let Owney run it.'

'You think so? You really think so?'

'Now! Tonight! When Dolly and I are doing the dishes you'll tell him. The merger will be the biggest thing in *salchicha* history. Heller & Hazman's Own Wurst Inc. How can you miss, dolling?'

Owney wasn't at all happy to be invited to dinner at his in-laws.

'You should have heard the names he called me, Dolly. In Cuban, he said, because the Cubans had invented the worst insults.'

'What do you care? You couldn't understand them.'

'He didn't yell at me entirely in Spanish. He said some pretty rotten things in English and German, too. And he fired me! I built sales for that company, Dolly. That's a matter of record.'

'Of course you did. And he knows that. He just has a terrible temper. That doesn't mean he *means* what he yells when he's all upset because no one had bothered to tell him when we were separated.'

'Tell him? Fahcrissake, how couldn't he know? You were in Hollywood. All the papers and all the television said you were in Hollywood. He saw me in the office every day in New York. How couldn't he know?'

'We're going to dinner to make my mother happy. She's always been on your side. So you'll compromise a little.'

Mrs Heller arranged things so that there would be a minimum of need to chat before dinner, but they could begin to eat almost immediately, because eating sausages in any form always cheered her husband up.

It was a wonderful meal. Bologna kebabs as an appetizer with *kalerei*, a pâté made of pig's ears, trotters and tail; *garbanzo* soup with *chorizo*; a frankfurter rice bake made with green beans, corn kernels, chopped onions and peppers, grated Cheddar, an egg, tomato juice, garlic powder, Spanish salami, rice, and four pounds of frankfurters.

Mr Heller began the meal coldly distant, but while he ate the frankfurter rice bake he hummed softly to himself.

'You all right, Paco?' his wife asked.

'It's ever so spicy and ever so good,' Mr Heller said happily to everyone.

After dinner, while the women cleared the table, Mr Heller took

Owney into his study, which had once been a maid's room at the back of the apartment. He gave Owney a cigar and poured him a small schnapps.

'So? How's business?' he asked.

'We went into our eighteen-thousandth supermarket today.'

'Supermarkets!'

'It's where people are buying food.'

'Packaged frankfurters!'

'Well, we have our share of the outdoor market, too.'

'Your share? *My* share. You stole the business from me – the ball parks, the racetracks, the political picnics.'

'Mr Heller, be fair. I built that business. I worked day and night to cultivate Mr Olgilvie.'

'You see it one way, I see it the real way ... but the main thing is, I ain't as young as I used to be and Bonita would like to travel a little. I want the business to go on even though I'm not there. I want you to run the entire business which I am gonna sign over to my grandchildren to make sure they can afford a college education, and I want you to run it.'

'Me? Run Heller's Wurst?'

'Who else? When my company is merged with your company it will be the biggest single frankfurter conglomerate in the history of the world. Nothing in Germany or Belgium or Switzerland can come near it. We'll set the styles and originate the taste and texture trends and all the others will have to follow whatever we do. Don't you see it, Owney? Don't you realize you will be the frankfurter tsar of the world?'

Owney felt an on-rushing of power but he was humbled. He would control the production and distribution of more frankfurters than had ever been eaten by all of the countries of Mittel-Europa. He had gone from a door-to-door salesman of luxury novelties, forced to live off women so that he could conserve his capital to be able to find his mother, to become a millionaire; the husband of an idolized multi-millionaire; a man who was about to become a multi-billionaire if the count were done in frankfurters. Life was good.

Chapter 44

Freddie Fanshaw was having a happy holiday at a sublimely comfortable small hotel in the Florida Keys with an exceptionally sensual and beautiful woman named Hermione Rooney whom he had met on an escalator at Bloomingdale's in New York and who was quite a remarkable tap dancer. She had, Freddie thought, the sort of legs which look realler than real in opera-length black hose under a pair of rather brief panties when tap dancing at three or four in the morning after an intense bout of Mum-and-Dadding-it. As he rested back on the pillows to restore his body fluids, he was overtaken with admiration for her energy.

'Tap dancing is no sluggard's art,' he said. 'Hermione is such a meaningful name for you.'

The phonograph was playing 'Avalon' in a double-time tempo. The inspiring young woman was doing the Bubbles part in a Buck and Bubbles middle routine which required some one-legged cross-over work and a good deal of arm swinging. She never seemed to get out of breath.

'How do you mean, Freddie?' she asked, concentrating.

'Hermione is a derivative of Hermes, the quicksilver messenger of the gods, isn't it?'

'I thought it was the feminine of Herman.'

'Heavens no. The German Hermine, which is the feminine, is an entirely different name. And Hermione was a daughter of Helen of Troy, wasn't she? Shakespeare dined out on the name.'

The weather had been splendid, showing more sun than he had ever thought there could be (looking back on his schooldays near Little Swell in the Cotswolds). The food was just right. The juke box was packed with golden oldies. The bartender knew how to do something with rum which could only be said to be remarkable. Things were so perfect that he wasn't surprised at all when the

Centre called him at 5.25 a.m. to ask him to investigate an oil spill about eleven miles out in the tiny Keys.

'I shouldn't have thought that was my sort of thing at all, Alan,' Freddie said to his control.

'Nonetheless. It isn't a maritime or an engineering problem, you see, Freddie. In actual fact no oil is involved.'

'You did say oil spill.'

'Technically, yes. One of the tankers – *those* tankers, if you follow, the former tankers of Mrs Noon – hit a reef and ripped open its number four tank, approximately amidships. No other tank was damaged.'

'But you said no oil spill.'

'No. And very strange. Something did spill, though. And it has caused havoc among the marine life. They are leaping out of the water. They are trying to walk on the beach. And quite a few of them are floating belly-up.'

'But how does that involve us?'

'Madam has been expecting the worst ever since the – ah – word Mafia came into this. I am told that if it is what she thinks it is, she wants us out of there without a trace and any connection with the tankers and anything but oil expunged for ever.'

'Really?'

'What is wanted is that you have a recce instanter. You are empowered to ask all the questions. You have full authorization from the People's Republic of China, the Inter-European Consolidators Ltd, and the Bahama Beaver Bonnet Company to make any announcements you see fit to make. Forty minutes after your visit is completed, the American television networks will be notified of the disaster. They will need to wait until daylight, at least until eight ack emma before they can get organized and move south to the tanker. That will give you approximately a three-hour start for the recce.'

'Will do.'

To save himself anxiety about anyone attempting to interfere in any way with his friend Hermione, Fanshaw put four stout sleeping pills in her delicious rum drink and she nodded off within moments. It was a pitiable thing really to watch her slowly run down, moving from the staccato taps required by the music from *Broadway Melody of 1938* into just flapping her feet as if she were dusting the floor, then to drop off into a deep sleep with Freddie catching her on the way down and carrying her to the bed.

He was on his way to the wrecked tanker in a hired helicopter within fifteen minutes, expanding his lead time to the maximum. He was put down on a beach which overlooked a pavonine sea on which slumped the guilty tanker, *Bergquist*, impaled on its villainous reef. He was alone on the beach when he got out of the chopper. He walked to the water's edge to stare down at the debris which was washing up. Dozens of cellophane bags containing white powder were accumulating on the beach. He examined a bag and its contents, then called the two-man crew of the chopper over. He scored and identified the contents of the bag with a marking pen and signed his name. He handed the bag to the chopper pilot, then to the shotgun, and asked them to sign their names.

'This stuff came off that tanker?' the pilot asked.

'This is a two-kilo bag,' Freddie said. 'How many bags would you say have been washed ashore?'

'Twenty? Thirty?'

'OK,' Freddie said. 'Remember the sight well. We may have to so depose. Right now we'll document about ten of these bags and put them in the chopper, then I want you to put me aboard that ship before this whole beach goes black with the Coast Guard, environmental people, and television crews.'

They loaded ten documented and counter-signed bags of cocaine into the helicopter, then Freddie had himself flown out to the tanker. He was winched down to the deck from the chopper. The ship's captain and the first mate were waiting on the number two hatch as he came down. 'Who the hell are you?' the captain asked. He was wearing a peaked cap which had a message from the Dutch Boy White Lead Company printed on it, a robin's-egg blue polo shirt and a white Turkish towel wrapped around his middle.

'I am Frederick Fanshaw, representing Bahama Beaver Bonnet and Inter-European Consolidators, as owners, and the People's Republic of China as lessees,' Freddie said. 'We want some answers.'

'What answers? We hit a reef.'

'But where's the oil spill?'

'I don't understand it either. We been tryna figure that out for twenny minutes.'

Freddie motioned the two men to the ship's rail. He pointed to the contents of the sea around the midships section. Hundreds of bags of cocaine were floating or suspended in the water showing up like the white bellies of dead fish.

'What's that in aid of?' he asked.

*

211

Within forty minutes a Coast Guard cutter had arrived and within seventy minutes choppers carrying television cameras, crews, and equipment were on board. Freddie identified himself as the owner's representative.

'I am shocked by what I have found here,' he said on camera. 'This ship has been found to have been carrying an extraordinary secret cargo, well over seven thousand kilos of cocaine, with a street value of hundreds of million of dollars, which was intended to be landed at the port of Boston. I have impounded ten of the sacks, witnessed by an independent helicopter crew, and I am going to fly those sacks to the Drugs Enforcement Administration in Miami to demand a full investigation. An unforgivable hardship has been imposed on the companies which own this tanker and a great ally which had leased this tanker in good faith to transport crude oil to the United States as a faithful service. In the case of the Bahama Beaver Bonnet Company – well! – they have been transporting oil in tankers such as this for over seventy years, haven't they? There is no more responsible oil entity in the world. I am charging that someone, with someone else's connivance, has somehow managed to substitute this – this contraband – in the number four tank of this vessel in the place of the oil – and only oil – which my principals had contracted to transport. It is not my place to say this, in anticipation of the findings of an official Federal investigation, but it is my belief that the investigation will show that the sinister traffic in this – this contraband – may be the doing of the recent, former owner of this tanker fleet, Mrs Osgood O. Noon.' Even the case-hardened television crews gasped as they watched and listened to Fanshaw wrap up his story and make worldwide news.

Freddie kept his indignation at white-heat until the television crews were finished with him, then he was winched aboard his chopper and flown away to the north.

On arrival back at the small hotel, it was ten minutes to noon. Freddie undressed, got into pyjamas, requested an alarm call for six o'clock that evening, slipped into bed beside the admirable young woman and went to sleep. At six they were both awakened by the telephone's ring.

'Ah,' Freddie said. 'Soon to be dinner time then.'

'Dinner time? We really did get to bed late,' Hermione said. 'And I'm still sleepy.'

Chapter 45

The news media in eighty-two countries blared out the charges against Oona Noon in 103 languages, implicating by inference her husband who, until that morning, had been the leading candidate for the Presidency of the United States. Wherever television was broadcast, the tapes showing Freddie Fanshaw making his charges were played over and over again on every news show throughout the day and into the night. Newspapers called in every kind of authority from government, education, abstract science, and marine biology to keep the story alive and well up on the front page and above the fold.

Goodie Noon, habitually out of touch with any news which did not relate either to the American Flag or the Pledge of Allegiance, was at work on another typewriter portrait of an American President, the now-famous self-portrait, done with a red and blue typewriter ribbon which, when printed on white paper, rendered the meaning of Old Glory within the features of a great American leader. As he worked intently, an aide dressed as a footman came in to tell him that a large number of television and print press had arrived on Bland Island and were not only sitting on the horseshoe pitch and surrounding turf but had asked if Mr Noon would please come out to consent to be interviewed.

'That's a lot of razzmatazz!' the candidate said. 'Mrs Noon has told me nothing about this. How do such people even get on this island? I really am put out by this. And they must be told straight off that any questions about abortion will be off-limits because Mrs Noon hasn't formulated my position beyond denying abortions to the desperately poor who had been impregnated through incest or rape.'

'We think it's just an informal, getting-to-know-you sort of interview, sir,' the aide told him.

Reassured that it was just another unexpected photo opportunity Goodie graciously agreed to appear on camera.

The mass interview had been set up on the rolled and manicured lawn surrounding Goodie's own horseshoe pitch. As he came out of Flag House he was puzzled by the number of cameras and crews and by the extraordinary turnout of print press because his wife hadn't told him that anything unusual was about to happen, but he put it all down to an early start of the primary race and bore up as a good soldier should.

He went into his standard talk about the Flag, the Pledge of Allegiance, the Constitutional right of housewives to own and shoot automatic assault weapons, and told the press of his abomination of abortion because it could, in one generation, strip the country of its pool of cheap labour, when the harsh voice of an interviewer startled him with a totally rude question: 'How long has your wife been the Cocaine Queen of the world?'

'I'm afraid I don't understand the question,' Goodie said.

'Sir,' a handsome lady interviewer who was standing in total St Laurent beside the CBS camera said, 'your wife is charged with massive cocaine-smuggling operations, using tankers which she had sold to American and British companies who had leased them to China. Preliminary findings suggest that it is the largest single narcotics smuggling operation in history.'

'*Cocaine*? My *wife*? Oona *Noon*?'

'Please comment, sir.'

Goodie's face was reddening deeply over his shocked indignation. 'Even if not a word of this is broadcast,' he said, 'as it most certainly will not be, that is actionable, madam. What is your network affiliation?'

Another interviewer took up the assault. 'Federal warrants have been issued for the arrest of your wife, sir. May we have a statement from you about your knowledge of your wife's criminal activities?'

At the word 'statement', Goodie cleared his throat and went into an automatic response from the rote of answers which his wife had prepared for him on almost every topic which could possibly come up at any interview. 'The national community is in general agreement,' he said, 'that it is essential to deal promptly and effectively with emerging tendencies which seem to support the use of controlled substances. In order to prevent any sustainability of the current expansion, and it is noted that action in this direction has been taken in many industrial countries, the evolving process of economic policy coordination provides an appropriate framework to develop an adequate mix of enforcement modes and moral precepts, supported by structural policies, in order to maintain a disciplined position and reduce internal imbalances. Thank you, ladies and gentlemen.' He turned away from the cameras and walked with grave dignity across the even green lawn to disappear into Flag House.

In Washington, Carter Modred, jr, Chairman of the Republican National Committee, switched off all three of the television sets he had been looking at, pushed the newspaper away from him and leaned back in his chair. 'Jesus,' he said, 'Goodie Noon was the best financed candidate we ever almost got to the primaries.'

'We were lucky all this hit the fan now,' his assistant said.

'You win some, you lose some,' Modred said.

Dolly Hazman came running into the bedroom. She was the early riser in the family and she had just listened to the seven o'clock newscast on the *Today* show. She had to shake her husband awake while she yelled his name, standard waking procedure.

'Owney! OWNEY!!!'

'Wha'?'

'Your friend, Mrs Noon!'

'What about her?'

'The police are after her.'

He sat straight up. '*Whaaaat?*'

'They say she's been smuggling cocaine.'

'Cocaine? Why should a woman like that smuggle cocaine? She owned seventy-nine supertankers.'

'That's how she smuggled the cocaine.'

'Has she been arrested?'

'She's skipped. She's gone.'

'Gone where?'

'Nobody knows. Obviously somebody tipped her off and she just picked up and ran.'

'I can't believe it. She was a wonderful friend to us, Doll.'

'I know.'

'From the first day I ever met her, she did everything she could to help me. Cocaine! It's just unbelievable. Just the same, we owe her.'

At two o'clock that afternoon Owney received a baffling, consternating and utterly incomprehensible call from his bank, the

215

Yamamoto First National, saying that it was of vital urgency that he come to the bank immediately. He took a bus across the bridge from Long Island City and made his way to the bank on Madison Avenue at 56th Street. At the mention of his name, Owney was whisked into a private elevator and ushered into the office of the branch vice-president, a Mr Kiyosho Fujikawa, a short, earnest and forthright man originally from the town of Fukushima, who wore rimless eyeglasses. Owney was received by Mr Fujikawa with so many bows that they constituted extreme awe as expressed in Japanese ritual. The banker seemed to be trembling as Owney shook his hand.

'What's up, Mr Fujikawa?' Owney asked.

The banker was breathing shallowly but he summoned up the ability to speak from the depths of his character. 'At 12.21 hours today', he said hoarsely, 'four billion six hundred and twenty million dollars was transferred to your savings account in this bank from sixteen banks and brokerage houses in North America.'

'Isn't that a lot of money for a savings account?' Owney stopped short. '*Four billion six hundred and twenty million*? Mr Fujikawa, have you lost your mind?'

'I think so.'

'Who? Who did such a thing?'

'We are trying to find out,' Mr Fujikawa said weakly. 'I had hoped to know by the time you arrived here but I am told it will be at least until four o'clock before we can know.'

'This is outrageous! What am I supposed to tell the IRS?'

'That, at least, is in order. All of the asset transfers were made in bearer bonds, in Triple A, tax-free municipals.'

'No *taxes*? On four billion six hundred and twenty million dollars of income?'

'No.'

'How can that be? I had to pay taxes when I was earning five thousand dollars. And when I was earning twenty-five thousand dollars. This is almost five billion dollars.'

Mr Fujikawa shrugged. 'That's how it is,' he said. 'For almost a decade the government fought a heroic battle against the possibility of swelling the ranks of the poor. The only way to do that is to protect the people who have substantial incomes – to try to contain the ranks of the rich – and, at last, our President seems to be winning the battle.'

'How much will the interest be on that kind of money?'

Mr Fujikawa took a calculator out of his jacket pocket and

punched in a series of numbers. 'About 280 million a year,' he said.

'Tax free?'

'Tax free.'

'How much is that a week?'

'About five million four hundred thousand.'

Owney sank into a chair. The figure absolutely dwarfed his wife's measly income of $940,000 a week. Somehow, without his knowing how, he had become the head of his family again. 'There has to be some mistake here, Mr Fujikawa,' he said weakly.

'No mistake, Mr Hazman. If it had come in all in one piece I would have said that someone in Michael Milken's book-keeping department had gotten careless and made a slip and I would have instructed our people to return the money. But sixteen different transmitting banks from sixteen different areas of the country, all to the same account – your account – it simply cannot be a mistake.'

'Municipal bonds? I don't know the first thing about bonds. They didn't teach bonds as an Economics major at Eureka.'

'They're just a form of money, Mr Hazman.'

'But – how could such a thing happen? This is a *terrible* burden.' Owney was deathly pale. He had developed a tic in his left cheek.

'By all means, Mr Hazman, you must consult lawyers before you accept this money.'

'Please stop bowing, Mr Fujikawa! Forgive me, but I'm really very upset about this – this shocker. It was a very, very irresponsible thing to have done.'

Nonetheless, as he said it, Owney felt the glimmerings of a gloat. What was Dolly's $47 million taxable pittance a year compared to $280 million a year? No matter how many hit albums or movies she had, no matter how much money she made she would have to pay taxes on it, but with the interest accumulation on $4 billion-odd tax-free he would always be $233 million a year ahead of her. A proper relationship would be restored. There would be no doubt about who was head of the house. Not only that but jointly they would easily have enough to pay for the college education of even their grandchildren no matter what the university fees had risen to by then.

'A package also came for you,' Mr Fujikawa said.

'A package? Not more money?'

'I don't think so. But I'm sure you'll want to examine it. Come this way, Mr Hazman.' Mr Fujikawa bowed several times,

217

indicating which door Owney should go through. They entered a small conference room off Mr Fujikawa's office. A rather makeshift bundle had been placed at the end of a long table, next to a pair of scissors and a telephone.

'I'll leave you with it, and see if I can get the identity of the donor with a little more despatch.' Mr Fujikawa left Owney alone in the room.

Owney sat in front of the package. It was wrapped in brown paper and secured with heavy twine. He used the scissors to snip the cord. He unwrapped the package. The contents seemed to be two large books. They were albums. He opened the top volume. On page one, in large letters which had been formed by a small boy's hand, he read the inscription:

OWEN HAZMAN'S STAMP ALBUM
Handle With Care

A chill locked into every surface of his skin. Owney stared at the open page. He felt himself beginning to sweat through the chill. He could smell the family kitchen in the house at Meier's Corners on Staten Island. He thought he heard his mother laugh so clearly that he turned in the chair and looked around him. He began to turn the page but his hand stopped. When his mother had gone away she had taken this album with her. He closed his eyes and tried to control his calamitous heartbeat. What was happening to him? Had he found her at last? Had he found his mother?

He opened his eyes and lifted the second album to the top. He turned the cover. On page one, just where he had pasted it twenty years before, was a photograph of his mother, lovely, smiling sweetly, encouraging him to be happy. Her beauty, as the memory of exactly what she had looked like was returned to him by the photograph, exalted him.

Mesmerized, flung far back into the past, he leafed through the pages. There was picture after picture of his mother, a few of his father, and many of himself. He sobbed chokingly as he came to a snapshot of his mother holding him in her arms. She had black hair and eyes.

He remembered. He recognized her.

Everything about her came back to him like a gust of perfume from the pot roast – boiled beef, really – she had made for him every Thursday, every week as the weeks had become years until he was nine years old and she left him. He recognized who she had been; he knew at once who she had become, but nothing helped him to unlock the mystery of why she had suddenly given him $4,620,000,000.

There was a light knock on the door. Mr Fujikawa entered. 'We have the names of the donors, Mr Hazman,' he said. 'They're all business companies but maybe they'll make sense to you. In alphabetical order they are: the ABC Janitorial Services Company of Butte, Montana; the Acme Literary Agency of Essex, Massachusetts ...' Mr Fujikawa read sixteen company names off the list he held, while Owney stared at him dazedly, hardly hearing what the banker said.

'I must make a telephone call, Mr Fujikawa,' he said. 'Excuse me.'

He picked up the phone and dialled. 'Jeshurun?' he said into the phone. 'This is Mr Hazman. Where can I reach Mrs Noon?'

Chapter 46

Mrs Noon had been asleep at 5.47 a.m. in the Louis XV bedroom of her New York apartment when her private telephone rang mutely inside the compartment of the *étagère* beside her bed. The telephone rings were soundless but each ring was transmitted by wire to an electric stimulator attached to the sole of her right foot. She was wide awake on the second ring.

'Hello? This is Miz Noon?'

'Oona? Wambly Keifetz.'

She looked down at her wristwatch.

'Early for you, Wamb,' she said.

'The tanker *Bergquist* hit a reef in South Florida. Its number four tank was ripped open. The cargo is floating all over the sea and is about to wash up on the coastline over what might be a wide area.'

'Who says?'

'The captain came in on the radio telephone a few minutes ago. So that's that. Within the next hour or so I have to notify the Coast Guard and the Environmental Protection Agency – if ten Floridians haven't already done that. Captain says three planes have already circled over the ship's position on the reef and the sea is awash with two-kilo bags.'

'Anythin' you kin see that we kin do about it?'

'No. Nothing, I'm afraid. Those bags will be up and down the beaches and the tanker will be hooked on the reef and all kinds of people will be looking into that ruptured tank.'

'Hard times for somebody.'

'For you, Oona. The number four tank was your concession and it was unknown to any of the rest of us. It's your trip.'

'Oh, Jesus. Poor Goodie. There goes his chance of ever bein' elected to anythin'. Thanks, Wamb. I better git outta town.'

Everything had happened at one time. The idol of her young womanhood, of her life, the Ayatollah Khomeini, had died the day before and the world was going mad with grief. She was marooned here on the Great Satan's shore, to accomplish the mission which that dear old man had marked for her with his personal vision. 'Destroy the Great Satan,' he had told her in his gentle way. She had not been permitted to be with him since Paris but she would never forget the wonderful years she had had at the side of the most darling old sweetie the world had ever known.

She had been deeply depressed over the death of the Cuddly Mullah, as she thought of him, sitting beside the television set and devouring the hourly news bulletins of his funeral. Everything had piled on her. First the death of her dear old dad and now this injustice of the shipwrecked tanker. It was too much. She broke and wept while she brushed her teeth and combed her hair. When she had pulled herself together again, she made a decision to get out of this life as she had escaped from other lives.

She put her emergency plan into action. It is the least I can do for my grandchildren, she thought. Her grandchildren would face brutalizing tuition fees when their time came to attend universities. She drew a credit-card-sized data bank with an 8K memory out from under her pillow. She called up the phone number of a banker in Council Bluffs, Iowa, and dialled the number.

'Harry. Miz Noon. You better git wide awake. Jes' don't look at the clock. I ain't got much time but this call is to tell you to put Plan A-One into operation as soon as you can raise them bankers. You hear me, Harry? Good. OK.' She hung up.

She swung her legs out of the bed, got a light suitcase out of a closet and began to pack travel things. She showered and then began to dress thoughtfully, looking grim as she thought of what she had just told the Council Bluffs banker to do. She dressed. She walked into the kitchen and, sitting at the table, wrote a note on a lined pad. The note said: *Dear Goodie: You are practically grown up now. I have done all I can for you. Now my turn has come and I am going to find out whether there is any life left on the planet. There is hamburger in the fridge. Love, Oona.* She sellotaped the note to the refrigerator door and, picking up the bag, left the apartment without disturbing any of the stricken Shiite staff.

The doorman got her a taxi. Loudly she told the driver to take her to Grand Central Station. She switched cabs at 47th Street, took the second cab to West 59th Street, took a subway to 168th

221

Street and Broadway, hailed a cab and had it take her to the Teterboro Airport in New Jersey. At Teterboro she hired a chopper to take her to Newark Airport, got aboard a flight to Houston where she changed to a Mexico City flight (using a French passport to get her Mexican entry card) and, on the Air France flight to Mexico City, ate a delicious meal.

She spent the night in Mexico City. The next morning she flew to Rio de Janeiro and settled into a suite at the Ouro Verde Hotel on the beach because the food was good there and the public rooms were quiet enough in such a noisy country that she could converse without shouting. She loved speaking carioca Portuguese, swallowing consonants. She wondered whether she could still wear a *tanga*, the male-dazing string bikini.

She also had some conversing to do in Farsi, she remembered. At 4.15 p.m. on the afternoon of her second day in Rio, she was visited by Nedjatollah Mahboubian, an expressionless man with a nose like a large comma who was the head of the Bureau of Fisheries & Wildlife at the Iranian Embassy. They had a short, grim talk, the results of which Mahboubian agreed to transmit to Tehran. When he left the hotel, Mrs Noon strolled to the writing desk, took up a coloured picture postcard of the hotel and, addressing it to Mr Owney Hazman, 395 West End Avenue, New York, wrote: *Having wonderful time, wish you were here*, and signed it, *Love, Mother (Hazman)*.

Chapter 47

Owney was too confused and numbed to call for Dolly's limousine to get him back to the factory from the Yamamoto Bank. He could only think of one thing: to get home and try to sort this whole blessing/disaster out with Dolly. He took the 57th Street crosstown to 8th Avenue and somehow found his way back to the Apthorpe by bus and foot. He let himself into the apartment with a key. He could hear Dolly vocalizing scales at the piano in the living room. He tottered in. She was startled to see him at such an hour after weeks of his having worked at the factory until eight every night, but also because he looked as if he had been canonized at the same moment he had been hit by a large truck.

'Owney! What happened?'

'You're going to find this hard to believe.'

She looked at her watch. 'But it's executive staff meeting time at the factory.'

He made a feeble wave-away with his right hand.

'Owney! What? Tell me this minute what happened!'

He shook his head with an eccentric looseness which made it look as if it were about to fall off. 'I don't know where to start.'

'At the beginning. For God's *sake*, Owney!'

'The bank called me at two o'clock.'

'Which bank?'

'The company bank.'

'Yamamoto?'

'Yes. The vice-president said I had to go right over there. So I went. Then – then – two things happened. Someone left me four billion six hundred and twenty million dollars and I found my mother.'

'You found your *mother*?'

'Besides all that money – the money is in tax-free bearer municipal

223

bonds – she sent me a package that had two albums in it.'

'Albums?'

'One was my stamp album which she took with her the day she went away. When I was nine. And the other was an album of snapshots. Of her, and of her and me.' Tears began to stream down his face but he didn't sob or choke up. 'So I know who she is, but I don't know where she is.'

Dolly put her arms around him. She kissed his throat and his cheeks. 'Why not?'

'Because she just sent the stuff and when I called her, the man said she had left the country.'

'You called her? Did it say on the album where to call her?'

She led him to the love seat and sat him down gently. She sat beside him. She lifted up his limp arm and put it around her neck like a dead fur piece.

'That's the extraordinary part, Dolly. The pictures in the album – my mother – you know who she was – is?'

'Who?'

'Mrs Osgood Noon.'

'*Whaaaaat?*'

Owney nodded dumbly. 'Now she's gone.'

'No wonder she had tried so hard, over and over again, to do the right thing by you. She was appeasing her guilt.'

'She was giving me her love.'

'Sure, Owney.'

'She left us four billion six hundred and twenty million dollars.'

'Yeah.' The real meaning struck her. 'You can find her! You finally have the money to hire all the detectives in the world and you can find her! With that kind of money behind you, the government will treat you like a royal duke. You'll have the CIA and the FBI looking for her all over the world. She'll never get away from you now, Owney.'

'You think so? You really think so?'

'Owney – four and a half billion dollars! How can you miss?'

He buried his face in his hands like a watermelon in a rush basket.

'Whatsamatta?' Dolly asked.

'Don't you remember the news on the *Today* show this morning?'

'So?'

'That money she gave us was squeezed out of the souls of ten million American junkies. That money has dirt and blood all over

224

it. That's a thousand squalid crack houses and fifty thousand secretaries snorting a quick fix in the company ladies' room. That's the snow-tooting American wounded, Dolly. The mentally sick and the dying.'

'No. No, Owney. Money is only money. It has no qualities. It doesn't carry judgements with it wherever it goes.'

'I can't follow that.'

'Money is only money, not rottenness or glory or whatever was attached to the people who had it before us. That's all it is, it's money, not consequences.'

'That's a woman's viewpoint, whatever it means. I just don't know, Doll. I have to think.'

'There is nothing to think about. Don't get me mixed up.'

'I want to find my mother just so I can talk to her. All my life practically I've been thinking about what I would say to her when I finally found her. How could you run away from me is what I thought I was going to say, the main part of what I was going to say. But now I want to ask her how she could do what she did just to get money. And, doing what she did, why did she have to have so much money? My mother! Jesus, Dolly, how could she do it?'

He sat very still and he wept silently. He manufactured tears. His eyes behind the distorting lenses of the tears were so filled with pain and shame that, as Dolly knelt on the floor in front of him and looked up into his face, she wondered how what had been marked in gold to have been the most shining day of his life could have been transformed into the worst he had ever had.

Three days later, Owney was at the factory having a session in the Meat-Mixing Procedures room with the foreman on duty about a 2.6 per cent production increase.

'I was thinking we could cut down on the sodium silicon aluminate and the BHA oxidant without any loss of quality,' he was saying when Dolly's call came in.

'Cosmetically, that's risky,' the foreman said.

The foreman was winning the discussion so Owney was glad to have to take the call. He took it in a nearby office.

'Owney? Dolly. Don't panic. A postcard just came in for you from Rio de Janeiro signed Mother.'

'Signed ... *Mother*?'

'It says: "Wish you were here."'

'It's a cry for help!'

'That's what I thought.'

'Was there an address?'

'It's a standard hotel postcard. A hotel called the Ouro Verde. She's registered under our name because that's how she signed the postcard.'

'What does that mean?'

'What?'

'Ouro Verde.'

'Ouro means hour, I think. Verde is an Italian composer. It probably means the Verde Hour, like the Telephone Hour on television.'

'I've got to go to her.'

'Today is Friday. You've got the whole weekend.'

'Pack for me. I'll send the driver to get the bag.'

'I'm going with you to the airport.'

'Maybe you should come with me to Rio and bring the kids. She's their grandmother.'

They were calm and matter-of-fact as they spoke but Dolly ached for him because she knew that he was scared. They had been over the territory a thousand times when they hadn't known anything except that they hoped that somehow his mother was still alive and that he would find her. Now that he knew who she was and where she was, all the interior dimensions of his emotions had changed because they had taken the finite shape of a woman who was calling out to him from a known place on the planet.

'I could come with you, Owney. Mama can take the kids for a while.'

'In my mind I've always been alone when I found her,' he said. 'I think I have to do it alone. It would be a terrific comfort if you were there, but I think I have to do it alone.'

By the time he hung up he was almost intoxicated with his victory over his life. 'Do it your way,' he said to the floor foreman, and walked rapidly to the elevator. When he got to the office, he asked Miss McHanic to book an evening flight to Rio out of Kennedy and to send his driver to the Apthorpe to pick up his baggage. 'Mrs Hazman will be coming back with him to ride with me to the airport,' he said.

Doris Spriggs faxed the transcript of Owney's telephone conversation with Dolly to James D. Marxuach at SRS in Langley. He memorized the salient facts of the transcript, then shredded the message. He immediately applied for transport to Rio de

226

Janeiro and put in for a four-minute meeting with Eddie Grogan, the DCI.

'Hazman and the Noon woman have some kind of a kinky code going between them. She's in Rio, registered under his name. Now hear this, chief. She is posing as his mother and she wants him to join up with her in Rio.'

'Ugh! But good work, James D.'

'When I nab both of them, this has to be the biggest collar in narcotics *and* espionage history.'

'Signal me when you have them, James D. We're going to lay on heavy media coverage when you bring them in. This is a White House photo opportunity.'

Marxuach followed Owney aboard the plane to Rio. He sat in the aisle seat directly behind Owney all the way to Brazil.

Chapter 48

Due to the deliberate speed of the camel caravans across Syria the mail delivery from Damascus and abroad reached Mal Olgilvie in En Nebk five days late so, as usual, his copy of the *International Herald Tribune* was six days old. He stared at the story on page one, below the fold, whose headline said: WIFE OF WHITE HOUSE HOPEFUL ALLEGED DRUGS OVERLORD.

He read the story with growing sadness. Not only because the whole thing was going to cost him a heavy loss in income but because one of the most splendid women in the American oligarchy was being smeared. Oona Noon was a fine woman. Not once in the year that his new life had kept him away from the States had she missed a payment of his share of the expensive vegetable cargo her tankers had carried. He had to admire her for that. It had made all the difference to his establishing himself with his wife's relatives in En Nebk and Damascus, and it stirred within him the deepest feelings of loyalty. But, he sighed, that was water under the bridge. Life must go on. He made a mental note to find out whether it had been Mahomet or Johnny Carson who had said that first. Or was it the show must go on, he mused.

Four days before Olgilvie's *tristesse*, in Iran, in the capital city Tehran, three of the sixty-one governing mullahs had read the same news story concerning their key player in North America, and went into action. They sent a message to the resident head of Hizbollah in Syria and told him what had to be done. They called the Hizbollah chief instead of the head of the Syrian secret police because he was one of the nine brothers-in-law of Malachi Olgilvie.

Within twenty minutes of Olgilvie's reading the newspaper story, his beloved wife came wailing into his tent. Alarmed, he sprang to his feet to comfort her. After much soothing and cajoling in guttural Arabic he managed to get the facts out of her.

228

'Not only my brothers,' she wailed, 'but all of Hezb'Allah, the sword arm of the Ayatollah, demands that you return to America to help a woman – a woman!'

He had never denied her anything. Slowly, bit by bit, he got the scraps of information out of her and pieced them together. Somehow, and he found it impossible to understand how or why, Oona Noon was vital to the plans of both the Syrian Hezb'Allah and the rulers of Iran. No matter how he looked at it, it was his duty to take Oona's case and clear her of the charges he had just read in the *Herald Tribune*, and any number of separate parties would pay the going rate, his usual fee of $1,500,000. He held his wife to his bosom and vowed that he would do anything in his power to make her (and her relatives) happy. She dried her tears and left his tent after a long bout on the cushions.

Olgilvie took out a thick loose-leaf address book from a great iron-bound chest and turned to the letter M in the index. He ran his finger down the pages until he came to Monahan, Wiley. He took up the field telephone and began the agonizing process of making a phone call, further straining the system by seeking to speak to a telephone number across the ocean, in Washington, DC.

There was yet another delay while the operator patched in the required listening posts at the secret police headquarters in Damascus; with Hezb'Allah headquarters; with the monitoring mullahs in Tehran, and with the regional police authority for central Syria (who happened to be another brother-in-law of Mr Olgilvie). By whatever magic which was performed, the call to Washington was completed in seven hours, eleven minutes. Wiley Monahan was on the line.

'Wiley. It's Mal Olgilvie calling from Syria.'

'Hey, Mal. Long time no see.'

'I just read the story about Oona Noon.'

'Yeah. Too bad.'

'Yes. Just the same, a problem is just an opportunity in work clothes, as Henry Kaiser used to say.'

'How do you mean?'

'Oona's an old client of mine. And I'd like to make both Oona and me clients of yours.'

'They been talking about arraigning Oona here.'

'Where is she, by the way?'

'God knows. On the lam.'

229

'Call her wherever she is and get her back to Washington. Tell her I'll be there to protect her. Tell her she was actually off on a mission of mercy for her husband when the delayed news of these false accusations reached her and she flew straight home to clear her name.'

'What mission of mercy?'

'You've got to line that up. Find a giant sea turtle and get somebody in Brazil to carve the Pledge of Allegiance to the Flag of the United States in Portuguese on its shell.'

'Brazil?'

'That's where all the big lamsters go. No extradition.'

'Oh. Right.'

'Tell Oona she was in Rio to get this sea turtle surprise for her husband.'

'Will do.'

'Get the best PR people and the entire Institute for Television Gestures & Movements on the problem right away. Pay whatever you have to pay.'

'You want Goodie at the airport to meet her?'

'Goodie and all the network cameras. I want a circus of happiness at that airport. A complete press turnout with not less than three thousand Rent-A-Mob demonstrators carrying signs and protesting the injustice of some sinister force trying to railroad an innocent American woman. Or whatever the PR people figure out.'

'I'll take care of it,' Wiley said.

'I'll be on a plane out of Damascus within eight hours. I'll cable you the flight number and the arrival time. Tell Carter Modred I'm coming in. Alert the White House insiders that I'm coming in. Then set me with the Attorney-General and Eddie Grogan. We've got to straighten this out for Oona.'

'I'm in, Mal. What else do you need?'

'Find that guy who just happened to show up on camera aboard the tanker. The one who accused Oona. Very fishy. The paper identified him as a Bahama Beaver spokesman. Check Keifetz out on him. Find the helicopter crew that brought him there and nail them down. Get the name of the lab that did the bag analysis on the cargo he says he found awash on the beach. That tanker simply could not be carrying cocaine. A Bahama Beaver Bonnet tanker? It's just crazy. Set me up a telephone appointment with Goodie Noon after the White House and the session with the A-G. Find me two independent labs who will testify that the bags in the hold of the *Bergquist* were only sand ballast to balance the rest of the cargo. All right?'

'Got it, Mal. Will do.'

'Got to go now. The camels are waiting.'

Wiley Monahan might have had a certain amount of difficulty in finding Oona Noon somewhere on the planet had not a keen, trained American lawyer been on the case. Monahan consulted several well-travelled friends about the name of the best hotel in the most cosmopolitan city of that country and all three named the Ouro Verde in Rio de Janeiro. He put a call through to Oona and was connected immediately. 'But, my God, Wiley, how did you find me? I changed planes three times and used some old paper I had – this is terrible! If you could find me this easily, then –'

'It's all right, Oona. Mal Olgilvie has taken your case. Everything is gonna come up roses.'

'Mal? Mal's in Syria.'

'He musta read about it. Anyways, he called me and he put a few ideas to work. He'll be here this afternoon, then he's goin' straight to the White House and the A-G. With the amount of money represented here, they'll all understand. You got nothing to worry about. Mal wants you to come home on the next plane.'

'Go home?'

'Yeah. Goodie'll be at the plane to meet you. You just keep telling the press that you were lining up a big I Am An American Day surprise for Goodie in Rio when you were flabbergasted to read the charges against you.'

'Mal said to do that?'

'Yeah.'

'What's the surprise?'

'It's a giant sea turtle with the Pledge of Allegiance to the Flag of the United States carved in Portuguese into his back.'

'Wiley! Goodie will love that!'

'Yeah. And we'll put communications specialists aboard your flight at Miami to bring you up to the right form. Just do whatever they say and cable me the name of the airline and the arrival time from Miami.'

'Wiley, this is tremendous!'

'Thank Mal. He's had me and my people running around like red-assed birds. He knew where to look for the evidence and by this time tomorrow he will have proved that the whole thing was a frame-up by the Medellín cartel.'

'I'll thank him – and you, Wiley – with a big cheque. My God, my money!'

'What? What happened?'

'It – it's all right. Thank you, Wiley, and God bless you. I'll get the first plane out and I'll wire you the arrival time.'

'Enjoy,' Monahan said.

As soon as she disconnected, Oonà began to worry about her money and covering her trail. She put through a call to her apartment in New York. Jeshurun answered.

'Jeshurun? Miz Noon. Has Mr Noon been to the apartment?'

'No, ma'am.'

'You saw that note I taped to the refrigerator?'

'Yes, ma'am.'

'Take it down and tear it up.'

'Yes, ma'am.'

'I am in Rio de Janeiro, Jeshurun. So to save time and money will you please call Mr Noon on Bland Island?'

'Yes, ma'am.'

'Tell him I have been here finding him a giant sea turtle with the Pledge of Allegiance to the Flag of the United States carved, in Portuguese, on the shell of his back, and that I am having it shipped to Bland Island in time for his annual Memorial Day celebration.'

'Yes, ma'am.'

'And tell him how much I am looking forward to being with him again at the airport in New York tomorrow.'

She called Owney at the Apthorpe in the hope of heading him off in case he had got her postcard and had taken it seriously. She had already formed a policy about the money. She wasn't going to crowd him on it; slow and easy, but not too slow and easy.

Mrs Heller, who was sitting with the children, answered the telephone.

'*Sí?*'

'May I speak to Mr Hazman, please?'

'They aren't here.'

'Who is this?'

'This is Mrs Hazman's mother. Who is this?'

'This is Mr Hazman's mother.'

'His mother? I never met you!'

'Is he at the office?'

'How could he be at the office? He left over an hour ago.'

'Thank you. Goodbye.'

As Mrs Noon was being driven the eight miles to Rio's Galeao airport to catch the flight to Miami/New York, Owney and Dolly Hazman were being driven by her bodyguard-driver (with another bodyguard riding shotgun and a car carrying four more armed bodyguards directly behind them) to New York's Kennedy airport to fly Owney to Rio.

'I knew this day would come,' Owney said. 'I had faith.'

'Keep cool when you meet her, sweetheart. Try not to break.'

'I am going to walk up to her, smile, bow slightly, place my hands on her shoulders and kiss her on both cheeks. Then I'm going to look her in the eye and say, "Hi, Mom."'

'Don't bring up the business of the money from the – ah – cocaine. Not in the first few minutes anyway.'

'Sooner or later we're going to have to discuss those municipal bonds. That will lead directly to talking about the cocaine.'

Dolly opened her purse and took out an envelope. 'I brought these pictures of the kids. She's never seen them. She'll want to have them.'

'That was a sweet and thoughtful thing to do.'

'How are you going to handle the – the – ah, cocaine – ah – problem?'

'I thought it all over. She obviously needs me and needs my advice. I am going to give her a choice. Either give yourself up, I will tell her, and we will fight it through every court in the land, or be an outcast from your country and those who love you. Naturally, she'll opt to come home.'

As Mr Olgilvie made his way north by racing camel, he promised himself that he would buy his family the big Mercedes 600, if the government ever put roads in and if his wife would ever hear of such a thing. He was in Washington staring across the desk at the Chairman of the Republican National Committee within nineteen hours.

'Carter,' he said to Carter Modred, 'in about an hour I have an appointment with the Chief of Staff at the White House and, forty minutes after that, I will sit down with the A-G. This Oona Noon nonsense simply must stop. There is total documentary proof that she is absolutely innocent. The sinister charges must already have had an effect on the candidacy of her husband, the most superbly financed candidate ever to run for the highest office of this land, and that is saying something, as you know.'

'I can tell you it near broke my heart to think of losing Goodie –

with that kind of money – as standard bearer in '92. I served with Ronald Reagan. I have known Ronald Reagan. Ronald Reagan is a friend of mine. And, to me, Goodie Noon *is* Ronald Reagan.'

'Well, I'm on the case and it is all going to be cleared up by this time Monday. Oona gets in from Rio tomorrow morning. Goodie and the international press will meet her at the airport. I have the proof of how this entire nonsense happened. Goodie's campaign money is safe.'

'What do you want me to do, Mal?'

'Tell the White House that you are convinced that the whole thing is a criminal conspiracy to get the blame away from the Medellín cocaine cartel and to debase the Bahama Beaver Bonnet Company – if you, or the President, can imagine such a thing happening.'

Within thirty-five minutes Mr Olgilvie was facing the feisty Chief of Staff in the White House. He was establishing his case within slightly more than a day after the agony of getting the call through to Monahan from En Nebk.

'Don,' he said, 'a Federal Grand Jury on this thing can only end up by embarrassing the administration. In the longest day of your life could you ever believe the Bahama Beaver Bonnet Company, the biggest in Big Oil, the biggest in communications and banking, would countenance one of their tankers transporting controlled substances? The captain of the tanker is outraged over this. Wambly Keifetz and everyone in between is outraged over this. Here' – Mr Olgilvie opened his briefcase – 'are two reports from two independent laboratories who analysed the contents of the bags in the number four tank of the *Bergquist*, the tank from which the bags were said to have leaked out when the tanker hit that reef. Sand! They were the ship's ballast! And heaven only knows where the ten bags came from that fellow says he found on the beach, except that it was Florida – the Keys of Florida – the smugglers' paradise. He had to be there straight from the Medellín cartel.'

Fifty minutes later, in the Attorney-General's office, he produced documentary proof that the son of a bitch who had made the crazy charges against Oona Noon – *Oona Noon!* – was a British outcast who fronted for the Medellín cartel, a man named Fanshaw. He produced a deposition from one Hermione Rooney (a woman who just hours before, thanks to a tip to the head of the studio from Wiley Monahan, had been signed by a major motion picture company to appear as a featured dancer in a musical extravaganza), which said that Fanshaw had confessed to her that he had been the bag man for the Medellín syndicate in the United States for the past seven years. 'He's the biggest catch the DEA could make, next to the ringleaders in Medellín, Colombia,' Mr Olgilvie said.

The Federal Grand Jury investigating Oona Noon was dissolved. Frederick F. Fanshaw was arrested as he was loitering outside the British Embassy in Washington.

'The lightning work of getting that Rooney woman the movie contract was the decisive point, Wiley,' Mr Olgilvie said. 'You did a superb job there.'

'She was a very ambitious girl,' Monahan said. 'Then, when she tap-danced for me early one morning, I saw the solution. I got a lot of satisfaction seeing this thing work itself out.'

'It won't be forgotten, Wiley. All of this is what the Republican Party stands for and we have a great man in there as our leader. You could get the President's Medal for this.'

'Jeez, that's the same as a knighthood,' Monahan said.

Subsequently, in fifty-one days' time, Freddie Fanshaw was sentenced to forty years, without the possibility of parole, in the Federal Penitentiary at Winsted, Connecticut, for a criminal conspiracy to deal in illegal narcotics. The evidence was so damning that the British Foreign Office could do nothing; unable to admit internationally that the fiend who had ruined the lives of millions was actually a secret agent of the British government who had been charged with foiling the very criminal organization which would benefit from the distribution of the cocaine. Nor could Fanshaw explain in his defence why he had appeared out of the sky on the deck of the tanker or who had sent him, without compromising his allegiance. He knew the rules. Caught red-handed, no one could lift a hand to help him. Perhaps after ten or fifteen years his government would put a discreet word in with the right people in Washington and he would be paroled. He certainly hoped so.

In the tradition of his service, MI6, for the duration of Fanshaw's sentence 'someone' saw to it that a tin of Lyle's Golden Syrup was delivered to his prison larder on the first day of each new week. Fanshaw's pension rights were protected and he was decorated *in absentia* in a little ceremony in the Red Lion pub in Waverton Street in London, which was attended by six of Freddie's close colleagues, including his control, Alan Melvin.

The Fanshaw trial was an internationally sensational one which tripled American television advertising revenues for ten days. Freddie was dazed by what had happened but, in a vast way, grateful for one thing. He had been charged and sentenced under the name of Fanshaw, not Featherstonehaugh, so his sisters would never know of his shame.

Chapter 49

By the time Owney reached the reception desk of the Ouro Verde hotel in Rio, he had worked himself into such a state of anticipation of actually, finally, finding and facing his mother at last that he was close to fainting. As he approached the desk, James D. Marxuach, although seemingly disengaged, was right behind him. Owney's head throbbed at the base of his skull in the classical hypertensive manner, his steps faltered, his hands shook and his face was a ghastly mask. When the room clerk told him that Mrs Hazman had checked out that morning to fly to New York, Owney's legs gave way and he went down. Two page boys quickly helped him to his feet. Gripping the reception desk for support he asked if the clerk was sure that Mrs Hazman had checked out.

'We secured her air ticket to New York, sir,' the clerk said, 'and our limousine drove her to the airport.'

Marxuach was appalled.

'What is your name, sir?' the receptionist asked Owney.

'Owen Hazman,' Owney whispered.

'Ah, Mr Hazman,' the clerk said with professionalized joy, 'Mrs Hazman left a communication for you.'

He turned to a rack, extracted a stack, and extended a letter on hotel stationery to Owney. 'Will you be staying with us, Mr Hazman?'

Owney collected himself. 'No,' he said, 'but I would be grateful if you would book me on a return flight to New York to leave as soon as possible.'

While Owney took the letter to a chair in the lobby, Marxuach went to a telephone. He called the CIA station in Rio and spoke to the chief.

'Richert? Marxuach. Did Langley tell you I'd be here?'

'Yes, sir.'

'I'm in the lobby at the Ouro Verde. Send me the best pickpocket in Rio.'

'Yes, sir.'

Marxuach hung up and returned to his post across the lobby from Owney who was absorbed with reading the letter. The letter said:

Dear Son,

How I have longed to call you that! But so much time had gone by that I decided – although I tried to help you in every way I could – that I didn't have the right to come back into your life. Malachi Olgilvie has cleared up the mis-understanding about the burst oil tanker, about which you may have read in the newspapers, and I have been summoned home. When you return to New York please telephone me at my apartment. (Jeshurun will know where I am at all times.) We will want to know each other in our new, true capacities and to talk over the premature transfer of those bonds (although there will be a handsome bonus for you in any event). The porter is here for my bags. I must go. Do try the sausage at Mario's, the best churrascaria *in town. The concierge will tell you how to get there.*

With all of my love,

Mother

Owney read the letter through slowly four times. He had found her! It was real! She had acknowledged that he was her son so she had to be his mother. Who else beyond Dolly would know such a secret? Dolly had never, ever had any opportunity to talk to Mrs Noon. His mother! Mom! Twenty years later, years in which his life and mind and yearnings had been filled with dreams, schemes, plans and hopes of finding her and now, at last, that he had found her, she had been sweet and thoughtful enough to remember his interest in sausages at a very, very stressful moment of her life. There could be no doubt that he had indeed and at last found his mother. It was worth ten times the journey of five thousand miles.

He fell into a reverie of the Christmas mornings to come where, surrounded by his children, his adoring wife and his kindly mother, he joined into the thrill of happy-making carols, urging God to rest the merry gentlemen with nothing them dismay. He thought of his mom in the kitchen at the Apthorpe, flour up to her elbows, sliding pies and cakes out of the oven and telling him that he could

238

lick the bowl. He stopped to reconsider that one. He wondered whether his mother, after so many years of being Mrs Osgood Noon, still had the baking knack but he tossed the doubt out of his mind. Of course she could still bake! It was like swimming and bicycle-riding: once learned, never forgotten.

A page boy brought Owney a message from the desk which said that his air tickets would be available at the head porter's desk in two hours' time, and the limousine that would take him to the airport would leave at 5.00 for a 7.30 flight. When the page left, Owney wondered whether he should call Dolly with the news that his mother had left for New York, but he decided against it. He went back to the lobby chair and reread the letter.

A tall, thin, coffee-coloured man entered the hotel. He went to the desk and made an enquiry. The clerk directed him to James D. Marxuach who was seated nine feet away. Marxuach and the man met in mid-lobby.

'The kid reading the letter in the chair behind me.'

'*Sim?*'

'Get the letter.'

'*Sim.*'

Owney walked dreamily to the porter's desk, handed over his American Express card and received the air ticket to New York. He asked for directions to Mario's restaurant. The porter, an enormously stout, impressively uniformed man, wrote the address on a slip of paper and told him to give it to the cab driver.

On the way to the front door and the taxis, a tall, thin, coffee-coloured man bumped into Owney, was enormously apologetic, then disappeared towards the bar. Owney went out, asked for a cab, gave the address to the driver and went off to Mario's restaurant with James D. Marxuach in the taxi behind him.

The sausage was called *linguiça*, which he was told was also a word for sausage, or *longanzina*, which Owney decided he preferred because the long part signalled more value for the money. It was a magnificent taste sensation: finely ground; spicy; its casing gave it a wonderful crunchiness, that tell-tale barbecue pop; and it had a very strong perfume. It was a ponderously large sausage but, Owney reasoned instantly, there was no reason why it couldn't be tailored to a frankfurter size. He insisted on paying the head waiter the equivalent of ten dollars for the *longanzina* formula and bought four raw sample sausages to take with him. The *longanzina*, the maître d' explained with pride, was heavily

239

smoked; the ground pork cooked in vinegar pickle and stuffed into hog casings. The wonderful smell of it came from cinnamon, cumin, garlic, and red pepper. Owney rushed back to the hotel where he sent a cable to Gordon Manning who, since the merger, had been his full-time pork buyer:

HAVE DISCOVERED THE MIRACLE TASTE SEN-SATION WHICH WILL DOMINATE SUMMER BAR-BECUE SEASON. STAND BY FOR NEXT YEAR'S WEENIE AWARD WINNER IN NEW BRAUNFELS. WILL BE IN OFFICE WITH SAMPLES TOMORROW.

He had found a great new sausage and he had found his mom! Or rather, he corrected himself, he had found his mom and she had guided him to find a great new sausage. He settled back in the hotel chair to reread his mother's letter. It wasn't there! He went through every pocket he had but he couldn't find it. He felt a deepening despair and, for a moment, feared that he was going to burst into tears in public. The most important thing in his life had been settled by a letter written by his mom's hand, scented subtly and reassuringly by that hand. Why couldn't things just go along smoothly with things connected to him and his mom, the way they happened to other people? But on the other hand, he realized gratefully, he had a lot to be thankful for. Because of his mom, he had found a great sausage opportunity. The *longanzina* would be the sausage choice of America when the barbecue season began next Memorial Day. There could be another Weenie in it at the next Academy Awards. But even winning another Weenie and making another $4 or $5 million was nothing compared to the most wonderful thing that had ever happened to his life. He had that sausage because he had found his mom!

He went for a walk along Copacabana Beach to study the string bikinis which were utterly useless in trying to conceal the behinds on hundreds of beautiful ladies who had been arranged by the Brazilian Tourist Board all over the sand. James D. Marxuach followed him.

Staring out at all those fulfilling boobs and bottoms, Owney decided that he liked Rio. He was grateful to his mother for bringing him here. All at once in a great surge, the entire merchandising plan for the *longanzina* sausage came to him. He would change its name, add a slogan, and sweep the barbecue pits of North America. He would call it:

'LONG 'n' EASY'

Just Like Summertime

A Bar-B-Q Bonanza!

A densely built man with the physical frame of a fire hydrant appeared at his side, flashed a set of credentials, and spoke to him with a strong Massachusetts accent.

'I am James D. Marxuach of the Central Intelligence Agency,' the man said. 'We wanted you to know that we know that the woman who calls herself your mother is the key Iranian spy in the United States and that we have a complete record of your own complicity.'

'Are you some kind of homo-erotic?' Owney answered coldly. 'Is this how you think you can fill your unnatural agenda?'

'When the woman who calls herself your mother lands in New York she will be arrested and charged. If you set foot outside Brazil, you will be arrested and charged.'

'Since when has the CIA warned its suspects?'

'Listen, kid. You're young. You've got a life ahead of you. Tell me all you know about the woman and how she has used you, and you'll get a much better deal.'

'You have a warrant?'

'I have notified my people to arrest Mrs Noon when she lands in the United States. You are and have been an accessory to her crimes.'

'Crimes? What crimes?'

'She – and you as her agent – have flooded the United States with cocaine to sap the health and morale of the American people.'

'You are some kind of tourist crackpot, mister. Either you stay away from me or I'll report you to the US Embassy for impersonating a government official.'

Owney turned away from the beach, no longer seeing the orchard of beauty, knowing too well that the man's allegations had been true. His mother was deeply involved in cocaine. How she could be seen as an Iranian agent bewildered him, but whatever, he had to get word to her somehow because if what that man had said was true and she was going to be arrested when her plane landed in New York, that would subtract her once again from his life, just as he had (almost) found her. But he had no idea of how to protect her. He would have to ask the airline to wire the pilot of the plane, if she had not already landed in New York. What kind of a message could he ask them to send? He couldn't tell her to get off the plane in mid-flight. He couldn't ask the airline to radio a warning that the CIA would arrest her on arrival in New York. He had spent his life yearning for the moment when he would find her, when he would know who she was and she knew who he was, and now it was all to be snatched away from him again. It was too much.

Marxuach didn't follow Owney across the esplanada to the hotel. When Owney had left him, he had somehow turned involuntarily to face the garden of boobs and bottoms bulging out of hundreds of *tangas* on the beach directly below. He stood, transfixed, staring with lust in his heart at the great carpet of bosoms and behinds which were so barely concealed. He was dazed by what he saw. For a moment, he forgot what he had been sent to Brazil to do. At last, the discipline of a lifetime, a quarter-century of responding to duty, forced him to follow his quarry but he was bemooned, struck dumb by the overwhelming wonders of what he had seen on that beach.

He was in a trancelike state as he stepped down into the Avenida Atlantica to cross over to the hotel when he was hit by a large Mercedes 600 limousine, knocked nineteen feet forwards and nine feet upwards into the highway where he was struck again by an oncoming postal truck which returned him to approximately where he had started the cross-over. At some point between the two collisions he died. Owney was well inside the hotel when the tragedy happened. The chauffeur told him, much later on the way to the airport, that a man had been killed in front of the hotel that afternoon.

As Owney was driven away from the hotel towards the airport his elation/anxiety over the discovery, not only of his mother, but of a great new sausage opportunity, had left him as air leaves an open-mouthed toy balloon.

James Marxuach had forced him to remember the shame which he would never be able to cleanse from his memory. The thought of the $4,620,000,000 his mother had given him landed on his mind with the force of a battleship's anchor falling into the polluted sea. After twenty years of yearning for his mother, listening for her step, answering the telephone every time it rang hoping it was she calling, now that he had found her a terrible cloud hung over his victory. She had made $2 billion or more, she had said, out of the sale of her tankers, but all of the rest of the $4,620,000,000 she had transferred to his name had come from the death and degradation which went with cocaine. His mother, his own beautiful, beloved mother, had been spoon-feeding cocaine to millions of Americans as if she had wanted to destroy them to make the country die.

He wasn't sure he wanted to find her any more. She was the enemy who would have sold her cocaine to her own son if he had wanted to buy it. He decided that he didn't have to get the answer to the riddle – because he knew the answer. No acceptable human could do such a thing to get $4,620,000,000. Counting his inheritance which had been drawing interest, plus the $720,000 which had been his share to date from the sausage business, he had about $900,900 of his own. That is, his and Dolly's. Dolly had $20 or $30 million, after taxes. That was all hers. He didn't want a cent of it, but even if she insisted on contributing something to the family's overheads, such as the upcoming university fees, they could still only eat so much, wear the same fixed number of clothes, and spend so much, even ignoring what it was going to cost to send the children to college.

But his mother had accumulated $4,620,000,000 by climbing on a pile of American corpses and might-as-well-be corpses. He had to know what had made her do it. How *could* she have done it?

At police headquarters in Rio de Janeiro, Captain Eberto Sa Pereira stared mournfully at the letter which had been found on Marxuach's body. 'The poor son of a bitch,' he said. 'He had just found his mother and this had to happen to him.'

The body was claimed by the CIA station chief within two days and shipped back to Washington. Under agency tradition, it would be buried with secret honours in a covert cemetery on an out island of American Samoa. Eddie Grogan, the DCI, was puzzled by the letter. 'It's funny,' he said in passing to his Director of Operations, 'I never thought of a guy like Marxuach ever having a mother.'

'Still, it had to be, chief,' the DO said. 'It's a biological necessity.'

Chapter 50

Before Mrs Noon left Brazil the American news media had shocked and rocked the nation with revelation after revelation about the oil tanker which was allegedly spewing out cocaine upon a Florida beach. These sensational charges were sustained by the stark accusations of 'the mystery man' who had claimed on camera from the deck of the stranded tanker, within hours of its striking the reef, to be the representative of the Bahama Beaver Bonnet Company, operators of the ship. The total reversal, the actual turning point of public opinion, came when Wambly Keifetz, CEO of Bahama Beaver Bonnet, denied that his company had any connection with such a man who had charged that Mrs Osgood Otto Noon, wife of one of the leading candidates for the office of President of the United States, had been responsible for the deadly cargo and had profited extravagantly from it.

Wambly Keifetz, greatest of the great American business executives, a revered philanthropist and art patron, actually appeared as the leading guest on an all-star Sunday-morning talk show of American pundits to say, 'Sinister forces are at work here. Sinister foreign forces who live by murder and kill for profit. To attempt to put the blame for their crimes upon a helpless woman, who is the wife of a great American statesman, is criminally and poisonously reprehensible. I say whoever this man is who said he was speaking for my company, he must be apprehended, investigated, tried, and convicted, for he is a peril to the American meaning as we know it, a peril to everything we stand for, and I, for one, cry. "Shame!"'

The pundits, led by George Will, gave him the first standing ovation for any statement ever made in talk-show history.

Immediately after that, at a press conference attended by 317 members of the worldwide print press, and the cameras of all five American networks, as well as twenty-seven camera crews of

244

overseas television companies, the same Wambly Keifetz, the traditionally inaccessible board chairman and CEO of the Bahama Beaver Bonnet Company, coldly repudiated the mystery man's presence and plausibility, stating that, whoever the man had been, he had not represented the Bahama Beaver Bonnet Company nor any of the other owners or lessees of the tankers in question, therefore he had to be trying to manipulate the American people into believing heinous lies. Mr Keifetz brandished laboratory reports of the samples taken from the tanker accident, proving for all time that they had been bags of sand, used for the ship's ballast, and not controlled substances as the imposter had charged.

'This is a colossal mockery of everything America stands for,' he cried out into the cameras, 'that the devoted wife of a great patriot be so accused! That my company, in my family for five generations, should be another innocent party to such a slander. That the People's Republic of China could ever participate in such rotten, rotten crime! I have ordered that every record, every accounting of the Bahama Beaver Bonnet Company be turned over to any government commission which most certainly will be called to investigate this outrageous injustice. I demand such an investigation to clear Mrs Osgood Noon's immaculate name!'

The 'mystery man' had disappeared and, out of nowhere, the Vice-President of the United States, in charge of the Anti-Drug Task Force, and the Attorney-General, in charge of the Drug Enforcement Administration, identified the 'mystery man' as the representative of the Medellín cocaine cartel in North America, and proved that Mrs Noon was not only entirely innocent of such wild charges but that she, and through her her husband, had been the victims of a shocking attempt by drug overlords to influence the election to the highest and most sacred office known to civilization.

When Mrs Noon landed in New York, the entire airport, if not the entire world, seemed to be celebrating something as prodigious as Lindbergh's landing at Le Bourget in 1927 or Ronald Reagan's retirement from politics in 1989. Monahan had arranged for two extremely loud brass bands, one from the US Marine Corps playing Sousa's 'Semper Fidelis' and one from the Boy Scouts of America, which played 'Hello, Dolly' in unison, on either side of the wide tarmac which Mrs Noon would need to cross in a wonderfully choreographed series of waves. The bands, in uniform, had been flown in from the nation's capital.

Over four thousand Rent-A-Crowd people had been assembled with their printed placards saying 'Welcome Home, Oona Noon',

'Osgood Noon in '92' and 'Death To The Dope Barons'. Thirty-one television cameras and crews had been assembled on scaffolding which Wiley Monahan had had erected to ensure total coverage. The Vice-President of the United States and Mayor Koch were standing by inside the terminal with the Republican senator for New York and a lady general of the Salvation Army.

Goodie Noon, pale but composed, waited with them for his entrance cue, receiving instructions from the Director of Washington's Institute for Gestures & Movements, a Conservative think tank. 'We have a highly trained representative aboard the flight with Mrs Noon,' he told Goodie, 'and all of Mrs Noon's movements and gestures will be coordinated with yours.'

There were 273 print media reporters and photographers on the tarmac. The historian of the Republican Party stood with Goodie, notebook at the ready.

Monahan had put a make-up woman, a PR authority, and the country's top television Gestures & Movements arranger aboard the plane during its refuelling stop-over in Miami. From Miami to New York, the Republican National Committee had reserved the entire first-class compartment of the plane for the rehearsal operation.

'Everything depends on how you react to questions in front of those cameras, Mrs Noon,' Miss Mendelson, the PR authority said. 'One slip and ninety million people who will be watching will know you are guilty.'

'Guilty, honey? Guilty of whut?'

'That's it. That's good.'

The Gestures & Movements arranger took over. 'Mrs Noon, for the first shot, as you appear at the top of the ramp coming out of the plane?' She ended the sentence with a lift as if it were a question.

'What's your name, honey?'

'Julia. Julia Sweeney. We want you to seem to ignore the cameras when you appear at the top of the ramp, turn around, and shake hands or hug one of us to give the television audience the informal feeling that you aren't concerned at all about what is ahead, that you had a wonderful time on the flight, are totally relaxed about everything, and had almost forgotten to say goodbye to a new friend.'

'What about the other passengers?'

'They'll be taken off in the finger at the rear of the plane.'

'That is good thinking.'

'Then, smiling broadly, and we have a little Rembrandt kit here to paint your teeth up to a dazzling white, you wave at the Rent-A-Crowd which has massed all over the concrete apron, just as pleased as Punch because you have spotted your husband in the mob. He is battling his way through, trying to get to you – the key cameras will be cued into showing the business of his bursting happiness at seeing you again, et cetera, et cetera – our people are working with him now – then they'll cut away to you as you start down the steps. There won't be any passenger tunnel, just the usual stair-ramp that is used only by hatless politicians.'

Miss Mendelson broke in. 'Now the flowers schtick. At the bottom of the ramp a jolly fat man will hand you a bunch of flowers – we were able to get Willard Scott to do the bit at his usual commercial rates – you give him a big kiss *but* you don't keep the flowers, about two hundred dollars' worth, you hand the entire beautiful enormous bouquet to the 107-year-old lady who is standing beside Willard holding his hand. She'll be on the show this morning to get her birthday congratulations from Willard. She will stagger and almost go down under the weight of the bouquet, but you will catch her and the expression of gratitude on her face will win you more points with the viewers.'

'Oh, lovely, hon. What do I do with the flowers?'

'Hold them high, getting them in frame with your face – we'll be going into close-up here – unless you are allergic to flowers, of course. In that case hand them to the Vice-President when he comes on line.'

Miss Sweeney said, 'Now – you see your husband, he's about eight feet away, fighting to get through the most uncontrollable crowd since the 21-day Hindu festival of Kumbh-Mela at Allahabad, Uttar Pradesh, India in 1966, and the wonderful joy of it fills your face. You are really going to have to show it, Mrs Noon, because we have cued every camera for full close-up as you bring this handkerchief we are going to prepare for you up to your face, and what's on it will bring tears of happiness to your eyes – at least the ninety million will see it as happiness because of the way you'll be smiling – and the two of you will rush into each other's arms. Then comes the tough part.'

'Whut?'

'The interview,' Miss Mendelson said.

'Now don't you fret yo'seff 'bout that.'

'The Dixie accent is very good, Mrs Noon. Maybe if, when the time comes, you could lay it on even thicker?'

'I'm witchew, honey.'

'Mr Monahan and Mr Olgilvie have prepared this briefing book which would seem to cover everything.' Miss Mendelson took a 512-page ring binder out of her briefcase. 'We'll spend the rest of the flight going over this, line by line,' she said. 'It contains twenty-nine ways to deny that you had anything to do with ridiculous charges concerning what turned out to be sand ballast. *Oil tankers need to be stabilized.* Keep telling yourself that. You've got to memorize the sense of this whole study because it might not be exactly the way it happened.'

'Me an' Mal Olgilvie have been tellin' it like it ain't for many a long year, hon,' Mrs Noon said. 'Don't worry about a thang.'

When the plane landed the enormous Rent-A-Crowd surged forward with such violent force that the police were unable to restrain it. It was not until the National Guardsmen and the mounted police moved in that the great mass of rented bodies could be brought under control. Four satellite up-link trucks were standing by, feeding eleven world television networks, when Miss Mendelson got the OK from the White House television-liaison spokesperson, Juan Francohogar, over the walkie-talkie that the cameras were ready for Mrs Noon to come out. Mrs Noon appeared at the top of the embarkation ramp, blonde and beautiful, to thunderous cheers and the almost deafening music of the two bands playing their conflicting scores.

Instead of waving to the crowd and the cameras in acknowledgement, she turned at the top of the ramp to give a farewell embrace to someone directly behind her, then, moving with great good nature, she turned and executed a wonderfully gracious, movingly dignified but difficult wave (no. 12 in the Reagan canon) to everyone in view, including the ninety million television consumers in North America and in forty-one countries overseas. The wave was a basic variation of the emotional, enormously sincere Ronald Reagan wave which had been institutionalized by him in 1981 and used throughout his reign as he got on and off the helicopter which kept taking him and his wife to and from Camp David. The Gestures & Movements Institute had amplified the original wave and, if such were possible, had packed it with even more sincerity and emotion during the long experiments in its labs. The effect was electrifying. The Rent-A-Crowd roared out its affection and delight.

Mrs Noon descended the mobile staircase mixing a leitmotif of

248

no. 8 and no. 3 waves which had been rehearsed on the flight north from Miami. She accepted a huge bouquet of flowers from Willard Scott and, in turn, made the gracious gesture of presenting them to the extremely old lady at his side, then saved the dear thing from falling under the weight of them. Mrs Noon stood, head high, bestowing upon the cameras the gift of a smile such as had not been seen on a human face since the wonderful screen moment when Lassie came home. She lifted the prepared handkerchief to her face. Her eyes stung with the impact of it but tears of joy welled up as she stared out at her husband.

Osgood Noon was waiting at the foot of the ramp beside the Vice-President. 'Goodie, you look jes' wunnerful!' Mrs Noon exclaimed, enfolding his long, thin frame in her arms. While the cameras recorded her every move, Mrs Noon held her husband by the shoulders at arm's length and said, 'Looks to me as if your nasty old cold is a lot better.' Ninety million people looked at each other and smiled softly.

After shaking hands with the Vice-President and kissing the little old lady, the trio, Mrs Noon and the two men, moved along the red carpet, passing crowds which were 146 deep on each side, and entered the airport building where the combined international press was waiting for them.

The Vice-President made the opening remarks to the assembled press and television. 'This happening thing, the business of the oil tanker thing, is an all-too-familiar pattern of shame to me in my relentless work of strangling the narcotics thing which would, if it could, attempt to make its way into these United States. It reveals a dastardly plot by the Medellín cocaine crowd of Colombia, in South America, to attempt to shift the horror of – uh – drugs to one of the oldest and most respected oil companies in our history, the Bahama Beaver Bonnet Company. In doing so, they intended to ruin the candidacy of the leading candidate for the Presidency of the United States by manipulating the truth thing to make it seem that one dear woman, the candidate's wife, Mrs Osgood Noon, was the perpetrator of the whole of this shocking outrage. If it weren't so absurd, so cynically sinister, it would be the most comical charge of the year. Well, the facts have been revealed. What the paid Medellín messenger boy said was some evil kind of dope was actually bags of sand which were needed for ballast. And now, the beautiful victim of this conspiracy. Ladies and gentlemen, I give you Mrs Osgood Noon.'

'Mrs Noon!' a voice from the press yelled. 'How do you plead?

Innocent or guilty?' That got a long and hearty laugh.

'Mrs Noon!' another voice shouted. 'Why did you flee to Rio de Janeiro?' It was a humorous question, delivered in a kindly manner.

'Well,' Mrs Noon said, smiling abashedly, 'it's jes' sech a personal thing that it's gone sound silly to y'all. I heard about this giant sea toitle? – my husband is a patriot and a Flag historian? – which had the Pledge of Allegiance to the Flag of the United States carved into the shell of its back? – An' I said to muhseff that I jes' hadda git that ole toitle fo' Goodie Noon.' There was heavy applause from the assembled news media who, at heart, were a sentimental bunch. When it died away Mrs Noon said, 'So I flew down to Rio an' I bought the dang thang fer Goodie.'

Goodie Noon took a lot of soothing on the trip home to Bland Island aboard the Herkybird which had been designed to seat seventy-five troops, until Oona had finally persuaded Goodie to let her turn it over to an English decorating team who had gradually modified the Texas ranch-house interior into a really comfortable living room which was a replica of the large drawing room at St Bartholomew's in Dorset with its certain accents as they had been imitated in the country houses of the British royal family. Goodie had resisted at first when Oona brought him the sketches but she said, 'Pooh, Goodie, whatta you know about Texas ranch house decoratin'. You never been in one.'

'I saw *Giant*,' Noon said. 'You know how I am about Texas and Elizabeth Taylor.'

'That's exactly what I'm drivin' at!' Oona told him. 'These sketches not only represent the best there is, but they replicas of the rooms she worked in the movie *Ivanhoe*.'

'I can only tell you it was awfully confusing, Oon,' he said to his wife, 'when those television people invited me out on my own horseshoe pitch to ask me, on camera, what I thought of you being the Queen of Cocaine.'

'Bad staff work!' Oona Noon answered sharply. 'How could your people send you out there without a briefing?'

'They just screwed up, I guess.'

'All any one of them had to do was to call the apartment in New York and to find out where I was and why I had gone there. You know I never leave anywhere without overconfidin' everythin'.'

'Golly, it gave me a terrible turn to hear questions like that out of the blue, I can tell you.'

'Goodie, I cain't wait for you to see this turtle. It is *enormous*. It has a shell as wide as a Minuteman silo, and right across it, in carved-on Portuguese, is the Pledge of Allegiance to the Flag of the United States.'

'And to the nation for which it stands,' Goodie said.

'The danged thang moves so slow anybody can read the Pledge without squintin'.'

'Golly darn, I can't tell you how sweet you were to go all that way just to support my hobby,' Goodie said. 'When will it get here?'

'What with Brazilian red tape for the export and customs here an' this an' that, they told me it would be 'bout four months.' The carver had told Monahan it would take at least a month to find the turtle and at least three more to carve the translation of the Pledge into it.

'It could be here for my birthday! Oh, neat!'

'What you been doin' all this time I been away?'

'I reached a decision on assault rifles, Oon. For one thing, about the first thing I'm going to do after I'm elected is going to be to limit the ammunition clips for those things to not more than forty bullets. That would protect the public and yet be fair to the sportsmen of the inner cities. And I have a peachy idea to reduce the deficit.'

'How's that, sweets?'

'I think we should take the Department of Defense out of the national budget. Because of its unique status as defender of our liberties, just like other government sponsored enterprises, it is too sacred ever to be touched by the Congress so it should be off-budget just like the Postal Service.'

'Brilliant, hon. You gone make a great President.'

'Of course all that stuff is gonna have to wait till I can cut those terribly unfair capital gains taxes.'

Chapter 51

Owney went directly to his office in Long Island City from Kennedy Airport when he came in from Rio. He asked Miss McHanic to call his wife and to bring all department heads into the boardroom for an executive meeting. He handed her the package of *longanzinas*. 'These are six Brazilian sausages,' he said. 'Have Reyes grill two of them, give two to the lab for analysis, and serve the grilled sausages, three bite-sized pieces to a plate, as soon as all the department heads have been seated.' He strode into his office and stared out of the window until Miss McHanic had Dolly on the line.

'Doll?' he said into the telephone. 'I'm back.'

'You missed her.'

The brutalizing scene of grim-faced CIA agents putting handcuffs on his mother flashed across his mind. He wanted to weep for her but, even more than that, for himself and his heart-breaking need.

'I'm so sorry, sweetheart.'

'I suppose the whole thing was played out on television.'

'Oh, yes. They invited me to the airport to help greet her. Not as her daughter-in-law, but as one of the, you know, celebrities, but my security people decided that that much of a crowd would be too much of a risk.'

'*Greet* her? Ce*leb*rities?'

'It was tremendous, Owney. We all watched it on television. Although I haven't told the children she is their Grandma yet.'

'On *tele*vision? My mom? When? What is this?'

'Last night. It's on every front page.'

'Was she arrested?'

'Ar*rest*ed? How do you mean?'

'How do I *mean*?'

252

'How could she be arrested? The Vice-President of the United States, the man who has spent every minute in that office fighting narcotics, was there with the Mayor of New York and the official Boy Scouts of America Band.'

'I don't understand.'

'She's innocent. That's been proved beyond a shadow of a doubt.'

'But she can't be.'

'Why not?'

'All that money. Those bonds.'

'Oh.' There was a pause. 'I see what you mean. But, hey, she could have won it in fourteen or fifteen state lotteries.'

'The odds against that are pretty long, Doll.'

'I just hate to think ... we're going to have to sort this out, Owney.'

'I'll be right home. I have to have one meeting then I'll get out of here.'

He hung up and went into the boardroom adjacent to his office, joining the department heads who had begun to wander in.

They sat around a long directors' table, all wearing the three-quarter length white coats of their profession. Owney tried to carry on as if he only had one thing on his mind, the greatest single barbecue opportunity that had ever salivated the taste buds of a great nation, but he was so depressed and confused by the events which had swirled around his mother that the product had to speak for itself.

Craig Olsen, the chief butcher, Gordon Manning, the pork buyer, Carmen Figueroa, the spices specialist, and Armand Coudert, the stylist, were immediately joined by the sales manager, the merchandising chief, and the head chemist for a full-scale intra-departmental meeting. They had hardly been seated when Miss McHanic entered with a large tray which contained small dishes holding bite-sized pieces of *longanzina*. All five executives began tasting at once.

'Say! This is excellent!' Gordon Manning said. 'What is it?'

'I don't think this is gonna need much modification,' Miss Figueroa said. 'This is some kinda sensational hot dog.'

The enthusiasm was as great as if someone had opened the door a crack and had flung a half-basket of Burmese rubies across the carpet.

'This is it,' Owney said. 'This one is going to sweep the entire

253

barbecue market beginning next Memorial Day and we've got to
be ready for it.'

'But what is it?' the merchandising man asked. 'Whatta they
call it? Who eats it? I been in this business thirty years, how come
I never had it before?'

'I found it in Brazil,' Owney said to the hushed respectful room.
'They call it the *longanzina*. We're going to call it the "Long 'n'
Easy, The Barbecue Sensation". Always one phrase. Never said
any other way.'

All heads turned to Gordon Manning who was the elder statesman in the room. 'That is sensational,' Manning pronounced.
'The name will sell even better arreddy than the sausage. Which
is as it should be, the American way. Throw in a little television
advertising and maybe a coupon campaign and you've got an extra
twelve million gross to carry you over the summer.'

'Frankfurter size!' the stylist shrilled. 'And why shouldn't we
create our own line of barbecue sauce?'

Miss McHanic appeared in the doorway.

'Mrs Noon on line two, Mr Hazman,' she said.

Owney excused himself from the meeting and left the boardroom.

Chapter 52

Owney picked up the telephone on his desk. He felt dread that, if he said the wrong thing, he would lose his mother again, perhaps this time for ever, but at the same time he knew he had to say the right thing, which to her would be the wrong thing, all of which made him think fuzzily, and uncertain about what it was he should do. He wanted to throw his head back and scream. His anxiety made his hand as wet as a working mackerel and the phone slipped away from him before he could lift it, clattering back on its base and startling him so that, to steady himself, he made the long, slow, shaken walk to the kitchen refrigerator to get a pitcher filled with iced tea and to drink from it directly without pouring it into a glass. Some of it spilled all over his tie which had arrived two days before from a supplier in Charleston, South Carolina who specialized in ties that showed authentic British public school and university colours. Time was spent drying the tie carefully, then, taking a kitchen towel with him, he returned to the telephone in the study, wiped the instrument dry and dialled his mom's number.

He was trembling on the edge of the greatest moment of his life. Everything he had striven for since he had been nine years old was signified with each electronic ringing sound that alarmed his hearing within the telephone earpiece. Every moment – well, almost every moment – for 7,310 days he had planned what he would say when he found her and confronted her. Over the years the speech he had finally approved in his heart was slightly different from what he was able to say when he spoke to her as his mother. He had meant to say, 'So we finally meet? Long time no see. How have you been?'

Jeshurun answered.

'Jeshurun?' Owney said, deflated. 'Mrs Noon, please. This is Mr Hazman.'

'Mrs Noon is on Bland Island, Mr Hazman. Do you have the number?'

'Yes. Thank you.' Owney hung up and dialled the Bland Island number, Mrs Noon's private number.

When she answered the phone he blurted, 'Hello – uh – Mrs Noon? Ravi? Ah – Mom?'

'Owney. Mah babuh!' Mrs Noon's voice broke.

Owney couldn't speak.

'Owney, I'm out here on Bland Island with Goodie but I'm gone git inta the chopper right now and head inta New York. I'll probably git to my apartment before you kin, but I want you to be there as soon as you kin make it. Did you get my postcard?'

'Yes.'

'Did you go to Rio?'

'Yes.'

'Purty little place, ain't it? Well, we'll talk at the apartment. 'Bye now.'

Armand Coudert put his head in the doorway. 'Owney, what would you think if I put a stunning black stripe to contrast with the pinkish casing all along your Long 'n' Easy?'

'Coudert!' Owney was flabbergasted to hear such a proposition from his chief designer, a married man with four children. Then reality fell upon him to inform him again. 'Put it to a vote, Armand,' he said, 'I've been called into town.'

Owney dialled his home number.

'Doll? I'll be late. She called.'

'She called *you*?'

'Well, no. Actually, I called her. That is, I called her back.'

'You poor darling. It must have been a paralysing experience for you.'

'She's on her way in to New York from Bland Island. In the helicopter. She wants me to meet her.'

'What are you going to tell her?'

'I don't know.'

'It's so *hard*, Owney.'

'We'll see how it goes. I'll be right home after that.'

The Shiite ground staff at Mrs Noon's building moved him across the lobby and into the elevator. Owney had the feeling that they were being especially solicitous – but how could they know? he asked himself. Inside the apartment, Jeshurun settled him in Mrs Noon's salon but Owney refused the ritual glass of champagne.

256

Mrs Noon entered wearing a Gallanos modification of the costume of a light-refreshments seller in the Temple of Osiris of some five thousand years before. It consisted of a longish pink and white heavy cotton kilt under a short green tunic which, with her platform shoes, made her seem about seven feet tall as she filled the crystal-and-light-framed doorway.

'Owney,' she said breathily.

He took a deep breath, then let it go out of him slowly. 'Hi, Mom,' he heard himself answer. He could not believe he was saying those wonderful words. She was standing there. He could reach out and touch her. He could put his arms around her the way he had dreamed for most of the past twenty years. Twenty years of thinking of very little else and now she was here, beside him, more radiant than he had ever been able to imagine.

'Oh, Owney. What a cruel, hard time this has been.'

'Nearly all my life,' Owney said.

'I drove out to that racetrack that Satdee, nothin' on my mind but linin' up ole Mal, then – no warnin' – he introduces you. This Owney Hazman he says.'

'Then you knew? From the first day?'

'I thought I was gone turn to stone, or melt away, or start to cry or jump outta that car, throw my arms aroun' you an' lock you inta my soul. Nothin' ever hit me like that. There you was, my baby, a grown man, lookin' at me with the blank eyes people have fo' strangers. I wanted to yell at you, "I'm you Mama", but I couldn't do it.'

'Why couldn't you? If you had only done that, everything would have stayed the same as it was when I woke up that morning. Dolly wouldn't belong to everyone in the world instead of only to me. I would have had my children.'

'The thick glass walls of time had dropped down all around me, Owney,' she said, talking brokenly. 'They was jes' one way out – straight ahead, away from the past. I could look back through the glass, I could see where I had come from, where I had done you wrong – that was my punishment – but I couldn't go back, Owney. There was too much at stake.'

She saw his eyes harden. 'No, no! Not the money. The country! I was the wife of a great man, a future President. If you could hear him drillin' the servants in the Pledge of Allegiance every mornin', standin' there so tall with his hand over his heart; if you could see him working like a dog – he does massive aerobic lip exercises to be in complete control of his lip movements so that anyone, anyone

257

in this country, could read them the way he wanted them to be read – so he would never have to say that terrible word "taxes" to the American people who had been trained away from taxes and into that historical deficit and national debt by Blessed Ronald Reagan ... I knew I had to sacrifice. But when I saw you standing there so handsome, so much the same as that little boy I had lost, I knew I had to find a way around them sacrifices. I had to keep you near me. So I set it up with Mal to make you the contact man an' that's what started up all the trouble which I brought into your life from that day onwards.'

Not from that day on, Mom, he wanted to say. Until she had begun her terrible confession, he had planned to pour out on her the whole story of what his life had been like from the day she had run away from him, but he couldn't do it. He couldn't pour his misery on top of her misery. It wouldn't be right. So he just stared at her with eyes as shiny and unblinking as a duck's and wondered whether all the pain was just about over or would it go on and on and on.

'Owney, try to see it my way. I had to run out on you because your daddy was forcin' me to run out on my whole life. I wasn't runnin' out on you but they was no way I could take you with me. It wasn't nothin' else I could do. Yo' daddy said that he was gone turn the whole guvmint against me an' –'

'It's OK. It doesn't matter now,' Owney said, suddenly remembering what James D. Marxuach had told him in Rio, trying to be blithe because, no matter what, he had found his mom. 'But the mind sure plays tricks. I just don't remember you ever sounding the way you sound. I must have just blanked out. I had no memory at all that you came from the South. I had this crazy memory that you came from Indian Head, Saskatchewan.'

'Well –' Mrs Noon said.

'But then I don't remember you being blonde either.'

'Memory is a traitor, son.' She suddenly dropped the Dixie accent entirely as if she had always spoken with Canadian speech. 'But anyhow, we have the rest of our lives to talk over the Mother's Day stuff. What we have to get organized now is the bonds I turned over to you for safe keeping. It was a lot of money and you were the only one I could trust.'

He stared at her sadly.

'So what we have to do now is tell your bank to redistribute those bonds back to where they came from, but let me tell you that I don't expect you to have go through all that trouble for

258

nothing. You are going to get one per cent of the value of the whole securities package for what you did for me, but I need to get moving now, Owney, so please call your banker.'

'No,' Owney said.

'*No?*' She was not startled, she was horrified. She tottered backwards, reaching to a chair for support.

He had been steeling himself to say that to her since he woke up that morning. He had lain rigidly on his back in the bed all through the night, weighing every aspect of what he had to do. First he had to face his mother and make her realize that he had forgiven her for deserting him so long ago. Then he had to set her straight on those bonds. He took into account that his mother couldn't be alone in what she had done and that some other very powerful entity owned a share in all that money but, when he arose from bed to sit on a stool in the cold shower the next morning, because he was just too weak and weary to try to stand under the onslaught of the water, he knew that, whatever the cost, he was going to have to deny his mother almost at the moment he had found her.

'It's all dirty money,' he said slowly. 'Money that came out of the sanity of this country, so I'm not turning one penny of it over to you.'

She was shocked straight back into the Dixie accent which she had made a part of her life for almost twenty years.

'Four billion six hunnert an' twenny million *dollahs*? An' you think you gone keep it?'

'I'm sorry, Mom, but that's the way it is.'

'Baby, some people gone kill me, I don't get that money.'

'I thought about that, too. We've got to reach a compromise.'

'A *com*promise?'

'If I give you back enough money to keep your people satisfied with whatever they consider their share, providing it is within reason, then you have to agree to get out of the cocaine business. Totally. One hundred per cent. And to take them out with you.'

'How you expect me to do that?'

'Ask your people.'

'What are you gone do with all that money?'

'Maybe form a Foundation which would try to convince people that they shouldn't use cocaine.'

'Owney. Owney – you don't know nothin' 'bout people.'

'The Foundation would grant you whatever minimum amount

259

it has to to keep your people from bothering you. How much is that?'

'I don't know. It been runnin' about a billion a year for this an' that. But mainly they wanted to plough it all back into the whole operation so's we could widen the popularity of cocaine around the country.'

'Shocking.'

'Politics is a shockin' bidniz.'

'How does politics come into this?'

'I cain't go inta that. My people are in politics and they don't like the United States.'

'But that's crazy. How can anyone not like the United States?' It was an impossible concept.

'Well, they been ploughin' back about a billion a year into popularizin' cocaine in this country.'

'Part of that had to be your share.'

'Well – yes.'

'What did you expect to do with all that money besides getting a lot of people like your husband elected?'

'Goodie's never been elected to anythin'.'

'He's going to run for the nomination for President next year and that takes a lot of money.'

'I cain't git it through my head that you gone try to keep that money, Owney. It makes me frightened for you.'

'How come?'

'My people got goals. They different from anybody you know. When they fine out you got the money and you won't give it back, they gone lose they mind.'

'Are you going to tell them that your son has the money and that he won't give it back?'

'No. No way. But banks have to tell thangs. It's jes' money to them. I – I jes' cain't think how I'm gonna protect you, son.' She imagined she could see Jeshurun and Elek knocking Owney unconscious and stuffing him in a laundry bag then transporting him to a big plane somewhere and flying him out to Tehran. She could hear Owney's screams while the mullahs persuaded him to release the money.

'I'll arrange for my own protection, Mother,' Owney said stiffly.

She tried not to stare at him too hard. She sat at the piano and began some riffs, then moved into a medley of 'Mother Machree', Jessel's 'My Mother's Eyes', and Jolson's 'Mammy' while Owney went to a window and stared out towards his factory in Long Island City.

'You know what I'm thinkin', Owney?' she said dreamily while she played the hymns.

'No.'

'I'm thinkin' that my people might decide to have you killed if they knew you had that money.'

'If they did that they'd never be able to get the money, would they? Anyway, what are we talking about? It's just a bunch of bearer bonds. How is anybody going to prove they're mine?'

'They are not yours!' The Dixie accent was gone. Mrs Noon's speech had turned itself into the harsh, clipped accents of American television. 'You know what torture is? Well, that's what they're going to do to your mother if you don't hand that money over.'

'I know all about torture, Mom.' He couldn't believe what he was saying. He never knew he had the kind of resolve that had overcome him when he knew that his mother was one of the main cocaine pushers in the country. It was all so different from what he had thought it would be. It was like being invited to a great party then deciding not to mingle.

'But whoever it is you're talking about, Mother, they know you transferred the money so it seems to me as if they'd be coming after you.'

'They don't know yet, son.' She moved on into an emotionally chorded piano arrangement of 'M Is For The Million Things She Gave Me' with a lot of fancy right-hand riffs on the keyboard. 'What are you going to do with the money if you won't give it back?'

'I have to think about that. I have to talk to Dolly.'

'Your wife?'

'Yes.'

'That's nice.'

'You don't really think, in this day and age,' Owney said earnestly, 'that anyone would think of killing anyone for four billion six hundred and twenty million dollars?'

'You'd better run along now, Owney,' Mrs Noon said. 'I have a lot of thinking to do.'

He stood undecided about what he should do but he did what he had to do, what he'd thought so much about doing for most of his life. He went to the piano, leaned over and kissed her on the cheek. 'I'll call you tomorrow,' he said, 'after I've talked to Dolly.'

'That kiss was the nicest thing ever happened to me.'

Owney rushed out of the room before he began to weep. He knew he was right but he felt fifty ways a traitor to the woman who had meant more to him than his own life. But she had taught him from the earliest days that he was able to understand that no matter what happened he had to do what was right. He had done that. He was right and Dolly would support that.

Chapter 53

When Owney left, Mrs Noon called Wambly Keifetz on his very, very private number, so private that, although it had been installed in 1964, twenty-five years before, no one had ever called him on it.

A startled shout came through the phone to her. 'Who? What? Who is this?'

'Wambly? Ravi Noon.'

'Jesus! You scared the hell out of me. What the hell happened that you called this number?'

'Where are you, Wamb?'

'I'm in the vault at my house on 64th Street.'

'If I come over right now can we have a meet?'

'In the vault?'

'Absolutely in the vault.'

'OK. Come on over.'

'Ten minutes.'

Wambly Keifetz was the heir to the prodigiously powerful and chillingly successful Bahama Beaver Bonnet Company, which controlled most of the construction, communications, fossil fuels, insurance, downtown real estate and the banking business throughout the world. Money came in so fast to the Bahama Beaver Bonnet Company that even the astonishing skills of two Cray super-computers were two months behind in trying to count it. Nonetheless, as one of the people who owned a large share of Ronald Reagan, Wambly Keifetz had been taught to understand that he could never have enough of it.

The Keifetz residence was a knock-together of six former private houses on East 64th Street, each one with a forty-foot frontage.

The Keifetz Public Information Department had worked for 1,351 man-hours to establish, via the news media, that it was the most expensive square-foot-for-square-foot residence in the Upper East Side of Manhattan, humbling even Donald Trump. A simple comparison of building costs had shown that the Taj Mahal had been brought in for 327 per cent less than Wambly Keifetz's costs for his dwelling, allowing for the inflation over the ensuing 338 years.

A footman showed Mrs Noon into an elevator which took her straight down for seven storeys into the bedrock of Manhattan, then debouched her directly into the main Keifetz vault. Wambly Keifetz was waiting for her as he fondled packets of large-denomination currency notes.

'Would you like a cup of Bovril?' he said hospitably. 'An Orange Whistle?'

'I could use a stein of Jack Daniels, Wamb,' she said. 'I hadda rough morning.'

He put the order through an inter-com.

'This has all the earmarks of an emergency, Ravi,' he said perceptively. 'You've never come down here before in all the years I've known you.'

'You believed so much in the Reagan revolution,' Mrs Noon said, 'that I know how much you must believe in Goodie's cause, Wamb. So I knew I could turn to you.'

'I can't tell you how that flatters me, Ravi.'

A bell sounded. Keifetz went to a cabinet door built into the wall and slid its panel open. He removed a tray which held a bottle of bourbon whiskey, a tub of ice cubes, two glasses and a decanter of water. He brought the tray to Mrs Noon. She made herself a tall, very dark brown drink.

'Wamb,' she said, sipping, 'you remember those vegetables that made all that fuss when your tanker hit the reef in the Keys?'

'Indeed, yes. I thought you managed that awfully well.'

'Mal Olgilvie organized the whole thang, actually. I must leave you his phone number in Syria.'

'Damned good man.'

'Anyways, I got to get out of the vegetable business. What with the primaries only three or so years away and Goodie bein' right on the edge of greatness, I figure the best thing is to git out.'

'You're probably right.'

'I thought you might like to take the whole thang over – the coca plantations, the processin' plants, and the vegetable product itself. And I can turn the whole distributor-retailer organization over to you.'

'Mafia?'

'What else?'

'Damned good people.'

'It's a real goin' thing.'

'Well, I must say it's very tempting. Now that we're operating the tanker fleet, that is.'

'It's been turnin' over a nice, steady billion-six a year and the good Lord knows it's the fastest-growin' business in the country. My investment bankers' projections show it has to go to three billion a year in eighteen months and keep goin' up after that.'

'I'd like to see the figures,' Keifetz said amiably.

'I had a good run of it. When Nicky an' me went into the business fifteen or so years ago, it wasn't hardly doin' ten million a year an' now look at it. But the White House means a lot to Goodie and that last ruckus sure gave botha us a bad scare so I decided to git out.'

'What did you have in mind?'

'The usual four times earnings, I guess.'

'Six billion four?'

'Let's round it out to six-five.'

'Well, I don't see why not. If the figures check out. Does Goodie know about the vegetable business?'

'Hell, no.'

'Then let's keep it that way. Let's keep him sweet for the history books. I know him and, as President, he's going to want to declare a crusading war on drugs. He's awfully dim but he is a predictable man.'

Owney sat facing Dolly in the living room of their apartment at the Apthorpe. The children were in Central Park with the two nannies and three bodyguards.

'So you found your mom,' Dolly said. 'I just can't believe it.'

'I'm still kind of in a daze.'

'And you never had to touch your capital.'

'No.'

'Was it everything you had always dreamed about, Owney?'

'Well, in a way I guess it was. But mostly she wanted to know about the money.'

'She wants it back?'

'There was some pretty crazy talk. She said her people were

capable of killing whoever had the money but that there was no way they could know who had it because it's in bearer bonds and she says she isn't going to tell them.'

'How can she not tell them if they torture her?'

'She mentioned that.'

'It's an awful lot of money, Owney. And after they get it out of her, they'll come after you.'

'Not with George Bush in the White House. No one is going to defy a law and order concept as mighty as four billion, six hundred million dollars.'

'Owney! Why are you so stubborn about accepting the money I make? We don't need their damned four billion six hundred million! Even after the children's college educations are paid for there will still be enough to take care of both of us.'

'No.'

'Owney, I'm making forty-seven million a year!'

'It isn't that. Let's remember that we have children and that we want those children to be able to say that, no matter what, their parents did what was right. Really, sweetheart. The rotten facts are that the money my mother transferred to me in bearer bonds came from the enslavement of the American people to a habit which wrecks their sanity, ruins their health, and is bringing this country to a standstill, all to get money. What do you think will happen to frankfurters if the men and women at my plant are moved effortlessly into the cocaine habit? Frankfurters will be gone from our culture. No! I cannot do it. I will not return that money. But I won't use it myself or for us and the children either because it is tainted money.'

'What are you going to do with it?'

'I'm going to have Schwartz, Blacker, and Moltonero form a Foundation and, while the money accumulates three or four hundred million a year in interest, I'm going to think about what that Foundation should do with it.'

Chapter 54

Dolly was disconcerted when Oona Noon telephoned from New York to ask if she could come to the Bel-Air house to see her. Dolly, with Owney's full agreement, was in California for cast readings of the script for her next picture, and for costume fittings. The children and their tutors and bodyguards were with her. What with the movie, the record company demands, the meetings for the following week's television show on which Donald Trump, Colonel North, and Charles Manson were to be guests, as well as the intensive planning required for the up-coming personal appearance/full scale performance tour of twenty-seven American and Canadian cities, Dolly scarcely had the time to spare for Mrs Noon. Nonetheless, she knew how important to Owney such a meeting would be (and she also wanted very much to meet the woman who was not only the grandmother of her children but would undoubtedly be the next First Lady), so she pushed the fittings back into what amounted to the early morning, did the reading with the principal cast from eleven until two, cancelled the rest of the schedule for the day, then showered and changed to be ready to meet her mother-in-law.

She dressed herself with great care: as the idealized conception of a wife and mother, with not a whiff of rock star anywhere, no screen idol, not a reek of the television force which brought her into 63,521,849 homes all over the world every Sunday night. She was about to meet her mythologized mother-in-law for the first time, but she was determined to do it on humble, everyday terms.

Dolly had forbidden any of the bodyguards to answer the door when Mrs Noon rang the bell, even though two of them had been dressed as footmen. She opened the door herself, wearing an apron and with just the hint of a smudge of flour on her left cheek. 'Oh! How nice!' she said when she saw Mrs Noon standing there, but

267

she made the extraneous movements she had gone over with the dramatic coach to show that she was flustered until she could get out of the apron and lead her mother-in-law across the foyer to the drawing room.

Dolly *was* flustered, in a way. In her wildest dreams she had never thought she would be entertaining the woman who had scored so many photographs in the W magazines she had pored over in earlier days when the world had been new, before she had played golf with the Pope or had brought Mike Tyson and Henry Kissinger together for a charity bout on her television show. This legendary woman who was standing on her threshold not only controlled America's cocaine supply but was an intimate of Nancy's and of Jerry Zipkin's, and wife of a man who might well be the next President of the United States.

'I made some scones,' she said in greeting. 'They're a Puerto Rican delicacy. I hope you like scones.'

'I adore scones,' Mrs Noon said. She had abandoned deep Dixie to speak with the purest Saskatchewan clarity and precision.

When they were seated, the two housemen/bodyguards came into the room, one tottering under an extraordinarily heavy antique silver tea service, the other wheeling a sweets trolley which had been copied, trolley and cargo, from the wagon at the Chewton Glen Hotel in deepest Hampshire, England, where Dolly had rested during one of her UK tours, with Lee Iacocca and Raisa Gorbachev.

Mrs Noon had taken equal care with her style of dress. She had retained the services of a theatrical costume designer (who had two current hits running in New York) to create clothing for this meeting to project a sober, stable, yet friendly image. As the costumier had said, 'What we are reaching for here is a cross between the conservatism of William F. Buckley, jr and the flamboyance of Cher.' Mrs Noon wore a dowdy Republican hat complete with a garden of milliner's flowers over a natural chinchilla body stocking which was worn under a severe navy blue suit jacket, cut in the style of those worn by New England whaling captains in the last century. Her shoes were sensible low-heeled brogans with diamond-crusted heels and buckles in the Pilgrim Fathers' style. As they were seated, ready to face the enormous tea, the front doorbell rang. The taller bodyguard went to open it. He returned at once. 'Packages, madame,' he said to Dolly. 'We will need to X-ray them.'

'Ah,' Mrs Noon said, 'no need for that. They are just some toys and things I brought along for the children.'

'How very kind of you,' Dolly said.

Mrs Noon had flown to LA from New York in one of the new supersonic Stealth fighter-bombers, transport which she had set up through Wiley Monahan and the White House without bothering Goodie, because she hated commercial airline travel. With the noise suppressors over each ear and by thinking constantly about how she might get her money back from Owney, she had had a pleasant hour and twenty minute ride. A nice little family heli-copter which Dolly had sent along to meet her took her from the LA airport to Dolly's landing pad which was just twenty-six sweet feet higher than the Reagans' in Bel-Air.

Dolly did her best to be welcoming because, despite the implied but jagged threats her mother-in law – her mother-in law! – had made to Owney, threats which now surrounded the prodigious tea like cannon peering down from a fortress, this was, nonethe-less, the mother whom Owney had been denied for most of his life and for whom he had given up most of his thinking hours as he had desperately sought to find her again. The intensity of Owney's yearning had carried over to her so she felt that she had suddenly come upon something as mythical as a politician's conscience; as rare and as priceless as clean air.

Mrs Noon, unaware of her son's gigantic sense of loss since he had been nine years old, was – while not as all-encompassing in her compassion as her daughter-in-law – uncharacteristically for a woman of the world, uncertain how she should say what she had come to say or even how to begin the conversation without having to ask after her grandchildren who were not her primary interest. She compromised by starting with small talk, looking for the opening which would allow her to say what she had to say; studying Dolly intently as she nattered on.

'I wonder if you will agree,' she said, sipping tea from a shell china cup which had cost $195 (wholesale), 'that the most utterly captivating ladies' room in the world is in the Parrot Club, in London.'

'Really?' was all Dolly could answer. The statement had an opposite effect from that which Mrs Noon intended. Instead of disarming her it made her wary. This was a devious, dangerous woman, she thought. She is trying to set traps for me.

'It's a private club for women in the Basil Street Hotel which is well worth joining for its lavatory facilities alone.'

269

'I'm really happy to hear that, Mrs Noon.'

'Should you wish to join – for you never know when you'll have the need while in the Knightsbridge area – I should be happy to put you up for membership.'

'I had always thought the very best world-class facilities were in the Palace Hotel in Lucerne,' Dolly said evasively, 'where my parents took me one summer. All that immaculate marble, lavish mirror work, the profusions of cut flowers, the undeniably efficient electronic flushing systems, as well as the built-in toilet-bowl fountain bidets were just the most well-thought-out conveniences I had ever seen. But I was just a child then.'

'Well! I must look into that,' Mrs Noon said.

'Why do you admire the facilities at the Parrot Club?' Dolly asked. She sensed that the Parrot Club was the key to this woman's intentions.

'It's just that – they're so *different*! The setting is so bizarre. It was actually a converted passenger platform from an abandoned subway station – a really long cavernous room, painted pink, with pink stalls and pink pull chains at the far end. Along one wall they have laid out a counter with every sort of hair spray, deodorant, and, as a blessing for the weary shopper – the club is very near to Harrod's – foot powder.'

'The English know,' Dolly said, watching her every word. 'My father often speaks of a men's room in a pub in the St John's Wood section of London which had huge water-filled transparent glass tanks over the urinals. The tanks also contained exotically coloured tropical fish and when the urinals were flushed and the water was emptied from the tanks, the fish would almost – but not quite – be left entirely dry until the renewing floods of water would refill the tanks and the fish would swim to the top.'

'How perilously theatrical!' Mrs Noon said. 'What a pity we will never see it because we are women.' Two very real tears, pressed out by the tensions of the meeting, welled over and rolled down her flawless porcelain cheeks.

'Mrs Noon!' Dolly said with dismay that was compounded by the overwhelming notion that her mother-in-law was about to ask for something which she would be unable (and unwilling) to deliver.

Mrs Noon patted the air in front of her with the fingertips of one hand while she dried her cheeks with a tiny lace handkerchief. 'Please forgive me. It just came over me that Chandler Hazman, my late husband – Owney's father – had been overcome with

270

admiration for the men's room next to the coffee shop at the Madonna Inn in San Luis Obispo – here in California, that is.' She sniffed noisily. 'He told me with awe in his voice that it was all copper: copper washbasins, copper paella pans as mirror frames and the most overwhelming urinal he had ever hoped to see. It was one long, enormous copper trough which was flushed at one end by a stupendous copper waterwheel.'

'Fascinating.'

'Oh, my dear. It has been wonderful talking with you today. You are so understanding. You have brought me great comfort. How are the children?'

'Just fine. Really fine.'

'What are they called?'

'Molly, Franklin Marx, and Bonita. Molly after you – that is the name Owney remembers you by from when he was a little boy.'

'He was a sweet little boy, heaven knows. Now he has become a difficult man.'

'Difficult?' Dolly asked innocently.

'Oh, it's all a mish-mosh. I had to go to South America to track down a sea turtle for my husband. Because travel can be dangerous I left some bonds with Owney and now he refuses to give them back to me.'

'He told me about it.'

'It is a terrible misunderstanding and Owney has placed all the blame on me. It just isn't fair. My late husband, Nicky Nepenthes, owned all those oil tankers as you may know. Unbeknownst to me, he was using the tankers to move certain – ah – vegetable products to the United States. When he died I inherited all that and I thought the rather enormous income which kept going into my bank accounts was just profits from the tankers – which, of course, it was . . . in a way.'

'Yes,' Dolly said.

'Do you think Owney really intends to keep all that money? Four billion six hundred million dollars?'

'Owney is determined to use the money.'

'*Use* it?'

'He is with his lawyers now. He is going to form a Foundation to combat the use of narcotics.'

'But – that is un-American!'

'I don't understand.'

'Honey, Americans live on narcotics! They start the day with caffeine-packed coffee or tea. They chew prescription speed to stay awake, then they need downers – which their doctors prescribe. All day long they stay whacked out drinking caffeine-packed Coke or Pepsi. They look at an average of 6.8 hours of straight fantasy every day on television. The hard cases even watch C-Span! If that isn't a hard narcotics addiction, what is? And another thing that makes the whole thing un-American – the same people also smoke tens of billions of dollars' worth of cigarettes every year.'

'If I may say so, Mother, the issue here is cocaine, not cigarettes.'

'Of course it's cocaine! How do you think those teensy little South American Indians make cocaine? Eighty per cent of the chemicals used to process the cocaine in Colombia, Peru, and Bolivia come from the United States. And it's not me saying that, it's the Drug Enforcement Administration talking. Acetone, toluene, methyl ethyl ketone – all American made – that's what makes cocaine.'

'But you were making the issue cigarettes.'

'The issue, where Americans are concerned, is, has been, and always will be only *money*! Last year in this country, two thousand people died from cocaine. In that same year, cigarettes killed 390,000 people. And that's *government* statistics! You think that's all? A government study found out that nine out of ten people who try cigarettes become addicted but only one in six who tried crack did. But none of the countries of the world can get the United States to stop exporting cigarettes – it's a matter of conscious American national policy. That makes the United States the most deadly drug-trafficker in the world today. Lemme tell you that my people are so bugged about this that they are thinking of filing a formal protest against the US barriers to free trade in cocaine with a petition against the unfair trade practices of the cigarette companies.'

'But – really – how can you compare the two?'

'How? Are there really any differences between cigarettes and cocaine? They are both major US health problems. They are both addictive. They both cause disease and disability and death. But Americans have to have them both. And on top of that they load their heads up with booze and beer and wine – known narcotics – then, to be able to sleep at night, they have to drop Valium or sleeping pills. Does Owney's Foundation think it is going to wipe all that out?'

'I think – I may be wrong – that Owney will concentrate on the hard drugs.'

'But, honey, if fifty billion dollars' worth of hard drugs is sold every year – and that's how they score it – who exactly is using them? The American people, that's who is using them! The voters, and I'm talking millions of voters, not just the poor folks and the black folks. Like one out of every four drivers between the ages of sixteen and forty-five who were killed in New York City traffic accidents tested positive for cocaine use. That was just between 1984 and 1987, God knows what the figures are today. That's from the Chief Medical Examiner of New York. Fourteen per cent of New York's population uses cocaine regularly. Multiply that by the whole country and you've got almost thirty million people.'

'That's shocking!'

'But why is it? How come that figure got so big all during the Reagan Administrations? Because he got the people thinking only about how to get the money! He put heavy pressures in this country – have you priced *bread* recently? That steady pressure is unhealthy, sure, but no politician is going to knock the American way of life. So, if the American people aren't to blame, who is? A bunch of foreigners, that's who is: Colombians, Peruvians, and Bolivians who grow it and ship it; Mexicans, Panamanians, and Cubans who smuggle it in – they are the ones who forced our innocent people into using drugs. So which end of that whole puzzle is Owney's Foundation going to tackle with my money? And when are these warlike government agencies going to do anything about cigarettes?'

Dolly started to try to answer but Mrs Noon poured more words over her.

'Jesus, honey, do you realize what Owney is going to be up against? Do you know how much the banking industry is taking down while they wash billions and billions of dollars in and out of their banks from Miami to California and all points north and south in between? And don't ask who they are washing it for – it isn't just the Medellín cartels and the Mafia, you know, there is also some very big money involved, and I am talking the biggest. Ever wonder why insurance premiums is so high? Cocaine isn't good for the health. It shortens the life. The insurance companies suffer if they don't keep raising the premiums. You want your husband to tangle with people like the banking and the insurance industries and the other heavyweights who own this country? Let that bunch protest by pulling their stocks and bonds out of the market and they'll make their point because you'll see a big depression. Political campaign money will dry up overnight.

Politicians who are not capable of thinking about anything else but getting re-elected are going to panic. Overnight, you'll see packaged, nationally advertised, legalized cocaine in every super-market in this country. Is that what Owney wants? Owney and his Foundation with his tiny four billion six hundred million is going to be steam-rollered like you never saw it happen anywhere.'

'Owney believes – I think – that the people caught buying cocaine should have their driver's licences confiscated.'

'Jesus, I must talk to Owney. He's getting in way over his head.'

Chapter 55

Owney had had a bad shock that morning. Unable to sleep, he had risen early, discovered that they were out of bread, and had gone to a German-American bakery where he had been charged $2.39 for a loaf of oat-bran bread which he felt he ought to eat because the television programming, commercials, and commentary had gone berserk about recommending anything made from oats or bran.

'My God, Mr Kuby,' he said, 'when I was a boy this bread cost thirty cents.'

'Lissen,' the baker said, 'when I was a boy this bread was a dime. But who had a dime?'

Owney hadn't been able to sleep well because of the excitement generated by the almost incomprehensible yet unassailable fact that he had found his mother. In all the years since she had left, each time he had decided to spend his inheritance to hire investigators to look for her he had hesitated and had believed he had not sent people out to look for her because of some innate thriftiness. But in his heart he had known that he had not taken the step because he knew that he would never find her, not that way, the world was too large; but now, due to cocaine, the abomination which was evaporating the mind and will of his country, she had been delivered to him. He was also overstimulated by the interest of the partners at Schwartz, Blacker, and Moltonero, the law firm charged with forming his Foundation. On hearing the amount of the proposed endowment for the Foundation, all three partners had attended the meeting at $1,550 a hour each. Owney was on a high. He had not only found his mother, he would redeem her.

When he got home from the bakery there was a message on the

answering machine to call Dolly in California. He called her immediately.

'Owney? Your mother was here yesterday afternoon, then she stayed right through dinner. She didn't leave here until almost one o'clock this morning.'

'My mom? In *California*? At our house?'

'You better believe it. I mean – it put me in serious trouble with my work. Over 117 people had to be held out of meetings.'

'You've got to learn to delegate, Doll.'

'Delegate? She filibustered me! Nine hours! She flew out and back from New York in a fighter-bomber – Jesus!'

'But what did she *want*?'

'She wants her money back. She had about nineteen separate arguments on why you had to give her the money. They involved every aspect of American life, plus all the mullahs of Iran, the Libyan-connected IRA, various Mafia hit persons, the CIA, and big bank reprisals – oh, Owney! – except she never made any threats, it was just sort of like she was a very, very sophisticated civics teacher.'

'Well, if she stoops low enough to try to get at me through my family, I have to say that I am very disappointed in her. But ...'

'But what?'

'Well, maybe she didn't want to just charge in on me cold. Maybe she wanted to tip me off that she was upset by talking it over with you.'

'For nine hours? By ignoring the children? By telling me that Colonel Ghaddafi has thirty-seven hit squads in this country and that the Iranians control Ghaddafi and that the money you now have is fifty per cent of fifty per cent owned by the Iranians.'

Owney laughed. 'How could my mom get mixed up with the Iranians?'

'I am telling you what the woman told me.'

'Who owns the other half of the fifty per cent of fifty per cent?'

'God knows. I mean, if she told me Santa Claus I'd believe her. Your mother is some salesman, Owney.'

They talked for forty-seven minutes, resolving nothing. Not more than ten minutes after Owney had hung up, just when his oat-bran toast was ready, buttered and warm, the phone rang again. It was Mrs Noon.

'Owney? This you mothuh.'

'Mom? I just talked to Dolly.'

'Well, then. You got some idea of the spot I'm in.'

'What spot?'

'What spot? She didn't mention Ghaddafi's people and a certain Brooklyn organized crime family?'

'You mean – *you*? They're after *you*, not me?'

'Not on the phone. We've got to meet and talk.'

'When? Where?'

'One hour. I have a vintage double-decker open top Fifth Avenue bus in some garage on the West Side. I'll pick you up in one hour in fronta your place.'

'Why a bus? Why that kind of a bus?'

'Nobody can bug it.'

'Mom!'

But she had hung up.

They rode up Riverside Drive through the lovely summer morning past the Sailors' and Soldiers' Monument. It was chilly-warm, which is how New York offers it in the early summer when the air comes in off the friendly ocean to bounce against the thick wall of smog and bound back again over the polluted Atlantic. Once upon a time the same ocean breeze had laundered everything in its path.

Mrs Noon and Owney were two of the passengers on the open top of the No.5 bus with its marked Fort Tryon Park destination. Four of Mrs Noon's armed Shiite building employees sat eleven rows behind them.

She held his hand, smiling happily. 'We haven't had an outing like this for a long, long time.' Her voice and her speech were the way Owney could now remember them. She sounded like the Canadian girl from Indian Head, Saskatchewan which she had once been so long before.

She could not remember ever having been happier, riding with the breeze in her hair with her adorable, wonderful son by her side.

'Remember the day we went all the way to Van Cortlandt Park on the IRT,' she said with a gentling voice, 'because you wanted to find out what it looked like when people played cricket and because you wanted to eat ham sandwiches sitting on the grass?'

He grinned at her. 'We took some pretty far trips from Meier's Corners,' he murmured. 'The Bronx Zoo, Jones Beach, Bear Mountain, but we had some wonderful bus rides just like this – up on the top.'

'I bought into this little bus just because of those bus rides.'

277

'You did?'

'I thought about you all the time, Owney. It was very hard.'

'Mom, why did you run away from me?' His voice cracked.

'I panicked. Then, when it was done, it was too late to ever go back and get you.'

'But *why*, Mom?'

'It's all a mish-mosh. I was born in Iran – I guess you didn't know that . . .'

Owney looked up at her (she was long-waisted, he was short-waisted), startled.

'My mother was a Canadian opera singer who fell in love with – with a young Iranian clergyman.' In actuality her father had married a Frenchwoman, a niece of Marcel Proust's. Owney's mother had spent the rest of her life concealing that because word buffs would have swarmed all over her trying to find out about cork-lined rooms and madeleine cookies.

'Anyway – when the CIA overthrew the Iranian government and put the Shah on the throne so the Bahama Beaver Bonnet Company could get the oil pipeline contract instead of the Soviets, I was already married to your father and we were living in Meier's Corners. Out of the blue, your father said he was going to expose me – that's what he called it, Owney, exposing me – to the FBI, because I hadn't registered as an Iranian.'

'Well,' Owney said, thinking with horror of the charges James D. Marxuach had made against his mother in Rio. 'I mean – why hadn't you?'

'I never thought of it! I mean, after all, the Iranian citizenship was only a technicality and I was married to an American citizen! My son was an American citizen!' She patted his knee. 'After all, the law is the law, but I think your father had his eye on some woman and he just wanted to get rid of me.'

'I never knew that,' Owney said. 'But he was pretty sick by the time I did know him.'

'Did you have a nice meeting with your lawyers?' Owney's mother asked, staring out at the traffic which was struggling across the George Washington Bridge.

'Excellent.'

'I suppose your plan for your Foundation is to lobby the Congress to send troops into Colombia, Bolivia, and Peru.'

'Good heavens, nothing like that. Not after Vietnam.'

'I suppose your Foundation will hire planes to spray the coca crops in Bolivia and places like that.'

278

'Nothing like that ever occurred to me.'

'Then your Foundation will plan to advocate the arrest and jailing of cocaine users in this country?'

'Mom! That would be unconstitutional.'

They were talking dreamily as if they were drifting in a canoe on a lazy summer afternoon, just talking to let each other know that they were there.

'What's your Foundation going to do then?'

'Well – the only thing there is to do. We will work with the young people. We may have to lobby but if we do it will be to secure housing and help for families. We want them to have good health care and an education for a rewarding kind of a life – including the truth about drugs. We'll want to help them get established in meaningful jobs, giving them a commitment to freedom, equality, and justice. If we can do it – and inspire the government to do it – children will be born and raised in healthy, loving families. None of them will feel the need to abuse drugs or hurt one another.'

'That's nice, Owney.'

'Well, it couldn't be done without that money.'

'Let's talk about the money. No, no!' She put a restraining hand on his forearm. 'Just quiet talk. No problems.'

'What is there to say?'

'Owney, listen. I've had enough time to think this all the way through since we talked the last time. First off, right at the front of the pack, I'm going to be in deep, deep trouble – maybe dead – if I don't come up with some of that money.'

'Mom! If anyone harms a hair of your head I'll –'

'I know, sweetheart. I know.' She patted his hand.

'Who in heaven's name would want to do such a thing?'

'It's better that you don't know. Just saying a couple of names might blow up this bus. If you want to protect me, and I know you do, you've got to give me back some of that money.'

'But, Mom – Jesus!'

'No, no! You listen to me. You keep the part that came from the – the vegetables – after all that's the part that has you so upset – and just give me back the money I got for the sale of my tankers.'

'How much was that?'

'Two billion four. I'll settle for that.'

'That would leave the Foundation two billion two.'

'Then we split the difference. We each take two billion three.'

'That's a lot of money.'

'Would Ronald Reagan think it's a lot of money?'

'No. I guess not.'

'I'm going to find you Foundation experts to tell you how you can get money from other Foundations, from the government, from foreign countries. I bet you we can raise another billion one for your side just from outside money sources like that.'

'That would bring the Foundation up to three billion four. But most of all, you'd be safe.'

'Yes sir, sweetie, I would be one hundred per cent OK.'

'Then that's what we'll do, Mom.'

'You're a good boy.'

'I just want you to be safe.'

'There's something else I want you to do for me.'

'Anything.'

'I want you to consider going back into politics.'

'Mom! How? After what happened the last time I'd be tarred and feathered.'

'Don't you believe it.'

'Mom! The entire news media of this country branded me as a pervert who was also plotting to blow up the Pentagon!'

'Now, Owney, you might as well learn now that the American news media accommodates itself. It sides with authority and the establishment.' She smiled at him fondly. 'Because the people who own the news media *are* the establishment.'

'How come?'

'I'm talkin' 'bout the news media as an institution. Individually, even the lowest writers earn more money than ninety per cent of the public, an' the stars with the by-lines, an' the talk shows, an' the book deals, and heavy lecture fees – shucks, they're ranked in the top two per cent of the country's income groups so they ain't gone rock no boat when we tell them whut we want. And they the ones who do the thinkin' for the people.'

Mrs Noon had shifted abruptly out of Canadian speech cadences because as she became rapt by her subject she tended to return to the habitual speech patterns of her past twenty years. 'They know that they bread an' butter depend on how well we do in bidniz. Who's gone pay for all them ads and commercials unless they keep the country proud of all the bidniz it does? That's whut the White House is there for – to protect bidniz with the help of the news media.'

'I can't accept that, mother. To me, the American press is either a bunch of hot-headed liberals fighting for the common man, or relentless crusaders.'

'As Calvin Coolidge – to whom my husband, Goodie Noon, bears a remarkable resemblance – said, "The bidniz of America is bidniz", not fillin' the American people with a lotta facks that is only gone confuse 'em.'

'Freedom of the press is not only our law, Mom, it is a Constitutional duty.'

'Well, you new to guvmint, son. But when you in there with the rest of us, snug an' cosy with the news media, you'll understand that we all members of the rulin' political class. The news media is an arm of the American state.'

'Then what you are saying is that, if the right people send the right messages to thoughtful people in the media, even though they had once called me a dangerous revolutionary, who – they claimed – not only wanted to blow up the Pentagon but also preferred sex with lesbians, I can still be elected to whatever it is you want to run me for?'

She answered him soothingly. 'After we get the right PR people telling the country about how you are the single contributor to a three billion four hundred million dollar Foundation which is dedicated to fightin' drugs, how set you are against the evil of drugs and convincin' them that you were framed by the CIA the other time you ran for office, you are going to be a very, very desirable candidate.'

'Candidate for what?'

'With the CIA exposed as bein' against you, voters will be reassured that you're anti-establishment, except that runnin' on the ticket with Goodie, they will also be reassured that you absolutely cain't be.'

'On the ticket? With Goodie? What ticket?'

'You remember the day we met again at my apartment except that although I knew it was you, you didn't know it was me?'

'Yes.'

'You told me you weren't meant to be a frankfurter salesman, an' that's the whole truth of it.'

'Please, Mom, what do you want me to be?'

'An' now, even though you own half the company you are still just a little frankfurter salesman compared to your wife. You think she has taken your place as the head of the family. Am I right or am I right?'

Owney nodded mutely.

281

'Therefore, to change that condition wholly and for ever, I want you to consent to run for Vice-President of the United States of America, and be on an equal footing with your wife, that's what I want you to be.'

'Mom! For heaven's sake! Come *on*!'

'Not only do I mean it but that's what we gone do.'

'What about the Constitution? It says a native born citizen of the United States has to be at least thirty-two years old to be a Vice-President. I'm only twenty-nine.'

'So? I still have all that paper my people ran up for me – forged birth certificates and all the rest, beautiful work – from the last time you ran for office.'

'How in heaven's name are you going to get the second place for me on a national political ticket? This is really crazy!'

'Owney, sweetheart – I am married to the man who is gone be the next President of this country. He has a big say – not the entire say but a big say – about who goes on that ticket with him. An' I have one very, very big say with him. I also have Wiley Monahan and Mal Olgilvie and Wamb Keifetz on my side. We control the people who control the convention.'

'In a de*moc*racy?'

'You better believe it. An' by the time Goodie tuckers hisseff out all through the primary campaigns and gets to that nominating convention in New Orleans, I am going to have him – an' everybody else that counts in the Republican Party – convinced that you are the only possible candidate to run with him on that winnin' ticket. An' you gone make a really *great* Vice-President . . .'

. . . as Mrs Noon explained to Wambly Keifetz and Wiley Monahan in her suite in the New Orleans hotel during the nominating convention when she was ready to confide in them that Osgood Noon wanted Owen Hazman as his running mate. Neither man could believe his ears. They were speechless, staring at her in shocked disbelief.

'When you think about it,' she said, 'you gone see that Owney is the best choice in the whole country for the slot.'

'He's not much more than thirty and looks even younger,' Keifetz sputtered.

'He's one of the dumbest and most passive kids I've ever seen,' Monahan said.

'Maybe so, but he's got the papers to prove he's thirty-five,' Mrs Noon said.

'I don't get it, Oona,' Monahan said. 'The country will be dumbfounded and the media will go outta their minds.'

'You show me somethin' botha them two cain't get used to an' you'll have to get into a different business. Look – last year when we was tryin' to position Goodie, he ran a few errands for the Reagan people.'

'What does that have to do with this kid being Vice-President?' Keifetz demanded.

'Thass jes' it. You know how crazy Goodie was always to try to git inta the loop with Reagan. It was Goodie's idea to send the Bible and the birthday cake to the Ayatollah. Man, he was *deep* into that Iran-Contra mess. When they gave him those few months working at the CIA, Goodie in*vent*ed Noriega! So, don't you see what I'm drivin' at? We'll have Goodie in the White House lookin' after our interests and the interests of our friends and if any crazy Democrats from left field think they can impeach Goodie for what he may have done here and there for Reagan, well, what alternative will they have? Make a president out of a kid who is really just a kid and who knows nothing about anythin'? Don't you git it? Owney is Goodie's impeachment insurance.'

'Jesus!' Monahan said as the full realization of the golden El Dorado overcame him. 'That is absolutely brilliant!'

Chapter 56

That is the full (if amazing) story of the profound national mystery of how an unknown, inexperienced 32-year-old man came to be nominated as candidate for Vice-President of the United States of America at the Republican Presidential nominating convention of 1992 at New Orleans, the youngest and, some would say, the callowest, man ever to be chosen for that high office which, as every American child knows, is only a heartbeat away from the Presidency. The man named to be Vice-President had had no experience beyond the field of frankfurters and novelty cigarette lighters, a background which few would have felt qualified him for such an awesome rendezvous. Fortunately the news media didn't emphasize that part of his background. They referred to him as 'a food processor for the twenty-first century whom three countries of eastern Europe sought out for counsel on modern sausage production and distribution.'

When the nation was told the news, at first, very early on, as it looked up from the sports pages and the Wheel of Fortune, it was stunned. People stared at each other glassy-eyed in the streets. The news media babbled brokenly trying to explain the decision. The heavy thinkers of Sunday television pundit shows went overboard rehashing the whole (discredited) CIA frame-up again which had involved, so unbelievably, a lesbian revolutionary and a plot to blow up the Pentagon. Three of the five women who had lived with Owney (or rather with whom Owney had lived) came forward. One, the computer programmer with whom he had refused to go skiing, sold sensational memories of her life with Owney to the *National Enquirer*, detailing in a spectacular manner Owney's brutality and ruthlessness on the day he had deserted her. However, the frankfurter industry people who were interviewed were forthright in their admiration of him. 'No man wins four Weenies on his looks,' Gordon Manning was quoted as saying. 'Owney Hazman is a great frankfurter executive.' Owney was photographed again and again with the candidate, Osgood Noon, whose paternal good-fellowship and outright belief in his running mate soon convinced the doubters just as the basketball and hunting seasons were starting, which would claim the attention of most of the males anyway.

There were, of course, vague (unpublished) hints generated by the other Party that the Republican Presidential nominee might have made a bad judgemental mistake, but the Conservative news media (98.2 per cent of the nation's press, radio, and television) proclaimed Owney as a business giant who had earned more than $1.75 million in the current fiscal year and shrilly demanded that all voters support him, regardless of Party. Then, at a signal from their television sets, the nation closed ranks behind their new Leaders.

Not only was Osgood O. Noon strong on flags and flag history, but the American people had been able to read his lips. There was no other way they could have misunderstood what had happened. They decided in their distracted way that in nominating Owen Hazman for the Vice-Presidency, the President-elect had been uncannily shrewd. For one thing Wiley Monahan saw to it that his name went on the ballot as O. Tompkins Hazman and persuaded the press to refer to him as Tom Hazman. As President of the Senate, where he remained passive and inscrutable, he was known as Big Tom Hazman.

After four years of the reign of Osgood Noon, because he had a pernicious compulsion to declare wars while simultaneously playing golf and speed-boating, because he had alienated the women's vote by his stringent opposition to abortion, and the minority vote by his veto of civil rights legislation, and the conservative vote because he had betrayed them by increasing taxes, the inevitability of O. Tompkins Hazman's incumbency (as well as the support of Wambly Keifetz, Oona Noon, Wiley Monahan and campaign funds of over $110 million) had Owney succeeding to the Presidency in the year 1997 to guide America into the new century. He would be what Thomas Jefferson had predicted would eventually happen under a democracy: the election of 'a representative President', representative of the average man.

O. Tompkins 'Tom' Hazman would serve two terms as President of the United States. In 2004, he was debarred by the Constitution from succeeding himself (the so-called 'Reagan

Amendment', by which a sitting President would be guaranteed six terms of office, having failed to be ratified).

Big Tom Hazman blazed new trails as the forty-third President of the United States. He was the first chief executive to appoint a woman as his Chief of Staff, the able, organized, no-nonsense Canadian-born Mrs Oona Noon, wife of the former American President. She had such a grasp of government problems as well as foreign policy that Tom Hazman became a President with whom history would be forced to reckon.

O. Tompkins Hazman was forty-seven years old (his published age) when he left the White House, an elder statesman. He returned to the helm of the frankfurter industry, to his considerable pensions, his office allowances, his Secret Service protection, and his towering sausage-shaped Presidential library at New Braunfels, Texas, superbly equipped by the Sony Corporation and the Japanese rice-growers association. He earned his substantial lecture fees, the occasional $8 million honorarium including considerable tax-free expenses each year for visiting and chatting with the Japanese, the Koreans, the Chinese, the Taiwanese, and the Filipinos as had become traditional for retiring American Presidents. His short talk before the Hamburger Franchise Dealers Association of Miami, Florida was said to rank with Lincoln's Gettysburg address and he was paid $237,000 for it plus 'expenses'.

To augment his income, dear friends insisted that visiting European and Asiatic industrialists and political contenders pay a fee of $250,000 to be photographed with Owney and Mrs Hazman in their gracious Bel-Air home. Surprisingly, these informal visits brought in an average of an extra $2,750,000 a year. The same group of dear friends who had pressed the Bel-Air home upon the Hazman family, including the Teamsters' Union, the Used Car Dealers of Las Vegas, and the schoolchildren of Meier's Corners, then purchased from President Hazman the Staten Island house which had been his birthplace, for $11,219,000 and presented it to the grateful nation. It became a national shrine.

The international publishing rights to his three autobiographies went for a combined $7,500,000. His fee for lectures (delivered from 5x8 cards) was $100,000 for an appearance and a government plane flew him to each engagement.

The obsolete 'other Party' succeeded to the White House after Big Tom Hazman's second term because, in partisan terms, he had left a vacuum when he was required by the Constitution to leave office.

However, the ravages to the American system of government which had been caused by the Hazman Administration were so deep and complete that the succeeding Party could not cope with the extent of the chaos, corruption, and cronyism throughout the government. The other Party was turned out of office after only one term in the White House. The American people, in their wisdom, drafted and swept into the office of the Presidency the most popular living American, Owen Hazman, him of the diffident manner, impeccable tailoring, and boyish smile.

Guided by a prodigious amount of campaign funds, and some unpleasantly vicious television spots, the American people were caused to realize that they wanted the comfort of knowing that O. Tompkins Hazman (as he was known on the ballot), still a relatively young man, would be the candidate who would, once again, grin them to glory.

By universal accord, Hazman was lifted back to the White House on the shoulders of the American people. What won the day for his third thrilling return to the Oval Office in what would be a broken accumulation of sixteen years in the White House, was an extraordinarily flattering shot on the cover photograph of the *National Enquirer*, the national newspaper of record, in which, wearing a teal-blue short-sleeved sports shirt, he filled the hearts of America with a grin which brought hope to the entire world and had them wishing they could somehow vote for him as he gazed off into the glorious future (as he saw it).

'I think he got some good press because he is an attractive human being,' his Chief of Staff, Mrs Oona Noon, said. 'He is perceived as a thinker for his people, a man with a great deal of common sense who will restore dignity to his country, bring prosperity to several, and eliminate the capital gains tax.' She became vehement as she answered a question which some troublemaker in the media had persisted in asking. 'People don't care whether he falls asleep at cabinet meetings or while chatting with the Pope, or whether he takes lots of vacations or doesn't seem to want to show that he has any understanding of what is going on,' she said hotly. 'They don't need that in a leader.'

Tom Hazman carried all fifty states and Guam in his third run for the Presidency, to retire at fifty-two (actual age) to accept the chairmanship of Noon-Keifetz International, a $50 billion 'development' corporation, which, adding in his pension benefits from the frankfurter industry, the Vice-Presidency and Presidency, and from the grateful Japanese companies who had sponsored his annual visits to their plants, offices, and theme parks, would pay him $4,734,921 a year, tax-free.

In his total of sixteen years in the White House as Vice-President and President, Big Tom Hazman did not disturb the funding of his Foundation because in his position he had been able to foresee the legalization of drugs. As a favour to his mother, to give her the chance to make the giant shift from private to public merchandising of the vegetables, by not using the Foundation to inveigh against narcotics use, he had not employed his Foundation's powers. In the ensuing twenty years, the money had earned almost $150 million in tax-free interest, but still Owney could not make the decision to spend any of it, other than buying members of his family, and his mother, really nice Christmas gifts from Foundation funds each year.

In his will, after setting aside for his children the $40 million he had earned from various opportunities which had emerged from public service through the canny advice of his Chief of Staff, he left the entire capitalization of the Foundation to provide housing (indirectly) for the inner cities through a chain of luxury hotels with 24-hour hot-meal room service and newly-legalized gambling casinos, a real money-maker, all income from which to go to the Molly Tompkins Foundation, a tax-free, perpetually sustained, public relations organization whose chartered purpose was to immortalize the achievements of Molly Tompkins Hazman, the symbol of motherhood, and a warm, caring human being, well into the twenty-second century and further if the funds held out.

At age sixty (actual age) he was appointed to the United States Supreme Court as Chief Justice of the United States where he presided until his eighty-fourth year (published age) when he returned to the frankfurter industry.

As President and as Chief Magistrate he had done more damage to the nation and the Constitution than can be readily estimated but he soldiered on as the idol of his people, grimacing and waving, distributing, on a wholesale basis, such smiles as nearly to break the hearts of the savage, simple-minded people.

His wife, Dolores Guadalupe Hazman, was to win three Oscars, four Emmys, five Obies, a Tony, a Wendy, and a Moey as well as sixteen consecutive Platinum records from the recording industry. Her income as a great rock star was never to flag below $55 million a year, almost equalling the emoluments the handful of her husband's aides and advisers had accumulated during the time Big Tom Hazman had served in the White House.

Every one of the Hazman children was able to graduate from college despite ever-increasing fees and charges. They were dressed by Lauren and flew Concorde throughout their lifetimes.

Cocaine was legalized in 1997 so that by 1999 its use had dropped to the level of ketchup. However, immediately, a new national addiction to a psychotropic drug called blanderoo, which compounded essences of the brooding uses to which the Bill of Rights had been put with the mystical cynicism of the Congress, all headily mixed with the redolent effluvia of Richard Nixon and Ronald Reagan. Blanderoo gave people the illusion that their politicians were not planning their destruction. It swept the country, enabling the White House and the Congress to assure the nation that all threats to life, liberty, and the pursuit of money would soon be conquered. They never were. Blanderoo, as with death, was the final addiction.